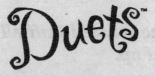

Duets™

**Two brand-new stories in every volume...
twice a month!**

Duets Vol. #49

Popular Harlequin American Romance author
Lisa Bingham will make you chuckle this month
with a wonderfully funny story about animal passions.
Joining her is Golden Heart finalist Susan Peterson,
whose *Everything But Anchovies* will leave you
smiling—and ordering out for pizza!

Duets Vol. #50

Bonnie Tucker leads off with a story to die for!
This writer always creates "wildly funny scenes
and memorable characters," says *Romantic Times
Magazine*. Reviewers at *RT* are equally pleased
with Lori Wilde, who "brilliantly weaves together
lovable characters, charming scenes
and a humorous storyline."

Be sure to pick up both Duets volumes today!

D0958602

Going in Style

Suzanne wanted Griff all worked up.

Only, after almost three weeks, nothing had happened, even when she'd insisted on playing strip rummy! She had gotten all the way down to her bra and panties—and not just any bra and panties, either. No, Suzanne was wearing her sex-until-you-die underwear. If she'd been Griff, she'd have been all over herself. Where in the world did he get his self-control?

Although...he did seem to be drinking an extraordinary amount of ice water, and was making an awful lot of trips to the kitchen to splash his face. He was also growing quite irritable—all good signs of a sexually frustrated man.

When she lost the game, she moaned, "Oh, I don't know what to take off next."

That's when Griff bolted out of the house.

A smile curved Suzanne's lips. It wouldn't be long now. She started humming, "I Got the Hots for You, Griff-ee" as she cleared off the table. Then her smile faded. She was running out of time. And although she knew she'd have Griff in her bed soon, she could only hope that "soon" was soon enough....

For more, turn to page 9

I Love Lacy

**_From the moment
Dr. Bennett Sheridan stepped
into the operating suite,
Lacy Calder was a grade-A
number-one goner._**

Never in all her twenty-nine years had she
experienced such an immediate reaction to
anyone. It was intense and undeniable. Sex
hormones twisted like Chubby Checker in her
lower abdomen.

Lacy felt an unmistakable clink, as if something
very important had settled into place. Something
that, until now, had been sorely out of kilter.

At long last it had happened.

Since she was a child, the women in her family
had promised that one day she would meet her
Mr. Right.

"But how will I know?" young Lacy had asked her
mother.

"The thunderbolt," her mother had replied. "It
strikes hard and fast."

And here at last was her thunderbolt. In the flesh.
With a mere smile, Dr. Bennett Sheridan had
knocked her out with a clean one-two punch.

For more, turn to page 197

HARLEQUIN DUETS

ISBN 0-373-44116-9

GOING IN STYLE
Copyright © 2001 by Bonnie Tucker

I LOVE LACY
Copyright © 2001 by Laurie Vanzura

This edition published by arrangement with Harlequin Books S.A.

® and TM are trademarks of the publisher. Trademarks indicated with
® are registered in the United States Patent and Trademark Office, the
Canadian Trade Marks Office and in other countries.

Visit us at www.eHarlequin.com

Printed in U.S.A.

Going in Style

Bonnie Tucker

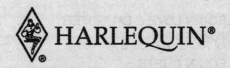

TORONTO • NEW YORK • LONDON
AMSTERDAM • PARIS • SYDNEY • HAMBURG
STOCKHOLM • ATHENS • TOKYO • MILAN • MADRID
PRAGUE • WARSAW • BUDAPEST • AUCKLAND

Dear Reader,

Romance writers get two questions asked pretty frequently. Where do we get our ideas? is the first. The other is, well...I'm sure you can guess. Ideas, however, can come from anywhere. The premise of *Going in Style* came from a truly original source. A few years ago, I had a medical scare. And even though the doctors told me I'd be all right, I didn't believe them. So, thinking I was going to die anyway, I ate and ate and ate! I even ate ice cream, which I hate. Well, it turned out that my doctor was right. I was absolutely fine...except that now I had to lose sixteen pounds!

So I decided that if something like that could happen to me, it could happen to my heroine, Suzanne, too. Only in Suzie's case, she wants something more delicious than ice cream. She's craving a little one-on-one with her gorgeous neighbor Griff. And after all, why shouldn't she have a taste of heaven on earth?

I hope you enjoy *Going in Style*. But stay away from that ice cream.

Happy reading,

Bonnie Tucker

Books by Bonnie Tucker

HARLEQUIN LOVE & LAUGHTER
18—HANNAH'S HUNKS
52—STAY TUNED: WEDDING AT 11:00

HARLEQUIN DUETS
2—I GOT YOU, BABE

For my friend
Cathy Maxwell.

Prologue

February 28, Nine Years Ago

THE SIZE OF Suzanne Mercer's bikini was every bit as itsy-bitsy and teeny-weeny as the one in the old song Grandma Hermia used to sing to her when she was probably no bigger than the bikini itself. The salesclerk had told her the yellow polka dots had been hand-sewn on the buttermilk-white silk.

Her best friends Christine and Nina had been with her when she bought it. They made plans to go to the beach today so she could wear it in public. They dared her, and she took dares seriously.

The bikini shouted out to her, *I'm daring. I'm proud. Look at me.* The reflection in her bedroom mirror of the brown-haired woman with the small waist and breasts that seemed too large for the tiny bikini top wasn't the Suzanne she knew herself to be. Her shoulders and back, which had been straight and sure, slowly slumped.

As Suzanne stared at her reflection, she wished her personality was more bikini and less navy tank suit.

Hey, what was she thinking? She looked good. She felt empowered. She was no tank suit. She gave herself a mental shake, and felt her blood start to rush through her veins with a zest for adventure she hadn't felt in longer than she could remember.

She covered her bikini top with her favorite long and loose navy shirt, her bikini bottoms with baggy white cotton shorts, and stuck her feet in a pair of old tennis shoes.

She could do anything she wanted. In thirty days she'd turn twenty-one. That was the magical age and, by gosh, she was gong to start celebrating right now. She'd wear the bikini to the beach and shock all her friends with the new Suzanne. She'd drink iced tea with a tablespoon of pure white sugar instead of the usual artificial sweetener. If she wanted to be really wanton, she could slather herself in baby oil instead of her usual SPF-45 sunscreen. This was going to be a landmark day.

Suzanne ran down the stairs, and as she went through the front door she shouted, "Bye, Mom, I'll be back late tonight."

She'd almost made it to her car when she heard, "Suzaaaanne!"

Her hands were poised over the car door handle, her key had almost made it into the lock.

Hermia called out again. "Come back here, darlin'."

Suzanne didn't rush back even though her mom stood in the doorway snapping and waving an envelope over her head.

"Now you've gone and done it." Hermia sounded hurt and a little angry when she handed the envelope to her. "Here. Read this."

"You read my letter? You know, this could have been from a secret lover." The envelope had been slit open.

"Really, Suzanne, this isn't the time for fantasies. We've got a crisis on our hands. A real emergency.

We can't let this go any further.'' Her mother's eyes filled with tears, and she delicately sniffled.

Suzanne saw the return address. Her mother's agitation could only mean one thing. She'd gotten the job. She practically ripped the letter out of the envelope, unfolded the heavy vellum paper and savored every word she read. *We at Merriweather, Watkins and Jones are pleased to extend to you an offer of employment.* She reread the letter, slower this time, committing each word to memory.

"I knew nothing good was going to happen when you passed that CPA test." She pointed her finger at her daughter. "I told you not to take that test. When are you going to start listening to your mother?"

"I have to call Dad." Suzanne headed back inside the house. "He's going to be so excited."

"Now, wait a minute, young lady." She gripped her daughter's arm, stopping her. "I can't believe you're going to consider taking a job at some accounting firm. My daughter? Working as an accountant?" Hermia's mouth pinched. "Didn't I raise you any better than that?"

"Mom, you've always encouraged me to work in numbers."

"Numbers, yes. But I never meant for you to get a job as an *accountant*. It's so...so...oh, I can't even think what it is. I'm devastated by this turn of events."

Her mother had drilled it into her brain since she was a toddler that she'd been born to pursue avenues of commerce and finance. What Hermia had in mind was something more in line with Suzanne using her mathematical mind to count cards at the blackjack table at the Red Rock Casino in Las Vegas. As far as Hermia was concerned, bankrupting the Red Rock was a matter of honor.

"Give it up, Mom," she said as gently as she could.

"That place is rightfully ours. It's your birthright."

"Mom, your great-great-great—or however many greats there are—grandmother didn't marry Red Jack Bourne. He married someone else."

"No, he didn't marry the first Hermia when she was pregnant with the second Hermia, who was his baby. The man is a scoundrel. His descendants are thieves."

"Thieves? Mom, the first Hermia Bourne stole Red Jack's name!"

"Minor technicality. Listen to me." She was pointing that finger again. "That happened over one hundred years ago. You need to put the past behind you, Suzanne."

"*I* need to! You're the one who needs to get over this…obsession. I'm not going to Las Vegas. I'm not going to play blackjack at the Red Rock Casino. I'm not going to win by counting cards. It's not going to happen."

"Where's my headache medicine? And don't you roll your eyes at me, young lady. You don't know the sacrifices I made for you. I married your father, didn't I? Even though no Hermia Bourne has ever married her mate. I could have lived in sin with him just as my mother lived with my father, and my grandmother lived with my grandfather, etcetera, etcetera. But did I? No. I chose to be different. I've never regretted my decision, until now. If I hadn't married your father, you'd have been named Hermia Bourne, too. You would have taken pride in your name. You would have gone to Las Vegas and broken the bank of those Bourne upstarts."

"I like being a Mercer," Suzanne said.

Hermia's pointing finger now shook right under her daughter's nose. "If only I had listened to my mother.

But did I? No. So she put the mother's curse on me. 'I hope you have a daughter just like you,' she said.'' She looked up into the blue sky. "I do, Mom. Are you happy?''

"Why are you looking up there? Grandma's not dead.''

"Awk! I'm anticipating she will be when she hears what you're planning to do. An accountant. Oh,'' she moaned dramatically. "This is a tragedy more tragic than any Shakespearean play.''

"Grandma will be happy for me. I'm happy.''

"You live in a dream world. Such a waste of talent.'' Hermia made tsking noises, then like her mother was prone to do, she went on using a different tactic. "My poor little darlin'.'' Motherly fingers brushed aside the curly brown wisps of hair that had escaped from Suzanne's thick ponytail and onto her forehead. "You belong in Las Vegas. You were destined for great things. Bankrupting the Red Rock would be the ultimate in greatness.''

"Oh, Mother.'' Suzanne wished she could be more sympathetic, but all she could think about was what a relief it would be not to have to come up with another reason to add to the six hundred and ninety reasons she'd already given her mother why the revenge of the Texas Bournes against the Nevada Bournes was a bad idea.

"There's only one thing to do,'' her mother said. "We both must see Sir James. Right now. He's at the Houston Livestock show this week. I did tell you they've added a fortune-telling area this year, didn't I? Tarot cards, palm readers, numerologists.''

"I can't go. You know Nina, Christine and I are going to the beach.'' Underneath her clothes, the yellow polka-dot bikini clung to her body, reminding her she had found her courage.

"I know, darlin'. But this is so important to me. We need to get an unbiased opinion as to what your future will be. An accountant at some stuffy accounting firm, or a free spirit, who will bankrupt the bad people, then take all that newly acquired wealth, hire her own accountant to pay her taxes, and meet a man and live happily ever after."

Suzanne knew what her future would be, she had it all planned, right down to the time and day. She didn't need Sir James, her mother's personal astrologist, to tell her. She was sick of Sir James. She barely had enough fingers and toes to count the number of vacations her family had canceled after Sir James had predicted that dreadful accidents would befall them. Just because the airplane they didn't take because of his prediction *did* crash, just as he said it would, and just because the earthquake in Mexico did happen, just as he said it would, didn't mean that he was right one hundred percent of the time. He was only right ninety-nine percent. Suzanne took comfort in his one percent margin of error.

"You can ask Nina and Christine to join us," Hermia sweet-talked her.

Suzanne made a conscious effort not to slump. "Fine. We'll get my future read."

"Wonderful, darlin'." Her mother clapped her hands together.

"But under no circumstances am I going to Las Vegas. I'm going to work at Merriweather."

"Of course you are."

"As long as you know that." Well, she felt better now that that was taken care of. After all, even cowards like her had to put a foot down—well, maybe a toe down—sometimes.

Three hours after they'd arrived at the Houston Livestock Show and Rodeo, having toured almost every fortune-telling booth there was, one thing was clear. Those people did not wish Suzanne well.

Her mother looked confused and dazed, two attributes that Suzanne would never have associated with her mother, especially not when this whole morning had been her idea in the first place. "No, it can't be," Hermia mumbled over and over.

"What did that numerologist know anyway?" Nina tried to slough it off. "Nothing."

Hermia held up three fingers. "Three. How can that number be so unlucky for my baby girl? How?"

"It's not unlucky," Suzanne said. Yet.

"Oh, yes, it is," Christine predicted. "And your birthday's on March 30th. Three, thirty. Poor Suzanne." Then she brightened, her face alight in pure joy. "You'll have to agree though that it sure is something the way all those fortune-tellers predicted the exact same thing."

Nina shot her friend the "you're worse than a worm" look. "Shut up."

"What's wrong with *you?*" Christine looked befuddled at her friend's hostility.

Suzanne had to ask herself how real all this was. Did a person like her, a sane, well-adjusted woman, believe what all those people told her today? Those tellers of the future, the palm readers, tarot card interpreters, numerologists, astrologers and crystal ball readers? Every inch of her screamed, *No!* "Nothing's wrong with anyone except the people who are telling fortunes at this place. I want one more opinion."

"I suppose you're right." Hermia didn't sound

pleased. "But, Suzanne, Sir James has always been so accurate." Sir James, her mother's guru, had given Suzanne the same prediction as the numerologist, the tarot card reader and the woman who was only a clearinghouse for the messages delivered by two psychic ants.

Twenty minutes later they came out of the last crystal ball reader's tent shaken. "What does Madame Bovier know anyway?" Suzanne asked. "She couldn't possibly see into the future. Her crystal ball was filthy."

Hermia linked arms with her daughter, patting her hand reassuringly. "Of course she couldn't, darlin'. Why, no one could accurately predict such a terrible thing happening to you with a dirty crystal ball."

"That's right," Christine and Nina agreed.

"And the palm reader's a fool," Hermia went on. She grabbed Suzanne's limp hand and flopped it over. "Look at that lifeline. It's going all the way up your arm."

"Mother," Suzanne groaned, pulling her arm from her mother's clasp, "that's a vein."

"Vein, line, what's the difference?" Hermia waved dismissively. "They're both going up."

"I am not having a good day," Suzanne told her mother, "at all."

"I know, I know. But, on the bright side, at least you have time to prepare."

"Bright side? I've had tarot cards read. I've been to a numerologist, crystal ball reader, palm reader, astrologist, and who knows how many other fortunetellers. They've all told me the exact same fortune. In nine years, on March 30th, on my thirtieth birthday, I'm going to die."

1

February 28, Nine Years Later

IT NEVER FAILED that when Dr. W. Griffin Scott's shift came to an end—as he made final notes before the patients were moved to a room, gave last-minute orders, answered remaining questions—something always cropped up that kept him from heading home. He'd consider it nothing short of a miracle if he ever managed to leave the hospital within an hour after his shift ended.

A schedule for trauma surgeons like him was dictated by the whims of fate, drunk drivers and the full moon. Nine-to-five schedules might work for the surgeons who scheduled gallbladder surgeries around Wednesday golf games and adenoid removal based on their own kid's need for orthodontia or rhinoplasty. That wasn't for him. Griff scorned the game of golf. The only gallbladders he operated on were the ones that came to him via ambulance. He had no kids, so the need for braces or a nose job wasn't an issue.

Normally the long hours never bothered Griff. He wore them on his chest like a badge of honor. But tonight, for some reason he couldn't figure out, he wanted to get out of the place. He wanted fresh, not disinfectant, air. He wanted—no, needed—to see a friendly face and have someone lend a sympathetic ear, listen to what was bothering him, tell him everything would be all right.

He wanted to talk to Suzanne. He needed someone calm and sensible in the bloody, violent, insane world he called his life. There was no one more calm and sensible than Suzanne, and he depended on her for that. Good ol' Suzanne. Always there with a nonjudgmental ear and a ready smile.

He wanted to tell her about the six-car pileup along Highway 90 fifty miles due west of Sugar Land. He needed to tell her about the helplessness he'd felt when he'd found out four people were already dead, before anyone could have gotten to them. A waste of life. He wanted to tell her about the fourteen that were brought in alive. About the twelve that his team had been able to save.

Mostly he wanted to talk to her about how the guilt was eating at him because of the two he couldn't save. Never mind that nothing but life-support systems had gotten them to the hospital and that no doctor could have possibly saved them. Suzanne would help him work through the guilt he knew he shouldn't feel, that he had no reason to feel, but that he was feeling anyway. She'd tell him he wasn't supposed to perform miracles that not even God saw fit to do. He'd believe her, too, because she was Suzanne, and she wouldn't lie to him.

At one in the morning Griff finally headed toward the door. It opened automatically, waiting for him to pass through, but instead he made a U-turn and went back inside. There was one more person he wanted to see before he left and he'd almost forgotten about him: Matt Ferguson.

He headed toward the closest bank of elevators, saw an M.B.M. Pharmaceutical salesman hanging around and opted for the stairwell instead, taking two steps at a time to the third floor cardio-pulmonary wing. He had nothing against the M.B.M. salesman; in fact, he gave away great coffee mugs as an incentive to use the company's products. Thick, navy ceramic, big handles a guy could get a grip on, beige letters spelling M.B.M., lest anyone forget where the mug came from. Griff respected a drug company whose sales force worked the same hours doctors worked. Thing was, he already had a full set of mugs. Besides, he wanted to check on Ferguson and then get out of here. The sooner he left, the sooner he could see Suzanne.

SUZANNE HAD never regretted taking the job with Merriweather, Watkins and Jones. It usually took ten years to make partner, and she knew that if she'd only had that one more year to live, she would have succeeded.

Her mother though, at any and every opportunity that presented itself, told her she'd made a mistake. So, despite how much she enjoyed her work, her mother's constant harping had inspired a daily ritual— to repeat to herself, "I love my job, I love my job." She said the words as soon as she woke up in the morning, before she even stepped out of bed.

Then, because saying the words somehow didn't seem to be enough to ward off Hermia's years of negativity, she also added a daily meditation to really hone in on all the reasons why she had chosen to go into the field of accounting.

Tuesday's mantra, "Numbers are logical," seemed so appropriate for what she had planned to do this month. If numbers in her life were King, then logic would be Queen. She only hoped that when she asked Griff the big question, he'd give her the logically correct answer, which would, of course, be a "yes."

She had nothing to lose by asking him. If he said no, she'd only have a month to live with the embarrassment, rejection and humiliation. But if he said yes, then she would have a memory to hold on to and cherish forever. Even if forever for her was only a short time away.

Suzanne, who lived by her day planner, who had everything written out minute by minute, found that the approach of March 30th was a real trial. She knew her end would come that day, but she didn't know when. It could be during the daytime, or it could be at night. That uncertainty of knowing the exact time was proving to be a test of her character.

She soon realized that there wasn't any way she could change that one aspect of the whole ordeal, so she would have to work around it. She would have to take care of all the loose ends that she could control. Making sure that her will was in order, and that her life insurance polices were in a place her parents could get them. She emptied out her safety deposit box, and put all the contents—her stock certificates, the real estate papers on some land she owned—in a strong box for her father to take care of.

Then there was Griff. Dr. W. Griffin Scott. Her neighbor. The man who made her body hum and strum. Her lust object. Her love object. Both unrequited.

Talk about total failure. She loved him with her heart and soul and had since the day he moved in next door to her, five years before.

It was sunny the day he moved in. A bevy of beauties surrounded him, giggling and cavorting as they helped him move boxes. There were a few men helping, too, but the women mostly ignored them and competed with each other for Griff's attention.

Suzanne had watched him, too, peeking out from under the brim of her straw hat as she pulled more flowers than weeds from her garden. She could understand why those women were going bonkers over the guy. The magic of Griff heaving up the heavy boxes, his body heated, his muscles tensing and relaxing, made the simple chore of planting begonias and peonies an impossibility.

He came over to meet her that afternoon, carrying a beer in each hand, and offered her one. His tan skin glistened; his light blue eyes were like cool water. She knew she was drowning and no life preserver could save her.

"Howdy, neighbor," he had said in that cute Bostonian accent she had grown to adore. He had stretched out his arm, and she reached for the beer. Their fingers touched briefly during the exchange, but the fire was born then and there and she had fallen instantly and passionately in love.

But then she'd bet her whole stock portfolio that so did every other woman whose path he happened to cross, and over the years there had been many. Although, now that she thought about it, Griff had been spending a lot more of his free time with her lately, and his swinging door was hardly swinging at all anymore.

So maybe, she reasoned, she did have a chance. Maybe he had a crush on her, just like she had on him. After all, five years of being best friends can make a person grow on someone.

So she would ask him to make love to her, and he would say yes. No problem at all. He wouldn't reject her. Not if she presented it right. Not if she caught him in the perfect mood.

In fact, now that she thought about it, there had been

a few missed opportunities, times when she could have asked him. But the mood never seemed right. Or the stars weren't lined up just so. Not that she knew anything about stars and how they were supposed to be lined up, but they didn't look very straight up there in the sky and she certainly wasn't going to ask her mother.

She gazed at her reflection in the mirror. On the outside she looked more like twenty than thirty. Make that *almost* thirty. Still, she hadn't had sex in a long, long time, and her insides were probably all shriveled up. When she died, her autopsy report would read, "Ms. Mercer died with a young-looking face and shriveled up insides. Probable cause—lack of usage." No way was any pathologist going to be able to write about her dissected insides in that disrespectful way. She wanted him to find a healthy female with a wealth of plumped up insides all pink and vibrant from being used as they were intended to be used. By Griff.

She'd have to convince Griff to take an active part in making her pink and plumped up. That's all. And if anyone could persuade him to help her, she could.

If she told herself that often enough, she might even come to believe it, too.

The sun had almost set by the time Suzanne got home from work and changed into blue jeans and a blue shirt from the blue shirt section of her closet. She poured herself an iced tea and took it with her into the living room. She loved this room, but she hadn't used it much in the seven years she'd lived in the house.

She sank to the floor, sitting cross-legged in front of her couch, settling against the soft floral cotton fabric for only a second before retrieving the magazine stuck between the cushions.

When she asked Griff the sex question, she wanted

to sound, and act, like a sex goddess. If she studied hard, learned to walk the wiggle walk, and talk the coochy-coo talk, the rest would surely follow. Griff would soon be drooling over every single one of her ten toes, and while he was at it he would be drooling all over her fingers, too.

He would take one look at the new sexy Suzanne and be so overcome by lust and desire that he'd take her to his bed. Or her bed. It didn't matter whose bed. Or it could be a floor, or a couch, or even the kitchen table. She didn't care where, as long as it was somewhere.

She ran her hand over the slick magazine cover, smoothing the wrinkles as best she could. She wasn't embarrassed about the magazine, that's not why she had hidden it between the cushions. The cover screaming promises of "Multiple Orgasms—A Woman's Second Coming" just didn't seem to match, in an aesthetic way of course, with the *Accounting News* and *Tax Preparer's Digest* she already had on her coffee table. Somehow "Ten Ways to Help Your Clients Avoid Paying Inheritance Tax" didn't look quite right sharing space with "Ten Ways to Help Your Man Find Your G-spot." Suzanne didn't know what the G-spot was, but she had a fairly good idea that G didn't refer to the Global Expenditures of Capital Gains Tax.

She turned off the lights as she walked to her bedroom, leaving the house dark. When Griff knocked on her door tonight as he always did when he came home from work in the middle of the night, she was going to do something she'd never done before. She wasn't going to answer. She didn't want to see him again until she went through every single article, page by page, and had her proposition all worked out so she could ask him the *S-E-X* question without blushing and stuttering.

By the time she finished reading "How To Get a Man To Say Yes To Anything," there'd be no way he could turn her down.

Suzanne checked her closet as she did every night to make sure everything was ready to wear the next day. Tuesday's navy suit was right in front of all her other navy suits. She tore the plastic laundry bag off the shirts, taking a blue one and placing it in front of the suit. Her briefcase and computer case were both packed, her shoes lined up and polished. She was ready for Griff. She was ready for work. She was ready for tomorrow.

Suzanne pulled on her nightshirt and crawled under the quilt with the magazine and a flashlight. If the house was dark and he thought she was sleeping, then he would know not to come over for their Monday night card game.

By tomorrow he'd understand why the lights were out tonight.

THE THIRD FLOOR was quiet except for the beeps and buzzes of the machinery. Griff took Ferguson's chart from the carousel at the nurses' station, and took a seat on one of the short, swivel stools as he scanned the notes.

"Hey, Griff, you're here late."

He swiveled around slightly and smiled at the nurse. "I wanted to see Ferguson before I went home." LuLu had been working the night shift at the hospital as long as he'd been there. They had dated on and off for a few of those years, and then she'd gone to California to marry some movie stuntman. He liked LuLu, and was glad she had come back. The hospital needed nurses, and she was one of the best. "How'd he do?"

"He's going to be fine, Griff. Quick fingers, if you know what I mean." LuLu lifted the side of her mouth in a half-pained smile and pointed to her behind.

"Now, LuLu. You know it's the effect you have on those men."

"Maybe not the right men."

Griff pretended not to know what she was talking about when she pinned him with one of her looks that were designed to make career bachelors like himself feel guilty. It hadn't worked before she left for California, and it wasn't going to work now. As far as he was concerned marriage was another word for heartache. He wanted nothing to do with it.

Griff quietly entered room 325 and stared down into the old man's face. He got quite a shock when Ferguson stared right back at him with eyes open wide. Griff took the man's wrist and felt his pulse. "You need to blink, Mr. Ferguson, or I might think you're giving me the dead man's stare."

"Where's my teeth?" the old man rumbled.

Griff pointed to the glass on the rolling table next to the bed. "So, Mr. Ferguson, you had a little excitement today."

The man snorted. "I didn't have any damn excitement, boy. You did. I was only along for the ride."

"Who found you this afternoon, sir?" he asked.

"Dunno."

"Who called the ambulance?"

He shrugged under the white sheets.

"Mr. Ferguson, who can I call to take you home when you're ready to leave? The information is missing from the chart."

"When I leave here, boy, it'll be in a box, and then

I don't care who the hell takes me." Faded brown eyes, full of meanness and something else, something Griff couldn't put a finger on yet, glared at him.

"You're going to be fine, Mr. Ferguson. Influenza A. Nasty strain. It's putting hundreds of people in the hospital. You'll feel like you're going to die for a few days, but when it runs its course you'll be out chasing the women again."

"I know what I got, boy. I don't need you telling me nothin'."

Griff squeezed the man's shoulder. No meat there. Just bones. "You'll be fine," he repeated.

"Leave me be." Ferguson's order came out like a croak. He turned his head away. Within seconds the racking cough that grabbed hold of so many of the flu victims attacked him.

Griff checked the I.V. Ferguson was already getting antibiotics. Hopefully they'd do the job and ward off pneumonia, something that would kill the old man for sure. "None of my patients leave in a box," he told Ferguson. "Dying under my care isn't allowed. If you want to die, you'll have to get your butt out of bed and go outside to do it."

"I will," Ferguson shouted. "But first I'm going to take a nap."

As Griff was leaving the room, Ferguson called him back. "Son," he said, sounding almost contrite. "Send that young nurse in here. I need to have my temperature taken."

"Okay, Mr. Ferguson."

"But first, give me my teeth."

Griff wrapped up his visit with Ferguson and then finally made his way out of the hospital. By the time he pulled into his driveway at two-fifteen in the morning, his body was asleep but his mind raced along on pure adrenaline. He glanced over at Suzie's house. There weren't any lights on, which was strange. She always had a light on for him. She knew he was going to come over and they were going to play three complete games of gin rummy. They'd been doing this same routine for almost the whole five years he'd lived next door to her. He'd bet his next month's salary Suzie had the schedule written in that day planner she carried with her everywhere. And that it was penned in, not penciled in. Plus it was his turn to win, and she probably had that written in that day planner of hers, too.

She had to be up. She was too dependable not to be. He walked to her back door and knocked. When no one answered he turned the knob. When the door didn't open, and he realized he'd been locked out he felt hurt. What did he do that she'd lock him out? He peered through the slats of the kitchen's mini blinds as best he could, talking himself into believing she hadn't locked him out, that she just wasn't home. Yes, that had to be it.

Now what was he supposed to do? He depended on her to answer the door when he knocked. She always had. Suzie was dependable. He depended on her dependability.

Where could Suzanne be? He paced quickly up and down the driveway, going past the side of her house. At every opportunity he looked into her dark windows, trying to see if he missed some light coming in from even the smallest crack in the blinds. No such luck.

Maybe she had a date. A date? Suzie? No way. Well, maybe she did. Nah, not good ol' Suzie. She hadn't had a boyfriend since that guy Trent. No, it wasn't Trent. Tom. No. Not Tom. Troy. Yeah, Troy, that was it. The Troy toy was a jerk and Griff had told her so from the get-go. But did she listen? 'Course not. Took her a couple of months before she finally dumped him. Griff was proud of himself. He had shown real restraint by only saying, "Told you so, Suzie Q," three, or at the most four times, since he wasn't the kind of guy who got pleasure from rubbing a person's nose in her mistakes.

Now all he could do was pace up and down her driveway, and the more he paced the harder he tried to figure out where she could be. Since she didn't have a boyfriend, there could be only one reason she hadn't answered the door.

Damn, he'd been a fool. What if Suzie was lying inside the house hurt? What if she had been robbed at gunpoint? Or murdered? What if she were lying inside there dying on the kitchen floor with a bullet hole through her heart? Here he was, a doctor, and all he was doing about it was getting angry because she hadn't opened the door. Oh, yeah, one selfish bastard, that was him all right.

He started pounding on the door, shouting, "Suzie, open up, Suzie!" at the top of his voice. He didn't care if he woke everyone in the neighborhood. *Come on, Suzie. Get up. Be up. Be okay.*

If she didn't answer then he'd bust the door down. He'd save her. That was his job.

"Suzie!" he kept shouting. "Open the door. *Suzie!*" His voice escalated louder and louder, the pounding got harder and harder.

He had himself so worked up he didn't realize she'd opened the door and his fist, propelled by the momentum he had used pounding on the door, whizzed past her face, barely missing her. "What are you doing here?" he shouted.

"I live here." She rubbed her eyes and yawned all sleepy-like. "Why are you shouting at me?"

"I thought you were dead."

"I will be soon enough. Shouting isn't going to change things."

"Don't even joke about things like that."

She shrugged, and mumbled almost to herself, "Who's joking?"

The only light he had to see her by came from the streetlamp which was at the end of the driveway and out in front of her house. He couldn't see her face or expression that well, but her words sent shivers of dread up his spine. He wanted to ask her what she meant. Only she wasn't acting at all like she was in the mood to talk.

So he asked instead, "If you heard me shouting, why didn't you open the door?" What he didn't ask, and what he really wanted to know, was why she had locked him out.

She yawned again. "I was sleepy."

"You're never tired. I was worried." Now that he was getting used to the dim lighting and could see her better, he noticed that she didn't look at all sleepy.

"Really, Griff? Were you really?"

She looked at him as if she were surprised, when she shouldn't have been. "Of course I was worried. You're my buddy. My friend. I worry."

"A buddy." Her forehead scrunched into a frown.

"Yeah, I was worried. Me out here shouting, you not answering.

Suzie, who'd been leaning against the doorframe, out of the clear blue asked, "Do I remind you of Jennifer Aniston?"

"Who?" What was she talking about?

"You know, the actress. In *Friends*."

"I've never seen it. It must come on when I'm at work."

"What about Julianne Moore? Do I remind you of her?"

"I don't know her. Does she live in town here? Have I seen her at the hospital?"

Griff didn't appreciate it when Suzanne rolled her eyes at him and gave him a disgusted look. "Hey, I'm sorry if I'm not answering your questions right. What do you want from me? I work." Okay, he told himself, he had to stop sounding defensive. It had been a long, hard day, and just because Suzanne wanted to make it longer and harder, instead of being the sweet, loving friend she always had been, well, she was a woman. She had that right.

"Meg Ryan?"

He shook his head. "Sounds kind of familiar, but not sure."

"Nicole Kidman, Catherine Zeta-Jones, Julia Roberts, Emily Watson. Any of those?"

"You know I don't go to movies. I fall asleep."

"Marilyn Monroe?"

"Finally, a name I recognize." He felt so proud of himself. "Yes, Marilyn Monroe."

Suzanne stopped leaning on the door and seemed to perk up. "I didn't know I reminded you of Marilyn Monroe." She looked up at him quickly then back down at her feet.

"You?" He almost started to laugh at that one, because he had no idea what they had been talking about, but he was sure he never said she reminded him of Marilyn Monroe.

"You said—I just thought, well..."

"Yeah, but...I was..." He stopped before he could stick his size twelves down his throat. He'd been up for thirty-six hours and was in no condition to read the kind of female thoughts he needed to be reading in order to keep her from getting mad at him.

"You don't have to say anything. I understand."

What did she understand? He didn't know what was going on. He chose his words carefully. "Good. Because there's only one Suzie Q."

"Right." She not only sounded cold and distant, she took a step away from him.

Now what had he done? What did he say that pissed her off? He replayed the words in his head, only his head was full of cotton and getting stuffier by the minute. He put his hand on her shoulder and squeezed gently. "Come on, Suzie. Let's go play rummy." The muscles in her shoulder tensed under his touch so he let his hand drop away.

"You want to play cards?" she asked, sounding incredulous.

She knew that's what he was here for. It wasn't like they didn't do this every Monday night. And Thursday night. And most Saturday nights, too. "I'll let you win," he offered. It must be her time of the month. That was the only logical explanation. Man-oh-man, what men had to do to please women. "Even though it's my turn. Offers don't get any better than this."

Her smile got so big, so happy, he thought he was in the kitchen and shuffling cards for sure. He took a step forward. Then she said, "You've got to be kidding."

He took another step. He had never been more serious.

"I'm going back to sleep." She wiggled her fingers in a gesture that looked suspiciously like a wave goodbye. That, along with the two steps she took away from him, sent him a clear message.

"How about a compromise? We'll play two games instead of three." He put a foot in forward motion, and what he got he never saw coming, because if he had, he never would have let the door slam in his face.

"What's gotten into you?" he yelled, despite now having what he was sure was a broken nose. He felt around and came away with something that felt like blood, which sent a sick feeling into his belly. This sucked. Everyone knew surgeons could handle all kinds of gory situations, except when it came to themselves. Then they fainted. And he was feeling light-headed already.

Here he'd been all worried about her, thinking she was dead in there, shot up, robbed, beaten, raped. There were all kinds of crazy people running around this world and she was one woman living all by her lonesome. What did he get for all that worry? Almost a broken face, that's what he got.

He tromped across their driveways to his own house. When he got to his back door, instead of pushing it open, he turned toward his neighbor's house and shouted, "I don't need you and your gin rummy, Suzie. I'm going to play solitaire. I *always* win at solitaire."

He didn't need Miss Suzanne's company tonight. He was too tired to make conversation with anyone anyway. Besides, he was only doing her a favor, going over there night after night. If he hadn't shown up like he usually did, she would've been disappointed. And lonely. Yeah, that was it. She would have been real lonely.

Now that he'd gotten all that straightened out in his mind, putting everything in perspective, so to speak, he felt a lot better. He let out a ragged breath, and slammed the door behind him. Then walking to the bedroom, he stripped off his clothes, leaving them wherever they dropped.

Naked and exhausted, Griff climbed between the cool sheets. He shut his eyes and let each group of muscles relax, starting at his feet and working up to his head.

His last thought as the blanket of sleep finally dropped over him was Suzie. He buried his head in his pillow and smiled. She was kinda cute, stable and friendly—except for the way she'd acted tonight, which was very out of character for her. Still, he'd chalk that up to female estrogen levels.

Yeah, Suzanne was many things, but she was no Marilyn Monroe.

2

THE NEXT AFTERNOON, Suzanne waited for her mother, Christine and Nina at Mrs. Wong's Hunan Dragon Garden Chinese restaurant. This was their ninth, and last, annual anniversary lunch since the fortune-tellers made their prediction. For such a momentous occasion, she would have thought they'd be on time.

They were already six minutes late.

She didn't want them to be late because that gave her too much time with her own depressing thoughts. Not about her last month on earth, which was where they should have been focused. But about how Griff didn't find her appealing in a womanly sort of way. Her only appeal to him was as a friendly confidant, and that, by its very nature, was the dirge of sexual attraction.

She should have been thinking about what exciting things she was going to do during the month of March, and all she could think about was trying to figure out a way to get Griff to discover the woman beneath the navy suits and calculator brain.

The revelation of how he truly saw her was a big blow to her womanly self-esteem. This was not good, not good at all. Just when Suzanne had thought she was making progress with him, he had to go and throw her into a backward spiral. She'd never read so many how-to-get-a-man manuals before. Those alone were enough to make an ordinarily frustrated woman, which she knew she wasn't, into a screaming, raging, maniacal, horny woman, which she had become. Forget romance. She and Griff had already been together for five years, and they were as romantic as an old married couple, which is exactly how they acted together. Comfortable, like a pair of worn-out house shoes.

She wanted his body. She wanted his sex. And she wanted it now.

There was no doubt about it, she was going to have to get aggressive, and it wasn't going to be a pretty picture. She put a time limit on what she now referred to as the Griff assignment. Miles away from his magnetic power, she could plan what she wanted to do as she would with any assignment. She had to do that because, as much as she loved him and wanted him, she had business obligations she had to take care of, and she could only waste so much time on something that could very well turn out to be a lost cause.

Suzanne glanced at her watch when her mother finally showed up, nine minutes late, not that she counted.

Hermia didn't apologize for being late, or offer an excuse. Her only comment was, "You really should see my yoga master, darlin', before you go on to that better place. You look very stressed."

"I'm not stressed, Mom." Suzanne's clenched teeth and lipstick-covered lips were frozen in a wide smile.

"Now that I look at you, I can see you're not." Hermia kissed her daughter's cheek. "My mistake."

"If I'm stressed, it's because you're late. You're always late. You know how I feel about schedules."

"I know, darlin'. We were having a caucus." She waved her arm behind her to include Nina and Christine.

Suzanne wasn't very pleased with herself when she realized that she hadn't noticed her friends had arrived right behind her mother. She, who noticed everyone and everything, could only chalk it up to how focused she was on Griff.

She wasted little time on small talk when the food arrived, and got right down to her General Tso's chicken.

"Why don't you eat slower, Suzanne?" her mother scolded.

"I have to get back to work."

"I thought you could take the afternoon off." Hermia sounded disappointed. "We were going to the caterers to plan the food for your wake."

"I've got appointments." Whether her end was near or not meant little to the clients who expected their taxes filed with the IRS on time. "I trust all of you. You'll take care of it."

Christine clasped her hands together. "It's going to be so wonderful. I've already made arrangements with A Catered Affaire and they're thrilled at the idea. They're even giving us a discount and—"

"I've hired the Houston Symphony to play," Hermia said. "Since we don't know when—"

"—or what time—" Nina interjected.

"—we've made arrangements for different parts of the symphony to arrive throughout the day. The music will never end."

"Only I will." Her voice caught.

"Don't talk like that." Hermia looked first to her left, then to her right, before leaning closer to Suzanne and whispering conspiratorially, "Your father thinks we're all crazy but, you know, he's a man, and men don't understand how important appearances are. Making sure your final soiree is more than just an ordinary party is so very important. We can't have guests leave your home with the memory of a tacky wake, can we?''

"No, absolutely not," Suzanne agreed.

"That's right." Hermia nodded at everyone at the table. "If that happens, long after you're gone all they'll remember is that Hermia Bourne Mercer didn't give her daughter the proper send-off. They'll whisper over their grocery carts, and scurry to the other side of the department store when they see me coming. You wouldn't want that for me, would you? Of course not."

Suzanne wondered what Griff would think when she invited him to her wake. Probably that she was crazy.

"Oh, my!" Hermia's eyes widened. "I suddenly remembered one thing. We've all decided that you should have a few dates before the end of the month, so we're all going to fix you up."

Suzanne's fork dropped on her plate with a loud clank. Her head started shaking before she even got the words out of her mouth, "No. Absolutely not. Call them back and cancel."

"Don't be silly, darlin'." Her mother patted her hand again. "We can't do that. We all knew you had so many other things to worry about. We thought getting yourself a date or two would help you relax. Go to a movie, out to dinner. Some dancing. Make you forget your troubles. Right, girls?" She gave Nina and Christine their cue, and the other two nodded encouragingly. "Our Suzanne needs a man to help her forget these are her final days."

"I don't need a man." She needed only Griff. And she was working on that.

"I knew you were going to argue. Didn't I, girls?''

The little puppets, who used to be her friends, nodded again.

"Listen to a little motherly advice, darlin'. A man can take away the loneliness and heartache that's goin' to eat at you this month. You're going to get to a point where you feel empty inside, and a man can fill that void with happiness and joy. When the end comes, you can go out knowing you've made someone happy—your mother."

"Mom, if I want a man, I can get a man. Any man. Men are begging for me."

"Yes, dear, I'm sure they are." Hermia went back to eating. Nina and Christine were busy chewing, too.

"Well, they are." Suzanne gave her head a toss, flipping her ponytail behind her shoulders for extra emphasis. "I have men at the office begging for advice from me. I have men at the grocery store begging to take my purchases to the car. I have men in the mall calling out to me, begging to shine my shoes. Men are begging to be with me all the time," she said.

"Being around all those columns of numbers has finally addled your brain," Hermia said. "I knew the day you passed that horrid CPA exam you'd go downhill. My own daughter, thinking someone yelling out to her in the mall, offering to shine her shoes for a price, is begging for her. Suzanne, I'm worried about you."

Her mother was right, and everyone at the table knew it. She most of all. No men were standing in line begging for anything other than the use of her brain. Even if she had hundreds of men begging for her attentions, it wouldn't matter anyway. Griff was the only one who could fill all her romantic fantasies.

Suzanne looked down at her chest, which was well hidden today, like every day, under a starched blue shirt and navy jacket. Now her breasts were always hidden away, never to come out and play. The only time she could remember revealing them was nine years ago, when she'd so briefly let loose and put on that polka-dot bikini. But then she'd found out she was going to die, and snapped right out of it. Where had that thought come from? She had gone crazy, and she hadn't even realized it until now. She looked around the table at her mother and friends. Her insanity was all their fault. Between bites, and their nonstop talk, they kept casting covert glances in her direction. When she had caught them at it, they had either smiled or turned pink, or both. It was as though she had Dead Girl Walking tattooed on her forehead.

Except Hermia. She only sighed. Tears dropped from the corners of her eyes. Suzanne wasn't sure if it was the knowledge that her only child had such a short time left to live, or if she'd bitten into one of the red-hot chili peppers that so liberally spiced General Tso's chicken.

Suzanne took in a deep breath, and would have bitten her nails, but she purposely had them covered in acrylic so she could get out of the habit. Instead she grabbed a piece of hair from her ponytail, and twirled it around her finger so tight it cut off the circulation.

Her mother finally dropped her fork on the plate and rescued the finger. With a huge sigh, she said, ''Please don't take it personally if I take out a life insurance policy on you.''

Suzanne, who had just put another piece of chicken in her mouth, stopped chewing. Christine stopped slurping her soup, and her head jerked up so quickly at Hermia's words that a piece of wet tofu caught and hung off her bottom lip. The water Nina had been swallowing went back into the glass and she started to cough.

"Now, now, girls." Hermia pounded on Nina's back at the same time she said in her soothing, matter-of-fact voice, "I know we only caucused about Suzanne's lack of a love interest, but this is something I've been thinking about. I'm nothing if not pragmatic. If Suzanne's still alive on March 31st, then all that'll be lost is a month's insurance premium. If not, well, I'm going to use that money to hire someone to break Red Jack's Red Rock Casino. If Suzanne isn't going to do the job she was born to do, then I'm just going to have to find a way to do it for her."

"How can I be sure that you're not going to try to kill me?" Suzanne asked. "You want that casino destroyed so badly."

"No need to be sarcastic, Suzanne Hermia Bourne Mercer." She looked indignant. "You're my daughter. I love you more than life itself. More than any casino." Without taking a breath, she added, "Although taking out an accidental death policy is a good idea, too. Thank you for reminding me of that." She pinched Suzanne's cheek, then patted where she'd pinched. "You're such a smart girl."

Christine pointed her finger, scolding the others. "How can you talk about such things in front of Suzanne? That's so rude." Out the side of her mouth, she said, "Hermia, I'll call you later. My brother sells insurance."

"I have an idea," Suzanne said, "to save you a few dollars, so you don't have to take out all that extra insurance. Why don't you have a séance and figure out exactly how I'm going to go? I'd be interested in knowing that, too."

"Didn't I teach you anything at all while you were

growing up, dear?'' Hermia's lips pursed in disappointment. ''You know we can't have a séance until after you're gone. However...'' She glanced at Christine and Nina. ''...we'll plan on it the first week after Suzanne's passing. How about that, girls? We'll be able to make contact with Suzanne as she's floating in the here and now, before she gets shipped to heaven on one of those angel birds that take people to meet St. Peter at the Pearly Gates.''

''How do you know that's where I'm going?''

''Where else would you go, darlin'? But that reminds me, since we're not sure how you'll go, only that you'll go, I'll take out some double indemnity along with the accidental death. No point in taking out disability, since that won't even be an option.''

''Do what you want.'' Suzanne gave the lot of them her blessing. ''Take out all the life insurance you can afford. I've already taken out insurance myself. Quite a bit as a matter of fact, and I may go ahead and take out some more.''

''You're so wonderful and generous. And prepared.'' Hermia sighed. ''Those traits come from her father's side of the family. My side is purely focused on revenge. That's why one of the insurance polices I'm taking out on you is earmarked for the 'Breaking the Bank of the Red Rock Casino Fund.'''

Suzanne stopped listening to them as they huddled close together to finish planning what they seemed to picture as the party to end all parties. The wake where the corpse would be awake until she died, whenever or wherever that would happen. They were in for a twenty-four hour party. She, who had always lived her life in the background, was the guest of honor. There was nowhere to hide.

AT ONE O'CLOCK that morning, Griff knocked on her back door again. Once again, she hid under her comforter, which did little to comfort, with a flashlight and read the chapter on ''Taming the Playboy'' from what was fast becoming her favorite advice book, *The Ultimate Guide to Understanding and Securing the Alpha Male*.

She had to admit that while reading *The Ultimate Guide* it crossed her mind several times that her head had been buried under a rock for all of her formative years. When she was dating in college, which really wasn't all that long ago, and there weren't all that many dates, either, boys were called boys, and men were called men. There were jocks and geeks and mama's boys. The only Greeks were in fraternities. But there sure weren't any alpha, beta or gamma males that she knew of.

By the time she finished Chapter Two, she knew the authors could have used Griff as their example of the perfect alpha male, since they described him perfectly. She found the book and its authors to be credible, so she decided to take their advice. That's how she had found the strength not to answer the door when Griff knocked, despite every part of her being that screamed, ''Suzanne, you crazy idiot. It's Griff. Let him in.''

Tomorrow night she'd let him in. Tomorrow she'd watch his strong hands, the same hands that saved lives, that performed microscopic operations with the lightest, most delicate of touches, shuffle the well-worn cards they played with and deal them out in his own snappy rhythm.

Tomorrow night she'd hear his warm, deep voice and let its timbre cloak her in a warm, man-scented blanket of familiar security while he'd speak with quiet intensity of his day. She would be with him until his eyelids drooped, and his lips slackened into that sloppy smile that caused her heart to palpitate. When he finally got into his goofy joke mode, she would do something that she'd never done before. Instead of telling him it was time to leave for his own bedroom, she would take his big bear hand within her own and lead him into hers.

A lot of hard work had gone into this plan. There wasn't any room for error, so everything had to be choreographed to the exact beat. Her trash baskets were overflowing with revision after revision of her plan, until finally she had gotten it right. She was so confident she had written the final version in her day planner. In ink. Not just any ink, either. Black, permanent ink. Nothing could change her plans now. Her insides were on their way to being pink and plumped.

When her alarm went off at five-thirty the next morning, she bolted out of bed, rushed to the closet and pulled out her Wednesday clothes. As the time neared closer to six, her stomach, chest and head were as tightly wound as she was sure her clients must feel just before a tax audit.

Finally, the knowledge of what she was about to ask him, the impact of what would happen if he said yes, the idea of spending a night locked in passion with one Dr. Griff, just about did her in. She needed fortification. She needed the instant gratification it would bring.

She tried to talk herself out of it, but in the end, the lure of how it would relax her won out. She pulled open the bottom drawer of her nightstand. Here she kept the bottle hidden under a dozen accounting magazines and one or two gardening almanacs. She took it out. "Don't drink it," she told herself. But like any addict, in the end, she couldn't resist the lure of the bottle.

She sat on the edge of her bed, bare feet dangling to the floor, toes scraping across the wood planks and the fringe of the blue throw rug. She lifted the bottle and hesitated a brief moment. If she wanted to change her mind, this was her last chance.

Well, forget that kind of self-righteous nonsense. She lifted it to her lips and let the sweet elixir pour into her mouth, down her throat, and coat her stomach. No frills. Not even a glass. Straight-up. No other way would do for her. Not now.

Hershey's Chocolate Syrup.

Wonderful. Decadent. A nice coat of fat across the hips. Men liked curvaceous women. She took another swallow. Her heart beat faster, and her eyelids fluttered as the sugar high kicked in. She set down the syrup bottle, now sucked dry, next to the clock.

Her palms were moist and cold. She touched her cheeks. They burned. Suzanne closed her eyes and waited until the grandfather clock's chimes started ringing. *One, two, three*—she jumped up and ran to the back door—*four, five, six*—threw it open and hurried outside.

Griff had opened his back door and came out of his house at the same time she did. "Suz," he said gruffly, barely nodding at her.

"I guess we should talk." She didn't blame him for being hurt, but according to her book, alpha males didn't stay hurt for long. If they did, they became gamma males, and there was nothing gamma about Griff. "About last night."

"Last night?" His look. Furrowed forehead. Lips in a straight line. Eyes squinted in concentration. "What do you mean?"

Total phony. Cute though. Real cute.

She watched him take in a deep breath of moist morning air, his broad chest expanding under his T-shirt. Griff, over six feet of solid muscle and strength. Griff, with the startling crystal blue eyes that could easily seduce as well as deduce a woman's innermost secrets, now stared at her.

"When I didn't answer the door."

"Oh, that last night."

"Or the night before," she added, then about kicked herself. Sure, Suzanne, add salt to his wound.

He dismissed her concern when he said, "I don't know what you mean." As he said the words, all nonchalantly, he scratched his upper arm, totally unconscious of how she stared at the muscles rippling under the cotton shirt. "What are you doing home now?"

"I thought I'd go in late this morning."

"You?" An eyebrow lifted in disbelief.

"I wanted to talk to you." She looked down at her bare feet and her pink painted toenails. She couldn't believe she had run out of the house without her panty hose and shoes. What had she been thinking? Oh, she knew what she had been thinking, but still, it bothered her that thoughts of him had consumed her to such a degree. "Can we talk?"

She walked carefully down her back steps, worried she'd trip over her own toes out of sheer nervousness. When she reached the driveway, she was only a few feet away from him. He stretched his arms up high until his hands were lifted over his head and yawned. His T-shirt rose over his taut stomach, showing muscles, tendons and a fine line of dark male hair that swirled around his belly button, then descended into his loose-fitting blue jeans. He knuckled sleep from his eyes, then gave her one of those heartbreaking

Griff smiles that turned her insides into nothing more than warm melted dark chocolate. The real Swiss kind. Even better than Hershey's.

He walked to his garage and pulled open the door. "Sure we can talk. At our usual time. When I get home from work. Right now, I'm going to take the garbage can out and go back to sleep."

Oh, he was mad, real mad. Now that was pure alpha male. She tingled at the thought of her making him get all alpha on her. This was almost worth changing her work schedule for.

"Griff? I really need to talk to you." Then she remembered about alphas thinking women were the weaker sex. Totally ridiculous by anyone's standard, but still, to get what she wanted she'd have to be strong and play weak. "I wanted to apologize."

He looked over at her, giving her one of his loopy, sexy smiles. "Yeah?"

She smiled demurely and shrugged, which wasn't an act at all, but a reaction from what his smile did to her heart—made it thump. There was a difference she now knew between a beat and a thump, and hers was actually thumping. He didn't even realize he had a smile like that. Boy-oh-boy, it was sex in the making. No wonder she had such a case of lust for him.

"Sure, Suzie. I have time for you. Not like you didn't for me. When I needed you."

She could read him like her *Guide* book, without needing to go under the covers and read by flashlight. Were all men this easy? How come she never knew this before? All the years she had wasted being a buddy when she probably could have had him doing her bidding years ago just by being demure. Wasted years. She'd been a fool.

Suzanne opened her garage door, which was an ex-

act duplicate of his, only, painted a dusty rose instead
of beige. They both hauled out their trash cans. Griff
swung his up and over his shoulders, carrying it as if
its contents weighed nothing, which it probably did,
loaded with empty pizza boxes as it was. Using his
other hand, he took her plastic can away from her and
carried both to the curb.

"Well—" Griff smiled through another yawn, his
crystal blue eyes looking sleepy but still on the alert.
Years of medical residency probably had given him
that look. "Let's go."

She wanted to go to bed with him. Only he looked
at her like a nonentity. A friend. The girl next door.
Suzanne didn't want to be that girl. Very deliberately,
but praying it didn't look calculated, she fiddled with
the first button on her blue shirt until it became undone. She went for the second. She looked at him and,
unfortunately, he was looking right back at her. His
gaze hadn't moved any lower than her nose. What was
she? A nonwoman? Were her breasts so neutral to him
that he didn't even see them? Apparently. This was
awful. She had a lot of work ahead of her, work she
hadn't planned for, hadn't scheduled in.

She shifted her weight from her left foot to her right
foot and back again. Her feet were cold.

Griff wasn't wearing shoes, either, but the cold con-
crete didn't seem to bother him. Neither did the chill
of the early morning air, although she could see that
under his T-shirt his nipples had hardened. She swallowed hard and looked up into his face. God, what a
face. His jaw, so square and strong. His nose, broken
twice while he had been growing up, was a bit
crooked. Endearing. Such virility standing so close to
her became her own version of heaven and hell right
here on earth.

"Well, nice seeing you. Have to go," Suzanne said, and cringed at the purely business sound of her voice.

He reached out and grabbed her wrists. "You're the one who wanted to talk." His forehead wrinkled as that blue-eyed gaze of his scanned her face. "What's the matter?"

"I was going to ask you a favor."

"Anything for you, you know that," he said. "We're best buds."

Buds. God, this was bad. She moistened her lips. A bud was a flower not yet in bloom. A bud was a dud.

Her throat felt parched and she wanted a glass of water. Make that another bottle of Hershey's Chocolate Syrup. Straight-up, no ice cream. A banana, on the other hand, according to the book, would be okay. She tried to get the words out, only it took several moments to get her thoughts off the size of the banana. When she finally spoke, the sentences weren't even audible and she was babbling, not making any sense.

The smile on his lips slowly turned into a line of concern. He gripped her upper arms, leaning down, looking into her eyes. "Are you okay? You don't look so hot."

She was hot all right, but not from any fever. She could feel the warmth of his hands all the way to her skin when he touched her through the wool gabardine jacket. Where the pressure of his fingers and palm rested on the cloth, she burned beneath it. She wanted to move in closer to him. To melt into his arms. God almighty, she wanted him with a fierceness that even she didn't know she'd been capable of harboring.

His tone was deceptively casual. "Come on, Suzie. Whatever's bothering you can't be all that bad. Tell Dr. Griff."

She wanted to lean into him, to use his strong arms

and hard body for comfort. Only she couldn't. Not yet. Taking a deep breath for courage, she tried again to speak. He waited. Doctors like Griff waited for their patients to talk. She knew Griff would never rush a lover either. He wasn't rushing her. Still, she couldn't just blurt it out. Her courage had left her, and she clung to the knowledge that she still had twenty-nine days after today. "Never mind. I have to go to work." She stepped away.

He pulled her back. Where his hand touched her arm, flecks of flame shot out. Fire alert, fire alert.

"Oh, no, you don't. Not after all this. Come on inside. I need something to eat. I need coffee. You need coffee, too, right?"

He was knowingly bribing her, but she was on to him. She had strength of character to fall back on when female hormones were trying to get her to do other things. Like take her clothes off. "I've only allotted a certain number of minutes to see you this morning, and we've already exceeded them. No fault of yours. Mine, all mine. So, bye." She was such a coward.

"Later?" he asked.

"Sure. I'll run home and get my day planner. We can set up an appointment to talk."

"You want to make an appointment to talk to me? Me? Since when do I need to make a date to talk with you? Huh, Suz? We talk now."

Suzanne had never ever seen him get like this before. A perfect textbook case. She would have to write the *Guide* authors about this, too. "The night shifts are finally getting to you, Griff. You've been so grouchy all morning."

"You're the one who's been in a mood." He said the word "mood" as if he really wanted to say something not quite as politically correct as that. Probably something more in the line of how she had turned into some PMSing bitch. It's a good thing he hadn't.

"I just have a lot on my mind." She had to tilt her head way back to look into his face. She breathed deeply, wanting to inhale his scent. Her hands clenched behind her back to keep from running her fingertips over the dark stubble covering his jaw.

"What's on your mind?" he asked.

She didn't answer, because how could she say that it was him? Griff was so magnificent. A lion. A grizzly bear. A lone wolf. She then remembered the pack of wolfettes that were always sniffing behind him. She took a step back. She wanted to be a wolfette in the most basic kind of way. She didn't know what she'd do if he refused her.

"Well?" He stomped his bare foot.

Suzie touched his shoulder in the same friendly gesture she'd always used when touching him. Only this morning her heart raced as she felt his muscles tense under his skin.

"Now, are you coming in?" It sounded like an order.

She would be stupid and a fool not to obey. "I'll see you later. I'm going to work."

He didn't say anything for a few seconds, just stared into her face, as if looking for a sign that she'd cracked up. She smiled at him.

"Come on." He took her by the arm and walked her up his driveway toward the back door.

"Okay, Griff, I'll postpone my appointments for this morning, move things around a bit." She tried to bat her eyelashes, but he looked at her kind of funny, so she figured that flirting wasn't working. She lowered her voice. "I'm only doing this because you asked me to.'' She would have postponed an appointment with Mr. Merriweather himself if Griff had asked her to.

He put his hand on the doorknob. "Hey, Suzie Q, that's my girl. We're friends, right? What're friends for if not to listen to each other's problems?"

"Exactly."

"You know," he said, holding the door open so she could walk in, "I'll do anything for you, Suz. Whatever it takes to make you happy."

Those were just the words Suzanne had longed to hear. As she entered his kitchen she knew she'd soon have Griff eating out of her hands. All she had to do was ask.

3

"ABSOLUTELY NOT!" His voice rose two octaves.

"Is that a no, Griff?" she asked softly. All she had asked him to do was have sex with her. The rejection rocked her all the way to the very tips of her toes. To the center of her heart.

She looked down at her clothes. Could it be what she was wearing? No, she doubted it. Her standard navy suit was very fashionable in the accounting world. It had been specially tailored to show off, well to show off nothing feminine. Thinking about it, she realized that could be a problem. But two buttons on her shirt were undone and she wasn't wearing panty hose. That had to count for something.

Maybe not. He'd never had a glimpse of her feminine side. He couldn't know that underneath the suit jacket were two breasts that were a pretty good size, a small waist and other womanly parts.

She occasionally wore her hair piled on top of her head in a makeshift topknot. Simple and easy. Only this morning she had rushed to get out of the house, so she had forgotten to comb it out before she put it back up. Now, she felt the strands curling and falling all over her face, neck and shoulders.

She wouldn't even think about her horrible freckles. No wonder he was turned off. She always wore makeup to hide them, but this morning she hadn't had time, so those freckles were probably popping out all over the place.

No wonder Griff had never thought of her as a desirable woman. No wonder he'd never had the kind of fantasies about her that she'd harbored about him all these years. He thought of her as a nonwoman, a sexless being, not a woman he might have secretly lusted after. This was…was…, well, it was just depressing, that's all. "I have hidden surprises," she informed him haughtily. "And, not that *you'd* notice, a couple of extremely large assets."

"I know all about your assets," he said dismissing her. "They're all tied up."

"They can be unbound."

"Not anytime soon. I keep my assets in easy reach, because you know, Suz, I keep telling you, that you never know when you're going to need some of your assets. In an emergency. To help a friend." He clearly was in his doctor-lecturer mode and he didn't look happy.

Well, neither was she. "You don't know what I'm talking about." Suzie had the urge to shrug out of her jacket, rip open her shirt, flash her assets and do a cheerleader shout, "Ah one, and ah two! Hey, big boy, these are for you! *B-R-E-A-S-T-S!* Breasts!" She didn't though, because if he just stood there and stared at her like she'd sprouted another head, she'd just lie down and die. Only she'd still have thirty days to suffer the humiliation before it happened.

She wasn't the spur-of-the moment kind of person who'd do things like that. And she wore a bra, so flashing him wearing a white cotton bra would be less than thrilling.

Oh, brother. She thought she had the whole Griff

seduction planned to the minutest detail, but she now realized she hadn't done any of this right.

"I don't see why we can't," she said, her tone surly. "We're friends."

"Friends. That's the key word here, Suz. My policy, and it's firm, is never have sex with a friend."

"You've made love to hundreds of women." She poked him in his chest with her finger. "I've seen them coming and going from here."

"There's a difference between making love and having sex."

"What's the difference?"

"You really want to know?" His lip curled into a smug smile.

His hair, long and rakish, fell over his forehead. She gulped, then nodded.

"The brutal truth? Can you handle it?"

"Yes."

His fingers jerked through his hair, pushing it back. "Every day I operate on people whose lives are put in these very hands." He held them out. "They have no choice about being there. They didn't say, 'Hey, I think I'll get myself in a car accident today so I can go to Sugar Land General and have Dr. Scott, the man with the magic hands, operate on me.'"

"I know that," she said softly, compassionately. They had five years of friendship between them. She knew him better than anyone and she knew how much he loved his work. But she also knew that he had let her into a part of his life few if any others were allowed to enter. The part that struggled with an occasional sense of helplessness.

"Every day there can be ten, twenty, maybe even thirty people. I never know. Little kids, old people, babies, so many people pass through the doors. Healing the patients is tantamount. I have no personal life.''

She didn't agree. She was part of his personal life. Friends were just that—personal. Couldn't he see that?

"The one thing that I do know for sure is that life is short and sometimes the end can come in the most unexpected way.''

"There's truth to that," she agreed. "On the other hand, some people, like me, have years to prepare for the end. Which is why I asked you to—''

"This isn't about having sex with you, Suzie," he said, his voice very low, very gentle. "For me, all those other times, it was about numbing my brain.''

"I can numb your brain as well as the next woman. Better even.'' She didn't see a problem, and wasn't at all happy that he did.

"No, you can't.''

"Yes, I can. I can have sex, too. I know how to have sex. It's just sex.'' What she wanted was sex with Griff. Before she died she had to fulfill her one and only fantasy. "Sex. Easy as one-two-three. In-out-in-out. Bang, it's over.'' She shrugged her shoulders. "Simple. What's the big deal?''

"In-out-in-out," he repeated slowly, as if he were mulling through the whole concept. "Then it's over?''

"Close your mouth, Griff. Why are you looking so surprised? You've done it millions of times. You know the drill.''

After a moment, he found his voice. Strong and sure, just like him. "Absolutely not. Not with you. You understand, don't you? I care about you.''

"Care?'' She didn't understand.

"Not only that, I respect you. In fact, I love you.''

"Love me? Then why no? What's the problem?''

"Because I respect you too much to have sex with

you. You're my best friend. I don't want that to change.''

"Only once Griff. What would change? You'd go your way, I'd go mine." She raised her gaze to the ceiling. "We could still play cards."

"Sex with you wouldn't be moral. It wouldn't come under my code of ethics." He puffed out his chest, his magnificent chest, all smug and self-assured.

So, the good doctor thought his wiggle worm was so good only a few, select women would get it, and she hadn't made the list. Well, it probably was. But she was deserving, too. More than most.

"I'm on a very limited time schedule." She finally gave herself permission to get angry. She only wished she had the kind of personality that would allow her to stomp her feet and throw china cups at the walls. "You, Dr. Stick-It-Anywhere, except at me, are talking morals? Do you see something wrong with this picture?"

"First of all, I don't stick it anywhere, and I resent the implication that I do. Second, I've never been indiscriminate, and third, I've always had morals," he defended. "Don't use my way of dealing with pain, and stress, and make it personal against you. You and me—" he pointed his finger first at her, and then at himself "—it'll never be. You make me relax," he yelled. "I depend on you to keep me calm." His voice escalated. "I depend on you to talk to. I come to you when I have problems. I need you, Suzie." His face had turned purple and his hands were clenched into tight fists. "You're my best friend, dammit, and best friends don't have sex." His breaths came in short gasps.

"Okay, then. Fine." She shrugged her shoulders and pretended disinterest. "I certainly understand your position." Even if it was stupid. She smiled at him, as if she had not a care in the world.

"Good," he said huffily. "I don't want to hurt your feelings."

"Hurt by you? Pah-leeze. You're no big deal."

"Good." His purple look had changed to a questionable shade of green. "I'm glad we understand each other."

Her grin got larger. "We do, we do." The doctor idiot was believing the smile. Men. Were they all so gullible or was it just the alpha males that believed anything that made their position the right position?

"Let me ask you something," Griff said.

"Sure. Ask away."

"Why do you want this sudden change in our relationship? Why did you want to do this...this...you know, with me? It's never come up before."

And that was the problem. If only Griff had *come up*, even a little, they would be in bed right now and not having this conversation. "The truth is, I'm going to die on March 30th, and I thought I'd like to try you out and see how you were before I go." She said it so casually. "Just once."

Apparently she made the announcement too casually, because it didn't register. All he said in response was, "Just once? For cryin' out loud, Suz."

"I know, I know, once may not be enough, but I was only going to have time for once. It's on my calendar, and well, I thought I wanted to try everything before I go."

Finally it clicked. "Die?" He leaned down and looked closely into her eyes and said angrily, "If this is your idea of a joke, it's a bad one. Tasteless. Not at all like you, Suz. I thought you had more class."

Ouch! The insult hurt. But they were friends, and

he could do that. She would have fought back, verbally, word for word, except all she wanted to do was find the guts to move her mouth a little closer to his so she could place him in a very extensive lip-lock. "I don't mean now, as in today. It'll happen on my thirtieth birthday. March 30th."

He abruptly spun around, went to the counter and plugged in the coffeepot then pulled open the refrigerator door.

"Griff?"

"What?" he snapped. The upper half of his body hidden, the lower half exposing extremely muscular calves.

"You didn't put coffee grinds or water in the pot."

"Damn." He threw the box with yesterday's pizza on the counter, slamming the door shut. He unplugged the coffee, filled the cylinder with water, threw grounds into the basket, then plugged it in again. "You're making me crazy, Suzanne. Crazy. I know and you know this is some kind of joke, and it's not April Fools' Day yet. You don't really believe you're dying."

"I will die." She sat on one of his kitchen chairs, her chin resting in the palm of her hand, and watched him toss the pizza in the oven right on top of the wire rack.

He switched on the oven to bake and the temperature to five hundred. When he came back to the table he had that heart-melting goofy grin splashed across his mouth. "I wasn't born yesterday. I went to medical school. You don't have the symptoms."

"Don't you think you should put the pizza on a pan or something?"

She couldn't look at those lips anymore. They made her want to act in a very non-Suzanne way. So it was back to business for her. "If you don't, you'll get cheese all over the bottom of the oven."

"If you weren't such an anal accountant you'd know that burnt cheese gives the oven character." He chucked her under the chin and moved back to the counter. He pulled two cups from the cabinet and set them next to the coffeepot.

"I *am* an accountant..."

He looked at her for a second, a smirk across his lips.

"But I'm not anal," she bit out defensively.

"Whatever you say, Suz. Except you haven't answered the question."

"Well, I'm not."

"Not what? Dying or anal?"

"Anal," she bit out.

"You know, you look real cute when you do that." He reached out and brushed his finger, which smelled like coffee and cheese, across her lip. His voice deepened. "Sticking your lip out like you're having a temper tantrum." Then he backed away. "And you're acting like you're twelve, too. Telling me that story about you dying. Ha! What do you take me for anyway? A sucker?"

"I'm not dying today." She breathed deeply and looked into his too handsome face. She wanted him something so fierce it took her breath away.

"See. I knew the smell of coffee would get the truth out of you." The tiny lines in the corners of his eyes, barely visible except for the tan, crinkled up, accentuating the blueness. He crossed his arms over his chest and looked all self-righteous.

"Believe what you want." She stared into those warm blue eyes. "I asked you what I asked you because of what I know to be true. I never would have

put myself in such a vulnerable position otherwise."
Although she never imagined his answer would have
been so humiliatingly negative.

"Suzie, you and me, we're not like that." His voice
had turned from gruff to gentle. "You know how
much money I make. We have a great personal relationship. It has nothing to do with sex."

"It's okay, Griff. You can drop it now."

He wouldn't. He kept going on and on. "If you and
I had sex, it wouldn't be sex, it would be making love.
And if we made love it would mean commitment. I
don't do commitment."

"I'm not asking for a commitment. You weren't
listening to me."

"You're right. You didn't. Tell me why you think
you have a month left to live."

"Oh. That. Well…yes." She hesitated.

He got up from the chair and went to the counter
and brought back two steaming mugs. "I've got all
day," he said lifting the mug to his mouth. "Have at
it."

She looked at her watch again. "Time," she stated,
"is only an illusion."

"What?" he hooted. "This coming from you? The
woman who lives by eight-minute increments?"

Her face went up in flames. She asked haughtily,
"May I have some cream? Sugar?"

He waved his arm towards the kitchen counter behind him. *"Mi casa es su casa."*

How true. She did know his house as well as she
knew her own. Just like he knew hers. Suzanne
scrounged around in his pantry, flipping through the
little packs of powdered creamer and sugar. Some people pocketed matches from restaurants, Griff was into
the staples—cream, sugar, salt, pepper, forks, knives.

She took two packs of creamer stamped with the Sugar Land General Hospital logo. The sugar had come from Mia's, Sugar Land's new Italian restaurant. She wanted to ask him how the food was, but figured pizza was pizza wherever you bought it.

She ripped open the packages and slowly poured the powder and granules into the cup. Griff stretched his arm out to the side, pulled open a drawer and handed her a spoon. She stirred slowly, watching the white powder turn the black coffee to light beige, the swirls inside the glass became a whirlwind, mesmerizing.

"Suzie!"

The spoon dropped into the cup, splattering hot liquid on the table and her hand. Her hand went to her mouth and she sucked on the places the liquid burned, trying to cool down the pain. "You scared me."

He raised his eyebrows. "I'm waiting."

"It happened about a month before my twenty-first birthday," she started. She looked above his head at the clock hanging on the wall. With a resigned breath, she told him the story. When she was through, she asked, "Do you believe me now?"

"I believe this all happened to you, but I don't think that means you're going to die. You can't really believe that, either. Not you. You're too sensible. Accountants don't believe that kind of crap."

"Really? You know so many accountants that you can make that kind of blanket statement?" She sighed. "On March 30th, I will be dead. Nothing is going to change that."

"Suzanne, stop talking like that," he ordered.

"I can't, because I believe this with all my heart and soul. I'm not going to die now. Or tomorrow. Or the next day. Nothing can kill me now." She grabbed his hand. Long, lean fingers. So strong and powerful. "Don't you see, Griff? Don't you understand? Even my mother thinks I'm going to die. They're all planning a wake."

"That's sick," he said, his face all twisted. "No one can know what the future will be. No one. If people knew, they wouldn't get in their cars and have accidents, now would they? They'd have an 'on purpose' instead. I'd be out of a job as a trauma surgeon because if everyone knew what was going to happen, there wouldn't be a need for trauma."

Suzie heard the garbage truck coming down her street. "Okay, fine. I'll prove it to you."

She stood up and went to the back door. "Watch me from the window."

Griff decided that the woman he had known for all these years, he really didn't know at all. She had a screw loose and he wasn't watching her from any window. He followed her out the door and trailed her as she walked to the front of the house.

The garbage truck had picked up the trash from the last house on the block. It now headed toward their houses. The truck wasn't going fast, but it was powerful enough and had enough tonnage to do some damage even at twenty miles an hour, especially if the driver slammed on the brakes and the truck went into a skid. It would be messy. Garbage dumped, flesh spilled. He'd seen too many end results of accidents like that. Accidents he knew would happen when Suzanne, standing on the curb, yelled out, "Watch me."

The truck crossed the intersection, picking up speed, barreling toward their houses, Suzanne left the protection of the curb and ran into the middle of the street and stopped, staring at the giant engine. The horn blared in the early morning hours, and the truck moved forward, giving no indication that it would slow down or stop.

Griff's legs, which had carried him through many a marathon, now acted like jelly trying to run through water—breaking apart and not getting anywhere.

And Suzanne stood in the middle of the street with a stupid serene smile on her face and her hands folded in front of her as if in prayer.

GRIFF COULD NOT believe that Suzanne had just put him through hell. Then, to top it off, she didn't look as if she had any remorse. She could've gotten them both killed, smashed on the street like a couple of roadkill armadillos. He was still shaking inside. His arms and hands, so steady in surgery, couldn't even hold the coffee cup without sloshing the brew. "What the hell are you trying to prove?"

"I told you I wasn't going to die until the thirtieth. Maybe now you'll believe me."

She sounded so self-righteous, she made him look like some kind of idiot. He wouldn't let her get away with that. He was no fool. "If I hadn't been there to lift you off the ground and carry you out of the street, you'd be nothing but fertilizer right now." He didn't believe this dying story of hers for one instant. This was not what he had learned in medical school.

What had gotten into her anyway? Suzie, his buddy, his friend. The one person whom he'd always counted on to be consistent. To be levelheaded. Never to change.

Never to act so damn...damn...*female*. "You're turning all weird on me," he accused, shaking his head at the horror of it all.

"I'm exactly the same now as I was yesterday. I'm exactly the same now as I was nine years ago. The same as when I met you five years ago."

Griff narrowed his eyes and really studied the woman sitting next to him. The woman he'd thought he knew. Why did she have to go and get all goofy on him? "You know what I think, Suz? You need a physical. I happen to know a great neurologist. He'll do an MRI of your brain, see if there's any kind of swelling. Maybe you have a concussion."

"I am so insulted that you think I need to get my head examined." Hurt tinged her words.

"I didn't say psychiatrist, although that's a thought, too."

"Stop that right now."

He could see things weren't going to be easy. He reached out and took her hand. So very small, and very soft. Without thinking he rubbed her fingers and palm between his own and said very gently, "Stress can do strange things to the brain. There's nothing to be ashamed of here. Isn't this your busy season over at that number-crunching place where you work?"

"I'm...not...stressed." She bit out the words at him and pulled her hand from his grasp. Crossing her arms in front of her, she gave him the evil eye. "I hate that all male doctors think that every time someone has a condition and you can't scientifically explain it, you chalk it up to stress."

"I never do that." Poor, poor Suzie. He didn't want to frighten her, but he'd seen it before. Grown men and women falling apart, becoming delusionary, going down the tubes all because of stress from their jobs or money or family problems.

Suzie's mother was slightly wacko, but she didn't cause Suzie much stress. At least he hadn't thought so.

He did know that she had a lot of stress from her job. She'd risen to the top in her company at a very

young age. Staying on top, when there were many
ready and willing to try to topple her, could get to a
person. Suzie told him only last month that she felt as
if she had to prove herself worthy of her lofty position
every day. That kind of stress and pressure would get
to anyone. He should know.

He'd decided to do what he could to examine her
on a very basic, cursory level, and do it in such a way
that she'd never know she was under his mental mi-
croscope.

He could pull it off, since he was known as a suave
kind of doctor. He had his own bedside technique
down to a science.

Griff stood up and walked around the kitchen. She
followed his movement with her eyes, which he took
as a good sign. He picked up the only stainless steel
cooking spoon from the plastic container sitting on the
counter and slapped it in his hands a few times, until
he had distracted her. Before she knew his intention,
he hit her knee with the edge of the spoon.

"Ouch!" she yelled, as her leg flew in the air and
her foot connected with his groin.

He cringed in agony and she didn't even have the
decency to look contrite. After all he had done for her.
After all he was still doing for her. House calls. For
free, yet.

"What do you think you're doing?" she asked.

"I don't know what's wrong with you, Suz, but the
clonus, those reflexes in your leg, are working just
fine," he croaked. "So it has to be a brain injury.
Have you fallen down? Hit your head? Been getting
enough sleep?"

"Sleep?" She started to giggle.

"Never mind. I know that answer." He leaned forward a little and gazed into her eyes. Clear and angry.

Those green eyes had gold specks and they were spitting anger right back at him. Good sign, good sign. "You better take this seriously."

"What makes you think I'm not?"

"Concentrate." He already knew her motor functions were in fine working order, since not even fifteen minutes ago she had been running, completely even and balanced, out into the street.

Yet, Suzie waiting in the middle of the street, no matter how steadily she stood on both feet, waiting to get run over by a garbage truck just to prove a point, was definitely the sign of some kind of trauma to the brain.

"Stop being a doctor, will you? There's nothing wrong with my brain." She rubbed her knee. "I may never walk again though."

"I know good orthopedic doctors, too." He then asked casually, "Suzie, what time is it? Can you read the wall clock?"

"Six thirty-one. If you're testing whether or not I need glasses, the answer is 'not.'"

"Visual acuity seems fine." He scratched that off his mental list of possible trauma indicators. Then he realized that Suzie would know what time it was whether she had a clock around her or not. Suzie *was* a clock. "Do you have headaches?"

"Of course not. I don't need two aspirin, Griff," she said with an overabundance of patience. "I'm just going to die on the 30th. It's in the cards."

"Is that some kind of tarot joke?"

"No, it's the truth."

"Now, other than your mother, do you have a past history of any kind of neurotic or psychotic brain dysfunction?"

"Don't you dare bring my mother into this discussion." Anger and frustration came pouring from her. "You may not believe me, but it's true. I have no reason to make any of this up." With a determination and strength that hadn't been there moments before, she said, "I didn't ask you to make love with me as a spur-of-the-moment request. I've thought about this a long time."

"You don't want to do this, Suzie. When you make love with a man, it'll be for keeps. Like I said, I'm not a for-keeps kind of guy. You know that."

She grinned at him. "I don't see why you're trying to make such a big deal about it."

"Big deal? Me? Ha!" How could she think making love with him *wasn't* a big deal? This was Suzie and he. He didn't want their relationship to change. Ever.

"Yes, *you.* Trying to diagnose me with something that doesn't even exist. Trying to make something out of my asking you to spend one night with me. You're acting like some autocratic doctor."

"I *am* a doctor. But I'm not autocratic."

"You have to trust fate sometimes. Some things don't have a scientific name. Or a reason for being. Or need a doctor. Or two aspirins. They're just here in this universe and need to be accepted."

Griff watched Suzie twist the gold watchband around her slender wrist until she could read the numbers on the face, then she glanced at the clock on the wall above the sink as if she needed to confirm the time on her watch. She took in a deep breath, and her lips formed a straight line while she drummed her fingers rapidly on the table for several seconds before repeating the clock-watching cycle all over again.

Now this finger-strumming, clock-watching Suzie was the same Suzie he'd always known and cared about. Suzie the time clock. He could deal with this woman. Griff forced the tense muscles in his shoulders to relax a notch.

He didn't think she looked any different than before either. She only wore two types of clothes. Her going-to-work uniform, a sexless navy power suit like she was wearing now, or her just as sexless relax-at-home uniform, the big blue shirts that swam around her body at least eight sizes too big and the baggy blue jeans that didn't fit any better.

Her brown hair looked the same, too. Today, she had it piled on top of her head in one of those knot things women seemed to be able to twist their hair into. In fact, in the five years he'd known her, he'd only seen her wear her hair two ways: in a ponytail and in that knot thing. "Suzie, let me put this in terms I think you'll understand." He didn't even know how long, or short, her hair was.

"I understand perfectly. No need to explain."

"No. I want to. This is my own theory, but I'm sure you'll agree with me." He couldn't help feeling smug. "I said it before and I'll say it again. You're under stress. All those things that happened nine years ago came rushing back. Your mind couldn't take it. You had—now this isn't the medical term, but it's descriptive—a brain burp."

"A what?" Her mouth and eyes popped open.

"I like that term actually," he said almost to himself. "And because you and I are such good friends, I want to help you recover."

"You're not funny, Griff."

"Yes, I am. I've always said accountants have no sense of humor. Doctors—now, we're really fun people."

"Oh, really? You don't think I'm a fun person?"

Griff's breath caught as he scrutinized her closer.

"I always thought you were fun," he said slowly. Except for her bare feet Suzie looked the same as always. Yet she was somehow different. He stared into her large green eyes, noticed the dark eyelashes framing them, making them seem even greener.

She stopped talking and stared right back at him, not blinking.

"You never make demands on me," he said. "I can always count on you to be here when I need someone to talk to. When I want to relax, but don't want to be alone. There's never a time when I'm with you that I wish I were somewhere else." He had never really thought about it before but knew it was true. She was special.

The morning sunlight peeked through the window behind her, shining through her hair.

"Suzie, your hair!"

Her hands flew up to her head, her eyes widened. "What's wrong?"

"Plenty." The Suzie he knew, his buddy, his friend, prided herself on always being so fastidiously neat. She never would have allowed one piece of hair to escape from that bondage knot. This morning, however, curls were falling out all over the place. They scattered across her forehead, down her cheeks and hung in enticing little ringlets along the back of her neck.

Enticing? What a strange word for him to think of in connection with Suzie. He'd never thought of her in that way before. It had to be from the shock of her having asked him to do the sex deed with her. That was not a Suzie thing to do.

But still, in the five years he'd known her, not until this moment did he know her hair had curls. Curls that were enticing. Curls that spoke to him. Curls that said,

"Yoo-hoo, Griff ol' buddy, you're a sucker for curls."
Then again….he thought as he gazed over all that hair,
hair that he just this moment discovered was not plain
brown, but a golden-reddish brown.

And that wasn't all. He rubbed his eyes. All that
morning sunlight must have done a laser surgical job
on his corneas. That's why he now saw pale freckles
scattered across her small nose and sprinkled on top
of highly flushed cheekbones. He had never noticed
her freckles before, either. Where had they come
from?

Griff pointed a finger at her. "You're doing this to
me on purpose. You know how much I hate change.
No, you wouldn't have thought of this yourself. You
don't have it in you. It was my mother, wasn't it?
Admit it."

"You know your mother's in Boston." She
sounded frustrated.

Yeah, right. "I know where my mother is. I know
about telephones and long distance, too. Do you think
I was born yesterday? And stop changing the subject.
I'm talking about you, not my mother." He didn't care
if she was staring at him as if he'd lost it. She was
the one who had something missing, not him. "Your
hair is all over the place. And…" He paused for effect,
"…it's not the same color as it was yesterday. Did
you think I wouldn't notice?"

"Oh, God." Her fingers flew to her hair. "I knew
it. You found a gray hair, didn't you? Gray before my
thirtieth," she moaned.

"On top of that, you grew freckles. Freckles! You
put them on your cheeks with some freckle pencil,
didn't you?"

"A true gentlemen wouldn't mention a lady's freckles."

"Oh, yeah? Well, you know I'm a sucker for freckles," he accused her. "You know everything."

She smiled at him. Oh, that smile. He knew that smile. Perfect white teeth behind full lips. That superior smile all women used on men who they thought were acting like little boys. She wouldn't get away with it.

Griff leaned back into the chair. "I've got your number." And that number didn't include golden-red curls springing from bondage or freckles his fingers yearned to play connect the dots with.

"I hate to disappoint you, Griff, but what you see is what I am. I was in such a rush to see you this morning, I didn't put on makeup and I forgot my panty hose." She lifted her foot and wiggled her toes at him. "Can you believe how distracted I was? Not to put on panty hose?" She blew out the last sentence as if it were a promise for passion.

His glance traveled from her pouty lips, down to breasts hidden from sight and which he'd rather not imagine right now, to those naked toes dancing in front of him. He loved toes. He loved to suck on beautiful female toes. He loved to massage toes. They were sensitive. Sensual. "Put your foot down," he ordered. He didn't need her foot turning him into some kind of male powder keg, ready to explode at any moment. And those perfect toes might just set him off.

This reaction he was having for her wasn't good. Not good at all.

He spoke to her, issuing the order as if he were asking a nurse to hand him a clamp, and he expected to be obeyed. "The next time I see you you better have those freckles covered and your hair combed. Understand?" She'd better. He willed his body to relax. He refused to have even the beginning of desire for her. He wanted his good, old Suzie Q back. *Now*. "And cover your damn toes."

She cocked her head, so he knew she'd heard him, but she didn't answer with a yes or a no. She only smiled. He scowled back.

He didn't want to see her smile anymore. He glanced at the wall, at the ceiling, at the sink, then looked down at her hands. There. Finally something about her that hadn't changed. Her fingernails were naked of polish, her hands cuddling the hot mug. *Naked and cuddled*. Oh, he had it bad. He waited until his heart slowed, then carefully raised his gaze to her face again, feeling stronger. She looked back at him with that same sympathetic smile he'd come to expect from her on Sunday mornings when he slogged his way up the driveway after logging in another weekend shift at the hospital. She always spent Sunday mornings out there playing in her garden doing whatever it was people did out there in the dirt, and when she saw him, he'd get that welcome home smile from her.

He would try to be more understanding. He'd get to the bottom of this even if he had to turn her upside down and shake it out of her. "Let's talk about this whole dying situation," he began.

"That's what I've been wanting to do." She fiddled with her watchband.

"We still have a-a-l-l-l-l day," he drawled, knowing it was only a matter of time before the old Suzanne, the human time clock, would take over where this new Suzanne sat twirling her watchband. It was already going on 7:00 a.m. and the Suzie he knew and loved should be about ready to bolt for the door.

"Okay, sounds good."

This couldn't be happening. "It's almost seven."

"I know." Her fingers moved to the table and she

picked up a paper napkin bearing the Bertha's BBQ logo.

He watched her fingers work at shredding the napkin, mesmerized by their movement. "What other plans have you made for the big departure? Or was I it?"

"Oh, no, you weren't all that's being planned."

He should have known that. Suzie would plan for her supposed future demise as if she were preparing for a tax audit. "Can you tell, or is it a secret?"

The smile on her face performed voodoo magic and he found himself returning her grin. She leaned forward in the chair. Her breasts, which he'd never paid attention to before, hugged the rim of the table as she reached out, her small, soft hand grabbing hold of his larger one. "You won't believe who agreed to play at my wake."

"You're having entertainment at the wake?" His smile left as quickly as it had appeared. Hers remained. "Who?"

"The Houston Symphony Orchestra. Well, not the whole symphony, since not everyone could possibly fit into my living room, but I've got part of the strings, part of the winds and a pianist will play my piano. It's going to be so beautiful. Promise me you'll come."

"There's not going to be a wake and you know it." He wished she'd get off this kick. "This is the most ridiculous, stupid, asinine, outrageous—"

She held up her hand. "Okay, I understand, Griff. Really, I do. No point in dragging this on. Thanks anyway. For listening that is."

What was this? A midlife crisis at her tender age of twenty-nine? She wasn't going anywhere. The thought of losing Suzie simmered hot beneath the surface of his heart for only seconds before his anger spewed forth faster than the Mount St. Helen's eruption.

He wouldn't lose her. He couldn't. Griff pounded his fist on the table, and coffee sloshed over the sides of both cups. "What the hell's wrong with you?" Anger and fear burned in each word. Suzie and death didn't mix. Suzie and sex did not mix, either. Even if she did look kind of sweet and huggable. Then again, he told himself, so did a kitten. "Fortune-tellers are quacks. They can't predict the future anymore than I can."

She didn't blink. Her smile never wavered, then her nose twitched. "I predict the pizza's burning," she said softly.

Loud sizzles and pings came from the oven as melted cheese dripped and splattered over the top of the hot electric burners.

"See," she said. "Predictions do come true."

Griff swore softly as he pushed back the chair, crossed the room and jerked open the oven door. Looking at Suzie, he bit out, "This doesn't prove anything."

"Except you should have used a pizza pan." She looked down at her watch. She took a few paper napkins from the pile he kept stacked in the middle of the table and wiped the puddles of coffee. "Told you so," she murmured.

"Can it."

She giggled.

"It's your fault anyway. You're not supposed to distract me from business." Griff looked around for something to use to protect his hands from the hot wire rack. He grabbed the dish towel off the sink. Using the terry cloth square, he pulled the rack toward him. With one end of the towel he shoved all the pizza inside the other half of the towel, then threw the whole mess in the trash.

He opened the window and back door so the smell of burning cheese and pepperoni could blow outside and give the neighborhood air some character.

Griff sat back down in the chair and rocked on two legs, then dropped the chair back down on all four. He leaned across the table and placed his finger under Suzie's chin, gulping down the lump that came from nowhere and clogged his throat. His skin, where his fingertip connected with hers, burned as hot as the oven. He ignored the heated lightning darting through his arm and into his gut and lifted her chin until she could look him in the eye again. "No pizza. Want a beer?"

She squinted her eyes at him. "For breakfast? Don't think so."

"My fridge is empty." He shrugged and moved back.

She twisted her watchband again, looking down at the face. "Thanks anyway. I've got to go." She took a deep breath, nodded her head slightly. "Now that I rethink this, the idea of making love with you was a bad one."

"Bad?" he practically squeaked. "It would never be bad."

"It doesn't matter anymore. Granted, you were my first choice, but you weren't my last. In fact, I have a list of men who have offered to—how should I put this?—show me a bit of heaven before I leave earth."

Griff could feel his blood pressure taking a hike up the mountain and it was her fault.

"So not making love with you, while I may be sorry I missed the adventure, is no big deal. I—" she pointed her thumb at her chest "—have men standing in line, willing to take numbers."

"You're lying."

"Am I?"

There was that Suzie Q smile again, and Griff didn't like it one bit. He pinned her green eyes with his gaze. He watched a flush creep across the freckles on her cheeks, and knew anger put it there. Anger because he accused her of lying, and Suzanne never lied. He knew that.

And that meant she did have a list of men willing to meet her demand for a good time before she supposedly died, which he knew for sure she wasn't going to do, even if she believed she was.

Suzanne stood, stretched and waved her fingers. "See ya 'round."

"Wait."

"For what?"

He took a step in her direction and loomed over her, crowding her space. She peeked up at him from under her long black eyelashes.

"There won't be anyone else. It's me or no one," he said gruffly. "But on my terms."

"What are your terms?"

"You and I, we know each other as friends, and I don't do this with friends. So we're going to have to date, get to know each other as more than friends."

She looked puzzled for a moment, then suddenly her eyes lit up, her freckles danced across her cheeks. She threw her arms around him and gave him the biggest hug he'd ever had.

He had been hugged by Suzanne many times over the past five years but he never noticed feeling all of her before. Now, he noticed. Her breasts, large, soft, cushioning his chest, her hip bones jabbing into his.

His body, which he could always control, lost control, and he grew hard under his jeans. She gasped and he knew she could feel his reaction to her.

She dropped back as suddenly as she had come to him. Her eyes widened in wonder, her mouth formed a pouty "oh." Her hand reached up and grazed the stubble on his jaw. A muscle in his cheek twitched in response to her touch, and her scent, sweet as chocolate.

"That is so wonderful of you, Griff. I'm really touched. And more than that, I want to thank you for changing your mind. Because you don't know what damage you were doing to my ego."

"That's okay, Suzanne." He shrugged off her gratitude.

"But all I wanted from you was one night of sex. In fact, I only penciled you in for an hour next Monday evening. So as much as I hate to, I have to say no."

5

ALL RIGHT. She could admit it. She was weak. Her *no* to Griff hadn't lasted any longer that the word "no" itself. Who did she think she was kidding? He knew she wouldn't put him aside for a month, and she knew she couldn't ever put him aside, not even for a day. She didn't have time to play self-righteous games.

Instead, she'd tried to get him to change his mind about not making love. After all, she had books on the subject, and he seemed like easy prey. If the hug they shared in his kitchen was any indication, his body seemed to want her, even if he kept the gray matter locked inside his head from saying yes.

She went about seducing Griff subtly, hoping to get him so worked up he'd come to her begging for delicious favors.

Only, after almost three whole weeks, nothing had worked. Not even the most recent gin rummy night when she insisted on playing strip rummy, and had gotten all the way down to her bra and panties. Not just any bra and panties either. She had on her arsenal. Full ammunition. Her sex-until-you-die underwear. The lacy one that barely covered her nipples, and pushed her generous breasts so close together that she could've planted corn in the depth of her cleavage. If she were Griff, she'd have been all over herself by now. Where in the world did he get his self-control? Or was she that unappealing to him?

No, she didn't think that was it. He seemed to be drinking an extraordinary amount of ice water, and was making quite a few trips to the kitchen sink to splash water on his face. He was also growing quite irritable. All good signs of a sexually frustrated man.

When she lost the last game, she pulled down her blue jeans, revealing a scrap of underwear so minuscule some man, namely Griff, would have to get real close to see it. She sighed deeply, as if losing the last game and having to take off her jeans was the worst thing in the world.

"Oh, I don't know what to take off next," she bemoaned, shuffling the cards a few times. She sighed again, then crossed her legs Indian fashion on the chair.

That's when Griff, the poor guy, bolted out of the chair, knocking it backward, mumbled a few incoherent words and stumbled out of her house.

Suzanne, a smile across her lips, put the cards away. She made up silly songs with titles like, "I Got the Hots for You, Griff-eee," as she cleared off the table, and "You Sexy Thing, Griff-eee" which she sang in time with the dishwasher's motor.

She picked up her discarded clothing and turned the lights out as she made her way into the bedroom. If she only had more time, she'd have him in her bed for sure. Only there wasn't any more time. Three weeks had slipped by, marked off on her calendar, and no progress in the seduction of Griff had been made. She was at a loss as to what to do next.

She lay on top of her bedspread, still in her bra and panties, her hands behind her head, staring at the ceiling. Maybe she should give up. Only she didn't want to let Griff go. Not until she had no other option. And that wouldn't be until March 30th. Quitting was not part of her nature.

She had almost drifted off to sleep when the ringing phone startled her back awake.

"What are you doing tomorrow?" Griff asked.

"It's my last day at work." She had told him that earlier—about the time she had lost the second-to-last gin rummy hand, and was peeling off her shirt. She took it as a good sign he hadn't paid any attention to what she had said.

"Want to go to a movie tomorrow night?"

"Are you still on that dating kick?" Why couldn't he just give it up and give in?

"I can't take anymore gin rummy, Suz. I'm dying here."

"A movie it is," she replied.

She hung up the phone and smiled. Maybe things were looking up after all. Tomorrow night. At the movies. In the dark. Her hand. Her roving hand. Starting at his knee and moving up his thigh, until she reached his jewels. She planned on giving him the crown.

SHE HAD GIVEN her notice at Merriweather, Watkins and Jones on the first of the month. Three weeks ago, her last day seemed so far in the future. Now that it was here, she didn't know where the time had gone. She sat at her desk, now devoid of all personal belongings, and looked at the bare walls and empty shelves of her office.

She picked up the telephone and punched in a very familiar number. "Mom."

"You sound terrible." Hermia could always get right down to the truth. "You're not sick, are you?"

"I'm scared."

"I know, darlin'. I'm here for you."

"I'll miss my friends."

"They're going to miss you, too."

"I'll miss you and daddy." Her voice cracked.

"My sweet baby." Hermia spoke softly, her voice full of sorrow. "You don't know how much you mean to me. To your father. This has been the worst month for us."

"I know, Mom. Me, too. I'm going to miss it here at Merriweather."

"Merriweather?" Hermia's tearful and shaky voice suddenly burst forth strong, spitting venom. "Don't you even mention that horrid place."

"I love it here. I would have made partner next year if things had been different."

"You should never have gone to work there. Never."

"Mom, it's been nine years."

"Wasted years. You could have been the owner of the Red Rock Casino. You could have been the one who finally avenged the Hermia Bourne name. Instead you wasted it in that place of legal numbers, tax numbers. Nothing useful at all."

"You'll live longer if you stop plotting revenge."

Hermia countered. "Oh, I'm not talking about me, darlin', I'm talking about your poor Grandma Hermia. Your poor great-grandma Hermia. The woes those poor women endured at the hand of those Las Vegas Bournes. You'll never know."

Suzanne knew very well, and her grandmothers seemed to have managed fine considering they were born and raised in Texas and had never met the legitimate Las Vegas Bournes. "Calm down, Mom. Please." She should never have mentioned Merriweather to her mother. She knew the reaction she'd get.

"What do you mean? I'm perfectly calm." Hermia spewed out with machine-gun precision. "Don't I sound calm?"

"Very calm." If you thought firing squads were calm. Then again, maybe mentioning Merriweather wasn't so bad after all. Her mother had gotten out of her weepy blue funk.

"You bet I'm calm. I just can't help thinking about what could have been had you taken after my side of the family...."

Hermia was still spouting forth "shoulda's" and "coulda's," giving examples of other ways Suzanne could have spent her adult life getting back at those Las Vegas Bournes, when Suzanne finally was able to get her to hang up. The call had exhausted her.

And saying goodbye at work wasn't going to be easy, either. She had friends she'd become close to. But more than anything else, she truly loved her job. Numbers gave her comfort. Even after all these years, numbers were still her friend. She had always gotten satisfaction knowing that what she had accomplished over the last nine years had benefited others. That her life had made a difference to many people.

This afternoon the firm would prove how much when she received the highest honor Merriweather, Watkins and Jones ever bestowed, an honor previously only given to a partner in the firm. Merriweather would close the office for the afternoon to host a going-away party at the Four Seasons in her honor.

THE BANQUET ROOM was large and filled to capacity. Suzanne sat next to Mr. Merriweather at the head table. After lunch, he stood, clanged his fork against the crystal wineglass and called the luncheon to order. When the noise quieted, he held up his champagne glass, and said, "Suzanne, my dear, your friends at Merriweather are going to miss you." There was a hum of agreement from her coworkers seated at the tables in front of her. Forks clinked against crystal.

"Normally when someone as valued as you retires—and we're calling your departure a retirement, and not anything else—we would give them the old gold watch. However, considering your situation…" Merriweather cleared his throat, but it took drinking three quarters of the glass of wine before he could continue. "You know, my dear, the watch isn't going to do you any good where you're going." The sound of clinking crystal once again filled the room.

"Since your departure is for a different and very sad reason, we decided to donate to your favorite organization what would have been spent on the watch." On cue her friends hummed their agreement.

Mr. Merriweather added, "Plus, we're going to add money to that donation and present to the New Hope Home for Abused and Abandoned Children—" More clinking, only louder now. Somewhere a glass broke, and someone swore. Merriweather went on. "—on behalf of Merriweather, Watkins and Jones, in your memory, a check to New Hope in the amount of ten thousand dollars."

"Speech, speech," her colleagues shouted. More crystal clinking and clanking, and a few more breaking.

There wasn't a strand of Suzanne's hair out of place. Her navy suit fit her with the usual precision. She looked over the people filling the room. They were all special to her. "I'm so grateful to all of you. To Mr. Merriweather, Mr. Watkins and Mr. Jones, for all the wonderful years I've had here. For your donation to New Hope. So kind and generous.'' She had to stop talking. A lump formed in her throat, tears ran down her cheeks. She looked down, then back to her friends. "I'm going to miss you all so much." Her voice caught. "I hope you'll all come to the wake so I can say goodbye to you one last time." Her friends began applauding, standing up at their places, giving her an ovation. She told them, "We're going to have a wonderful time, until it's over."

There was nothing left for her to do after all the goodbyes were said, the hugs and kisses exchanged. She went back to her house, and began the grueling task of cleaning her two bathrooms. There was no way that all those people who had applauded her at the Four Seasons were going to be snooping around in her medicine cabinets, and the cabinets under her bathroom sinks, looking for personal things to gossip about after she was gone. Out went the douches and condoms. Gone forever were the stomach acid medicine, her cucumber face mask and raspberry foot cream. Her stash of Hershey's Chocolate Syrup, that was a little harder to find. Those bottles were hidden everywhere, and they'd probably still be finding them years from now.

Everything in her life seemed to be winding down, drawing to a close. Except for Griff, and that was her greatest disappointment. Even though they had a date for a movie, she doubted they'd have dessert in either one of their beds. Well, they might, but it wouldn't be together.

She met Griff in his driveway. He held the car door open for her and, after she stepped in, they were on their way. They hadn't even driven a block when Griff told her they'd have to stop at the hospital first. "I left my wallet there. Somewhere."

He did that all the time. "Someday someone is going to really steal it, and then they're going to become you, and your credit will be ruined, and your life will be ruined, and you won't be able to fix it, and I won't be here to help you."

He glanced at her out of the corner of his eye. "I'm sure it's in the locker."

"That's good. At least it's locked up."

"Or it could be at the nurses' station. Or maybe in surgery. It's somewhere. I'm pretty sure I know exactly where it may be."

She settled herself more comfortably in the seat. She didn't really want to see the movie anyway.

"Do you want to wait in the car, or come in for a minute?" he asked when he pulled into the doctors' lot and parked.

A minute? All night is more like it. "I'll go with you."

He came around to the passenger side, and helped her out of the car. After placing her arm through his, they walked across the parking lot, side by side, hip against hip. She looked up at him at the same time he looked at her. His smile was so warm, so caring. Didn't he feel it, too?

They walked through the automatic sliding glass doors, and no sooner did they step over the threshold, than an announcement came over the loudspeaker. "Paging Dr. Scott. Dial 36-24-36."

"That voice is so familiar," Suzanne said, her head cocked so she could hear better.

"No, it's not," he denied quickly.

The page came again only this time a chill of doom

zipped through Suzanne's blood. That voice. She knew it from somewhere.

"Wait here," Griff ordered, pointing to a square of linoleum. "Or better yet, go into the waiting room." He pointed over her shoulder.

Suzanne glanced back, saw groups of people mingling in the room, and nodded. She understood the words *wait* and *here*. Still, as soon as Griff moved towards the cavity of the hospital, she followed behind him. Just because she understood the words didn't mean she had to agree or abide by them. Life was short. Live each moment. Besides, no one should be paging him because no one should even know he was here. Besides that, the female voice coming over the loudspeaker every few minutes made her feel creepy.

Griff, one second cheery, the next agitated, growled, "I told you to wait in there."

"If I wait in there, we'll never get to the movie. If I come with you, there's a better chance you won't get distracted." She gave him her biggest smile. Then he got paged again.

He placed a friendly, brotherly hand on her shoulder. The kind a doctor would put on a patient he didn't know, but was trying to act as if they had a history together. "Suzanne. Listen to me. I'm going to find my wallet and I'll be right back. Now go in the lounge like a good girl, okay?"

She glared at him. She loved him to pieces but hated when he got that condescending doctor attitude.

"I'll buy you a buttered popcorn at the movies. And a lemonade. Would you like that?"

The way he asked, like a parent trying to bribe a child, *if you're a good girl, I'll give you a candy bar,* sent a spasm of anger through her. "Don't patronize me."

"I'm not." He grimaced. "I apologize if it came off that way."

"All right." Did that mean she had to go into the big waiting room like a good girl, or could she follow him around like a little puppy dog and sit in his lap, and lick him all over? Maybe if he let her lick him, she'd get rewarded for good behavior, and then they could finally, finally, make love.

That page came again. Griff looked up at the ceiling where the amplifiers were positioned at thirty-foot intervals. She watched in fascination as every muscle in his arms and legs went rigid. His jaw twitched.

She almost felt sorry for him. Almost, but not quite. He looked too guilty. "Why don't you go answer your page?" she asked."

"I'm sure it's nothing. Probably another Dr. Scott." His words were precise and clipped.

"Doctor Scott, you are urgently needed by 36-24-36." The voice sounded like an advertisement for a 900 telephone line.

Suzanne's eyes became like slits as she glared at him. *Why, that slimy skunk. That low-down scoundrel.* "That's LuLu." Suzanne announced to him and the whole first floor at the same time.

"Damn," Griff swore under his breath. "Lower your voice."

This explained everything. Now she finally knew why Griff had been saying no to sex with her. LuLu had come back to town. Intellectually, Suzanne could match herself against any man or woman anywhere. But when it came to Griff's fantasy playmate, LuLu— of tight, spandex shirts, microshorts, miniskirts and breasts that defied gravity—obviously had been his plaything of choice.

Her ego had taken a hit over the past few weeks,

and she'd been wounded. She now knew with absolutely certainty that the wound was not terminal, because if it were, she wouldn't be planning ways to outmaneuver LuLu. LuLu had always proclaimed in her growly-purry alley cat voice, *Whatever LuLu wants, LuLu gets, and LuLu wants the big, bad doctor.* "When did she get back in town?"

"Oh..." He casually shrugged his shoulder as if when wasn't a big deal. "About three weeks ago."

Suzanne saw red and she wanted to kill. She knew what LuLu had meant to him, and it was a big deal. LuLu and Griff had a history. She'd been there the first day Griff moved into the house next to hers.

She remembered that day as if it were yesterday. How he'd come over to her fence and given her a beer. LuLu had come out of his house, futzed around with her straps and then spotted the two of them together. She sashayed across the lawn toward them. LuLu with that unmistakable breathy voice. Possessive, blond, big-breasted LuLu. He had said goodbye to Suzanne and gone back into his house with LuLu.

The following Sunday, he had come back to her yard, this time dragging a lawn chair, stretching out his long legs, putting his bare feet near where she sat on her knees planting little marigolds around her vegetable garden. She had learned he was the new trauma doctor.

They had become friends that Sunday and their friendship had grown over the years. But it wasn't until LuLu had moved to California that they had become the best of friends. "Did she move back to town with her husband?" Suzanne asked him.

"Not exactly," he hedged.

"Either she did or she didn't." Did she sound like

a shrew, or was that her imagination? Must be her imagination.

"There's a possibility she never married the guy."

"She said she was getting married. Why would she lie?" *To make Griff jealous. Admit it, my man.*

"You know women, Suz. They say a lot of things to get a guy to commit to marriage." He stared pointedly at her. "Like offering sex with no commitment, when it's totally not in their nature. Or saying they're dying."

"You're accusing me of lying." She couldn't believe he'd do that, the low-down skunk. "You're saying I'm only telling you I'm going to die on the thirtieth to get you to commit to marriage? To me?"

"No," he said without a lot of conviction. "Not really."

"Listen to me, Griff. All I want from you is sex." Her voice rose higher because somehow, she got it in her mind that if she talked loudly, he'd believe her. "Is that so hard for you to understand?"

His gaze darted back and forth around the foyer area and the meeting rooms feeding off the hallway. He put his finger to his mouth and shushed, "Quiet."

Not likely. "Sex. S-E-X." With each letter, her voice rose. "Sex, sex, sex. Is that just a terrible thing to want from you?"

"Shhhh! Suzie. Please." He would have covered her mouth with his hand, only she anticipated his move and backed away.

The hospital din appeared to quiet down. People seemed to be moving closer to them. LuLu's trampy voice came over the loudspeaker again, paging Griff, using her 36-24-36 measurements as a calling card. "And her—" Suzanne pointed to one of the speakers in the ceiling "—she's so unprofessional. I should report her to the AMA, the CIA, the FBI, the Bureau of Vital Statistics!''

Now his face turned a bright red. *Oh, Griff. How can you be so...so...male?* How could the suave, worldly doctor react to silicone and bottled blondes in such a way?

The answer was as simple as the 36-24-36 LuLu continued to seductively advertise. Testosterone ruled and men under its influence had no sense when it came to what was good—or bad—for them.

Well, Suzanne had measurements, too. And hers weren't the store-bought variety, either. Hers were utterly genuine, even if they were hard to see in her oversize clothes. Why, if she were in a boat and it capsized, unlike LuLu who would float, Suzanne would sink right to the bottom like other treasures worth diving for. And if she weren't worth retrieving, she didn't know what was.

Oh, Griff, Suzanne silently moaned. *Why aren't you thinking with your head? The one attached to your shoulders.*

Griff's gaze darted over the top of her head, looking behind her. ''Suzie, it's okay. Calm down.''

''Calm down? If it weren't for the fact that we were such good friends, I wouldn't even want to have sex with you. I just don't want to die all shriveled up inside. You're nothing but a means to my end,'' she practically shouted. She had to, because if she didn't she'd cry; the rejection and hurt she felt ran that deep.

God, she hated LuLu and all women like her. So sure of themselves. So sure of their own appeal to the opposite sex. So sure they could get any man they wanted. LuLu, by her mere presence, made someone like Suzanne, an average working woman, who looked average, who acted average, who was average, seem, well, nothing more than average.

She didn't want Griff to know how much she hurt. She didn't want to show any weakness. So she changed tactics. She mentally stiffened her upper lip and gave him a casual shrug. With a little laugh that didn't sound too brittle, she said, "I can't believe the kind of impression I have given you." She spoke quieter and ignored the LuLu pages, although that was hard to do. "So you and I, well, we wasted these past couple of weeks getting to know each other as, um…how would you say…"

"More than friends?"

"That's it. I guess it was just frustration running over. I wanted to have sex, and I thought you and I would have had it by now. But, well, time is up. Onward and upward so they say. Move on."

"Suzanne—" Griff started.

"No, really, it's okay. It's not as though you're the only person I could have sex with. I was only doing you a favor by giving myself to you before I die. Kind of like a virgin giving herself to a man for the first time. I thought you'd be grateful."

Suzanne, knowing that she had his complete attention, looked behind her scanning the faces of the people in the waiting room. There were a lot of men milling around the lounge. Good-looking men. Men without women attached to their arms. She did one of those limp wrist shoo-shoo gestures at Griff. "You can go find your wallet now," she told him. "I'll wait for you in there." She tossed her head toward the lounge.

Griff looked over her head and fixed his gaze on some men in the corner.

She followed his gaze and asked, "Who are they?

The men over there by the coffeemaker?'' She pointed. "They look so familiar.''

"They should. Those are the Duvall brothers.'' He said the name Duvall as if he'd eaten a sour lemon.

Suzanne stared in awe. Those were the big, bad Duvalls? She had heard about that family all of her life. Everyone in town had. They had a history that was as long and colorful as her own Bourne family, with one notable difference. While her mother and grandmother talked about bankrupting a casino and running the Las Vegas Bournes out of town, the Duvalls would have just killed them all.

"Why are they here?'' Suzanne whispered.

"I don't know. I don't have to tell you, though, to keep your distance from them. No sense courting trouble.''

"Sure, Griff.'' Maybe her luck had taken a turn for the better. The Duvalls, right here with her in the same building. "Whatever you say.''

"Maybe you should come with me,'' he offered.

"Don't be silly.'' She waved her fingers at him. "Go. Go.''

"But—''

"I'll be fine. If you don't get your wallet, we're going to miss the movie.''

"Right.'' He still hesitated.

As LuLu's seductive voice called to him again, Suzanne knew her dreams of having Griff would never happen.

She looked over at the Duvall brothers. Maybe her dream would never happen, but she had it in her power to make her mother's dream come true. The Duvalls held the key. Once again she said to Griff, "You can go now.'' Only she wasn't watching him, she had become so focused on the Duvalls.

Last week she had added two more life insurance polices to her already heftily insured self. As she remembered or heard about a good cause or a needy organization, she'd purchase another policy and make that organization a beneficiary. By the time she died next week, she'd make many organizations and fine arts groups extremely wealthy and happy. The policy she had purchased for her parents was really only to help defray the cost of the wake and the funeral itself. They didn't need the five hundred thousand dollars.

But that money would sure go a long way in breaking the bank at the Red Rock Casino, and if anyone could break the bank, she could. If anyone could help with the funding she'd need to reach her goal, it would be the Duvalls. If they'd agree. Suzanne had no reason to doubt they'd agree.

The Duvall brothers were huddled together, keeping themselves apart from the others in the waiting room.

"Suzanne." Griff's tone sent a warning. "Did you hear what I said about keeping away from those men?"

She almost jumped out of her shoes. "You scared me. I thought you were gone."

"Suzanne?"

"Yes, I heard you." She took her gaze away from the Duvalls and concentrated on giving Griff a big, beatific and most innocent smile. "Now go. I don't want to be here all night."

"I'll be back soon."

Suzanne didn't leave her place in the corridor until Griff was out of sight and she couldn't hear his footsteps any longer. She still waited a few extra minutes just to make sure he wasn't coming back, then she sauntered into the waiting room, trying to look as if she hadn't a care in the world, when the whole time her heart was about to hammer right through her chest.

First impressions were so important, and she had to make a good one. She had everything to gain, and everything to lose. She tried to concentrate on the big picture as she made a beeline for the Duvalls.

Suzanne did what the magazines she'd studied in her quest to make herself irresistible to Griff suggested she do in order to get what she wanted from men.

Not that any of it had worked on Griff, but these guys weren't her friends, so she might have a chance at wooing them. She started by smiling prettily at the men. At the same time, she stood straight and tall, shoulders back, her generous breasts displayed to their greatest advantage, even though she knew that these men would need a good imagination to react to what was under the oversize blue shirt. This little fact had her slightly worried, because if their reputations were justified, and she had no reason to doubt that they were, an imagination was something they didn't possess.

The Duvalls were known to be straight shooters, not the kind who liked to think about new and innovative ways to kill their prey. They just aimed and fired.

Murderers. All right. She wouldn't think about all that right now. They had no reason to kill her. Not yet, anyway.

"Gentlemen." Suzanne held out her hand to the man who looked to be the oldest of the brothers. "I'm Suzanne Mercer."

The tallest and best looking Duvall brother didn't hesitate for a single moment. He took her hand in his own, and said, "Ambrose Duvall."

"I don't want to be forward, being a stranger and all—"

"We may not have been introduced properly, but you're not a stranger. We all noticed you over there." He nodded his head in the direction of the entryway.

"Really?" She propelled her chest out more and sucked her tummy in until it hit her spine. "I'm honored."

"We're the honored ones. After all, you're the lady looking for sex, and if this weren't such a sad time for us now, we'd all volunteer to help you find it." He turned to his other two brothers. "Right, boys?"

The other two made noises of agreement, although neither looked happy. She worked on trying to convince herself that their reactions were only two opinions, and not the world's. Their opinions meant nothing. The sinking, nauseous feeling in her stomach wasn't caused by their rejection.

Besides, sex wasn't what she wanted from them, and it stunk that they turned her down when she hadn't even asked. "I don't want sex."

"No?" Raised eyebrows and skeptical expressions.

"Absolutely no," she said leaving no doubt.

"How could we have misunderstood? We all heard you say you did." The Duvall brothers nodded and Ambrose continued. "Everyone here heard, too. Quite entertaining for such a somber environment as this."

She looked around the waiting room, where every single person had his or her gaze focused on Suzanne and the Duvalls. If today was the day she was supposed to die, die she would have, of embarrassment. Then again, the few women waiting seemed to look at her with understanding and sympathy. Was every woman as frustrated as she? Suzanne hoped not. She lowered her voice to a conspiratorial whisper. "Sex is a code word for life insurance."

Ambrose made an extremely profound comment.

"Ah." The other two brothers took their cue, and echoed him. "Ah."

"My friend, the doctor who I came here with, thinks I'm too young for that kind of insurance, but you know, things happen."

Wyatt, the middle Duvall brother, just a shade shorter than Ambrose, and with light brown hair instead of jet, took her hand, brought it to his lips and kissed it gently. "So true, so true," he said. "Maybe too young for life insurance, but definitely not too young for sex."

Suzanne took her hand back. She was out of their league and she knew it.

The youngest Duvall brother, Mickey, who couldn't be more than eighteen, came to her rescue. Sort of. He looked at her adoringly. "I wish I could help you with your sex life insurance, but my brother said I have to keep the testosterone inside me so I can become mean like them."

"A man, Mick, a real man." Wyatt slapped his little brother's back, almost knocking him to the ground.

"Curious this life insurance that insures sex," Ambrose said thoughtfully. "Does that mean if your sex life runs out, you collect the life insurance? If so, the sex life insurance companies must be cursing the day Viagra came out. That drug ended a lot of sex deaths."

Suzanne looked up at Ambrose. Dark, deep brown eyes, swarthy skin. His shoulders were large, his hips narrow. If she weren't so in love with Griff, the man standing in front of her had the capacity to melt. Only she didn't feel a thing. Not one little spark. She took a deep breath, and came clean with him. "We were talking about sex, the doctor and I. You see—and this is a secret, it's to go no further than you and I—"

Ambrose leaned down, and Suzanne whispered in his ear "—the doctor's impotent. Can't lift a thing."

Ambrose looked at her as if the concept was inconceivable. Which it truly was, especially for Griff, the most virile man alive. She went on, though, really getting into her fiction, "I've been trying help him, but he won't let me. And, well, you see, I don't have much time left. So I decided I can only help those who want my help—which is why I wanted to talk to you." She gazed at him adoringly, through half-closed eyes. "I need your help so I can help someone I love very much. My mother."

Ambrose took her hand, turned to his brothers and ordered, "Wyatt, Mick, get an update on Momma, and don't let them give you any of their doubletalk."

"Is your mother all right?" Suzanne asked. She had been so wrapped up in her story, she'd forgotten they were in a hospital and that the men were here for a reason.

"Heart problems. She was alive when we brought her in. If she's not now, my brothers and I will take care of the doctor in charge."

"I'm sorry about your mother. This is probably a bad time for you."

"No, no. It's perfect." He still held her hand. "I'll help anyone who wants to help their mother. Mothers are special people." His voice caught, but he cleared his throat until he sounded normal. "Come into my office, and let's talk business."

Ambrose guided Suzanne to one of the sofas and waited for her to sit, then settled next to her. He took her hand again, kneading her fingers between his. "What can I give you?"

Suzanne closed her eyes for a brief moment, wanting to gather her thoughts, to make sure everything came out the way it should. Wanting to make sure she really did want to give up the Griff seduction plan, and move on.

LuLu back in town meant she really had no choice in the matter. It was time to go forward. The least she could do before she died was do what her mother had been asking her to do for years. Break the bank at the Red Rock Casino. The Duvalls were known as high-interest moneylenders. Then again, so were credit cards. The only difference was the Duvalls didn't have a grace period. But she wouldn't need one.

"I need you to take my life insurance policy, five hundred thousand dollars, which will be paid in full on my death, and advance me half the funds. You can use the policy for collateral."

"That's a lot of money and you look healthy. I don't loan money that takes years to pay back."

"You won't have to wait to get your money back any longer than a week." Suzanne gave him her best smile. "Because it's a sure thing. I'm going to die on March 30th."

"Why should I believe you?"

"Keep an open mind, okay? Because stranger things have been true." Suzanne told him everything and he listened as if he were captivated. And believed her. When Mickey and Wyatt returned from checking on their mother, she explained everything again. She told them about the Red Rock, about how she was going to play blackjack and bankrupt the casino bank, how she was going to win back her family's good name. Family and reputation were concepts the Duvalls understood.

"Do you know how to play blackjack?" Wyatt asked.

"No. But I'm a numbers person. I've read about

counting the cards. There's all kinds of books out there
on how to win at blackjack. My mother's been giving
them to me for years.''

"Doesn't it take practice?"

Suzanne thought a minute about that. She'd been
practicing playing cards, albeit gin rummy, with Griff
for years. When Griff won, it was because she let him
win. She was a card wizard and she knew it. She truly
believed what she said. "I'm going to break the bank.
There's not a doubt in my mind."

She was still sitting next to Ambrose, his arm now
draped around her shoulder, when Griff found her
there fifteen minutes later.

The brothers stood first. Ambrose took Suzanne's
hand and helped her from the couch. "Ambrose, Wyatt, Mickey, this is Dr. Scott."

The younger Duvalls shook Griff's hand. Ambrose
looked at him speculatively, before returning his gaze
to Suzanne. He winked at her, leaned down and whispered into her ear as he kissed her cheek, "The doctor's problem is our secret."

Griff glared at all of them, looking as if he wanted
to eat everyone for lunch.

"I'll see you all tomorrow," Suzanne said as she
and Griff were leaving.

"The Café Beignet at nine in the morning. We'll
finish our business then." Ambrose took her hand
once again and kissed it. "You're lovely," he murmured.

"Thank you so much." The clouds in the sky
opened up, and the sun came shining through. Or so
it seemed, even though the sun had set hours before.
At least her mother would be happy.

"What was that all about?" Griff asked as they
walked to the car.

"Oh, Griff," she said dreamily. "Remember when I said I wanted to have sex with you?"

"I'm not likely to forget."

"Go ahead and forget, because that's all in the past." She gave him a big smile. "Those Duvall brothers are taking care of everything."

6

GRIFF HADN'T TAKEN a vacation from the hospital in the five years he'd been there. Since most of his colleagues were married and had kids, Griff, and the few other single doctors, were the ones who were always called for favors. They were the ones who worked Christmas and Thanksgiving. They were the ones called first to cover someone else's duty when a family emergency came up.

Suzanne had done a Dr. Jekyll and Mr. Hyde on him and he was the one turning into a monster. Last night, from what he could gather, and he was pretty proud of his great instincts, she and those Duvall hoods were planning on having a group sex orgy. This morning, Griff knew he'd have to come to her rescue. He got up early, and hit the phone, calling in favor after favor from colleagues who owed him much more than he was asking for in return. After an hour, he'd finally managed to get ten consecutive days off. He needed every one of them. He was going to become Suzanne's bodyguard. Her protector. He wouldn't let her out of his sight.

Griff knew Suzanne well enough to know if she were meeting the Duvalls at nine, she'd be out of her house by eight-thirty. He wasn't sure exactly what he planned to do to stop her, all he knew was that he had to stop her. She was not going to have an orgy with the Duvall brothers, no matter how much she wanted it. The very idea of Suzanne and those three hoodlums, romping in a bed together, was so disgusting he almost lost his breakfast thinking about it. He'd save her and even if she didn't thank him now, she would someday.

He couldn't understand what had happened to her all of a sudden. He knew her mother, and Hermia was crazy, in her own unique way. He had thought, though, that Suzanne had a few good years left in her before she turned out like her mother. On February 28th she was fine, and then on March 1st, she'd gone fruitcake on him. To top it off she wasn't playing by his rules and his rules were simple and easy to follow. Suzanne was not allowed to change, ever, and she definitely wasn't allowed to go bonkers.

Now this happened. Not only did he have to put up with her believing she was dying, he also had to try and take their relationship, which had been fine for five years, and give it a new dimension. He'd tried to take their dating slowly. He wanted to give her time to change her mind. Mostly, although he'd never admit it to Suzanne, he wanted to go slow because he had become so attracted to her, it scared the bejesus out of him. And now, for all his saintliness, she was planning to cheat on him.

He wouldn't let her get away with it. If anyone was going to be her sex toy, it would be him, and he was doing his best to control his own urges when he was around her. It was really hard, in more places than one. During the past three weeks, sometimes, without any kind of advance warning, when he should've been thinking about his patients, he found himself thinking about the last time he'd seen her wearing her night-gown. How her breasts had been outlined under the thin flannel material with the washed-out rosebuds. He never thought about the rosebuds until now. Her breasts had swayed gently under the material. He remembered the time they were playing rummy and eating ice cream. She had covered the vanilla ice cream with half a bottle of chocolate syrup. When she took a spoonful, the syrup dripped on her nightgown. Both of them went for the syrup at the same time. His finger brushed against her breast, her nipple, and it hardened under his brief touch. He had apologized to her, and hadn't thought about it anymore. Until now. The memory of touching her nipple, of the brief contact with her warm, full breast, was as clear as if she were standing in front of him eating cold ice cream and dripping chocolate syrup. He could imagine her nipples getting tighter under his touch, until they stood in proud points. He didn't want to think about her breasts and certainly not her erect nipples. Nipples he could almost imagine touching and laving, bringing them to even greater heights.

He had to stop. He'd seen thousands of nipples. Men's and women's. Perky nipples, sedated nipples. Brown, pink and tan nipples. A nipple was a nipple.

Then why the hell could he only concentrate on Suzanne's? Those erect nipples under the faded flower flannel with the chocolate syrup stain. Damn. He was in deep trouble now.

He gave himself a mental shake, and finally started coming to his senses. He had it all wrong. Suzanne was in trouble. Not him. He had to stop thinking about her breasts and concentrate on making sure she didn't bare her generous assets to those Duvalls.

He went to her house and knocked on her back door. This door knocking was becoming a ritual he didn't like. He wanted to go back to the good old days when he could walk in and yell out, "Yo, Suz, where's the java?"

When she didn't answer after a few minutes, he got a little more aggressive. He banged on the door with his fist. Still no Suzanne. She could be in the shower. Naked. Washing herself with slippery soap. *Stop this right now, you pervert. This is Suzanne.* He wasn't doing it on purpose, he told himself. He hated thinking about Suzie's breasts naked. He didn't want to imagine her naked at all, only that was all he could think about, ever since she brought up the two of them making love. Now, the thought of her naked, and him naked with her, in the shower, slipping and sliding around, drove him into a state of male frustration with no release in sight.

Obviously though, for Suzanne, she planned on getting her release this morning. This time he pounded the door so hard the frame shook. She opened the door just as his fist headed for the door again. "If you don't stop opening the door when I'm in midknock, you'll get hurt," he growled, lowering his fist.

"Why are you knocking anyway? It's open. You always just come in."

He swallowed hard and tried not to look below her neck. His efforts strained his every natural instinct. If he'd been an Olympic athlete, he'd have won the gold medal for concentration alone. "I can't come in anymore. Things are different."

"No, they're not."

Sure. Now that she was getting satisfaction from the Duvalls, he could go back to being her good ol' buddy Dr. Griff. He was having none of it.

Once he was in the kitchen, he looked her over, and she was all dressed up. Still in blue, but not baggy. "New clothes?" he asked.

She pirouetted for him. Her shirt was tucked into a slim-fitting pair of pants, the kind that went below the knee and stopped. She wore high-heeled, open-toed, slip-on sandals, which made her taller and her legs look long and slim. "You like?" she asked, all cutesy.

"Where do you think you're going in that getup?" he demanded to know. The woman needed a keeper.

Instead of getting insulted and hurt, which he'd meant for her to so she'd go and put on her old baggy, sexless clothes, she got all happy on him. "I told you last night I was meeting the Duvall boys for brunch."

Boys? Suzanne who had always been so smart, so practical, so full of common sense, now, suddenly, couldn't see her nose in front of her face. How could she not know what kind of trouble she was getting herself into? He grinned at her, making sure he didn't let on that he was plotting her rescue. Stubborn accountants probably wouldn't like to be taken off course. The grin made his jaw hurt like hell. "I'm starved," he said. "Let's get going."

"You're not invited."

The grin disappeared. "What do you mean? Since when am I not invited anywhere you go?"

"Since today is a private affair."

"What kind of affair?"

She actually blushed. "These things are of no concern to you."

"All right then. Why don't you give me an example of what kind of affair isn't my concern?" Turn a girl like Suzanne down for sex and she cops an attitude. "Not because I'm nosy, but because I'm trying to learn how to be more sensitive, to have better bedside manner."

"I don't have to." Her nose stuck itself way up in the air. A real nasty attitude.

Well, he knew how to deal with women. Bluff 'em

and flirt. "Hey, Suzanne. I know why you're so ticked off."

"What in the world are you talking about?" Just like all women, she, too, got that shocked "Me? Ticked off?" look. "I'm certainly not angry."

"Sure you are." Uh-huh. He knew.

"I don't know where you come up with your ideas sometimes." She took her purse off the countertop and headed toward the kitchen door.

He gave her a look that said, "You can't put one over on me." Truth was, he couldn't tell what she was thinking anymore. He could only go with the facts. Fact one: She wanted sex. Fact two: She was going to see the Duvalls. If one and one didn't equal a *ménage à quatre,* he'd eat his stethoscope.

She opened the door and breezed through without a backward glance, leaving him behind. He choked back the retort he was about to blast her with, and followed. When she was halfway to the garage she turned back. "Can you close that door, please?"

Who did she think he was anyway? Her butler? He wasn't anybody's servant, he fumed as he retraced his steps to her back door. He slammed it hard enough to shake the already loosening frame. "I'm coming with you." He'd hear no argument.

"You can't."

"Why not?"

"Many reasons, but two of the minor ones, the only ones I'll discuss with you, are that you're not wearing any shoes and your clothes look like you've slept in them." She lifted up the garage door.

"There's a reason for that, you know. Some of us work hard, and fall asleep hard. Some of us, especially those of us who sleep naked..." He paused and watched as her eyes got a dreamy look. Good. "Yes, when you're used to sleeping naked, and you fall asleep before you can get your clothes off, you forget you're not naked and so you toss and turn in your clothes.''

"So you say." Her voice sounded husky. Then he wondered if it always sounded like that and he'd just never noticed before. Probably not, because if it had, he would've noticed. What he wished was that he didn't find it so sexy. "Yeah, it's either take the time to get out of everything, or pass out. I guess I passed out." He'd better shut up because he sounded as if he were babbling, and men didn't babble. Boys did. The last time he checked he was all man.

With barely a glance at him, she said, "See you later. Maybe."

"Maybe? What do you mean, maybe?" He followed her to her car, and got into the passenger side.

"Griff, get out," she ordered. "You can't go with me."

"I'm going." He leaned back, settled in, crossed his arms over his chest. A man, that's what he was, right down to his toes. And he had fine toes. They should never be covered in shoes. "I know what you're up to and someone's got to protect you," he said smugly.

"You don't know anything about it."

Then again, he didn't want those Duvalls to think Suzanne's friends had no class. "Wait for me." He took the keys out of the ignition and dangled them in front of her. "Be just a sec."

Her mouth opened. Her eyes widened. She looked mighty mad. And cute as hell.

Suzanne started to move her lips, as if she were trying to get words out, and Griff knew her well enough to know that when she was really angry, and the words started to flow, a tanker truck couldn't stop her. He bolted from the car, taking her keys with him, and went back to his house to get dressed.

SUZANNE WAS OKAY with the fact that Griff knew her about as well as anyone possibly could. That he knew her innermost secrets. Secrets no one else knew, with the exception of her mother, of course. Not that she *wanted* her mother to know all of her intimate secrets or anything. It was just that Suzanne couldn't seem to keep any secret from Hermia, much to her regret.

Then again, neither Griff nor her mother had known how much she had loved Griff. That secret she had kept harbored inside her for five years.

Now that she thought about it, until three weeks ago, he hadn't known about the horrible day at the livestock show. The day the fortune-tellers predicted her dying. She would have told him about it; it wasn't really a secret. Only the topic had never come up in all the years they'd been having conversations. Until she asked him to make love to her, that is.

She really didn't keep too many secrets from him. There was no need. She felt underneath the driver's seat until she touched the little plastic bag she had taped there. She pulled the bag free from the tape and brought it out from its hiding place. She took the spare car key out of the bag and placed it in the ignition.

Griff didn't know about her spare keys. It wasn't a secret either, only another topic that had never come up in conversation. Now she realized it was a good thing, because if it had, he would have taken this key with him, too. Along with the other two keys she had hidden around the car.

Poor Griff. He'd probably be a little angry when he came back outside and found her gone. She started the car and was halfway down the driveway when he came running out of his house dangling her key ring in front of him shouting, "Stop!"

She braked, leaned out the window and yelled above the running motor, "I'll see you tomorrow night and we'll talk over gin rummy."

She knew she should keep backing out, only she couldn't. There was something about watching Griff move. The way he slung one leg in front of the other and advanced toward the car. And her. Sleek and strong like a lion. Goose bumps rose on her arms and legs and sent a shiver through her veins. Her breath came in short, rapid spurts. Normal thoughts got fogged over with something akin to pure, primal lust. It had to be the way his jeans hugged his body, outlined his crotch, etched every detail, the bulges and shadows giving her imagination free rein.

His sculpted face didn't show strain, only determination. And the way he looked at her. Oh, God. He'd never looked at her like this before. A mixture of uncertainty, caring and, even though she probably only imagined it, craving, too. She wanted him to crave her as much as she did him. So much that it hurt.

If she hadn't been so caught up in the aura of Griff, she would have been halfway to the restaurant by now. Yet her need to be with him, for as many hours as she had left and that he could spare, overrode any other obligation. For the time being. As soon as she met with the Duvalls, everything would change.

Suzanne gestured for Griff to get inside the car. He talked and talked nonstop during the drive, but she didn't pay too much attention to what he was saying because having him next to her was enough to send her in a daydream that rivaled any conversation.

"Are you listening to me?" he asked.

She didn't know how many times he had asked the question before it finally registered that she needed to make a response. "Of course."

"Good. Then you understand." He sounded satisfied. About what, she didn't know, but at least he was content for now.

They were only a few blocks from Café Beignet when his arm, in a casual, friendly way, reached across the back of her seat. The heat of his skin scorched her shoulders. She almost ran a red light when his fingers kneaded the back of her neck.

A friendly gesture. She would have thought so, until she glanced at him out of the corner of her eye, and saw he had a clenched jaw and dagger-sharp eyes. Maybe not so friendly. Maybe proprietary. Men. Even if she didn't understand why they did what they did, she was pretty good at predicting what they would do.

Suzanne parked and the two of them walked side by side toward Café Beignet's double doors. They'd almost made it when he stopped, grabbed her arm and brought her to a standstill. "You can't go in there. You don't know what you're letting yourself in for. I would be a pathetic friend if I let you do this to yourself."

"I appreciate your concern, but I'm fully prepared." She had to do what she had to do. She had no choice in the matter.

"I have no doubt you're a responsible adult, Suz. That's not what I'm talking about. You don't know those guys. You'll never be the same when it's all over. Things like this change a person forever."

"Oh, I know." She sighed. "I'll be a richer person for what I'm about to do. For helping those that need me."

His Adam's apple bobbed, and the way he looked

at her, as if she were some kind of nut, hurt deeply. He only made it worse by piling guilt on her with his next words. "If you want it that bad, Suz, I'll give it to you."

"I can't let you make that sacrifice for me," she told him sadly. "The Duvalls—well, it's just a business deal to them." She couldn't let him ruin his financial future for her mother's silly revenge. "It's all been arranged, the terms set." She took his hand in hers and gave it a squeeze. On an impulse that she didn't know she had, since she was not in the least bit impulsive, she reached up and gave Griff a kiss on the cheek. Her lips lingered briefly on the day-old stubble, and his scent—faded woodsy aftershave, minty toothpaste—filled her with yearning. She loved him so much.

"They're scum."

"They have what I need."

"I'll change your mind. You'll see." He held the door open for her.

Tantalizing scents from cooking bacon and eggs assaulted her. Her stomach growled in response. Griff had placed his hand lightly on the small of her back, and it took all the willpower she had not to lean back into him.

They were seated at exactly nine-thirty. "Maybe they won't show up." Griff looked hopeful.

"They'll be here." Men like the Duvalls took risks all the time. That was their business. What she offered was a sure thing. She knew that, and even if they didn't believe her now, they would on the 30th.

"Okay, Suzanne. I offered this to you before, but you said no. This time I'm not taking no for an answer." Griff let out a deep, tortured breath. "If you're that desperate to have sex, so desperate that you'll hire the three Duvalls to service you, then I have no choice.''

"Sex?" What in the world was he talking about? "Me? With the Duvalls?"

"That's what this is all about. I know it is. You said so yourself. You told me that since I wouldn't take care of you, you were going to get it somewhere else."

"You misunderstood." Could this possibly mean that all these weeks since she asked Griff to make love to her, he'd been thinking about it? Hot-slide-abacus! She hadn't a clue.

To think that every time she'd seen him over the past few weeks, making love with her had been in the back of his mind. And, apparently, if what he was saying was true, he was now imagining him and her together, in every way. That put old LuLu out of the picture. For now.

She liked that. In fact, she liked it so much, it gave her so much hope, that when she came home from Vegas, she might find time to work him into her schedule, for a few minutes at least. She slipped off her sandal and rubbed her toes along the top of his foot and up past his ankle. All the magazines she'd read said foreplay should begin before the act, so maybe if she started foreplay now, by the time she came back from Vegas, he'd be ready for her.

"Thanks for offering to service me, but I'm not a charity case, and I don't need handouts."

"I didn't mean it like that," he tried to explain.

"I'm going to Vegas."

"For sex? When I'm offering?"

Suzanne rolled her eyes. She'd call him Dr. Doofus, but he was so cute. "No, to win the casino for my mom."

"So Hermia finally wore you down." He wore that

superior smirk, now that he knew she wasn't going for sex.

"She didn't do anything. I'm doing it because I want to do something for her. It's my last chance to give her something that she's wanted all her life. No one else can do it, so it's me or no one." Her mother's obsession wasn't a secret.

"It takes a lot of money to buy a casino."

"Yes? So what's the problem?"

"No problem for me. But how are you going to get the front money?"

"The Duvalls. That's why I'm here."

His belly laugh was rude. "No way."

"It truly amazes me, Dr. Know-it-all, that when you thought I was coming here for sex with the three of them, you readily believed that. But a logical reason, to borrow money, and you're laughing at me. Do you not think that a legitimate business transaction deserves respect?"

"No insult intended. But understand, Suz, no one in their right mind would borrow money from those thugs."

She raised her eyebrows and glared at him. He was getting deeper and deeper in dog poop. "Let me explain the economics of this transaction to you. In layman's terms, so you'll understand."

He looked insulted. Good. She explained how the brothers had agreed to take the $500,000 life insurance policy as collateral, and give her $250,000 in cash. "I'm going to turn that two hundred and fifty thousand into millions, and break the bank, and win the casino for my mother, my grandmother and all the Bournes before them." She held her head high, put her hand over her heart, and expounded her covenant as if it were the Pledge of Allegiance.

Griff laughed all over again, which deflated the high-pressure air in her lungs. "It's not funny." She gave his smirking face the evil eye.

"I'm not laughing at you. It's just that it's so ridiculous. You and the Duvalls. Why would you want to put your life in danger?"

"You don't get it. I'm going to die on the 30th. Not a day before."

"Right. Right. I'm sure the guy whose body they found in Buffalo Bayou didn't think he was a goner, either. Rumor is it wasn't a drowning. The Duvalls killed him."

"It makes no difference. For me, it's a sure thing."

"If you wanted money to go to Vegas, I would have given it to you."

"I wouldn't take money from you, Griff. This is a business transaction." She put her foot back on the floor, and spit his own words back at him. "We're friends. Friends don't have sex with friends—you said it yourself. Well, they don't borrow money, either."

"One thing has nothing to do with the other." He leaned across the table, bringing his face close to hers. "Not when they say that last night Skip Wilson's son was hit by a car and left for dead. He's in the hospital now." Griff leaned even closer. "He's not talking, but everyone says the Duvalls ran him down. Is that who they were in the hospital to see last night, Suz?"

"No." She leaned towards him, too, until they were practically nose-to-nose. "They were there to see their momma."

"So they said. But are you sure?"

"All I want is the money. Nothing else matters."

"Well, they're not here yet." He leaned back again. "Maybe they won't show up."

Suzanne studied him intensely, blocking everything

in the restaurant out, until a big brown paper bag dropped down from above and landed in the middle of the table with a loud, gunshot bang. She gasped, covered her chest protectively and glanced up into the faces of the three Duvalls. When her heartbeat slowed to almost normal, she said, "Hello, everyone."

They all sent wary glances toward Griff as they mumbled their greetings to her.

"How's your mother?" she asked.

"As well as can be expected."

"I'm sure she'll be fine." She touched the bag. "Thank you for the money. Here. This is for you." She handed Ambrose the insurance policy.

"When are you leaving?" Ambrose asked, looming over her.

"On the two o'clock flight."

"Back tomorrow?"

"I plan to be. Thank you so much for trusting me."

Ambrose Duvall, wearing a dark suit, dark shirt, white tie and fedora, took her hand in his and brought it to his lips for a kiss. "I like you, Miss Mercer, but I'm a businessman."

Suzanne got her hand back and folded both in her lap. She didn't want this Duvall brother to see her shake. "Like I said, this is a sure thing."

"As we discussed, if you don't return the investment, plus interest, by the end of the month..." He held up the policy. "Whether by natural causes or not, no matter how much I like you as a person, no matter that I think you're beautiful and exquisite, one way or another, you will be dead."

"Told you so," Griff hissed, after the Duvalls left. His hands were balled into fists and he looked like he could attack. "They're killers, and you act like this is recess."

She had to work hard to calm him down. "They don't mean anything by it." They meant every word.

All the way back to their houses, she had to tell him over and over that she wasn't going to lose the money in Vegas. She had packed all her books on winning at blackjack and counting cards in her carry on bag. She'd memorize them on the airplane going to Las Vegas. She had a photographic mind. The whole thing should be so easy. "Everything will be okay," she reassured him as she drove her car into the garage.

"You don't understand," he argued. "You're not taking this seriously."

"I'll see you later, Griff," Suzanne said, turning off the engine.

"Now, wait a minute." He looked as if he were trying to relax, stretching out his long legs, his arm over the back of her seat, grazing her shoulder, tickling her neck. Keeping her from opening the car door. "You know, Suz, I've been thinking."

"That's great. Thinking is good. You can tell me all about it when I get back from the trip." She reached for the door handle. She had to get away from his magical power, or she'd find herself stretching out and relaxing, too. She could already feel her ability to escape weakening. "I've a plane to catch."

"That's what I wanted to talk to you about."

He touched her cheek. Shivers of need washed through her. She knew that as long as he touched her she wouldn't be moving. His touch had the power to hypnotize.

"I've never been to Las Vegas, and I want to go with you."

And she really, really wanted him to go with her, too. "I don't know, Griff," she said, sounding doubtful. No way would she come off to him as some eager young coed out for a good time. "It's not a good idea."

"It would mean a lot to me."

"Why?" She really wanted to know. All these years of silently living in frustration because she let the relationship be the way he wanted it to be, not the way she wanted. And now that what she wanted, what she needed, was out in the open, she had to know why it was important for him to be with her. "It wouldn't be fair for you to come with me, and taunt me with your hugs and goodnight kisses. Your touches. Your promises of something more than friendship that you don't keep."

He shut his eyes and took a deep breath before opening them again to look at her. "As soon as I got up this morning, I called in my markers. I've got ten days off."

"I won't be alive for ten more days."

"I still have those days, though, and I want to spend as many as you'll let me with you."

"Spend time with me?" She couldn't possibly turn him down now. Any bit of time she had with him, she'd grab and hold dear to her heart. Griff never took time off of work, yet he did today.

He slowly nodded, as if he couldn't believe it himself. "I'm trying to get used to the new you. I've always loved you like the great friend you've been. Only, over the last couple of weeks, all these other feelings have been surfacing and I'm not used to it."

"Griff," she said softly, taking his hand. "You don't want to settle down. You don't want to get married. I don't, either. I've been telling you that for us to make love with each other would be a one-time experience. Once. No commitment. No marriage. No happily ever after. Just a happily right now."

"That's not you. You know that you're the type of lady who expects to marry."

"If it weren't for the fact that I'm going to die on my birthday, I would agree with you. But you see, you're safe from any kind of female talons. These—" she held up her acrylic nails, "—are not going to puncture your skin." He took her hand and kissed her fingers. "Would you like to join me in Las Vegas, Griff?"

"You know I would." He lowered his mouth to hers and gently kissed her lips. The kiss wasn't passionate, but it wasn't the kiss of one friend to another friend, either. It was the kiss given to a new lover, a kiss that promised more.

7

WHEN THEIR CAB pulled up to the Red Rock Casino and Hotel, she was sure the driver had brought them to the wrong place.

She had heard, but never really listened to her mother, grandmother and great-grandmother rant and rage about the original Hermia's misfortunes at the hands of one Red Jack Bourne. Those old stories had become background noise. Always there, never heard. They'd been telling the same story, embellishing the facts of displacement for so many years, that Suzanne, even if she could remember the facts, wouldn't know anymore which were true and which were not.

What she did know, and what had been abundantly clear all her life, was that her mother wanted what she claimed rightfully belonged to the Texas Bourne family. Most of what Hermia wanted seemed logical. The casino, the property the building sat on and all the assets of the gambling and hotel operation, oil leases, gold mines. Hermia had often said, "The hotel's probably a cockroach-ridden dump that'll cost a fortune to renovate, so they can keep the hotel, but even a few slot machines would bring in a little grocery money."

Wanting the casino was at least reasonable. Other things Hermia thought to be reasonable, Suzanne did not. Like her mother suggesting various ways to kill off all the legitimate Las Vegas Bournes. Poison, deadly spiders, a slithering asp were all possibilities in Hermia's mind. Suzanne vetoed murder.

Knowing the Red Rock was at least one hundred years old, Suzanne did not have high expectations for the condition or appearance of the place. So when the cab stopped at the tall glass-and-chrome building, which was anything but ramshackle, it came as a shock.

After they got out of the cab, Griff leaned in through the front window and paid the driver.

"Is this really it?" she asked Griff.

"That's what the sign says." He placed a hand on the small of her back. That one touch was so gentle, so confident, so knee-weakening. Her insides constricted into a tight knot. He held her overnight bag in his other hand, and guided her inside.

She stopped next to the first row of slot machines. A pink-haired woman, cigarette dangling from the corner of her mouth, deposited quarter after quarter, five at a time, into the machine, and each time she threw the handle, coins dropped down into a silver tray, making ping-pinging, ding-dinging noises. In fact, there were a lot of those noises throughout the place.

Shouts of surprise, screams of excitement and bursts of laughter came from all parts of the casino.

"People are winning," she whispered to Griff. "This isn't good."

"Of course it is." He moved to the next row of slot machines, dropping her bag and digging into his pocket.

"Don't," she said, blocking the slot where the coins were deposited.

He moved her hand, stuck in a quarter, pulled the lever and lost it.

Suzanne breathed a sigh of relief. At his strange

look, she said, "If people win, the casino can't make money."

He nodded at his losing machine. "Trust me, Suz, the casino makes lots of money."

"We'll see." By tomorrow, as the new owner, the first thing she planned to do was have a thorough look at the books. If those slots were causing the casino to go in the red, out they'd go.

Suzanne gave her name to the reservation clerk, and signed for her room. Griff gave the clerk his credit card.

SUZANNE PLUNKED the overnight bag in the middle of the king size bed. "I'm ready."

He smiled at her and started to unbutton his shirt. "Before blackjack? Okay."

Oh, that would be so wonderful, but no. "Business before pleasure."

"That's the Suzanne I know and love." He rebuttoned the button. "Afterward, though, I plan on making sure this is a night you will remember."

She started to get hot flashes just imagining what it would be like with him. "Let's hurry."

"Wait one more minute."

She thought he was going to try and convince her to stay and take a turn under the covers. Only he wanted to talk about the Duvalls again. He couldn't seem to let it drop. "You realize how much danger you've put yourself in, don't you? Your life is up for grabs."

She appreciated his concern, but he just didn't get the fact that she couldn't lose. Even if she lost, she couldn't lose. Except that she would have lost her mother's dream, and she didn't plan on doing that. "Life is a gamble and I'm going to win."

He snorted at that one. "You've turned into quite the little risk taker all of a sudden, except that the only blackjack you know how to play is what you read in a book. That's not going to help you. Not when you're playing with the money of known killers."

"I know how to count to twenty-one. That's all I have to know."

"There's a strategy to this game."

"I'm not worried. Let's go."

"Do you want to practice?"

"No. In fact, we should be done in an hour. Or less." She couldn't wait to get back to the room and Griff's promises.

"An hour?" His voice full of scorn.

"Too soon?"

"No one does it in an hour."

"Maybe no one did it right. See, I figure if I bet the $250,000 on the first hand and double it, then $500,000 on the next hand and double it, then keep on doubling..." Suzanne thought the whole plan simple and logical. "I'm surprised no one's ever done this before."

"Maybe they've tried and failed."

She shook her head. "I'll be holding the mortgage on the property in no time at all."

"No one wins that much at one time. The tables have limits."

"Then I'll max the limit at one table and go to the next." She had no idea what she was talking about, but logic prevailed.

"They'll see what you're up to and stop the game."

She thought about it for a moment. "You're right. Maybe that'll look too suspicious. How's this? What if I lose a few hands, to throw them off the track?" The more excited she got, the faster she talked. "Then

I'll win a few, lose one or two, win four or five, and then, before they even know what hit them, I'll have taken my original investment and wiped them out.''

''Suzanne, I hate to tell you this but it's not going to happen.''

''Suddenly I'm getting really sorry I brought you. You're too negative.''

''This from the woman who analyzes everything down to the number of cornflakes in a serving?''

''If you knew me at all, you'd know I don't eat cornflakes.''

''You've certainly turned into a flake.''

''If anything, Dr. Know-Nothing, I've become a very spur-of-the-moment, take-charge person. And you know what?'' She got right into his face.

''What?''

''You're reminding me of myself for my first twenty-nine years, and I don't like it.''

''Is this our first fight?'' Now he got in her face.

''Yes, I like it. In fact, as of this moment I'm keeping this new Suzanne and tossing out the old one.''

''That'll never happen. Your old self will come through,'' he said with assurance.

''What do you know?''

''I know everything there is to know about you. I am your conscience. I'm the voice of reason.''

''Then take your voice and go give someone else your reason. I don't need it.'' She loved him, but love had nothing to do with business. When he got all pompous like this, she wanted to give him a shot of his own antibiotic.

''All right. You're on your own.'' He flung up his arms. ''I'll have nothing to do with it.''

''No one asked you to.''

"I won't even practice with you, or give you my tricks of the trade."

"I don't need them. I've got the blackjack book. I studied the strategy."

"Aha!" He grinned at her in glee. "If I were a betting man, which I am, I would put your life insurance policy on the fact that if they had a blackjack certification exam, you'd pass it on the first try."

"And you'd be right." Well, that was just fine. She'd show him. "When I win, I won't even say, 'I told you so.'"

"That's something I won't have to worry about. Knowing the strategy and winning are poker chips of two different colors."

They walked to the cashier together. She didn't want to exchange all her money for chips at once lest she look suspicious. She started out small, ten thousand. The cashier didn't bat an eyelash.

"I have $240,000 left," she told the woman in the money cage. "Can you exchange that for chips? A few thousands, mostly five-hundreds and one-hundreds?"

The cashier set trays on the counter and started loading them with colored chips.

"I'm impressed, Suz." Griff whistled long and low. "This is your second spur-of-the-moment decision in the last twenty-four hours."

She thought about that for a second. "You're right."

"It's a good thing I came along. With this much excitement in your life, you might have a heart attack and I'll be right here to resuscitate you."

She looked up at him, her smile wistful. "I know I missed out on a lot of fun in my life." She touched his arm. "I'm glad you're here with me to give some of what I've been missing back."

She took the trays of chips off the counter and carried them through the casino. Griff walked behind her. "I want to be here for you."

This new Suzanne scared him. The Suzanne he'd known and loved would never have met with the Duvalls, let alone traveled to Las Vegas to gamble. The person standing in front of him was a stranger with a familiar face. Someone he knew, but didn't know.

He followed her around the casino as she made the circuit twice before stopping at one of the blackjack tables. Two men and a woman were already seated there looking serious, chips piled high on the players' side of the table. Suzanne sat next to one of the men, placing the chip trays to her right.

"You can go now," she said. "I'm fine."

Griff dug his heels into the carpet, crossing his arms over his chest. "I'm not going anywhere. I'll stay right here."

She smiled at him, all sweet and friendly. "Get away."

He couldn't believe she'd said that. But before he could question what he'd heard, she said it again. Still all sweet, but her eyes told a different story. He tried to get her to change her mind. "I came here to give you support."

"I wear a bra for support."

Why the ungrateful wench. "This is what I get for being here for you?"

The pit boss appeared out of nowhere. He didn't have a sweet smile. In fact, he looked downright nasty. "You heard the lady, mister."

Griff wasn't intimidated. "She doesn't mean what she says."

"Yes I do, Griff." Suzanne said the words quietly, looking straight into his eyes, imploring him to understand.

He looked down into her face. A beautiful face. He wanted to protect her. He wanted to pick her up and carry her and her chips away, back to safety. Back to February, before all this crap happened. The clock doesn't turn back though. He knew that. He reached into his wallet and took out a one-hundred-dollar bill. "I saw a slot machine over there that had my name on it."

He heard Suzanne say, "Goodbye," as he headed toward the opposite end of the casino.

Suzanne waited until Griff was out of sight. Then she placed her opening chips on the table and waited until she was dealt. A ten down, a seven showing. The other people at her table were drinking and looking very serious. But not as serious as she was. She was playing for the Bourne women's heritage.

She lost the first hand. The second hand she won, which made her feel a little more confident.

Each hand that came after, she thought she could win, but she didn't.

After losing half her money at the first table, she took her chips and found a better table. There were two others there, too. These people were having a better time. The chips in front of them were piled high, and the dealer seemed to be shoving more their way.

Suzanne's first hand was blackjack, and she won. The second hand she had eighteen, and lost to the dealer's twenty.

She didn't remember the time going so fast. She kept thinking that if she could win one more, she'd make up for her losses. Only she didn't win enough to make up for her losses. It had only taken four hours and eleven minutes to lose the whole two hundred and fifty thousand.

She didn't care about losing the money, she knew the Duvalls would get that back. She did care about disappointing her mother. This had been her last chance to give her mom her wish, and she'd blown it.

GRIFF HAD discretely checked up on Suzanne over the course of the evening. He knew she'd gone to several different tables. He didn't get close to her, but she didn't look around to see if he was there, either. She had one thing on her mind, playing that game, and her concentration on the cards was all encompassing.

He played the slot machines, he played his own game of video poker, and went to the craps table, and rolled the dice. He spent a good amount of change while waiting for Suzanne to bankrupt the casino.

When he had finished losing at keno, he looked for her again, only this time, she was nowhere to be found.

He circled the game tables for about ten minutes before he spotted one of the players he had seen at the last table she'd been playing at.

"The lady that was sitting with you over there." He pointed to where they had been. "Do you happen to know where she went?"

The man took a swallow of whiskey, then said, "It was over quick-like. Never seen chips fly around the table like that. Where do you think she learned to play?" He looked a little confused.

"She won then." It wasn't a question. He had been hopeful, wanting her to succeed for her own safety if nothing else. He pumped the man's hand. "Thanks."

Griff went straight to their room, bringing with him flowers and champagne. When he unlocked the door and walked in, the room was cloaked in darkness. Suzanne sat on the edge of the bed, looking anything but happy.

"Suzie Q," he said, dropping the flowers and wine on the dresser and moving quickly toward her. He kneeled in front of her. There was no reaction. Could it be shock? That was a lot of money. He picked up her listless hand, so cold. He rubbed the soft skin between his hands, trying to bring warmth into her. "The man downstairs told me your news."

She didn't utter a word, only stared into nowhere.

"Is the shock too much for you?" he asked.

Still nothing.

Then, he heard her whisper so softly he had to lean in closer to pick up all the words. "Aren't you even going to say, 'I told you so'?"

Griff frowned. He'd missed a connection somewhere. "Why would I do that?" The man had said she won so he didn't understand why she was so down in the dumps. Then he snapped. She was in her room, and not in the hotel business office taking over, telling the staff how to run their lives. Was it possible he'd misunderstood? That she hadn't won after all?

"At least," she went on, "I finally know how I'm going to die on the 30th. The Duvalls are going to have me killed."

Now the situation was crystal clear. "Suzie, it doesn't matter that you didn't win. I'll give you the money to pay back those scum."

"Is that what you think? That I'm worried about them killing me?" she sniffed.

"Aren't you?"

"I've been telling you for the last three weeks, I'm going to die on the 30th. It doesn't matter how it happens, it's going to happen." She swiped at her nose with her hand. "Paying back those kind men—don't call them scum—who loaned me the money in good faith isn't the issue. It's my mother. I wanted so much to give her what she's always wanted."

He dug his fingers through the hair at the nape of her neck. He had no idea that hair so curly would be so soft. "Your mom will understand." Suzanne leaned her head back into his hand. He gently massaged, whispering nonsense, wanting to calm her. "You know Hermia. She'll think you're a wonderful daughter just for trying."

"And my grandma, too. They both have spent lifetimes wanting to avenge the Bourne name. Here I had the opportunity, right in the palm of my hand. I lost it. I failed them, Griff."

She looked up at him. Her face so close to his, her lips full and kissable. All he had to do was lean down a fraction and he'd feel them on his. Would they be as soft as they looked? Or would they be as firm and determined as she was?

He could call himself all kinds of names. Sucker. Bounder. He could chastise himself for the lurid thoughts he'd been having over the past few days, thoughts of making love to Suzanne. He could chalk it up to her having brought up the subject.

Then again, if he were honest with himself, he'd have to admit that over the past five years, he had thought of it himself a time or two. Maybe three.

He touched her hair…soft. Massaged the back of her neck…warm. Her skin against the pads of his fingers…electric. He knew as a doctor his fingers had a magic touch, but until now, he'd never known what it was like to touch magic.

Suzie's head leaned heavily into the palm of his hand, and she closed her eyes, her smile wistful. She wasn't crying, yet her eyelashes were moist, as if her tears had somehow been captured and were being held prisoner.

He lowered himself onto the bed, sitting close to her. His thigh rubbed against the length of hers. He didn't know if it was because of all her weeks of persuasion, or if he'd been thinking the thoughts all along, but where their limbs rubbed against each other, a slow fire began to heat through his veins.

He leaned over slightly in her direction, so that he faced her. His chest met the softness of her breasts and that wasn't enough. He wanted to lay her down on the bed, he wanted to move over on top of her, he wanted to undress her, and have her.

Suzanne. How did this happen? When? Where had he been all these years that he hadn't noticed the feelings he had for her? Had they always been there? Had he hidden them from himself, denying them the same way he denied anything that might force him to come to terms with the idea of falling in love? He was afraid of loving and losing someone. He saw death every day. Loving Suzanne. Losing her. He refused to believe it.

He used the thumb on his other hand to gently brush the unshed tears from her eyes. Her closed eyelids fluttered under his touch. Her scent captured him. So familiar, all Suzanne. Maybe that's why he leaned down closer to her neck. Maybe he had to delve deeper into her body heat, into the essence that was hers and hers alone.

She turned her head, her lips barely touched his and she sighed. Or maybe it had been him. Her eyes, still closed. His body, hard, strumming.

He gently tilted her back onto the bed. He heard her say, ''I want you so much.''

The palm of his hand rested on her chest as his

fingers undid the first button of her shirt. Her breasts rapidly rose and fell beneath his touch. He felt like a schoolboy undressing a girl for the first time. He wanted her out of her clothes. Now. But he had to give her the chance to back out. He had to warn her. "Nothing will ever be the same between us again."

"I don't want anything to be the same."

He undid the second button, then the third, until finally she lay exposed. She sat back up and did to him what he had done to her, one button at a time. Only with each button undone, she kissed the exposed skin. "I've never kissed you before, not like I've wanted to. Sometimes I would think about it, and the idea of kissing you would send chills through me."

He cupped her face in his hands, lowered his mouth to meet hers. He couldn't kiss her enough. One kiss turned into another, then another. His tongue slipped inside her warmth, hers danced together with his in a slow, sensual rhythm.

She shrugged out of her shirt, her lips still clinging to his. When her hands were free, she ran them down his shoulders, gathering the material of his shirt and taking it down his arms until the material stopped at his wrists, held captive by more buttons.

He finally broke their kiss. She opened her eyes, and stared at him dreamily, her lips swollen, full and moist. Her tongue peeked out, licking her lips where his mouth had been, taking his taste and bringing it in.

He couldn't stop looking at Suzanne, from her slender neck, to her round shoulders. Her breasts were restrained in a yellow polka-dot bikini. Barely. One move and she'd be out of it. He couldn't wait. "Did you want to go swimming?" he gulped, hardly able to get words out. Never had he suspected what she'd been hiding from him all these years.

She looked down at the bathing suit. "This is my courage."

"Did you need courage for me?"

"No," she said softly. "Not for you. Maybe courage isn't the right word, or maybe it's only part of what I'm trying to say. You do something to me, to my insides. I feel like a coil that hasn't sprung and I don't know what to do."

He reached behind her and unsnapped her courage, tossing it somewhere behind him. Suzanne was a gift, and he planned on opening her carefully. She leaned forward, her chin on his shoulder, her naked breasts cushioned against his chest. He took her hand and placed it on his erection. Her hands curled over his member, and he groaned. "This is what you do to me."

"I could do more, if you took off your pants." She let go of his sex, then slipped off the bed, standing in front of him.

He gazed at her for several moments, his finger and thumb, skimming the indentation between her waist and hips. He moved his hand down the side of her hip, then followed the fabric of the bikini down until he reached her inner thigh. He fingered the material there, before slipping his finger inside, touching her wet center. She moaned, rotating herself around his hand. He watched her eyelids close, her lashes fluttering. Her breathing came in rapid bursts of air.

He was glad he had on his jeans. His own erection was so hard, the confining material felt painful, which kept him from exploding. He didn't want to come yet. He wanted to watch Suzanne. To give pleasure to her, before seeking his own.

Only she had other ideas. She put her hand on his shoulder and squeezed. "Stop." Her eyes were glazed over.

"I don't want to."

"And I don't want to do this alone." She took his wrist, and pulled his hand away from her. She unbuttoned the cuffs of his shirt, and helped him out of the material, then threw it behind her, just the way he had tossed her bikini top.

She crooked her finger, without saying anything, letting him know she wanted him to stand. It was more difficult for her to concentrate on seducing him, when all she wanted was some kind of release and she didn't know how to get it. He did stand, but he kept kissing her breasts, laving and suckling one nipple, while massaging the other to a peak with his thumb, sending spasms from there to her belly. No part of her body lacked his attention.

Despite her shaky fingers making the task more difficult, she finally got his jeans unsnapped, and the material slid down his legs. He stepped out of them, never once taking his mouth from her breast. She had to pull away from him, because she had to look at what she'd uncovered.

Suzanne had imagined a lot of things about her and Griff, and what they would do together, but in her mind, she never actually imagined what he'd look like naked. She'd seen parts of him though. His muscular shoulders, and a tight, flat abdomen where the muscles were corded and pronounced. She knew he had long legs, and she could tell from his jeans he had a great butt. However, the one major important part of him, the manly thing, she had never even begun to imagine.

When she finally saw him, stiff, proud, she was not disappointed. Griff, naked, was a man made to pleasure a woman, and tomorrow, when she could actually think coherently, she might tell him how angry she was that he kept his attributes a secret from her all these years.

She gently guided him back to the bed. He sat down, his erection exposed, tall, thick and proud. She stood in front of him, and he slipped his fingers back into her bikini bottoms, but this time he pulled them down her legs. She stepped out of the bathing suit, and stood in front of him completely naked, suddenly feeling vulnerable.

He could see all of her now. The shadows, indentations, peaks and valleys. There were no secrets.

He reached out for her center, cupping her, putting his hand where it had been moments before, slipping two fingers deep inside her, touching, rubbing on her nub.

He took her hand and placed it on his erection. When she didn't move, he guided her, showing her what he wanted. She ran her hand down the length of him, hard and silky soft at the same time. She could feel his blood flowing through his sex and when she squeezed him at the bottom, he sucked in his breath, as if his heart had stopped beating.

She positioned herself on the bed, sitting on her knees, facing him, straddling his legs between hers. She placed his arousal on the outer edges of her womanhood and rubbed his tip into her wetness, until, with one slow movement downward, she captured him inside her, then slowly slid down the length of him, relaxing her legs, until she sat in his lap. The feel of him pulsing inside her took her breath away.

"Oh, Griff," she sighed, not moving yet, only laying her head on his shoulder, breathing in his scent. "This is so good." And had come so late.

He gently guided her face to his until he could capture her lips. He didn't stop kissing her, not when she leaned into him until he was flat on his back and she was lying on top of him. Her body and his took on a rhythm of their own. He held her bottom tightly, to keep her close to him.

When the tremors began to go through her, she thought something was wrong, her stomach muscles were coiled so tight. Then a plug got pulled and explosions inside her went off. She could hardly breathe, her legs and arms had lost all muscle mass. She had become a rag doll. Griff rolled her over until she was on her back and he was on top of her. Her legs, which she didn't know could move anymore, seemed instinctively to stay wrapped around his waist, capturing him as he had captured her. She ran her hands down his back, cupped his buttocks, kneaded his flesh. His sex was deep inside her, sliding up and down. She could feel him everywhere, he filled her with all that was him. Finally he, too, worked up to a frenzy, bringing her once again along with him, until they both collapsed, him on top of her, sated. Not going anywhere anytime soon.

He opened one eye and gazed at her. "Thank you." He made butterfly kisses along her neck and shoulders.

"No, thank you," she whispered, playing with the hair at the back of his head.

"I guess you're mad at me."

"Why would I be mad?"

"Because if I hadn't been such a jerk, we could have done this three weeks ago when you first asked and had three weeks of this. Now we wasted all this time."

"No, it's not wasted. Because we're only going to do it once, just like I promised. So whether it was three weeks ago, or today, doesn't matter. We did it, and now I can die a happy woman."

Apparently, Griff had other ideas about her one-time-only plan, and proceeded to tell her all the other ways he planned on making love to her. She smiled and nodded, and tried to keep up with him as best she could, only she fell asleep with him still deep inside her.

SUZANNE WOKE UP the next morning at the same time she did every morning, except in a different time zone. Griff, naked, slept by her side. Just the way she'd dreamed, only now the dream had come true.

He slept on his stomach, his head facing her. With each exhale, warm air puffed from his mouth, gently fanning her shoulder. He had one arm flung across her waist, holding her captive to the bed, and to him.

Her bikini bottoms was on a chair somewhere and he'd thrown the top across the room, where it had landed on a lampshade. Griff's clothes were strewn like cookie crumbs across the floor, the trail ending at the bed.

They had been in such a hurry the first time, folding and hanging didn't even figure into the picture. Yet for all the hurry they'd been in, for all the rush, for all the horrible, terrible yearning her body begged to be released from, Griff had done anything but rush. He had slowly, painstakingly, made love to every part of her body, parts she hadn't even known she had. He'd lavished attention from the top of her head to the tips of both her baby toes. There wasn't one part of her he hadn't kissed or touched in some way.

She had spent the past five years pretending to Griff and to herself that being good friends was what she wanted and expected. She had put on a convincing show for him, but she knew that was only half of what she wanted. She had been afraid to ask for the other half, the loving part, because she knew if she did, it would change their relationship forever. As much as she wanted him, asking him to go a step further would have risked everything they had together, and it wasn't worth that risk. Until she had asked him on March 1st. By then, she had nothing to lose, and everything to gain.

The five years of waiting and wanting him to make love with her had been worth the wait.

Making love with Griff had given her a glimpse straight into heaven. Leaving wouldn't be so hard now that she had this gift to remember and keep with her throughout eternity. And Griff, the king of no commitment, could be happy, too. He had given her the one thing she wanted most, and his life could still go on as it always had. No commitment. No emotion. No permanent relationship.

With him cuddled up to her side the way he was, so strong, so full of pleasure, Suzanne could feast on him all she wanted without having to worry about getting caught gawking. In sleep, the normally tense muscles in his face relaxed, making him look young and carefree. Not at all like a well-known doctor. Certainly not like a man who knew how to make a woman feel wanton, cherished, nurtured and sexy, all at the same time.

She had to tattoo the memory of their one night together on her brain. She had so little time left, and so much with which to nourish the part of her that had been empty. She would always remember Griff's kisses on her stomach, how he lowered himself to her center, and drank from her until she begged him, pleaded with him, to finish the deed.

Griff mumbled something in his sleep and pulled her toward him. She hadn't known there was room to get any closer. One long, muscular leg slid between hers, prodding them apart, until he had room to bend his leg, and rub his knee against her center. She tried not to breathe because he felt so good, and she didn't want the moment to end. She was afraid if she moved, he'd wake and if he woke up, he'd stop rubbing her, stop cuddling her. She wasn't ready for the new day to begin.

If he woke, they'd leave, and it would all be over. They'd get on their Texas-bound airplane. She'd go home and call the Duvall brothers, and have to tell them that she not only didn't get the mortgage on the Red Rock Casino and Hotel, but she also had lost their $250,000. She knew without a doubt they'd get their money back after the 30th. She wasn't worried about that. Pride though, that was another thing. She'd been so sure of winning, of breaking the bank, that failing to do that just about destroyed her self-confidence. What good did it do to study something, to memorize the formula, when failure was the end result.

Griff was doing a good job of nuzzling her neck while he slept. The more he nuzzled, the more she wanted everything else. If she didn't get control of the way she felt, she was going to do something she'd never done before. Make love to a sleeping man. And she had told him they'd only do it once, and she'd be breaking her own promise. Okay, so they did it three times last night, but since it was all in one night, she'd consider it as one time. They were, after all, her rules.

But his neck kisses were sending liquid fire through her, and all thought of once-only promises vanished.

Plus, she didn't know if it counted as a second time if the man was sleeping. Probably not. She hadn't read anything in her books about having sex with men while they were sleeping. She didn't even know if they were capable of rising to the occasion, and she couldn't tell if Griff was primed and ready to go because of the way he slept on his stomach.

Then she found out, when she slowly slipped her hand between Griff's chest and the mattress, and slid it lower, and lower, until she connected with rock solid man. She had studied all those magazines about making love, and even if she said so herself, she was a pretty fast study. Last night could be considered the test, and she'd passed.

So maybe the books she'd read on winning at blackjack, on counting cards, were wrong. Because if they'd been right, she surely would have won. Flunking wasn't in her nature.

She looked into his face and was pretty surprised when she found him looking right back at her with one eye open. She smiled, and he smiled right back. "I thought you were sleeping," she said.

"I was having a dream."

"I want you so much," she whispered with an urgency that couldn't be denied.

"You can feel that I want you, too." He slid across the top of her, settling between her legs. "This is something we didn't try last night to start off with, but in the morning it feels real good."

"Ah, the missionary position, also known as the four-second job. The one where men say, 'Oh, baby, that feels so good. Oh, baby! Oh, baby!' and then *bam!* It's over and then the man always asks, 'Did that feel good for you, too?' Before I can even give him an answer, he's snoring. The missionary position is a conspiracy to keep women from knowing the pleasures of the body. I'm convinced of it."

"I don't know who your friends are, but check out the time right now. When you and I are finished, I can guarantee it will be way past four seconds."

The last words she uttered before he kissed her mouth were, "Promises, promises."

8

GRIFF TOOK the old hand-me-down rocking chair from his living room and then sat in it on the front porch. Rocking. All he needed to make the picture complete was a whittling knife and a piece of wood.

He didn't have a whittling knife or a piece of wood. So he only rocked and rocked. He'd been at it all day. Like some old curmudgeon. Like his former patient, Matt Ferguson. He'd hung around the old man a lot the past couple of weeks. Some of the old guy's habits must have sneaked in when Griff wasn't looking.

From where he sat, facing to the left just a smidgen, he could watch the house next door. Suzanne's.

Just as he'd gotten his rocking up to speed, had the rhythm going in the right direction, Suzanne's friend Christine came bouncing out of that house. The house of his "used to be" best friend and one-night and one-morning lover. She looked mighty happy for being at her good friend's wake. "Dr. Scott," she called out, skipping toward him, "aren't you coming over?"

He played all innocent-like. "Where to?"

"Didn't you get an invitation? I could swear we mailed you one."

He got an invitation all right, and he filed it right where it belonged. In the shredder.

"You're wanted in there," Christine said.

He crossed his arms over his chest and scowled at

her. ''Maybe later.'' No way was he going to that circus next door.

Christine finally went away to enjoy some more of her best friend's last hours on earth, leaving him at peace with his own misery, where he was very happy, thank you very much. Then Nina came outside.

''Yoo-hoo, Dr. Griff.'' Nina stepped gingerly across the grass in six-inch heels.

Why she didn't take the sidewalk, where walking would have been easier, he hadn't a clue. Then again, she was part of Suzanne's circus team, and logic and reason didn't have a place over there. If it had, that party would never have taken place. What would have taken place is Suzanne and him, making love. She knew the sex was incredible. She was the one who begged him for more and more, all in one night. And the next morning, too.

Oh, hell, maybe he'd been the one who had done the begging. Semantics. Didn't matter.

What did matter was that Suzanne had turned out to be every guy's fantasy of a love machine. It was only natural he'd want to continue what they'd started. Anyone with half a brain would know that, and Suzanne had at least two brains in her head.

Then again, glancing next door, watching what was going on, he changed his mind. Half a brain.

The real kicker though was when *she* told him she didn't want commitment. That was *his* line, and she had no right to use it.

She told him life is short, and she appreciated the good time.

He was no one-night stand. He wasn't just some plaything to use and throw away.

No sooner did they get off the airplane in Houston

and drive back to their houses, than she told him, "See you at the wake."

Not likely.

Then, instead of coming over herself and begging for his attention, she sent Nina and right before her, Christine. Like Nina could do what Christine couldn't? That wasn't likely, either.

He didn't tell Nina to go back where she had come from. He let her plod right over the gopher-hole minefield, also known as Griff's grass. If she didn't watch it, she was going to fall right into one and break an ankle, like she almost had when he heard her shout out, "Oops, sorry little furry animal down there."

She moved another few steps, stopped, put both hands on her hips and glared at him. "Don't watch me."

"Who's watching?" Like he had nothing better to do.

He had lots of things to do. Things like figuring out if it was worth expending the energy it would take to get off the chair and retrieve a beer. Nah, thoughts that required using his brain to think expended too much internal energy. He'd rather watch klutzy Nina trip over gopher holes. That was mindless. He put his hands behind his head and rocked and watched. He had a great life—yes, he did. He was only sorry he took ten days off work. He was ready to go back.

Nina, after long, grueling minutes, and he'd bet a lot of ankle and foot bruises, finally navigated her way off the grass. Then she stood in front of him, looking like she wanted something from him. Was waiting for something from him. Approval, maybe? Not from this doctor she wasn't getting it.

"Why didn't you take the sidewalk?" He had to know the logic behind what she'd done.

"The grass is so much faster," she said. "And Suzanne didn't send me to get you, in case you're wondering."

"I wasn't."

She looked at him funny, like she knew he was lying, which he was, but she'd never prove it. "Suzanne needs you, Griff. Are you coming?"

"Why can't she come over herself and ask me?" She didn't need him, or want him—not even in her bed. She'd made that perfectly clear.

"She would if she could get away. There are so many people in there. They're wanting to toast her. She won't participate unless you're there."

"I'll be there later," he lied.

When Nina started back to Suzanne's along the same route she had come, Griff called out to her, "Take the sidewalk."

She actually had to stop and think about it before she finally strutted next door by way of pavement.

Car after car drove down their street looking for parking and there wasn't any. More than one car stopped, its occupants asking if they could park in his driveway. He gave them all the same answer. "No way in hell."

Suzanne lived such a quiet life, or so he thought. He had no idea she knew this many people. People apparently weren't deterred by the lack of spaces on the street. They were finding somewhere to drop off their cars, because they were walking to her house from all directions.

He should have known, after their incredible night in Las Vegas and then her rejection of him, that she had been leading a secret life. He was going to watch out for those quiet accountant types from now on. He had their number.

"Oh, boy," he muttered when he saw Hermia come out of Suzanne's house. He shot out of the rocker, wanting to get out of Dodge before she spotted him. Only Hermia, with her laser vision, saw him before he made his escape and effectively put up a roadblock. "Griff, darlin' boy, we need you next door."

She came over, taking the pavement. When she arrived at the bottom of his porch, he held out his hand and she used his assistance to walk up the porch steps. Not that she needed help, it was her old-fashioned Southern upbringing that demanded the niceties of gentlemanly behavior, even from slobs like him.

He told her flat out, "She's not going to die. You know it and I know it."

"Yes, she is. It was in the fortune. All of them. Did she tell you about that day?"

He nodded.

"You don't know what it's like to be a mother," she sniffled, "knowing that your only child is going to die. I've lived with this for nine years, and every year a little of my heart is eaten away."

"You sure have a funny way of showing it." He nodded in the direction of the house. He lived with death on a daily basis and had never seen anyone have a pre-dying celebration. It was morbid.

"Oh, you mean the wake? Well, you see, since Suzanne knew the exact day, but not the time, it gave us the ability to plan ahead. We made this party for her. I wanted her to remember this day forever," she said dramatically. "Even if forever for her is only another hour or two." She pulled a lace handkerchief from her sleeve and sniffled into the white square.

A black limousine pulled into his driveway. Griff took all three steps at once, and made it to the car in record time. He tapped on the driver's window, yelling, "You can't park here."

The driver opened the door and if Griff hadn't backed away, he would have been slammed. Ignoring Griff completely, the driver got out and opened the back door for his passengers. Ambrose, Wyatt and Mickey, dressed in identical black suits, each with a red carnation on his lapel, stepped out.

Hermia went to them, holding out her hand, introducing herself. "You're the nice gentlemen who loaned my little girl that money."

"Yes, ma'am," Ambrose said, taking her hand and kissing it like a true hoodlum.

Hermia twittered and held out her hand as if it had been kissed by royalty. "She's so sorry she lost it. She didn't mean to. You know that, don't you?"

"A deal's a deal," Mick said, doing the shoulder shrug thing that wannabe hoods like to do.

"Of course it is." Hermia brought out the tear blower again. "You have the insurance policy. She told me so."

They nodded.

"By tomorrow, my darlin' girl will be gone, and that five hundred thousand will be yours. Follow me, and I'll show you inside."

"Hermia," Griff said, reaching for her arm, "let the Duvalls find their own way." When she started to argue with him, he said, "They won't mind. I want to ask you something before you leave."

After the Duvalls were safely next door and out of hearing, although with the Houston Symphony playing, he doubted anyone in there could hear anything, he said, "I know Suzanne lost the money and I want you to know I offered to give her the money to pay them back."

Hermia patted his arm. "It's okay, Griff. She doesn't need it. They'll get the insurance proceeds."

"She's not going to die."

"Believe what you will."

"Now she's got those hoods after her, and they will kill her if she doesn't pay them back."

"They can't kill her if she's already dead."

"She's not going to die," he repeated, this time through clenched teeth.

"Okay, darlin' boy. Whatever you say. You're the doctor."

His body went rigid with anger. "Don't patronize me."

"I wouldn't think of doing that."

"Let's go." He took Hermia by the arm and marched her back to the house next door.

"You can't come to the wake dressed like that," she told him, staring at his lightweight cotton shorts and T-shirt. "It's not proper attire for this occasion."

"No offense, ma'am, but you'll have to take me as I come."

"You forceful men," she tittered, "you're all the same. Just like my darlin' husband Michael." She patted his arm when they arrived at Suzanne's door, then took off in the opposite direction.

He'd been watching members of the Houston Symphony come and go from the house all day. With every change of musicians, the music seemed to change, too. The long, classical pieces went on and on for hours in the morning and early afternoon. By midday the music became more lively. Now it positively hopped. A few couples were actually swing-dancing around a raised platform bed that looked to be Suzanne's final resting place.

After asking several people where she was, he was directed to her bedroom. He knocked. "Suz?"

He heard a muffled, "Go 'way."

"It's me."

"I know."

He tried the handle, and the door opened. "Suzie Q, where are you?" he called out. "Come out, come out and play." He felt like he was getting ready to give a shot to a five-year-old, saying stupid things to throw them off guard, lying to them, telling them it didn't hurt, then sticking it to them. It pained him to give it as much as it pained them to get it.

He glanced around the room, and at first didn't see her. Then her head peered out from behind the bathroom door. Then a shoulder. Finally, she must have decided to stop trying to hide from him. With her head held high, her shoulders back, and with a strong, determined step, she walked into the bedroom.

He couldn't believe what he was seeing. No way would anyone else, either, if he had his way.

"What are you wearing?" he demanded. He knew exactly what she wore and he wouldn't allow it. That yellow polka-dot bikini had no business being seen out in public. The skin she showed, those breasts that were practically naked, were for his eyes only.

"You know what this is." She looked at him with this puzzled look on her face. "Don't you remember?"

Oh, she was a sly one, that girl. "Take it off." His body's reaction to her in that bathing suit was no secret. His shorts were made of lightweight cotton. Suzanne wasn't stupid, and she knew just where to look. And she did.

He stood tall and proud and he wasn't going to back

off. She wasn't taking off the suit, either. "Right now," he ordered.

She walked toward him, her hands outstretched, and she kept walking until she stood right in front of him. She put her hands on his hips, gripped the elastic of his waistband and pulled down.

"Now you did it," he told her.

"I did do that, didn't I?" she said with obvious pride at what she was able to do to him merely by wearing that bathing suit.

Poor Griff, Suzanne thought. She would have smiled if he hadn't looked so sad. Even if other parts of him were happy to see her. "This bathing suit means a lot to me. It's special. I want to die in it because the memories are so happy that it will let me concentrate on the happy thoughts and not on being scared."

"You should be scared all right. The Duvalls are out there, waiting for you to go." He pulled up his shorts, and got satisfaction when she looked disappointed.

"They'll get what they were promised."

He leaned down, capturing her mouth. He kissed her gently at first, then parted her lips with his tongue. She opened further, and he took the invitation. He slid his tongue over hers, then around the roof of her mouth, and her tongue again. He nipped her, he sucked her as if she were a lollipop and he was looking for the chewy center. His hands lowered the straps of that bikini. His bikini. He pulled it down until her breasts were exposed.

Then he raised the straps and covered her again. "Suzanne, I don't want to share the bikini with anyone. It means a lot to me."

"It means a lot to me, too."

He nodded. He realized that if she really thought she was dying, and the bikini gave her courage, she should wear it. He was being selfish. "Maybe, if you wore a terrycloth robe over it, it would be okay."

She turned her back on him. "Unsnap it, please."

He did as she asked. She put the top on the bed, peeled her bottoms off, and placed it next to the top. She went to her closet and put on her terry cloth robe, just like he'd asked her to do.

"I won't put on the bikini tonight." She picked up the two pieces and handed them to him. "Do you have a pocket?"

He twisted around, and pointed to his backside.

"Keep the bathing suit and savor the memories. That night meant a lot to me."

"There're going to be more nights."

"Please, take it with you. I want you to have it."

He brought the bathing suit up to his face. "It has your scent."

"I have to change," she said gently, touching him one last time. "I think it would be a good idea if I were alone right now."

He took the bikini and crumpled it back in her hand. "It isn't just your scent in this suit. There's mine, too. Us together. Take it with you. Bury it with you. Keep the memory."

Suzanne would keep the memory, all right. She'd carry it with her, close to her heart, all the way to heaven. When he left the room there was anger all bottled up inside him. She could tell, and she hurt for him. She wasn't angry. She was sad because of all the wasted opportunities.

But, he'd have his memories, too.

9

GRIFF ROAMED aimlessly through the rooms in Suzie's house. Each was filled to capacity. The Houston Symphony had switched from romance songs to Broadway show tunes. Someone in the house had requested *Steam Heat* and he could swear this was at least the third time they'd played it.

The Duvalls were lined up like penguins against the west wall. Even though the sun had set hours before, that was still the one side of the house that rarely cooled down. In fact, those Duvalls couldn't have picked a more appropriate place to roost—or roast. The hot wall of hell.

Nina and Christine had taken charge of the buffet. They'd moved the dining room table against one wall and had brought in two temporary tables to line the other two walls. There was enough food to feed the population of Sugar Land, and that's basically who they had roaming around the house. He had never seen so many people packing away so much food.

Griff was one of the few doctors he knew who got involved with his patients. Consequently, most thought of him as a friend and invited him to their weddings, births and loved ones' funerals. He'd been to a few Irish wakes, too, but never had he seen anything like this. The people in Suzanne's house were having a celebration unlike any he had ever witnessed before and doubted he'd witness again.

Suzanne finally came out of the bedroom, and this time she was dressed in something more appropriate. A white nightgown. Not flannel, either, but at least she was covered up. Not that that made any difference to his mate down there. Suzanne made his temperature and everything else rise. Interesting, since he had a feeling all along it wasn't just the bikini that caused his constant state of arousal. Suzanne had done this number on him, and he didn't see a cooling off period anytime soon. She looped her arm through his and asked, "Did you get something to eat?"

"I'm not hungry," he said. "There doesn't seem to be anyone mourning. Are you sure they know this is a wake?"

"Oh, yes, everyone knows. We're getting ready to start right now. Let's go into the other room, shall we?" She turned to the crowd. "Let's go everyone. Time to say...goodbye."

She looked up at him with the saddest, most woebegone pair of eyes he'd ever seen. "I love you, Griff," she whispered with a catch in her voice. "I always have. From the first time I saw you, the day you moved in."

"You never told me. Never even gave me a hint that you felt that way." He brushed back wisps of hair from her forehead then leaned down and kissed where his hands had just been.

She had given him plenty of hints about how she felt. Maybe she hadn't hired a biplane to fly in the sky with a sign proclaiming Suzanne Loves Griff. Other than that, though, she had been almost blatant about her devotion and lust. He hadn't gotten it. "I guess I'm shy," she said demurely, lowering her lashes, looking at the floor lest he see how she really felt— that he had to be totally dense.

He cupped her face in his hands, and waited until she looked at him, then lowered his mouth and captured hers. He kissed her, long, deep. When someone in the crowd did a "Wooo-wooo, Go-Go-Go" he broke away. "I've always loved you, Suzie Q. You know that, don't you?"

"You love my bikini."

"That's not true."

Liar.

Griff said, "How about I come over, and you greet me at the door, wearing nothing. Just you in your birthday suit. I'll prove to you that you turn me on when you're naked, too." He wiggled his eyebrows at her. "You know that I've seen thousands of naked people, so being naked is not a big deal to me at all. But *you* naked—" he leaned down and nuzzled her earlobe "—now that's a whole other dimension, something they didn't cover in med school."

She didn't find him amusing. "I won't be here tomorrow."

"Yes, you will," he said with certainty.

"I'm feeling weak already."

"You've been living this fantasy for so long, you're believing it yourself. The power of suggestion."

"My heart is beating slower."

"I know how to make it beat faster." He stood tall and took a step backward. She didn't even rise to the bait, only stared at him as if he were the saddest, or maybe the most dense, man on earth. He snapped at her, "You're not dying."

She came forward, touching his hand. "I don't want to go. This is something I have no control over. But you should be happy. You won't have to worry that I'm going to make demands on you, that I'm going to want something from you that you aren't ready to give.''

''I wasn't worried.''

''Because you know I'm not going to be here to-morrow. So whatever we have now, whatever magic happened to us that night in Las Vegas, is something you can carry with you always, just like I'm going to do.''

''You don't know what you're talking about,'' he said angrily.

Hermia came over to Suzanne with a glass of champagne in each hand. She handed her daughter one and tried to give the other to Griff. ''Not for me,'' he said, turning away, heading to the opposite side of the room.

''That man is so forceful,'' Hermia said, her voice all swoony. ''Like a lion ready to pounce. Too bad you two didn't have time to really get to know each other. I bet he would have been lovely.''

''Our relationship was fine the way it was.''

''Suzanne, darlin', you were always satisfied with so little.''

Her mother was wrong. Dead wrong.

Hermia called out, ''Toast, everyone.''

Griff watched Suzanne's mother gather the crowd of pseudo-mourners around her. He couldn't think of them as being anything but fake. Despite what she believed, he knew she wasn't going anywhere. This whole thing was ridiculous.

Yet one after the other they toasted Suzanne. And Suzie, who didn't normally drink, was packing away the champagne like it was apple juice.

The orchestra played ''Ol' Lang Syne,'' ''Till We Meet Again,'' ''I'll See You In My Dreams'' and a bunch of other sappy tunes.

After every toast the crowd shouted "Hoorah" as if this was some kind of Texas football event.

Griff retrieved a glass of ginger ale, chewed up two maraschino cherries, and put the stems on the plate of brownies. He found an empty place to roost against the wall opposite the crypt bed they had set up for Suzanne. He leaned back, holding the wall up. Suzanne's dad, carrying a glass of wine, walked over and took a place next to Griff, sharing the weight of the wall. "To you, Mr. Mercer, on hosting a great party." He held up his glass of ginger ale.

"This is one of the saddest occasions of my life, Dr. Scott. I miss my little girl already." Suzanne's father sobbed, then drowned his tears in half a glass of wine.

Griff's jaw nearly dropped to the floor as he stared at the banker. "You can't believe what's going on here."

"I believe it all right." He took a final swig of wine then set the empty glass in the middle of the brownie plate, next to the cherry stems. "Good night, son. I would have been happy to have had you in the family, had circumstances been different."

Griff watched Mr. Mercer weave his way across the room and finally take his place next to his wife and daughter, leaving Griff to support the weight of the wall all by himself.

There were more toasts made to Suzanne, and she apparently felt the need to partake in the festivities along with her guests, taking a sip after each one.

Griff felt it was incumbent upon himself to shout out to anyone and everyone who would listen, "It ain't gonna happen, folks. You can all go home." Nobody paid attention to him except the three people standing in front of him, who were unlucky enough to be getting Griff's predictions right in their ears. They booed him.

At exactly 11:45 p.m. his little Suzie, the conservative, no-nonsense, dependable woman he'd known for five years, staggered to her final resting place, the draped bed, table, platform, or whatever they were calling it.

By now, after all that toasting, the crowd had gone from laughing it up to drunken tears. Some women, and a few men, were wailing so loudly they drowned out the orchestra, who only played louder as a result. Griff's wall vibrated with the sound.

He was surprised the police hadn't been called in by the neighbors for disturbing the peace. Except he'd spotted all his neighbors in Suzie's house, along with the two neighborhood patrol officers.

Suzanne, standing next to her final resting place, motioned everyone to silence. "I don't know why I have been chosen to leave my friends and loved ones and lover-for-one-night—" she gave Griff a weak smile, wiggling her fingers at him "—at this time." She took a swallow of champagne, and hiccupped. "I'm too young. Have too much to do." She gazed at Griff, tears filling her eyes. She raised her glass to him. He waved an empty hand right back at her. She hiccupped again. "Found my true love." She grinned at the audience. "Am I blushing?" Hiccup. "How utterly un-accountant like." She turned to Hermia. "Mamma, I don't feel so good."

Griff shook his head at the antics going on.

Hermia and Grandma Hermia ran up to Suzanne, cooing, "We know, darlin'. We're here with you, sweetie pie."

Suzanne needed a lot of help getting on the table-bed. Her foot kept slipping off the platform, and her nightgown kept getting tangled between her legs.

"She's not going to die," Griff called out.

"Shut your trap," the lady standing in front of him ordered. "You don't know nothin'."

"I'm a doctor." He knew a lot.

"I'm president of the United States."

"What a liar," Griff said in disgust. He was serious here, and these people were acting like the whole thing was really going to happen.

The lady standing to the side of him got close to his face and hissed, "Shush." No one had "shushed" him since Miss Olson in third grade, and he hadn't deserved it then, either.

Those Duvall gangsters were moving closer toward Suzanne, probably to get a better look at their pigeon.

"I guess this is goodbye," she said forlornly, then hiccupped again. "I'll miss you all. But I'll see you before too long. In a better place."

People called out their final goodbyes right back to her. Only this time, instead of loud and boisterous, these farewells were quiet and sad.

She glanced around the room until her gaze found his. He stared right back, defiant, angry. He thought this whole thing a farce and she knew he did. He couldn't believe Suzanne and everyone in this place actually believed what was going on here. But they did and he knew they did. From the Duvalls sipping their own stash of booze from a flask they had brought with them, to the Merriweather gang of accountants, including old man Merriweather, they were all here paying their last respects to Suzanne.

The guest of honor was drinking that champagne, hiccupping, crying and accepting the condolences as if they were her due.

She comforted those around her, telling people it was all right. That she was going to a better place. That she'd meet them in heaven someday. She shook her head as if all was lost.

As the minutes ticked down, the house of noisy, partying people grew more silent, glum.

Hermia and Michael did their best to help their daughter get comfortable on the blue satin-covered table-bed. They fluffed up her pillow. Hermia tried to straighten the nightgown that kept riding up Suzanne's legs, which she couldn't seem to keep together, showing everyone how long and shapely they were. And giving them a pretty good indication of what else was under there.

Griff, being the gentlemen he was, never mind jealous and territorial, made a quick run to her bedroom, and took the quilt off her bed. He brought it in the going-away room and covered Suzanne up, placing the quilt right under her chin, wrapping it around her feet, and letting the sides dangle to the floor. Now, that was better. He headed back to his wall, was just ready to hold it back up again, when she kicked off the covers. "Hot," she moaned. "So hot."

Griff was going to head back to her, and wrap her up again, when someone absconded with the quilt.

Nina handed Suzanne one lone lily, which she held clasped between her hands. "It's a hothouse lily, Suzanne."

The lights in the house were being dimmed, the living room lights turned off, and candles lit. The room, now awash in gentle candlelight, brought an uneasy silence to the crowd. Two candles placed on a raised platform near Suzanne's head, flickered with each of her breaths. The light cast an eerie glimmer across Suzanne's stilling body.

The only sound now heard in the house was the grandfather clock ticking down the minutes.

The guests began to chant. "Five. Four. Three. Two. One."

The clock struck twelve.

Griff wanted to call out, "Hickory, dickory dock." Only he didn't, because people were crying, and someone wailed, "She's dead, she's dead."

Griff picked out the whispers. "It must have been a heart attack." "No, a fatal stroke." "Consumption." "Gas. She probably exploded."

They were all whispering, but no one was going near her. Even from where he stood, at least fifteen feet away, he could see she wasn't moving. Even her lily wasn't. And the candles near her mouth weren't moving, either.

That was ridiculous. She had to be breathing. She must have put herself in some kind of trance. He elbowed his way through the crowd to Suzanne. He'd take care of this charade and he'd do it right now.

He grabbed Suzanne's wrist, feeling for a pulse, not finding one.

Mr. Mercer tried to hand Griff a piece of paper. "Here's the death certificate," he said. "Since you're the doctor, please take care of this for us."

"You hold it for now," Griff said. He leaned his ear over her mouth, and didn't hear or feel breaths. Her chest wasn't expanding and contracting. "I love you," Griff said, speaking so softly only she could hear. If she could still hear. "I can't tell you that enough."

He pinched her nostrils, tilted her head back, lifted her jaw, then covered her mouth with his own. He gave her two, slow, full breaths, paused, then repeated it again.

He felt for her pulse, and once again, couldn't find it. Her chest still wasn't rising or falling. He yelled at her father, "Call 911."

"There's no reason to, son, if she's gone," Mr. Mercer sobbed, tears rolling down his face. "My daughter."

Griff placed the heel of his interlocked fingers and hands over her breast bone, near the bottom of her rib cage. He looked at Suzanne's father and threatened, "If you don't call 911 right now, I'll have you arrested."

"All right, all right." Mr. Mercer headed toward the kitchen, and the closest phone. "Waste of the good EMT's time. I know my little girl's gone."

Griff locked his elbows, and firmly pressed down into Suzanne's chest. He repeated the compressions only twice when Suzanne popped straight from the table and folded over on top of him. "Ouch," she moaned, drawing in oxygen. "Are you trying to kill me? You sucked the air right out of me. I can hardly breathe." Instead of sounding grateful that he'd saved her life, she was downright rude.

"What time is it?" someone called out.

"What day is it?" someone else asked.

"It's the 31st," Ambrose Duvall growled. "And she's not dead."

"No kidding." Griff hoped he sounded agreeable. "I'm relieved the day is here. I want to put this all behind us."

"She's owes us money," Ambrose said. He looked at Suzanne and slapped the rolled up insurance policy in his hand.

"I'm so sleepy," Suzanne said and hiccupped. She closed her eyes and lay down on her side, curled up.

Griff gazed down into the now quietly snoring,

peaceful face of Suzanne. He couldn't wait for her to wake up so he could take her back to bed again.

He faced the crowd and delivered his final diagnosis. "I'm happy to say Suzanne's alive, and very intoxicated."

The symphony struck up a raucous version of "One Hundred Bottles of Beer on the Wall," and all of Suzanne's guests sang. The guest of honor, though, slept through the whole morning-after wake.

Griff left her house and was almost home, when he was called back by one of the Duvall brothers. When he turned around, he found all three of them there, surrounding him. Ambrose held up the rolled up insurance policy. "Give Suzanne a message from us."

"What if I won't?"

"You will."

They were right. Griff would, and they knew it.

"Tell her that we renewed this insurance policy for another thirty days. That means she has thirty days to pay us back five hundred thousand."

"She only borrowed two-fifty."

He slapped the paper in the palm of his hand. "But the policy is for five hundred, and she was supposed to be dead, and we were supposed to collect the whole five hundred."

"I thought you liked her. Why would you want to hurt her?"

"We do like her, don't we, boys?" Ambrose turned to his brothers who all nodded in agreement. "But this is business. We want the money by the end of the month, or Miss Mercer will be dead."

10

GRIFF SHOVED aside the almost empty pizza box and watched through half-closed eyes as Suzanne gnawed on a piece of crust. He didn't want her to know he was paying that much attention to her. But he was. From the first time he kissed her, not as a friend, but as the desirable woman wearing that bikini, he had been hypnotized.

Never in his wildest imagination would he have thought any woman could have that kind of power over him. He sure couldn't have imagined the woman would be good ol' Suzie Q. Only now that he had found his true love, the woman he wanted to be with forever, she wasn't cooperating. She'd gotten it into that stubborn head of hers that *he* didn't want commitment. Where she ever got an idea like that, he couldn't even venture a guess. All right, he could guess. But in all the times he talked the talk, he'd never had her in mind. She was different from all the others.

So he pretended not to look at her, not to pay attention to her, when all the while he watched her every move. He committed to memory how her small, white teeth nibbled on the crust. How, when she moved, her breasts swayed under her shirt. How every once in a while he'd get a peek at her cleavage. He would never forget how her breasts felt so full and heavy in his hands. How they felt when he was on top of her, or she was on top of him, and they grazed his chest, the skin flushed with passion, her nipples pink and engorged.

He did that to her. He could still remember how they tasted. Sweet. How she moaned in ecstasy, and how he had encouraged her, reveling in the pleasure they brought to each other.

As she took another bite, tiny crumbs clung to her chin. He reached out and brushed them off her skin, and when she flicked her tongue to lick crumbs off his finger, he immediately went from semi to fully ready to make love to her again. The image of her licking other parts of him didn't help, either. Her tongue on his neck and inner thigh. "If you're still hungry and tired of pizza, I can think of a few other things you can eat," he said innocently, already getting hot, just thinking about what they could do under the sheets.

"It's okay. The pizza's good."

"Hmm," he answered noncommittally, shifting in the chair, glancing at her with a lazy smile. "I wasn't necessarily talking about food." He pretended to close his eyes again.

"I know what you're talking about," she said. "Only I'm ignoring your innuendoes and your tight crotch. Because I'm not even going to think about unzipping your zipper and letting your thingie come out for air."

He groaned, frustration running rampant through him.

"Griff, it can't happen anymore. I told you in March I only wanted you to make love to me once and I went back on my promise. We did it at least three times."

"We did it five, but I'm not counting."

"And they were five great times," she said, putting

the crust down and looking at him in earnest. "I'll treasure them always."

"That's why you remembered the exact number."

"Sorry." She gave him that innocent little smile.

"You're a number person, someone who never forgets anything that has a numeral in it. Yep, I can tell our time together meant so much to you." He would have been insulted, but he knew Suzanne well enough to know she was hiding, that she remembered everything, down to the exact detail.

Ever since he kissed her, really kissed her, she had gotten into his blood, and it would take a lifetime—a lifetime he planned on spending with her—before it would dissipate.

"Forget sex for a moment."

"I'm not the one who brought it up." She reached for her crust again, but he took it out of her hand and put it back on the table.

"I want to talk to you about where you plan to get the money you owe the Duvalls."

"You already know that. We're going to Vegas to win it back from the Red Rock."

He let out an exasperated breath. "Look at me, Suzie. Concentrate. Where are you getting the money to take to Vegas?"

"I'm raising it."

"How?"

"I'm going to cash in stocks and liquidate my assets. A lot of what I have is real estate, and it needs to be sold. I've already talked to my stockbroker, and my father, and I should have the funds available in about ten days."

"No, you'll have it tomorrow."

She gave him a sad smile. "Now it's your turn to

concentrate. It takes longer than a few days to turn these things to cash. You know that."

"Suzie." He took both her hands in his. They were so soft and so little. "I've been single a long time. Okay, my whole life. Thirty-three years. I've worked hard at a job I love. I'm not a big spender. No fancy cars or fancy houses. I have nothing but money, and it's easy to get to. Hell, half of it's under my mattress." He wiggled his eyebrows. "Wanna go count my loot?"

"Griff. I do your taxes. How come I didn't..."

The look of horror on her face was beautiful. In all the years he'd known Suzanne, she'd always been so practical, rarely sharing extreme emotions. Now he'd finally, finally managed to shock her. He loved it.

"I'll never miss the money, Suzie Q. It's yours. I'm going to pay back the Duvalls. Get rid of them. The legal way. Period."

"You can't do that. I have to earn the money."

"Then, I'm going to front you. I'll pay for this betting binge. Either take the money to Vegas and gamble it, or I'm going to give it to the Duvalls myself. One way or another, that money's going to get you out of this mess."

Suzanne didn't speak for five minutes. That's a long time to listen to the hum of central air-conditioning and dogs barking at the moon. Finally she asked, "You would do that for me?"

"I love you. I'd do anything for you."

"I wouldn't let you give it to them though. I would have to borrow it, go to Vegas, win it back for the Duvalls and give you back your stake."

"If that's what you want to do."

"Under those circumstances, then it would be all right."

He stood and went around the table. With his hand held out toward her, he waited, and wasn't disappointed. She had accepted his conditions. She stood in front of him, wrapping her arms around his waist, her head resting on his chest. He waited a moment then took her face in his hands and centered his mouth over hers, kissing her. He heard her breathing come in short gasps, and his own was labored. He knew, as a doctor, that both of them were going to have to finish what they started, or they would die of frustration. "Suzie?" he asked.

When she nodded, he took her hand and led her down the hallway toward his bedroom.

"Griff," she said softly several hours later. "It was eight times before. Not five."

No matter how much she proclaimed she wasn't going to commit to him, as far as he was concerned, they were going to be together from now until forever.

Unless the Duvall brothers did what they had threatened to do if they didn't get their money. Kill her.

SUZANNE THOUGHT that Griff inviting her to meet Matt Ferguson was one of the sweetest, most wonderful, kindest gestures he'd ever made. With his clothes on, that is.

When he insisted that her Grandma Hermia join them, he went from being "hero" to "object of worship."

Griff had told her that Matt Ferguson had played professional poker in his younger years, and that he had offered to help her learn to count cards, to give her better skills to help win the game. For this trip to Las Vegas she was taking all the help she could get.

She didn't know how much help he would be, though. She didn't think anyone could possibly teach her what she hadn't already learned in the three books she'd read and committed to memory. Not that she was able to put any of those rules to good use.

Suzanne also knew that Griff was keeping a watchful eye on the elderly man. Although Griff would never admit it, she had a feeling that spending an afternoon at Mr. Ferguson's house was more to make his new friend feel needed. The fact that she needed to practice counting poker hands gave Griff the perfect excuse for a visit.

"Oh, my-oh-my," Grandma Hermia clucked when they drove down a long, winding driveway, finally stopping in front of a three-story Tudor mansion. "The way you were describing him, you made him sound desolate."

"Money doesn't buy you companionship, or keep away the loneliness," Griff said, looking at Suzanne.

She couldn't let him get away with that, giving her grandmother the impression that Griff was lonely and she was the cause. "I know what you're saying, and I'm telling you that you're the one I'm protecting. You'll never forgive me if I let you catch me. Or me catch you."

"I want you to catch me." He took her arm and pulled her over the bucket seat, as close to him as he could.

"You're only saying that because I'm not chasing you. If I change my mind and tell you 'yes,' you'll be on the first rocket ship to Mars." She looked up at his beautiful eyes. Those eyes that gazed back at her with love and yearning.

"You don't know that, do you? You're a coward." His mouth lowered, lightly grazing her lips.

She wanted to give in to him. She wanted to tell him she would marry him and live with him forever and ever. That she loved him more than life itself. It was all true. Only there had been too many midnight conversations with him, during which he had made it plain that he didn't ever want to marry or be stuck with one woman. Why, just a month ago, when she first asked him to make love to her, he had told her he wasn't the marrying kind.''

Still, she sighed as he captured her lips fully, nudging her mouth open with his tongue, gaining entry and deepening the kiss. He moved his hand from her arm, slipping it around her waist, pulling her even closer to him. She opened her mouth wider, giving his tongue more access, enjoying the way he was desperate to do it.

It wasn't until she heard her grandmother clearing her throat that she remembered they weren't alone. Her face heated, and she smiled sheepishly at the woman sitting in the back seat, gave a little shrug, and said, ''He just sends me, Grandma.''

Griff turned to her grandmother, too, only he wasn't smiling. ''Your granddaughter needs a talking to. When a man loves her and wants her forever, she'd better say yes. She may never get a better offer than me.''

''She's a Bourne. Bourne women don't marry. Her mother was always different, from the time she was little. So you can't go by her.'' Grandma Hermia cackled, lifted her handbag and whacked Griff across the shoulder. ''You're such a cutie pie. If only I were twenty years younger.''

''Try fifty years, Grandma,'' Suzie said.

''You shush your mouth, young'un. For a man, having a woman like me can only be compared to getting a Renoir painting. We Bournes become more valuable and beautiful with age.'' She puffed up her well-hairsprayed hairdo.

Griff got out of the car and opened the back door for Suzanne's grandmother. He offered the older woman his arm, which she accepted without a backward glance at her granddaughter. She leaned heavily on Griff, flirting outrageously, as if to show the younger generation how it was properly done.

Then Matt Ferguson opened the door to his home, and Hermia went from clinging vine to Venus flytrap. She straightened herself and marched up to the white-haired gentleman, giving him her hand. Matt took what was offered, bringing Hermia's hand to his lips for a proper gentlemanly kiss. ''Welcome to my home, Mrs. Bourne,'' Matt said.

''It's Miss Bourne.'' She batted eyelashes that looked longer behind the large glasses she wore. ''But you can call me Hermia.''

He took her grandmother's arm and escorted her into his home. Without turning around or looking at either Griff or Suzanne, he raised his other arm and waved for them to follow.

The Duvall's white Lincoln limo pulled up seconds after Mr. Ferguson had gone inside. Suzanne didn't mind—at least too much—that the Duvall brothers were taking turns watching her. Twenty-four hours a day, seven days a week, one of them sat in that big limo outside her house. A white limo by day, a black one by night. When she had started back at work, they were outside her office building. They were outside the beauty shop, outside the dry cleaners. If it weren't so morbid, the reason behind the watchful eyes, she would almost feel protected. As it was, she was nothing more than a pigeon being used for target practice. That is, if she didn't deliver.

She went over to their car. The back window lowered, and Wyatt stuck his head out, saying almost apologetically, "You know how it is, Suzanne, there's five hundred thousand dollars at stake here."

"I know." She nodded in agreement. "I thought you had a date tonight."

"It's my turn on watch," he said matter-of-factly, but looked so crestfallen.

"I'm sorry I messed up your plans."

"Business is business."

And lest she ever forget that, those Duvalls were right there, on the street, to remind her.

"Why are you so nice to those hoods?" Griff asked as they walked toward the house, sounding thoroughly irritated.

"So they'll kill me painlessly?"

"Be serious."

"All right. They're nice men. Just going down the wrong path. It could happen to anyone."

"They're not nice."

"They loaned me money when I needed it."

"And they want it back within thirty days, with one hundred percent interest, or they'll kill you."

"Which brings us back to why I'm nice. Painless, Griff. You doctors are trained to slice, dice, shoot those tetanus shots, and do it all with a little, 'this won't hurt a bit,' or maybe, 'you might feel a slight pinch,' as you're tearing guts out of these poor unanesthetized patients."

"I've never hurt anyone," he said, with assurance.

She stood on her toes and gave him a quick kiss on the cheek. "Trust me on this. You're a doctor. Your doctor's bill of rights allow you to do two things. Heal and torture."

He squeezed Suzanne in his arms. "You have so much to learn, my little Suzie Q. I'm a great teacher."

"I know you are."

"And so's Matt. You're going to win in Vegas. Or you can give them the money right now. I'd rather you just give it to them."

She shook her head. She hoped Matt Ferguson could help her, but she had a feeling that this was something she'd have to do on her own. She'd practice more, like she had with Griff over the past couple of weeks. Everything would be fine.

If not, well, just living past March 30th had been a gift she hadn't expected. If the Duvalls somehow caused her to have a tragic accident—no, she wasn't going to think that way. She would be positive. Matt Ferguson *would* help her succeed. Griff had told her so, and Griff never lied to her. Except for that commitment thing, but he was lying to himself first, so she could forgive him that.

"Call me Matt, young lady. None of this Mister crap. After all, we're colleagues in the pursuit of winning. Right?"

"Right," Suzanne agreed. "But it's been a long time since you've played, hasn't it?" He must be somewhere between eighty and one hundred and twenty.

He said very seriously, "The rules don't change. I can teach you what I know, and you'll prevail. That's the way it is."

"There are cameras all over the casino. Was the security as tight as it is now when you were last there?"

"It was a little different, but security and cameras shouldn't matter. You're not cheating. You're going to play an honest game by their rules and you're going to win.''

Her elbows rested on the game table, her face in her hands. She gazed at Matt, wanting to believe him. For the first time since she woke up on March 31st and saw Ambrose Duvall slapping the rolled-up life insurance policy in the palm of his hand, she had hope.

Matt dealt the cards, and they played a few hands, all of which Suzanne, using the rules that she had memorized in the books she'd read, lost. ''This isn't good,'' she mumbled.

Nor was it good that her calves and shins were getting battered under the table by her grandmother and Matt, who were trying to play footsie with each other, only they were missing their marks.

By the time she lost the fifth game, her nerves were strung so tight she was about to break in half.

''Mr. Ferguson,'' she said politely, ''do you have any chocolate?''

Grandma Hermia slapped her hand. ''Bad girl. Stop thinking of food and concentrate on this game. You're doing crummy.''

''I need some endorphins, Grandma. Really, really badly.'' The past few days had been harder to bear than she had ever imagined. Of course, she realized that part of the problem was that she hadn't been prepared to have these days. She'd thought she'd be dead. So, of course, her day planner was blank. That alone was unnerving.

''What you need,'' Matt said, ''is to concentrate on what I'm telling you.''

''Ouch.'' Griff reached under the table and rubbed his calf. A few of the towers of chips fell.

''Oopsy! Sorry,'' Grandma Hermia said with a shrug of her shoulders.

"I *am* concentrating," she said, extremely glad it was Griff who got the footsie whack from Grandma Hermia this time and not her. "I promise."

Matt nodded, then picked up the deck of cards and placed them faceup. He fanned them out in a straight line. With one finger he flipped the last card. Suzanne watched as the whole deck, in a domino effect, went from faceup to facedown. Without skipping a beat, and ignoring the cooing admiration from her grandmother, Matt asked, "How's your memory, young lady?"

"I do have a photographic memory, if that's what you mean. But only for numbers. I'm terrible with names, and awful with details like who the eighteenth president of the United States was."

"All right. Sit right there. I'll be back."

After fifteen minutes, Grandmother Hermia went to look for him, and when they reappeared in the game room, her grandmother's lipstick was smeared all over Matt's lips, and they both had sappy smiles on their faces. *Why Grandma,* Suzanne thought, *good for you.*

Matt carried a stained cardboard box to the table, placing it in the middle. With great care he untied the twine holding the cover flaps down, and opened one flap at a time.

Together, they peered inside. "There's nothing but scraps of paper in there," Grandmother Hermia said. "I was hoping for, I don't know, silver, gold, some kind of treasure. Diamonds would be good."

"This is a treasure, my precious," Matt said.

Suzanne took a few of the papers from the box and immediately recognized them for what they were. "Oh, Grandma, if these are what I think they are, this is a treasure that is priceless. For someone like me, it can be worth five hundred thousand dollars in blackjack winnings. Right, Matt?"

''Absolutely, young lady. I knew when Doc here brought you over, you had to have something going for you. Certainly couldn't have been the way you were playing twenty-one before.''

She studied one of the papers she held. It was dog-eared and yellow, but to her, it was like the finest vellum. The faded pencil numbers were more beautiful than the most intricate calligraphy. Matt sat back in his chair, arms folded across his chest, and watched her.

Suzanne recognized some of the patterns of numbers written on the paper from one of the books she'd read on how to count cards. Only, the way Matt had it written down, it made more sense to her. She held up the paper with the heading that read, My Basic Strategy.

''You see,'' she explained to Griff, ''he's written down here all the hands to bet on, and the hands to fold on. He has a column here for what to do if he gets a combination of these cards, and what to do if the dealer gets a combination of those cards.'' Suzanne pulled another scrap of paper from the box. She studied it for a moment, committing the combinations to her memory, then she showed Griff. ''When these combinations of cards are dealt, you fold. The other paper had higher percentages, but this one says under no circumstances are you to bet on these cards. Is that right, Matt?''

''That's it, Miss Suzanne. The box is full of years and years of my observations. I haven't played in thirty years, so the information is only as scientific as I could get through my own observations. No computer for this man.''

She took another scrap of paper. This piece only had a few lines. Written in pencil at the top were the words, When to Hit and When to Stand. Suzanne read the paper, closed her eyes, and repeated to herself what she'd just learned. She looked at Mr. Ferguson again. "This is a wonderful treasure."

"Take the box home and study the papers. Memorize the combinations. When you do, come back and we'll play some real poker." He took the paper out of her hand and placed it back in the box, then carefully retied the twine.

"Thank you, Matt." Suzanne clutched the box to her chest. "You've saved my life."

"Now, don't get all dramatic on me. Come on back in a few days, once you have it memorized. We'll see how much you've learned. Once you've learned your stuff, you'll be ready to go back to Vegas."

Matt walked them outside to Griff's car. Suzanne waved to Wyatt still sitting in the limo. He rolled down the window and waved back.

Griff's shoulders tensed and his hands formed into fists. "I hate that guy. He wants to hurt you."

"Don't be silly."

He took her by the shoulders. "You don't know how much trouble you're in."

"The problem, Griff," she said quietly, "is that I know exactly how much trouble I'm in. It's a frightening thought."

"You will let me help you."

"There's nothing you or anyone else can do. I have to do it on my own."

"Okay, you two lovebirds," Matt said, his dentures clicking. "There'll be plenty of time for that serious stuff. Now don't you even think about coming back here without your grandma. You hear me?"

Suzanne glanced at her grandmother's happy face. "I hear you."

11

THE RED ROCK Casino and Hotel lobby looked almost
exactly the same as it had when she and Griff left it
almost a month before. She did notice a few differ-
ences though. "It looks like they recovered the fur-
niture," she said to Griff. "I thought it was red before."

"Considering they're two hundred and fifty grand
richer now than they were when we first came, I would
think they could afford to cover the couches. And get
new carpet if they wanted."

"Please don't rub it in." She never should have
brought it up. She hated to remember her failures.

"It won't happen again."

"It can't."

"Yoo-hoo, kiddos, we're here." Grandma Hermia,
despite clinging to Matt Ferguson's arm, teetered on
six-inch open-back sandals.

"Look at your grandmother," Griff whispered.
"She's going to kill herself in those shoes, and if she's
not careful, she'll bring Matt down with her."

"Don't be silly. She wears a red pair just like those
for gardening."

"I don't believe you." Griff put his arm around her
waist and moved her closer to his side.

Suzanne felt protected near him, and she needed to
feel that way now more than ever. He lowered his
mouth to her ear and his breath tickled her. Then he

asked in a soft whisper, "Hey, Suzie Q, do you feel like you're some big-shot celeb with an entourage following you?" He gave her waist a gentle squeeze. His touch sent little tiny shivers radiating from the point of impact outward.

Over the past four weeks, whenever Griff had touched her, whenever she was near him, she had felt a sense of serenity, a peacefulness inside her that she hadn't known she was able to feel. Her whole life before the month of March had been one of getting to the top, climbing the career track, making partner, never stopping, always working. The only times she'd ever relaxed were with Griff, and those games of rummy had never been enough. She'd only accepted what she had thought she couldn't change. Now she wanted more. She didn't want to spend her life clawing her way to the top of Merriweather, Watkins and Jones.

What she wanted was to spend her life slipping and sliding over, next to, and underneath Griff. There were jobs everywhere for accountants like her. But there was only one man for her. She'd be stupid to keep denying what she wanted. What he wanted. She would be stupid to toss away a future of love and commitment. Yes, commitment. Because she knew they were committed to each other.

He'd told her a long time ago that he never wanted to fall in love. He'd told her that love hurts. But Griff had changed. She'd seen it happen. He cared about her. He'd called in more favors at the hospital so he could take the time to be here for her. He'd emptied his mattress for her.

He had told her on the airplane as they flew over the Grand Canyon that if the Duvalls came after her with a gun, he would jump in front of her and take the bullet himself. Suzanne believed him. Griff put all his patients before himself. He had more compassion in his little finger than ten people had in their entire collective bodies.

Suzanne didn't understand why it took coming to Las Vegas for the second time to make her understand all this. Maybe it was watching her grandmother flirt so outrageously with Matt. They were too cute together, the tall, tall man, and the short, short woman, who even with those high heels was still, well, short.

Maybe it was knowing that within the next twenty-four hours she wasn't going to break the Red Rock bank, but if she didn't win back the Duvalls' money, plus interest, the man she loved would be out his whole life savings.

Of course, she'd be out her life. But that wasn't important now.

Just as the money wasn't important to Griff. If it had been, he would have used it for the worthless, showy things that other people craved—boats, country club memberships, big houses and diversified investments. Instead he tossed it aside as if it had no use other than to buy food, clothing and shelter. She admired that about him.

Yet, no matter how much the money didn't mean to Griff on the outside, she knew on the inside it meant a lot. She knew he had come from a family that didn't have a lot of extras. He had bought his mom her house, and he had paid for his brother and sister to go to the finest universities.

Okay. So now that she had convinced herself that she wanted him forever, she only had to tell her parents and grandmother. They'd be thrilled.

Her mom and dad arrived in the next cab. Hermia

looked around the lobby and said to her husband, "It's been modernized since we were here last."

"That was thirty-one years ago, Hermie," Michael said, glancing lovingly at his wife.

Her mother blushed. Her hands slid up and down his lapel, and then she straightened his tie. "You were a wild man, darlin'."

If Suzanne's expression was anything like Griff's, then they both must have had the most shocked looks on their face. Her dad, a wild man? The banker? Not likely. Only he was eating up her mother's attentions. Who would have thought it?

The Duvall brothers, by their mere presence, invoked a myriad of feelings, most having to do with terror and fear. The powder blue limo, with the eight-foot guitar cemented on the roof and the huge "Elvis Rocks" painted on the side, took a lot of the deadly impact out of their arrival. From the way they slunk out of the limo, they must have known it, too.

"Oh, look who's here," Grandma Hermia cried out, teetering over to the brothers. "The reason we're all having this reunion. Welcome, boys." She patted three pairs of cheeks.

Ambrose, Wyatt and Mickey took off their fedoras and each took his turn bowing over Grandma's hand.

Her grandmother was in her element, and the Duvalls played right up to it. "Aren't they sweet?" Suzanne asked Griff.

He answered her just as she thought he would, with curse words that no woman should hear. And she didn't, since he mumbled them unintelligibly. Was she a lucky woman or what? Not only did Griff love her, he was able to express himself so eloquently. Someday soon, she was going to have to sit down and count her blessings.

Only now was not the time. Not with the cobra coiling in her stomach and getting ready to strike out at any moment. She pulled on Griff's shirtsleeve. "I want to get this over with. Let's go get the chips."

Griff took her arm and they walked toward the casino. "Are you sure, Suz? We can still just give them the money."

"No. If I do that, you're out a quarter of a million dollars, plus their interest. If I lose it, you're still out, and if I win, everyone will get paid."

Matt and her grandmother came up behind them. Matt pulled her shoulder and said, "You won't lose, my dear. You got trained by the best."

She smiled gratefully at her new friend.

Ambrose juggled the gun in his pocket and stared at the people around him as if daring someone to make a comment about his suit and tie.

The noise and smoke in the casino overpowered her, making the cobra in her belly do flips. She swore that once this game was over, she would never come back to this place.

Griff walked her to the cashier cage and lifted the carry-on bag filled with money. Like the last time they had come here, this cashier didn't show any emotion, either, as she filled tray after tray with colored chips and slid them through the gold bars to Suzanne.

Suzanne lifted the trays, but Griff immediately took them from her shaking hands. "We don't want to lose any."

"No." She shook her head. "Take them. I'm concentrating on what I learned. I'm trying to remember what Matt told me on the plane coming over here. I guess I drank too much coffee." They both knew that was a lie. She was scared spitless.

"You can do it, Suzie. I have all the confidence in the world in you."

"Oh, Griff. I just want it over." She also wanted to fall into his arms, which was a bad idea since he held the chips.

"Okay. How's this for a plan? Bet what you want, but when you get the perfect hand, bet it all."

"All?"

"Go for it, babe."

Matt tapped her on the shoulder. When they stopped walking, he pointed to a table. "That one."

The dealer, Peggy, welcomed all of them. Suzanne sat on the end, and Mickey took the stool next to hers. Griff squeezed his way between them and managed to somehow, accidentally, push poor Mickey, the baby of the Duvall family, from his throne.

"So sorry, Morris," Griff said.

"It's Mickey." He got himself off the carpet and shrugged away the embarrassment.

"Isn't that what I said? No. Well, hey, sorry again, dude."

Suzanne shook her head. "You're so bad," she whispered.

"No, baby doll. I'm good. In fact, I'm great." Griff gave her a kiss. "For luck," he said, then got Peggy's attention. "Can I have dollar pieces for this?" He handed her a one-hundred-dollar bill.

"Family, friends," Griff started, gathering everyone around him. He brandished a cup clinking with one hundred one-dollar coins. "Let's leave Suzanne alone and go have ourselves some fun. I'm going for that nine million megabucks slot machine. Who's going to join me?"

There were no takers. Finally Suzanne begged them to go. "You're making me nervous." When Matt started to leave, too, she grabbed his shirtsleeve and held him back. "I need you for moral support."

"What about me?" Griff asked, that wounded little boy look on his face.

"Not this time." Her mouth was dry, her lips cracking. "If I fail, I want to do it alone. If I win, I want to do it alone. This is something that I need to do myself." She had to know she could do it without anyone there. Except Matt. She needed Matt. And judging from the look of gratitude on his face, he needed to be needed.

Suzanne took all the racks of chips and put them in the center of the table.

"There's a house limit of five thousand at this table," Peggy said all snooty-like.

"Get your boss. There are always exceptions," Suzanne said, and was very grateful when Matt gave her the thumbs-up.

The dealer used an automatic shuffling machine and four decks of cards. Suzanne was the only player. Matt stood to her left. She swallowed the lump in her throat and waited for the cards to be dealt. The first hand, the very first, she was dealt a queen up and an ace down. Blackjack.

The dealer had a jack showing.

Suzanne knew she could either win or lose. If the dealer had twenty-one, too, then it would be a draw according to the house rules, and no one would win.

Did the dealer have blackjack, too?

Suzanne knew the cameras overhead were shining down on her. She knew they were focusing on her hands, her feet, everything about how she sat and what she did. With so many cameras stalking her at every turn, she almost had to sit on her hands to resist the very strong urge to pat her hair. So she sat very still and waited for the boss to come over to the table and decide how much she could bet on this hand. To decide whether she'd win or lose.

GRIFF LOST his hundred coins in a matter of five minutes. Maybe ten. He wandered around the casino, dropping quarters into any machine that looked promising, but he didn't do that hot on those, either. Finally the smoky air started to get to him, and he made his way back to the lobby.

Suzanne's dad sat on a couch reading the paper. "Can I join you?" Griff asked.

"Sure, Doctor." Mr. Mercer moved over to the left, leaving plenty of room.

Griff sank into the cushion and made himself as comfortable as he could.

"Suzanne told me you gave her the money for this, uh, adventure?"

"I had some extra lying around."

"Quite a bit of extra. You know, as a banker, I have to tell you that your money would work better for you if it wasn't stuffed under your mattress."

"But, according to an orthropedaeic specialist I know, all that green stuffing does wonders for lower lumbar support."

Michael's eyebrows came together. "Really?" He snapped the newspaper several times before resuming where he'd left off. "Never heard of that before," he mumbled several minutes later.

Griff liked Suzanne's dad. Only at this moment he realized that for all the years he had thought Suzanne to be just like her father, they had been friends. Then as soon as she turned out to be like Hermia, he had fallen in love with her.

Only she wasn't like Hermia and she wasn't like

her dad. She was Suzie. She loved him. He knew that. She cared about his well-being. He loved her and cared about her right back.

So what was the problem? He had already told her he wanted them to be together. Only like her grandmother had said, Hermia Mercer was the only one who had gotten married. Maybe he'd been wrong about Suzanne and commitment. Maybe she never planned on marrying. If that was the case, he'd change her mind. Immediately. After all, she was the only woman he had ever asked to marry him, and he didn't plan on ever asking another. She was the one.

Then, like a tuning fork humming in his brain, it dawned on him that maybe he hadn't asked her. Nah, of course he had.

Hadn't he? He couldn't remember.

He saw her coming from the casino, her timing perfect as always. He met her halfway, his arms wide open, and she walked right into them. "I did ask you to marry me, right?"

Suzanne backed away. "No, you didn't."

"Of course I did."

"I would know that."

"You never gave me an answer."

"Because you never asked the question."

"I told you commitment."

"That's not the same as marriage. Two different words."

"Well, will you?"

She didn't say anything, only looked at him with this funny look on her face.

"Suzanne, what do you say?"

"I won, Griff. I won."

His moment of speechlessness lasted only that long, one small moment, before she jumped into his arms, all soft, and warm and cuddly, and he lifted her up, twirling her around and around in a circle.

She was laughing and crying as he put her back on the ground. He kissed her lips and her neck, and anywhere else he could. "Keep my share," he said.

"Of course not."

"It's for our children's college fund."

"If we marry." She turned away from him when the Duvall brothers approached. "I've got your money."

"We knew you could do it," Ambrose said. "Put it in here." He unsnapped an empty black leather briefcase.

"Here's your two hundred and fifty thousand. That's the money you initially gave me. Now the interest you're charging me, well, we had to pay taxes on the whole five hundred thousand, so there's not as much here as you asked for."

"You had no right to pay taxes," Mickey growled. "That was our money." He reached inside his pocket.

Griff lurched forward, ready to spring, only Suzanne held him back with a light touch on his arm.

"Really?" she asked.

The three brothers grunted menacingly.

"Let me explain something. We all know that Al Capone was before your time." Suzanne spoke like a schoolteacher giving a history lesson. "But surely you remember him, or stories about him?"

All three brothers blanched.

"Wonderful! I see you do. You'll remember he murdered hundreds, maybe thousands of people, only they could never pin anything on him. Remember that? So what did he get sent to jail for?"

The three Duvalls mumbled in unison, "Tax evasion."

"You all are so smart." Suzanne counted out the Duvalls' initial contribution and placed it in their briefcase. "I had planned that one of my life insurance policies, the million-dollar one, was going to go to the New Hope Home for Abused and Abandoned Children. I donate to them all year long, but I never would have been able to give them that million-dollar gift unless it was in an insurance policy."

By the expressions on the Duvalls' faces, they saw it coming.

"It was one of my greatest disappointments that they didn't get any money at all."

Three pairs of shiny black wingtips were shuffling on the marble floor.

"I had a lot of fun winning back this money for you," she told them. "So much money."

Ambrose handed her the briefcase back. "Here."

"Oh, no, I couldn't."

"Yeah, take it. For the kids."

"You don't understand. You need to donate it so you can take the deduction off your tax returns."

"Suzanne." Ambrose's gaze shifted left and right, and he lowered his voice to a soft gravel. "We operate a cash-only business. Get my drift. Take the briefcase."

She gave him a tight hug. "Thank you. I really did enjoy myself, you know. I wanted to bet the whole amount, and the dealer had to get the pit boss, and the pit boss had to get the manager, and the manager had to get someone, and on and on, until, you know what?" The Duvalls shook their collective heads. "Mom, Grandma, listen to this."

Suzanne's mother and grandmother along with a large crowd of people circled around her. She walked the perimeter of the crowd and plucked a man from the middle, bringing him over to her family. "This is Red Jack Bourne the Fifth. Can you believe it? We're cousins."

"I can see why my great-great-grandfather fell in love with the first Hermia, Miss Bourne," Jack said to her grandmother. "Your family is lovely." His gaze turned to Suzanne.

Griff wasn't going to stand for another guy making goo-goo eyes at his woman. "You two are cousins," he said. "And this isn't the backwoods of Tennessee."

Grandma Hermia shook her finger at Griff, and said to Red Jack, "That rude man is Griff. He's our Suzanne's beau, and a doctor, to boot." Then she added, "Which explains the rudeness, don't ya know."

"We're getting married." Griff staked his claim, glared at Suzanne and dared her, without having to say a word, to deny it. When she didn't, he added, "As soon as possible. The sooner the better."

"How about right now? The Red Rock offers the finest Vegas weddings," Jack said. "You can have Elvis or Dolly Parton. We've got Julius Caesar if you're into Roman. Or maybe you'd like Fernando, he's our resident magician, and also a licensed minister."

"Why, isn't that nice of your newfound cousin?" Grandma Hermia said.

"Mom." Suzanne held her hand out as if to stop the bulldozing tactics they were using. "Griff has a family. His mom and his brother and sister should be here. Getting married now wouldn't be fair to them."

Griff, knowing the history of no marriages in this family, had a feeling that Suzanne was using a stall tactic. If she thought he would forget about this by stalling long enough, she was wrong. "Suzie Q, baby, I love you."

"Oh, isn't that sweet?" Grandma cooed. "Matt, isn't he just the most?"

"The most," Matt agreed, then went back to counting the overflow of coins in his casino cup.

"Suzanne, one of the things I love about you is that you're always thinking of others," Griff said. "We can get married here, and then as soon as we get back, have another wedding and invite my whole family and also everyone that was at the wake. The Houston Symphony can play again, we can dance, eat." He leaned over and whispered for her only to hear, "We can make love, all day and night, every day and night. I know a special bed in the hospital that you can come and use when I'm on night duty. We can make those springs jump."

Suzanne wrapped her arms around him and squeezed him tightly. "I do love you."

"I love you, too."

"All right, let's go."

Cousin Jack placed a call on his walkie-talkie to order up Elvis. The whole group then followed him to the lobby to wait for the arrival of the King. They didn't have to wait long.

Elvis, dressed in a powder blue tux, had a big brown guitar strapped to his back, and he arrived at the hotel sitting in the back seat of an old Ford convertible.

He swung his guitar over his head then stood up, gyrating his hips.

Suzanne looked at the Elvis outfit, then turned to the Duvalls, and they shrugged. Why, those thieves. They had stolen Elvis's limo.

Griff grabbed on to Suzanne's hand and held tightly. Not because he needed the moral support, but because he was afraid she was going to bolt.

They followed Elvis into the chapel. The family

lined up behind the bride and groom as Elvis began to sing "Love Me Tender," interspersed with his rhythmic "Dearly Beloved."

Griff couldn't wait to get Suzanne upstairs. For the first time in his life he felt complete. He felt whole.

He looked around him at her crazy family. Life from now on would be one hell of a roller-coaster ride, and he was taking a seat, strapping himself in and hanging on for the duration.

Epilogue

"THIS IS THE BEST possible day, Michael. Everything worked out just fine, better than we had planned." Hermia sat next to her husband in the first row, tears in her eyes as she watched Suzanne and Griff sing their vows, albeit off-key, as directed by the singing Elvis.

"Yes, it did." Michael took her hand and squeezed affectionately.

"What more could a mother ask for? Her daughter married. A doctor in the family. Medical care a phone call, a house call away. Life is good."

"You did better than you thought."

Hermia, a proud smile on her face, couldn't agree more. Nine years ago she and her astrologer, Sir James, planned for each fortune-teller to tell Suzanne the exact same fortune. *On the 30th day of the third month of your 30th year, your life, as you know it, will be over forever.* Sir James, the dear man, had forgotten to tell them the *as you know it* part, and consequently Suzanne assumed she was going to die. And her Suzanne, my-my, she did a mother proud, proving herself to be a Bourne through and through when she fell right into it.

"She never suspected a thing. And no one else did, either. At first I was going to tell her it was a fun birthday event, but you remember, Michael, she was so serious, and I knew if she didn't do something with her life she'd grow up like a dried-up old raisin. How tragic that would've been. There's just something about thinking the end is near that makes a person take charge of her life.''

"Suzanne's a lucky girl, having you as her mother.''

She stroked his cheek. "I'm a lucky woman.''

"You know, Hermia, you were lucky this time, but you're not planning on doing any of this fortune-telling mumbo jumbo stuff again in the hopes of getting grandchildren from those two, are you?''

"Oh, yes, Michael. Most definitely, yes.''

I Love Lacy

Lori Wilde

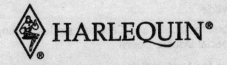

HARLEQUIN®

TORONTO • NEW YORK • LONDON
AMSTERDAM • PARIS • SYDNEY • HAMBURG
STOCKHOLM • ATHENS • TOKYO • MILAN • MADRID
PRAGUE • WARSAW • BUDAPEST • AUCKLAND

Dear Reader,

In nursing school I did my internship in the operating room. It's a heady environment, working with skilled doctors who literally hold lives in their hands. There's something irresistibly mysterious about meeting a pair of sexy eyes over the top of a surgical mask. This notion sparked the idea for a series of romantic comedies set in a hospital.

Nurse Lacy Calder, Dr. Janet Hunter and physical therapist CeeCee Adams each have contrary outlooks on life, romance and career. But they're the best of friends. They support each other through broken hearts and burned dinners, rotten boyfriends and bad hair days. Although each woman finally meets and marries the man of her dreams, none of them could have succeeded without a little help from her friends.

The fun starts with *I Love Lacy*. Shy scrub nurse Lacy Calder has waited for the *Thunderbolt* to strike—and strike it finally does in the form of sexy Bennett Sheridan. But whenever she's around an attractive man, Lacy turns into a klutz. How can she convince the man of her dreams that she's his Miss Right when he thinks she's the clumsiest woman on the face of the earth? It takes the Thunderbolt, two matchmaking grandmothers and a goat named Frank Sinatra to make Bennett realize that he loves Lacy.

Best wishes,

Lori Wilde

P.S. Look for Janet's and CeeCee's stories coming soon in a special Double Duets!

Books by Lori Wilde

HARLEQUIN DUETS
40—SANTA'S SEXY SECRET

To Ann Leslie Tuttle:
Everyone should be blessed with such an editor.
Thank you for caring so much
about books and readers.

1

FROM THE MOMENT Dr. Bennett Sheridan stepped into the operating suite at Saint Madeleine's University Hospital, his freshly scrubbed hands held up in front of him and a toothpaste-commercial grin breaking across his *GQ* cover-model face, Lacy Calder was a grade-A, number-one goner.

She glanced up from where she stood perched on her step stool spreading autoclaved instruments across the sterile field, preparing for an upcoming coronary bypass surgery, when she turned her head and saw him standing inside the doorway.

Her heart gave a crazy bump against her chest, and her breath crawled from her lungs. Never in all her twenty-nine years had she experienced such an immediate reaction to anyone.

It was intense and undeniable.

Endorphins collided with adrenaline. Sex hormones twisted like Chubby Checker in her lower abdomen. Excitement, approval and sheer joy sprinted through Lacy's nerve endings fast as electrical impulses skipping along telephone lines, wiring urgent messages to her brain.

It's him! It's the thunderbolt. Oh, my goodness gracious, Great-Gramma Kahonachek was right. He wasn't some myth like Big Foot or the Loch Ness Monster or the Tooth Fairy.

Lacy was not the sort of woman who lusted after complete strangers, and yet she was lusting after this one.

Big time.

Step aside, George Clooney! Outta the way, Noah Wyle! Cut a wide path, Anthony Edwards! Dr. Bennett Sheridan has arrived!

The man's Mr. Universe-quality physique begged her to caress him with her eyes. He was tall, well over six feet, and broad-shouldered. He wore green hospital scrubs, but the normally shapeless attire seemed to actually enhance his amazing body.

With his arms curled upward, still damp from the mandatory fifteen-minute Betadine scrub, she could see the hard ridges of his biceps bulging beneath thin cotton sleeves.

Spiced peach skin as dark as an itinerant beachcomber's, and a firmly muscled neck spoke of time spent pursuing outdoor athletic activities. A tennis player, she decided, or maybe softball. His nose, crooked slightly to the right, announced that it had been broken sometime in the past.

A fight, she wondered, or perhaps an accident? His teeth, straight and white, flashed like a linen sail behind his widening smile. An accompanying dimple carved a beguiling hole into his right cheek. When his chocolate-kisses eyes met hers, Dr. Feel Good made it seem as if she was the only woman on the face of the earth.

Be still, my heart.

She felt an unmistakable "click," as if something very important had settled into place. Something that, until now, had been sorely out of kilter.

At long last it had happened.

Lacy's knees turned to water. Her pulse hammered, and her tongue stuck to the roof of her mouth as surely as if plastered there by peanut butter.

"Morning, ladies," he greeted Lacy and the circulating nurse, Jan Marks. "I'm Dr. Bennett Sheridan, third-year resident on a study fellowship from Boston General. I'll be interning with Dr. Laramie for the next six weeks."

They had known he was coming on board, of course. Dr. Laramie had made a point of bragging about the fine young doctor, summa cum laude from Harvard, who'd flown to Houston specifically to study under him.

A young doctor who'd beaten out three hundred other anxious applicants for the prestigious opportunity. What Lacy hadn't expected was that Dr. Sheridan would melt her heart with that let's-break-open-a-bottle-of-champagne smile or that she would experience the most desperate urge to razzle-dazzle him.

But how could she ever hope to impress a man so obviously out of her league? He was Mark McGwire. She was the water girl.

His gaze landed on her and stuck.

Lacy gulped. Fully gowned and masked as she was, her hair covered with a sky-blue surgical cap and her feet slippered in matching shoe covers, Lacy couldn't help wondering why he stared so intently. Had she forgotten to put eye shadow on one eye? Did she have a smudge on her forehead? Was her mascara smeared?

Just her luck to meet the man of her dreams on the day she'd flubbed Makeup Application 101.

Unnerved, Lacy took a step backward and promptly somersaulted off her stool.

"ARE YOU all right?" Without even thinking about having broken scrub, Bennett Sheridan rushed to the fallen nurse's side.

Poor thing looked like a turtle flipped on its back. Her small legs were flailing wildly as she struggled to extract her toes from the hem of her scrub gown. Her scrub cap was knocked askew, revealing a hint of silky blond hair.

"Here," he soothed, kneeling beside her and placing one hand on her shoulder. "Let me help you." Reaching over, he tugged the corner of the gown from her foot. "There now."

He looked at her.

She stared at him.

All he could see was a pair of soft, beguiling blue eyes the shimmering hue of lazy summer dreams peeking at him over the top of her scrub mask. Sumptuous eyes framed by impossibly long lashes zeroed in on him with the precision of a laser beam.

Bennett blinked at the sudden sensation piercing his chest. He opened his mouth to speak but no sound emerged.

"Do you hear music?" she asked.

"Music?"

"Bells ringing, birds tweeting, angels singing?"

"Angels?"

"You know, those heavenly creatures with wings."

Bennett cleared his throat. Damn if he didn't hear a faint refrain of hallelujah somewhere in the back of his brain. "Did you hit your head?"

"I'm fine," she whispered.

"You've both broken scrub." The circulating nurse's voice cracked through the enchanting spell surrounding Bennett's mind. "Get off the floor. Scrub in again." She clapped her hands. "Hurry. The patient is in holding, and Dr. Laramie will be here within minutes."

Bennett rose to his feet and held out his palm to the cupcake-size scrub nurse. She reached up and took his hand.

It was an extraterrestrial moment. An R-rated version of *ET*. Out-of-this-world woman touches man, generates ethereal glow, causes hot sparks deep inside his groin.

Very hot sparks.

Impossible. He couldn't even see her face. This sensation had zilch to do with the young woman at his feet and everything to do with the fact he'd eaten a chocolate-chip muffin for breakfast. His blood sugar was high. Yeah. That was the ticket.

Not a testosterone overload. Not an endorphin rush.

He tugged her off the floor. She righted her cap and avoided his eyes.

"Thank you," she whispered and started for the door.

"Wait," he said. "You've got something stuck on the back of your scrub pants."

"Where?" She turned her head and tried to peer behind her.

"Allow me."

Not knowing what demon possessed him, Bennett placed one hand at her hip to hold her steady. A soft, inviting hip that could easily have modeled gauzy, blink-and-they're-not-even-there undergarments.

He took his other hand and grabbed hold of the sticky red label plastered to her world-class tush and pulled. Audibly, she sucked in her breath, and he was startled to discover she was trembling.

His heart stuttered, and he realized his blunder too late. He should not have touched her in such an intimate place. Not when he was having lascivious thoughts about that delightful bottom.

"Here you go." He cleared his throat and kept his voice neutral, belying the chaos rioting inside him. He placed the label in her hand.

It read, Volatile, Handle with Care.

Was that a message or what?

"Th-thank you," she stammered.

"Scrub in again. Both of you." The circulating nurse barked from across the room and pointed in the direction of the scrub sinks. "Now."

THEY STOOD side by side at the deep stainless steel sinks in the scrub area, scouring first their fingers, then their hands and last their arms with stiff bristled plastic brushes and reddish-brown Betadine solution.

Neither had spoken, but Lacy felt as if she was ready to explode.

Bennett began to whistle, and the sound pushed excited shivers under her skin. She cocked her head and listened, trying to identify the tune. When she did, she almost dropped her scrub brush.

"Hooked on a Feeling."

Was his whistling this particular song some kind of sign? Possibly a subliminal expression of his internal thoughts?

The thunderbolt.

This had to be it. Nothing else explained her reaction to him.

Wait a minute, Lace. Hold your horses. For all you know this guy is married.

She glanced at his left-hand ring finger. Bare. But that didn't mean anything. Most surgeons didn't wear rings. Then again, the guy was a surgical resident and few residents were married. Still, a naked ring finger was no guarantee.

Lacy couldn't believe fate would so cruelly lead her

astray. Surely Cupid wouldn't send her a married man. Because that's exactly what this felt like. As if she had been shot straight through the heart with the winged cherub's love-dipped arrow.

She recalled the feel of Bennett's hand at her hip, his fingers plucking the sticky label from her backside. An electrical thrill shot through her, tingling all the way to her toes.

Stunned, Lacy could not speak. How was it possible that the mystery man she'd been spinning elaborate fantasies about for half her life was poised a mere five inches away?

Since she was a young child, the women in her family had promised that one day she would meet her Mr. Right.

"But how will I know?" young Lacy had asked her mother.

"The thunderbolt," her mother had replied. "It strikes hard and fast. You'll just *know*."

"There's no mistaking it," her grandmother Nony had interjected.

"No point even looking around," Great-Gramma Kahonachek agreed. "If you don't feel the thunderbolt then he isn't the one. If you do, then nothing can stand in the way of true love."

Growing up in a large extended family, listening to the romantic tales from the old country, Lacy admitted she secretly wished the thunderbolt was real and not a figment of the grandmothers' active imaginations.

They had trained her to associate love with a strong physical and mental jab that could not be mistaken.

The magic had worked for her mother and her grandmother and her great-grandmother. If the thunderbolt theory was good enough for them, it was good enough for her. They'd all had long and happy marriages.

And here at last was her thunderbolt. In the flesh. With a mere smile, Dr. Bennett Sheridan had knocked her out with a clean one-two punch.

She accepted her emotions at face value. Dr. Bennett Sheridan was the man she'd been waiting a lifetime for. She knew it as surely as she knew her own name.

And yet, she was scared.

Terrified, in fact.

His sudden appearance in her world was a disruption of the status quo, and as much as she had longed to find her true life partner, now that the time was upon her she was afraid she would screw up her one chance at happily ever after.

Lacy experienced a breathless edginess, like a panicked swimmer dragged down by the ocean's hidden undertow. She wasn't sure what to do next. She couldn't very well say to him, "Hi, I'm the woman you're suppose to marry and I wanna bear your children."

"What's your name?" he asked in a James Bond voice that caused a ripple of slick heat to roll down Lacy's back.

"My—my name?" she stammered.

"I don't want to have to shout, 'Hey, you,' every time I need a retractor."

His eyes twinkled mischievously and his bold stare made her wonder if he had X-ray vision and could see past her outer clothing to her skimpy black lace matching bra-and-panty set beneath.

She had a thing for expensive underwear. Lingerie made her feel feminine, sexy, even when she wore baggy scrubs. She imagined his reaction if he knew what she had on right this very moment, and ended up embarrassing herself.

Lacy swallowed hard and concentrated on scrubbing her fingers until they ached, desperate to sever her gaze from his.

Did he feel it too? This heat? This energy? This inexplicable *something?*

"Lacy," she finally whispered, frustrated by her shyness.

"I'm sorry, I didn't catch that." He tilted his head as if straining to hang onto her every utterance. "You have such a soft voice."

"I'm sorry."

"Nothing to apologize for." His smile widened.

She knew it was dumb, but she had a really hard time talking to intriguing men. Her tongue turned to oatmeal, her hand sprouted all thumbs and she stumbled and stuttered. With the teenage bag boy at the grocery, no problem. Her middle-aged dentist with the bad toupee, no sweat. But give her a handsome, sexy guy, and Lacy morphed into the world's greatest klutz.

Maybe it was because she was the second of six kids and she'd sorta gotten lost in the shuffle. She wasn't the kind to speak up for herself, although she knew she should. Her friends told her she was too nice. Maybe that was true. Lacy only knew that it was difficult for her to make small talk.

She worried about sounding foolish, and she figured it was better to keep her lips zipped and let people wonder than open her mouth and remove all doubt.

So here she was standing next to a Greek god in human form and she could barely utter a single intelligent word. What good did it do to have found Dr. Right when she couldn't even speak to him?

"Lacy." She squared her shoulders and forced herself to speak louder, but she was still unable to meet his eyes. "Lacy Calder."

"Well, Lacy Calder, I'm charmed to make your acquaintance."

Quickly, she glanced over to see if he was looking at her, but he was rinsing his elbows. Lacy took advantage of the moment and allowed her gaze to linger upon him, absorbing his essence, rejoicing in his overt masculinity.

He exuded strength and power. A woman would never be afraid if she had a man like Dr. Sheridan to protect her. Then, as if feeling her eyes upon him, he raised his head and boldly winked.

Ack! Busted.

Lacy blushed and dipped her chin to her chest. Thank God for her mask. It covered most of her face. The only things that could give away her errant thoughts were her eyes. As long as she didn't meet his gaze directly she could get through this surgery.

Hurriedly, she kicked off the water with her knee then turned, hands up, and headed for the operating room.

She could feel Bennett's gaze burning her backside. Lacy gulped and hoofed it across the floor, willing her hips not to wiggle. She was concentrating so hard, she didn't even see the orderly pushing the supply cart.

"Lacy." Bennett called her name. "Look out."

His warning came too late. She turned, but not quickly enough.

Wham! The cart broadsided her.

Supplies teetered. The orderly swore.

Lacy reached out a hand in an attempt to keep the supplies from falling, but her sleeve caught on a shelf.

She jerked.

Boxes began their slow slide to the floor. Catheters and instrument trays, specimen bottles and packages of syringes.

An avalanche of equipment descended upon her.

Lacy tried to leap out of the way, but her sleeve remained snagged.

But before she could hit the ground, Bennett was there. His arms went tight around her waist, and his breath seared warm on the nape of her neck.

Lacy flushed to her roots. He must think her the clumsiest woman in the entire universe.

"I've got you," he whispered.

Yes, you do.

AFTER THEY FINISHED their third scrub of the morning, they regowned and entered the operating suite at the same moment Dr. Laramie strode in. Bennett started a conversation with him, effectively letting Lacy off the hot seat.

Mentally, she castigated herself for her oafishness. What was the matter with her? She had better get her head in the game. She couldn't be dropping instruments higgledy-piggledy during the surgery simply because the latest hospital heartthrob had distracted her.

She returned to her stool and her instrument tray.

Not long afterward, the patient, a sixty-five-year-old retired construction worker who'd recently suffered a heart attack, arrived on a gurney, and their work began in earnest.

Lacy tried to focus on her job, handing Jan the equipment she needed to prep the patient. Betadine swabs, sterile towels, normal saline.

On automatic pilot, she moved through the activities she performed with experienced ease several times a day. Her mind restlessly toyed with thoughts of Dr. Sheridan.

Calm down, Lacy. You can't afford to make rash assumptions. Too much is at stake. Give your emotions a chance to cool off. Maybe this is only happening because your thirtieth birthday is looming and your biological clock is ticking.

It sounded good, anyway. Her rational mind tried to slacken the stampede racing through her stomach. But her heart wasn't buying one word of it.

He's the one, he's the one, he's the one. Her blood sang through her veins.

Helplessly, her eyes sought him again. She observed Bennett from behind as he spoke in low tones with the anesthesiologist, Dr. Grant Tennison.

She admired how the material of his scrub pants stretched across his backside. She noticed that the hair poking out from the back of his surgical cap and trailing a short distance down his neck was thick, wavy and black.

More validation. Lacy had always pictured herself with a black-haired, brown-eyed man.

I want to curl up on the sofa and read the Sunday paper with him, she thought. *I want to roll over in bed every morning and find him snoozing on the pillow next to mine. I want to go to the supermarket with him and pick out favorite comfort foods together. I want to feed him ice chips from a spoon when he has a fever. I want to see how he brushes his teeth and puts on his shoes and butters his bread. I want him to ask my opinion—does his tie go with his suit? Or should he grow a mustache? I want him to worry when I'm not home in time for dinner.*

This man was everything she had ever wanted and so much more.

Ben Affleck good looks, stellar career ahead of him, a come-on-over-to-play-at-my-house smile, and most of all…

Fireworks.

Peering into his eyes had shown her a glimpse of what lay in store. An earth-rocking sensation she could not deny. Red-hot-chili-pepper sparks that took her breath and promised so much more.

Rapture skipped through her as she entertained thoughts of kissing him. How would it feel to have his full, firm lips snuggled flush against hers? His tongue eagerly exploring her mouth?

Bennett turned and gave her an I-know-what-you're-thinking-you-naughty-girl look.

Swiftly, Lacy feigned intense interest in her work. She repositioned the instruments on the table and breathed in stale air through her mask. The powerful lights beaming down on them seemed hotter than normal, stirring the flutters in her tummy.

Now that she had found him, how was she going to convince him that she was *his* Miss Right?

Her innate shyness had often hampered her in nursing school, and it was the main reason she worked in surgery. Here, she never dealt directly with the patients. She could help people without interacting with them too much.

It had taken her months to develop the working relationship she had with the surgeons and the other nurses. Her co-workers occasionally teased her about her introversion, but after six years she had at last become comfortable in her job.

She must overcome this accursed shyness. She absolutely must. Otherwise Bennett Sheridan, aka the thunderbolt, would complete his residency at Saint Madeleine's and be on his way without anything more having passed between them than a few meaningful glances.

Lacy could not let Mr. Right march out of her life. She had to do something to get his attention, had to force herself to conquer her natural reticence with the opposite sex.

But what?

And how?

2

"GREAT-GRAMMA, it's me, Lacy."

"*Drahy!* Is that you?"

"Yes."

"You sound so far away."

"I'm on my cell phone." Lacy glanced over her shoulder to make sure she was alone in the locker room before speaking freely.

She had a few minutes between surgeries and instead of taking a coffee break in the lounge, she'd felt compelled to give her great grandmother a quick call. As if there was such a thing as a fast phone conversation with her family.

"Oh, my darling, I'm so glad you call. I'm missing you."

"I miss you, too."

"Have I got a story for you." Her great grandmother's rich laughter rolled easily across the miles. "Frank Sinatra munched your cousin Edward's undershorts right off the clothesline."

Frank Sinatra, whose eclectic diet consisted of everything from spray starch cans to potato vines, was Great-Gramma's favorite ram, named after her favorite singer. She raised a small herd of Tennessee Mountain Fall Down goats, who were known for their odd defense mechanism of fainting at the first sign of danger.

Except Old Blue Eyes's namesake was so ornery he rarely fainted any more. Nothing seemed to scare him. Not even Great-Gramma chasing him with a marble rolling pin.

"Gramma, I don't have time to talk about the goat. I've got something important to tell you."

"What has happened?" Immediate concern tinged her great grandmother's voice. "Something is wrong."

"Nothing is wrong." Lacy took a deep breath. She could almost see the tiny eighty-eight-year-old woman hunched over the phone in the family's eight-hundred-square-foot kitchen in West, Texas. "Something is very right."

"*Drahy,* don't tell me...." She inhaled sharply.

"Yes." Lacy nodded. "It's happened."

Great-Gramma gasped. "The thunderbolt?"

"Uh-huh."

Her great grandmother let out another laugh. "At long last. But wait, let me call your mother and your grandmother Nony. They'll want to hear this, too."

"Gramma, I only have a few minutes."

But it was too late. Great-Gramma had already laid the phone down. Lacy heard the receiver clank against the antique oak table that had been passed down through five generations, and for a moment a wave of homesickness washed over her.

Just then the locker room door opened, and Jan sailed in. "Don't forget, the next surgery starts in twenty minutes," the circulating nurse said before disappearing into the adjoining bathroom.

Rats. Even with a closed door between them, Lacy was afraid Jan might overhear her rather private conversation. Pensively, she studied her locker. Hmm. She was small enough to fit.

She opened her locker, wedged herself inside and closed the door behind her. A spare lab jacket brushed against her face, and she had to balance on top of the street shoes she wore to work.

It was black as thunder, and hot and stuffy. Just when she decided this was a dumb idea, her great grandmother came back on the line.

"Now, *drahy,* tell us all about the thunderbolt."

"Hang on, Gramma." Lacy heard her mother's voice in the background. "Let me put her on speakerphone."

"These newfangled gadgets," Great-Gramma muttered.

"I can't talk long," Lacy reminded them. "I've got to get back to work."

"Sweetheart, this is your mama."

"And your Nony," Lacy's grandmother chimed in.

"Hi, everyone. I had to call to tell you I've been struck by the thunderbolt."

All the women on the other end of the phone began to titter at once. As quickly as she could, Lacy filled them in on the details.

"So what's the problem, *drahy*?"

"I don't know how to approach him. You know how I get when I'm around men I like. And this is ten times worse. I say stupid things. I fall down. I drop stuff. What can I do to make him like me?"

"You do nothing," Great-Gramma advised.

"He will come to you," Grandmother Nony contributed.

"Listen to your grandmothers. It will all work out," Lacy's mother said.

"But how can you be so sure?"

"Trust in the power of the thunderbolt!" all three chimed in unison. "It will never go wrong."

"Okeydokey. Thanks so much. I love you guys."

"We love you, too," Grandmother Nony said.

"Bring your thunderbolt to see us soon," Great-Gramma said.

"Enjoy being in love," her mother said. "You deserve it, darling."

"Goodbye." Lacy severed the connection and leaned back in the locker, her heart pounding.

Love.

Was she really, truly in love? Maybe she was reading more into this feeling than she should. Maybe it was just sexual chemistry and not the thunderbolt at all. That thought gave her pause.

She heard the outer door of the locker room close, and she figured Jan had left. Time to get back to work. Lacy pushed against the locker door.

It didn't open.

She fumbled in the darkness, her fingers grazing over the cool metal. No handle on this side of the door.

This was just ducky. She was going to be late for the next surgery. Jan would have her hide. Not to mention that she'd placed herself in a very embarrassing situation.

"Help," she said in a small voice. "Is there anybody out there?"

Silence.

She tried the door again without success. She would never live this down. She'd be the laughing stock of the OR.

The outer door creaked on its hinges. She heard footsteps.

"Hello?"

"Hello?" A deep male voice rumbled. "I heard a call of help from the hallway. Am I having a conversation with a talking locker?"

"Uh, could you open the door for me? I sorta got locked in."

"Lacy?"

"Yes." Then, to her utter chagrin, she recognized the voice.

The door swung open, and she looked into Bennett's laughing eyes. He diplomatically hid his smirk behind a palm.

She wriggled her fingers at him. "Hi."

"Should I ask what you're doing in there? Or is it better if I don't know?"

"Just making a phone call." She stepped from the

locker, head held high as if it were perfectly normal to sequester yourself inside your locker.

"I've got a news flash for you, Supergirl," he teased. "That's not a phone booth."

She held up her cell phone as proof that she had indeed utilized the locker as a phone booth, but not before wishing the floor would crack open and swallow her up. "Thanks for letting me out."

"Anytime."

"Well," she said, slipping her phone into the pocket of her lab coat and kicking her locker door closed with her foot. "I better get back to work."

"Ditto." He was still grinning.

Lacy inched toward the door.

"See you," she said.

"We're doing the same operation. I'm right behind you."

"Oh."

Feeling like a hundred shades of fool, Lacy turned tail and bolted down the hallway before she did something really stupid, like trip over her own shoelaces and go down in a heap at his feet.

"IT'S HOPELESS," Lacy moaned to her closest friends, CeeCee Adams and Janet Hunter. "He's been at Saint Madeleine's for five weeks, and I haven't worked up enough courage to speak to him outside the operating suites. Not only that, but I'm sure he thinks I'm a complete idiot. And I could swear he's purposely been avoiding me."

It was late Friday afternoon, and the women were in Lacy's living room at the River Run apartment complex where all three lived. River Run was a moderately priced development only three blocks from the hospital.

Lacy had lived here for the six years since she'd been out of nursing school, and until the past few months, she'd loved her little corner apartment with the great view of Washington Park. But lately she'd grown restless. Suddenly, she had a desire for more space. A house to call her own. A front yard where she could plant flowers and grow vegetables. A place to raise a family. Except she had no one to raise a family with, and unless she did something drastic to defeat her shyness, she might never get the opportunity.

She would live the rest of her life in this tiny one-bedroom apartment, a lonely spinster who had missed out on her Mr. Right because she had been too paralyzed with fear to pursue him.

Try as she might to reassure herself that she was simply following the advice of the women in her family and allowing the thunderbolt to take its course, in her heart, Lacy knew she'd embraced the path of least resistance. Deep down inside she'd known all along that nothing was going to happen between her and Bennett unless she got brave enough to open her mouth and have a conversation with him. She had to make this happen. That's what was so scary.

"It's not hopeless." Janet reached for an apple from the fruit bowl on the coffee table.

Tall and willowy, with chin-length dark hair and inquisitive indigo eyes, she was Lacy's physical opposite. Janet had lived at River Run for less than a year. She had recently completed her pediatric residency and was hoping to get in with the group of renowned pediatricians on Blanton Street whose offices were adjacent to the hospital.

"I'm proof of that." Janet smoothed imaginary wrinkles from her tailored gray slacks.

"What do you mean?" Lacy leaned forward. She and Janet sat on the sofa while CeeCee lay on the carpet doing crunches.

A physical therapist, CeeCee was fanatical about staying in shape. It paid off. In Lacy's opinion, salsa-haired CeeCee had a figure that could rival any movie star's and a sparkling personality to match.

"I used to be shyer than you are," Janet told Lacy.

"Nobody's shyer than me."

Janet snorted. "Oh, yes. In med school before I could work up the courage to go into my first patient's room, I had to stand in the hall and give myself a twenty-minute pep talk."

"It took me thirty minutes," Lacy confessed.

"See? If there's hope for me, there's hope for you."

"I would never have taken you for a shy person," Lacy said. "You're so self-assured."

"It's all an act. Or at least it was in the beginning. Perceiving, behaving, becoming. If you believe you're competent and outgoing, then you'll become that way and once you get over being shy, you'll never go back. Right, CeeCee?''

"Don't ask me." CeeCee huffed as she lifted her shoulders off the carpet and rolled forward. "I was born to socialize."

"I wish I could be like that," Lacy said wistfully. "I hate crowds and parties. It's tough thinking of things to say. I much prefer curling up with a good book any day of the week to the pressure of having to make small talk with strangers."

Lacy observed her friends. They brightened her life like fresh-cut flowers on the windowsill or homemade bread hot from the oven, slathered with butter, or soothing classical music on the stereo. She treasured them, and yet she envied them, too.

How she wished she could be more like breezy, fun-loving CeeCee or no-nonsense, down-to-earth Janet. Instead, she was a meek little wimp. Too shy to come out of her shell but hating her self-imposed isolation.

If it hadn't been for CeeCee stepping across the hallway three years ago looking for a cup of alfalfa sprouts, Lacy would still be friendless in Houston.

It had also been CeeCee who, ten months before, had invited Janet to join them for a run in the park. Since then the three of them had been inseparable. Currently, none of them had boyfriends. And until Lacy had met Bennett Sheridan, she'd been content with her life.

Since she'd first laid eyes on him, she'd been unable

to think of anything else. She'd confided her interest in Bennett to her friends, but fearing their ridicule in her belief in love at first sight, she hadn't told them about the thunderbolt.

CeeCee believed that you made your own magic no matter what partner you were with, while cynical Janet didn't believe in romantic love at all.

"Lacy needs our help," Janet reminded CeeCee. "Got any great ideas?"

"Makeover!" CeeCee shouted gleefully.

"Makeover?" Anxiously, Lacy reached a hand up to pat her honey-blond hair, which hung in a single braid down her back, and she glanced at her loose-fitting cream-colored floral jumper. "What's wrong with the way I look?"

"No offense, sweetie." CeeCee drew her knees to her chin in a characteristic gesture. She was wearing black Lycra leggings, ballet slippers and a stretchy pink crop top. Her tomato-red curls flowed like a flame across her shoulders, free and unfettered. "But you don't dress to attract the male of the species."

Lacy winced at her friend's honesty. True enough. She purposely picked outfits that would not draw attention. No flamboyant colors, no short skirts or plunging necklines. She preferred sensible clothes. Flats to high heels, stud earrings to dangly hoops, clear nail polish to scarlet. Yes, the more conservative her attire the more secure she felt.

Except when it came to her undies. There she indulged herself, allowing her fantasies free rein. She could afford to splurge on panties, teddies and bras. She had nothing to be afraid of. Men never saw her underwear.

"Why do I have to call attention to myself?" She frowned.

"Honey, why do you suppose flowers are so colorful?"

Lacy shrugged.

"To attract bees and butterflies."

"But," Lacy said, "I won't know what to say to a bee when he flits around my flower."

"You don't have to say anything," Janet told her. "You act cool, aloof, distant. Make them work for it."

"Nope," CeeCee argued, demonstrating the difference in their personal styles. "You smile and make eye contact."

"All right," Janet conceded, "but follow her advice only if you're interested. Give the rest of them the cold shoulder."

"I don't want to impress anyone except Bennett."

CeeCee sent Janet a do-you-want-to-give-her-the-birds-and-bees-lecture-or-should-I look and shook her head. "The girl's got a lot to learn."

"What is it?" Lacy glanced at her friends. "Tell me."

"How did you get to be twenty-nine years old without picking up on some of this?" Janet asked.

"You guys know how old-fashioned my parents are. They didn't exactly tutor me on becoming a blond bombshell. Both my sisters are younger. On the rare occasions I had a date, my folks insisted one of my brothers go along as chaperon.''

''And after high school?''

''It's always been hard for me to meet men,'' Lacy confessed.

''Things have got to change. If you want Dr. Sheridan to notice you, then you've got to get other men interested in you first. Guys are, by nature, commitment shy. You have to set the hook before you reel them in.'' CeeCee pantomimed casting with a fishing pole.

''I don't understand.'' Lacy moaned and covered her face with her hands. ''This is too complicated.''

''Come on, you can't hide out forever. Not if you want to win Dr. Sheridan's heart,'' Janet said gently.

''Yeah, get out there and have a blast.'' CeeCee nodded.

''Let me see if I understand you. In order to catch the man of my dreams, I have to pretend to be a carefree party girl who flits from man to man without a concern in the world?''

''You've got it,'' CeeCee exclaimed. ''That's the male psyche in a nutshell.''

''But won't guys think I'm easy?''

''Yes. That's the whole point.''

CeeCee's reasoning distressed Lacy. Couldn't Bennett just fall in love with her for herself? Why did she have to fake being a gregarious hedonist?

If he was only attracted to that facade, what would

happen when Bennett discovered that she wasn't like that at all?

"What if I attract him and we start going out? What happens when he expects things to, er, progress further than a good-night kiss?"

CeeCee blinked in disbelief. "You mean you've never..."

Lacy shook her head. "Never. And even if I wanted to go to bed with a man, I've got to be in love with him and I want him to be in love with me, too."

"Hang on." CeeCee zipped from the room and returned a moment later with a small square foil package. She tossed it in Lacy's lap. "A girl's got to protect herself."

Lacy thrust the condom at CeeCee. "I'm not ready for this."

"Keep it. You never know when it might come in handy."

Nervously, Lacy palmed the condom and dropped it into the pocket of her jumper. "I don't think I'm going to have to worry about a condom right this moment. I'm so shy. Let's start with that. How do I begin to overcome my bashfulness?"

CeeCee wrinkled her brow. "Can you think of a time you weren't shy?"

Lacy shook her head. "No."

"Wait a minute." Janet snapped her fingers. "Didn't you tell me you used to act in plays back in high school?"

"Yes."

"That takes guts. How were you able to overcome your shyness in order to get up on a stage in front of people?"

"Easy," Lacy said. "I was so busy playing a part I didn't have time to feel self-conscious."

It made sense. Acting had been her one social outlet in high school. She had enjoyed becoming someone else, forgetting herself, shedding her shell and emerging as the star. Could she actually do it in real life?

"How do we begin?" Lacy asked, excited yet hesitant. What was she letting herself in for?

"First we give you a makeover."

"Then," Janet said, "we put you to the test."

"A nightclub." CeeCee snapped her fingers. "Where you can practice talking to men you don't care about before you move on to Dr. Sheridan."

"You two will come with me, won't you? I mean I don't think I can traipse into a bar on my own."

"Sure, we'll be there," Janet assured her.

"Thanks," Lacy said gratefully. "You guys are wonderful."

"What are we waiting for?" CeeCee asked. "Let's get going. The night is young, and the men beckon."

"YOU'LL LOVE this place," Dr. Grant Tennison assured Bennett. They pulled into the parking lot of a noisy nightclub near the hospital district, aptly named the Recovery Room.

It was only seven-thirty but already the joint was packed. The thumping strains of heavy rock music jarred the walls of the large squat building decorated with flashing red-and-blue neon signs that simulated whirling ambulance lights.

Grant had offered to drive, since Bennett was staying at the visiting physician's quarters at Saint Madeleine's and hadn't bothered to rent a car.

"Some of the best-looking women in Houston come here." Grant flung open the door of his late model Porsche and stepped into the muggy night air.

"Sounds great." Bennett was glad to be out of the high-stress hospital environment. He was going to have a couple of beers, relax and enjoy the eye candy. "It's been a busy five weeks. Laramie's a brilliant surgeon, but he's also a slave driver. I'm ready for a little R and R."

"I thought you had the air of a resident who'd spent too many long nights alone." Grant winked and nudged him in the ribs with his elbow. "Don't worry, you'll find what you're searching for in here."

Bennett certainly hoped Grant was right. He was looking for something to take his mind off Lacy Calder.

For some reason he could not properly frame into words, Lacy fascinated him. Bennett had assisted Dr. Laramie with thirty-four cases, and Lacy had scrubbed in on twenty-eight of them.

Twenty-eight times in five weeks he had looked up to see those enticing astral-blue eyes across the table from him. And twenty-eight times he'd found himself aching to peel back that mask. Only once had he seen her without the paper covering over her face, and that was on his first day when she'd locked herself in her locker.

And each time he'd caught her eye, she quickly glanced away, but not quickly enough to hide the deep scarlet flush that rose to color the tops of her cheeks. Her shyness served to heighten his attraction. If mere eye contact made her so flustered, what would a kiss do to her?

The idea excited him to the point where Bennett had to chide himself for the direction of his inappropriate thoughts. He had no business pursuing his co-worker. None whatsoever.

First of all, they worked together, and it would be stupid to allow anything to interfere with their professional relationship. Second, he was only going to be in Houston for another week. Not nearly enough time to get to know a complex woman like Lacy. Third, even if by some wild stretch of the imagination he did manage to form a bond with her, he had another year left in his residency at Boston General. Then he'd be occupied setting up his private practice. But most important of all, he couldn't afford to be distracted during life-saving operations.

And then there was his personal credo—never, ever get sucked in by physical attraction. He was a man of science. He knew all about pheromones. They had their place in the scheme of human reproduction, but rational-minded human beings didn't choose lifelong mates based on sexual attraction. He knew firsthand the chaos unrestrained chemistry could cause.

His parents had met, been wildly sexually attracted to each other, married a few weeks later, created a baby and lived unhappily ever after for two miserable years before finally calling it quits. Over the course of time, both his father and mother had reiterated their lesson, and Bennett, seeing their distress, had heeded their words. Love at first sight is a myth. Lust, yes. Love, no. Never let your hormones rule your head. Make love to a woman if you will, but don't base a marriage on physical desires.

That was why he had dodged Lacy outside the surgical suite. He was afraid of the way she stirred his passion. If he saw her go into the locker room, he avoided it for awhile. If they passed in the corridor he pretended he had something so important on his mind that he didn't notice her. If they ended up side by side at the scrub sinks, he always started a conversation with anyone else in the vicinity.

Although he felt like a heel giving her the cold shoulder, it was for their own good. He could not afford to fall in love, get married and start a family for at least three more years. He refused to go through what his parents had gone through. He wasn't doing that to his kids. Nor to himself.

He had no time for a serious relationship. Particularly a long-distance one. No, much better to enjoy the simple pleasure of working with Lacy and let it go at that.

Determinedly pushing aside all thoughts of the shy scrub nurse who'd so unexpectedly piqued his curiosity, Bennett followed Grant Tennison into the crowded, noisy nightclub.

Grant waded past a dozen closely packed tables near the door, making a beeline for the bar, calling out greetings to several people as he pushed past.

Glancing around the room, Bennett realized Grant had spoken the truth. The place was crawling with beautiful women. To the right of the bar was an archway leading to the dance floor where a disc jockey played a jivey Van Halen tune. Numerous dancers bumped and gyrated in time to the music. To the left lay a room that housed pool tables, pinball machines and video games.

Leaning back, elbows against the counter, he ordered a beer and studied the crowd. Bennett found people-watching fascinating. When he was a boy, his paternal grandmother had loved to take him around with her because he could sit for hours in a shopping mall or an airport or a doctor's waiting room watching the crowds go by, wondering who they were, what their lives were like, where they were going.

Fond memories of time spent with Nanna were his most prized possessions. It had devastated him when she'd died of a heart attack five years ago.

His interest in people, their motives and problems was what had led him to become a physician. That and Nanna's absolute belief in him. He ached to be useful to mankind, to do something important and make Nanna proud.

It was only later, while he was in med school, that he realized he loved surgery best and cardiac surgery most of all. What could be more fulfilling than learning the secrets of the human heart? By helping to correct heart disease, he was giving people a second chance at life, another opportunity to love. In Bennett's estimation, nothing was more rewarding.

He eyed the front door. Customers came and went. He recognized several people from the hospital.

Bennett was about to spin around on the stool and ask the bartender for another beer when the door swung open and in marched three very attractive women. Every head in the place turned to stare at the compelling trio.

The redhead led the way. She bounced rather than walked. Her hair was shoulder length and curly. She was of medium height with a body that wouldn't quit. A bubbly smile graced her lips, and she swung her head from side to side, greeting everyone in her wake.

Behind her came the brunette. Tall, slender, cucumber cool. She looked neither to the left nor the right but kept her head high and her gaze to the front. She had piercing ebony eyes and a no-nonsense countenance, and she wore an elegant black pantsuit, low-heeled black boots and pearl jewelry.

But it was the petite blonde bringing up the rear that stole his breath.

"Mama mia," Bennett whispered under his breath,

his palm damp against the sweating long-necked beer bottle.

She moved with light, delicate steps, parting the air like water. Her hair, the color of moon drops threaded with gold, hung straight as a curtain down the middle of her back, and it was swept back off her forehead with a vibrant green bow. She was about five-one, certainly no more than five-two, and couldn't have weighted a hundred pounds soaking wet.

Her daintiness stirred his protective instincts. He had the sudden urge to scoop her into his arms and hold her safe from the rowdy crowd.

Her shoulders were squared, her chin up. She wore a barely there sheath of emerald green and matching three-inch high heels. A gold choker glistened at her slender throat, and she carried a small gold clutch purse.

Bennett could not take his eyes from her.

The redhead scouted them a table and hustled her friends into place. The blonde took a seat with her back to him. She laughed at something the brunette said. It was a sweet, melodious sound.

A man in a cowboy hat came over to talk to them. He leaned down to whisper in the blonde's ear. She raised her neck. The action caused her pale hair to swish against her ivory cheek, and she tugged gently at her earlobe.

The gesture was so subtly seductive, Bennett had to give her credit. Most women who frequented night-clubs were pretty obvious with their sexuality. Like the blonde's red-haired friend. But not this one. She exuded an elegant, old-world grace he hadn't seen in a woman since his grandmother.

He wanted to know her.

No. Wanted was too mild a word. He felt compelled to make her acquaintance. Something inexplicable was pushing him forward, urging him to procure her phone number.

Wrapping his fingers around his beer bottle, Bennett got up and strolled around the bar, hoping to get a better glimpse of her face.

But before he could reach a vantage point across from their table, she took the cowboy's hand and allowed him to lead her to the dance floor. She cast a tentative glance over her shoulder, and her red-haired friend gave her an enthusiastic thumbs-up sign. Apparently she approved the blonde's choice.

For some reason it bugged him that the blonde had selected the cowboy. If that's what she was looking for then he was out of the running. Bennett Sheridan was as far away from cowboy as one could get and still be standing on Texas soil.

Bennett went to stand in the archway leading to the dance floor. Several other men where holding up the wall, observing the dancers and waiting their turn to dance with the ladies of their choice. Crossing his arms over his chest, he casually grasped the long-necked bottle between his thumb and index finger.

The disc jockey had put on a country and western tune Bennett didn't recognize. He watched while the

cowboy two-stepped the blonde around the dance
floor, her feet barely touching the ground. She was
uncertain in her movements, as if she didn't two-step
very often, but graceful nonetheless.

She reminded him of someone. Whom, he couldn't
quite say. For no reason whatsoever he found himself
wondering if her eyes were whirlpool blue.

Who was she? He had to know. Soon as the cowboy
relinquished her, he'd find out.

Her hair swirled as she danced. Bennett found himself mesmerized, and he wasn't the only one. He
caught many covetous glances angling her way from
the men lined against the wall.

You're jealous, he thought, then immediately dismissed the idea. How could he be jealous of a woman
he didn't even know?

What was this unpleasant squeezing he experienced
deep in his gut as he watched the cowboy slowly slide
his hand lower and lower until he was almost touching
her firm buttocks encased so seductively in that snug-
fitting dress?

The blonde didn't seem to mind that the cowboy
was getting his fill. She didn't move his hand away or
slap his face. She probably liked being fondled in public, he surmised. No doubt she had come here intent
on lassoing herself a cowboy for the night.

Bennett fought the urge to punch something. *This
is completely irrational, Sheridan. Get over the
woman.*

Shaking his head, he turned away, unable to bear

another moment of watching the cowboy grope the soft flesh he yearned to nuzzle. It had been much too long since he'd had the pleasure of a woman's company if he was letting something like this upset him.

"How you doing, buddy?" Grant Tennison clamped a hand on his shoulder. "Having a good time?"

Bennett shrugged and wondered why he had come.

"I saw you eyeing that pretty little blonde. Very cute."

"You know her?" Bennett perked up.

"No, but she sure does catch the eye, doesn't she?"

"Yes," he agreed, disappointed that he wouldn't be able to wrangle an introduction from Grant. "How about her friends? Do you know them?" Bennett cocked his head toward the table where the brunette and redhead were surrounded by men.

"I know CeeCee. The redhead. Everyone does."

CeeCee was very attractive, Bennett had to give her that, but in his estimation she couldn't hold a candle to her fair-haired friend.

At that moment, the blonde returned from the dance floor. Sans cowboy, Bennett was pleased to note. She passed right by where he and Grant stood. Bennett narrowed his eyes, desperate for a closer look. Her scent caught his nose as she floated off.

Roses. He'd smelled that perfume before. Lacy?

His heart skipped a beat. Nah. Couldn't be. This dishy young lady simply could not be the shy scrub nurse.

Then she stopped, turned and met his gaze. There was no mistaking those Alps-blue eyes. He'd stared into them for hours at a time. Stared at those eyes and lusted after the woman who possessed them.

Coquettishly, she pursed her lips and blew him a kiss.

Stunned, Bennett realized that the bewitching blonde was indeed none other than Lacy Calder.

3

LACY FELT physically ill. Dancing with that cowboy and then blowing Bennett a kiss drained every ounce of courage she possessed. What had come over her? Hands trembling, she sat down at the table beside CeeCee and Janet.

Had Bennett recognized her? She had wanted him to, and yet the thought of holding a conversation with him caused her chest to squeeze so tightly it was a miracle she could breathe.

"You did great," CeeCee exclaimed, pounding Lacy approvingly on the back. "First time out of the hat and you dance with a guy! I'm so proud of you."

"He dragged me around the dance floor," Lacy muttered. "I don't really call that dancing."

"Jake's a nice guy, though, don't you think?" CeeCee glanced over her shoulder at the cowboy. "He was a good friend to help ease you over your first dance and break the ice."

Hmm. Jake the cowboy might be good friends with CeeCee but he had let his hands do a little more roving than necessary. Lacy, of course, hadn't had the courage to tell him to keep his hands to himself, so she'd suffered in silence.

Lacy sighed. It was this ridiculous eye-popping dress and these silly three-inch spike heels CeeCee had forced her to wear that caused the problem. In her scrubs, the cowboy wouldn't have glanced at her twice, much less tried anything.

"Are you all right?" Janet asked. "You're pale as a sheet and you're perspiring." She placed two fingers on Lacy's wrist. "Goodness, you're tachycardic, too, and your pulse is thready."

"I think I'm going to be sick," Lacy confessed, remembering what she'd done.

"Put your head between your legs, take a few deep breaths. You're going to be okay," Janet said firmly. "It's just an attack of nerves."

"I'll get you a glass of water," CeeCee volunteered and sprang up from the table.

Janet laid a comforting hand on Lacy's shoulder. "CeeCee doesn't get it, but I know how hard this is for you. Hang in there. I promise flirting gets easier the more you do it."

"He's here," Lacy whispered, ducking under the table and tucking her head between her legs. She studied the cement floor, noticed a piece of broken pretzel wedged in a crack and focused on it. She took several deep, cleansing breaths.

"Who's here?" Janet asked.

"Dr. Sheridan."

"Where?"

"Over near the rest rooms."

"Which one is he?"

"Tall. Black hair. Great build."

"Nice tan?"

"Uh-huh."

"Oh, my, Lacy, he is gorgeous." She heard the approval in Janet's voice. "He's definitely worth overcoming shyness for."

Lacy closed her eyes. The nausea wasn't getting any better. "I blew him a kiss."

"What?" Janet asked in disbelief. She lowered her head beneath the table and peered at Lacy. "You've got to be kidding."

"No," Lacy said miserably. "That's why I feel so shaky inside. I can't believe I did it."

"Well, that's great. CeeCee's right. You *have* made a lot of progress tonight."

"It was a stupid thing to do. He's going to think I'm some sort of hussy."

"He will not. And even if he does, that's the point. But tell me, how did you work up the courage to blow him a kiss when you can't even speak to him at work?"

"I don't know," Lacy wailed. "You guys had me all gussied up in this sexy outfit, and I guzzled that wine."

"You had half a glass," Janet told her.

"I took your advice and pretended I was a sexy actress. I don't know what came over me. It's as if I was standing outside my body watching someone else inside my skin. I stopped, turned and blew him a kiss.'' She covered her face with her hands and groaned.

''It's not the end of the world, sweetie. What's the worst that can happen? He doesn't ask you out.''

But he has to ask me out, Lacy thought desperately. *He's the one I'm going to marry! I felt the thunderbolt.*

Suddenly, a pair of men's shoes appeared under the corner of the table. Shoes that were presumably attached to a man.

''Did you drop something, Lacy?''

Bennett Sheridan's voice made her cringe. Lacy wished she could curl into a tiny dust ball and blow away. What to do?

Lacy's innate fear warred with her desire to get to know him better.

Janet was no help whatsoever. ''I'm off to the lady's room,'' she announced.

No, Lacy wanted to cry out, *you can't leave me.*

''Take my chair, Dr. Sheridan,'' Janet offered.

Janet stood up. Bennett sat.

You can do this, you can do this, you can do this, Lacy affirmed, then raised her head and peeked over the edge of the table to find him studying her with a bemused expression.

''Baywatch'' babe, she thought. *Pretend you're a gorgeous babe from ''Baywatch.'' Sexy, breezy, without a care in the world. You're irresistible to men. You wear toe rings and tattoos and string bikinis. Think wicked, Lacy.*

Sitting up straight, she painted a smile on her face.

"Do you come here often?" he asked, amusement in his voice. His eyes twinkled, and he folded his hands on the table.

"Fairly frequently," Lacy lied, surprised at her brazenness. Where was all this courage springing from? "I have a few other places I hang out at, too."

"That's odd."

"Odd?"

"I wouldn't have pegged you for a party girl."

"Oh, sure." She waved a hand. "I go out every night."

He looked surprised. "I've been wanting to ask you out, but I figured you weren't the type of girl who went in for temporary relationships."

I'm not, Lacy longed to say, but instead she kept her mouth shut and waited for Bennett to continue.

"Since I've only got a week left in Houston, I don't want to start something serious that I can't finish. But I certainly would enjoy squiring a beautiful lady around town. Especially a lady who knows all the hot spots."

"You would?"

"Yes."

His brown eyes met hers. Lacy gulped.

The thunderbolt galloped through her, quick and hot. Her great grandmother was right. There was no mistaking the sensation.

Bennett looked awfully good in his crisp white cotton shirt, starched blue jeans and casual penuchecolored loafers. This was the first time she'd seen him in normal clothing, Lacy realized, and he did not disappoint.

"Are you asking me out, Dr. Sheridan?" Her heart did a free fall into her stomach.

"Would you say yes if I did?"

"For fun only?"

"That's right." He cocked an elbow against the back of his chair.

"Nothing that would monkey with our jobs?"

"Absolutely."

"No strings attached?"

"None at all."

Darn it. Why wouldn't he stop staring into her eyes? Lacy felt as if she were falling, falling, falling into the abyss of his soul. Flustered, she peered at her hands and fought the heat rising to her cheeks. She was in trouble here.

Bennett leaned forward. He was so close she had only to reach out her fingers an inch or two and she could touch his firm skin. "You're not looking for entanglements, are you, Lacy?"

What was it CeeCee had told her? That all men were nervous about commitment. That they shied away if a girl acted too interested, too eager, too anxious to have a man in her life. The male of the species wanted a challenge, a competition, a prize.

"Me?" Lacy placed a hand on her chest and forced a laugh. "Want a commitment? Whatever gave you that idea?"

"I don't know. In the operating room you struck me as a very old-fashioned girl."

"And what gave you that impression?" Lacy was amazed at the ease with which she spoke to Bennett, but this was important.

He was *the one,* and she'd do whatever it took to convince him of that. Even if it meant pretending that she wasn't particularly interested. The logic was perverse, but CeeCee knew what she was talking about. Men battled for the honor of dating her.

"It's the way you blush every time I look at you. The way you can't hold my gaze for long. Like right now."

What the hell? In for a penny, in for a pound. She picked up her half-filled wineglass, downed the contents then swung her gaze to meet Bennett's.

It took everything she could muster not to cough and sputter. The tepid liquid burned her throat, and she tried not to blink. She had to maintain eye contact to convince him she was wild and bold, not shy and reticent.

He stared at her.

She stared right back.

The room seemed inordinately warm and humid, steamy almost, and the music was too loud. They were stuck in motionless observation. Glued.

His eyes peered deeper and deeper. He was inspecting her, scavenging her face for clues to her emotions.

He did not want to get involved in a long-term relationship. He was looking for something casual, light.

He'd made himself perfectly clear. To pretend she wanted the same thing was folly, and yet, if she did not, he would not ask her out. She harbored no doubts about that.

Getting him to date her was the key. Once they went out, once Bennett got to know her, then he would learn that he could not live without her. He would move to Houston and finish his residency here. He would discover there were no obstacles to their love.

According to the women in her family, the thunderbolt was never wrong. Going out with him on the pretext that she was expecting nothing more than a good time couldn't backfire.

This would work.

Then something horrifying occurred to her. What if he was married and looking to cheat on his wife with her? Maybe he just wanted an out-of-town affair.

Lacy narrowed her eyes at him. "You're not married, are you?"

He chuckled. "No."

She let out her breath. Thank heavens for that. But she had to act nonchalant, as if she wouldn't mind dating a married man because she was that disinterested in a long-term romance.

"Because it wouldn't matter to me if you were," she fibbed, and hoped the heavens would forgive her a few off-white lies. It was for a good cause, after all.

"Really?" He looked surprised for the third time that night.

"Yes."

"I would never have believed it. You're an enigma, Lacy Calder. Sweet on the outside, naughty on the inside." He wagged a finger at her and grinned. "My grandmother used to say, 'Always watch out for the quiet ones, Bennett, they'll fool you every time.'"

"Your grandmother is very wise," Lacy said.

"Was. She passed away five years ago."

"Oh, I'm sorry. Were you close?"

"Very. She practically raised me."

"What happened to your parents?" Relief washed over Lacy. Conversation was easier when they spoke of family.

"Mom and Dad are both physicians. Their work usually came before changing diapers. Or their marriage, for that matter. They got divorced while they were still in med school. I was two at the time. They were going to put me in day care, but Nanna had a fit and insisted she be allowed to take care of me instead."

"Do you have any brothers or sisters?"

"Only child. How about you?"

"I'm the second out of six. Two sisters, three brothers."

"Must have been fun growing up in a huge brood." Bennett sounded wistful.

"It had its moments." Lacy smiled, thinking of her boisterous childhood.

"Nanna was my best friend."

She liked hearing about his grandmother and how much he had loved her. It reaffirmed her belief in the rightness of her feelings for him. Bennett Sheridan *was* the man of her dreams.

"Nanna sounds like a very special lady." Lacy understood. She was very close to every one of her grandparents.

"She was." A sad expression crossed his face.

A bold thought occurred to her. *Touch his hand, Lacy. Comfort him.*

Her fingers ached to follow her brain's command, but did she have the guts? Mentally bracing herself, she reached out and covered his left hand with her right.

Mistake!

A big one.

Alarm bells went off. Fireworks of which she'd never experienced the like shot through her. Suddenly all colors shone brighter, all sounds were magnified, all aromas smelled stronger.

Disco lights flashed from the dance floor. The throbbing beat vibrated up through the floor. Voices buzzed around them. In the cramped room, she smelled beer and popcorn, cigarettes and aftershave.

He felt it, too. She saw the flicker of response in his eyes. They were instantly forged. She to him. He to her. Cemented. Bound. Joined.

No escape.

Her breath flew from her body. All moisture evaporated from her mouth. Her skin tingled at the feel of his muscular hand beneath her own. Her heart leaped at his spicy, clean scent.

"I want you," he said, "very much."

He wanted her. She saw the desire in Bennett's handsome face and knew it was true. She shivered. All her life she'd hoped yet feared that she would one day be the target of such stark desire.

Lacy had ached for the thunderbolt to crash into her life, while at the same time dreading the inherent loss of control that accompanied such a phenomenon.

She couldn't take it. Could not keep staring into those eyes. She dipped her head.

Lacy knew she should say something, should respond to his bold declaration, but her shyness flooded back, more vicious than ever. She simply could not speak.

Trepidation welded her teeth shut. She wanted him, too. More than he would ever know. But if she told him that she accepted his proposal, if she agreed to his no-strings-attached proposition, could she surely change his mind? Was the thunderbolt really as infallible as her family insisted? Could she, after all, trust her emotions? Was she willing to proceed on blind faith?

"Lacy?" He softly called her name. He'd taken her hand in his and was gently caressing her fingers with his thumb. "Did you hear what I said?"

"Uh-huh." That utterance was all she could manage.

"I want you so badly I can taste it, but I refuse to hurt you. If this isn't what you want, Lacy, if you are looking for something special, then now is the time to tell me.''

What to say? If she agreed to a frivolous fling, she could end up with a broken heart despite what her family said about the thunderbolt being a sure thing. What if this feeling she had for Bennett was not the thunderbolt at all but merely a severe case of unadulterated lust?

If that were true, Lacy had never lusted after anyone before, not even a movie star. This *thing* she had for Bennett was mental as well as physical. At least two dozen times over the five weeks she had anticipated his every need in the operating suite, handing him instruments before he had even asked for them.

A rational-minded individual like Janet with a healthy skepticism for something as fanciful as the thunderbolt might argue that Lacy was such a good scrub that she automatically knew what any physician would need under the circumstance. But it was more than that. In her mind, she could hear Bennett say ''Kelley clamp'' or ''Abbott retractor'' before the words came from his mouth. Once he needed a rarely used tool, and she'd placed it in his hand before he'd even finished asking if she had one on her tray.

That's how closely attuned they were to one another.

''I'd like to get to know you better,'' he said.

''Me, too. That is, er, you, I mean, not me,'' she stammered.

''Will you dance with me?'' He smiled.

Things were moving way too fast. Flustered by the pressure of Bennett's hand on hers, disturbed by her vacillating emotions, swamped by shyness, Lacy knew she had to get away from his distracting physical presence so she could think this through.

Frightened that she might say yes before she had time to consider the consequences, she pushed back her chair and got to her feet. The way she was going, if he asked her to shimmy out of her black lace panties she would break her neck complying.

"Lacy?" A frown creased his handsome brow. "Are you all right?"

"Bathroom," she said.

A rowdy drunk winding his way through the tables bumped into the back of her chair. Lacy teetered on her absurdly high heels.

"'Scuse me," the drunk mumbled, then lost his balance and stumbled against her.

"Oh!" Lacy breathed.

She saw alarm on Bennett's face, watched him push back his chair and lift his hands to catch her as she tumbled headlong into his waiting arms.

MOMENTUM drove Lacy's backside into his lap. Her legs flew into the air, exposing yards of creamy skin. Reflexively, Bennett's arm curled around her waist, and he cradled her against his elbow.

"You're all right," he whispered.

The sexy feeling of his rock-hard thighs beneath her soft buttocks robbed her of all speech. An acute throbbing sensation hummed straight up through her bottom, and unless Lacy was mistaken, she had raised an equally compelling reaction in him.

He wanted her.

Their gazes collided. She saw desire in his face—hungry, raw, dangerous. Her excitement vaulted into overdrive. Not even in her wildest fantasies had she imagined it could be like this.

Don't blush, don't blush, don't blush, Lacy mentally begged herself.

How could she convince Bennett she was a free-wheeling party girl if her cheeks turned crimson at the slightest provocation? She had to prove that she was brash, brave and bewitching. She could not risk retreating into her protective shell of shyness. Not unless she wanted to chance losing him forever.

Bennett had made it clear enough he wasn't interested in long-term commitment. Of course, he didn't know about the thunderbolt yet, but he would soon enough. Until the feeling caught him the way it had snared her, she had to convince him that she was anything but the marrying kind. All Lacy needed was a toehold. Once Bennett opened up and gave her the opportunity, he couldn't help but fall in love with her.

It was fated. She was his destiny.

But what to do? How would an outrageous, adventuresome, no-strings-attached girl act? How could Lacy convince him that she was spontaneous, free-wheeling and took life as it came?

Kiss him, some impish voice in the back of her mind

ordered. *Kiss him. Kiss him hard. Kiss him long. Leave no doubts about your intentions.*

It would be so easy. They were already pretty darned intimate with her body snuggled tightly against his and her right arm wrapped around his neck.

All she had to do was lean forward and gently run her tongue along his lips. Not that difficult, really, especially when she wanted to kiss him more than she wanted to breathe.

Lacy hesitated.

Bennett's respirations, she noted, were as erratic as her own, and he hadn't removed his gaze from her face since she'd tumbled headlong into his lap.

Kiss him. On the mouth. In front of everyone. That's what a vamp would do.

Lacy the vamp? The label felt unnatural and yet kissing him felt so right.

She was scared. If she were standing, her knees would be knocking in a deafening cacophony. Lacy could count the number of times she'd been kissed on one hand, and not once had she been the instigator.

Most of the kisses had been perfunctory good-night-after-a-date kisses. None of them had been mind-blowing. Truthfully, Lacy had never really *wanted* to kiss a man the way she wanted to kiss Bennett, but her natural reticence held her back.

Her shyness had always been a safety net, something she could count on when she got in over her head. Well, not any more. The time had come to take control of her future. This was the man she'd waited her lifetime for.

No more stalling. No more fanciful daydreams. No more lonely nights. Not if she acted now. She had zero to lose and everything to gain. Might as well plunge right into deep water and see if she could float.

Tentatively, Lacy dampened her upper lip with the tip of her tongue.

Ready or not.

Bennett gave her a knowing smile.

Lacy knew there could be no halfway measures. If she kissed him, it had to be all or nothing. No half-hearted joining of their mouths would do. If she wanted to convince Bennett that she was indeed a woman seeking a casual liaison, then she had to act that way.

Pretend to be someone else. You're acting. You're not Lacy Calder, shy scrub nurse, kissing Bennett Sheridan, handsome physician.

Lacy lowered her eyelashes and gave Bennett a come-to-me-big-boy glance from the corner of her eye.

His body tensed beneath hers, and his arms tightened around her waist. His gaze acquired a hazy, hungry quality like a starving man offered a full plate at the king's banquet.

People were watching. She felt the heat of their collective stares, and her skin prickled with awareness. Normally, Lacy would have been consumed by anxiety at being the center of attention, but resting here in

Bennett's lap, staring up into eyes as dark as a cayuse pony's, she felt so wonderful that all self-recrimination vanished.

If the crowd was wishing for a show, then by golly she would give them one.

Drawing in a deep breath for courage, she pursed her lips.

Bennett swallowed. His Adam's apple bobbed.

Anticipation. So sweet.

Later, thinking back on the moment, Lacy couldn't really say who kissed whom. She raised her chin. Bennett lowered his face, and their lips became one, melding into a blur of soft flesh—sizzling, powerful, electric.

Act the part. You're a femme fatal. A heartbreaker. A collector of men's affections. Give him all that you've got.

It was as if the entire universe was shoving her forward. An aching, urgent need she could not explain gripped her with primal lust. Amazed at her own boldness, Lacy poked out her tongue, urging his lips to part, to allow her entry.

Eagerly, he complied.

Her tongue slipped into the warm, moist recess of his mouth, and she inhaled his sigh.

He smelled heavenly and tasted even better, a soothing mixture of poppy seeds, soap and homemade bread. His flavor reminded Lacy of her great grandmother's kitchen.

Great-Gramma Kahonachek had come to America

from her native Czechoslovakia. She canned her own pickles, baked her own yeast bread and made her own soap. Why Bennett Sheridan should smell like that unusual concoction, Lacy didn't know, but the aroma produced in her the warm, welcoming sensations of home.

Home. Yes. She'd found home in his arms.

Greedily, Lacy quaffed from him. At last. At long last. Her fantasy man had come to life.

Her eyes drifted closed as she rode the rising wave of euphoria. The sensation transported her far beyond the bar and into a place so magical she'd have sworn she was dreaming.

Bennett's mouth roved over hers, deepening the kiss. He hoisted her flush against his firm chest. Even through their clothing she could feel the rapid-fire pounding of his heart.

He was so strong, so virile. He made her feel as treasured as a five-year-old's favorite teddy bear.

Everything in her responded. Her nipples hardened. Her breathing quickened.

Blood rushed to the surface of her skin, bathing her in exquisite heat. An intense wave of longing crested deep inside her.

Lacy had never known it could be like this. This all-encompassing love, this crazy, cockeyed thrill, this incredible sense of rightness.

There was no doubt in her mind that Bennett Sheridan was her other half, her soul mate, her true love, even if he wouldn't admit it yet. He was too caught up in his career, too worried about hurting her to take a chance on love, but Lacy knew better. She would use any means at her disposal to win him over, including pretending to be something she wasn't.

He would forgive her in the end. He had no choice. The thunderbolt had struck.

BENNETT SHERIDAN was a goner.

Kissing Lacy was like taking the express elevator straight to heaven. She lifted him up, gave his soul wings. Adrenaline and testosterone shot through his system, propelling him to a level of arousal usually reserved for sex-starved teenage boys. He was flying, gliding on top of the world. Unfortunately, that only meant he faced a long downward plunge.

His head reeled. His gut clenched. His loins flamed. His heart hammered.

And all for want of this wild little blonde thrashing madly about in his arms.

He had to break the kiss, had to get fresh air, had to do something before he ravished her right there on the table.

Gasping, he wrenched his mouth from hers.

Applause broke out around them, and Bennett found himself blushing. He had never been so influenced by his passion.

Ever.

He prided himself on being a rational man, fully in control of himself and his actions, and yet in one brief moment, Lacy Calder had stripped him of that illusion.

He was no better than a wild stag in the woods rutting for a willing doe.

His fingers were trembling. He jammed them through his hair and struggled desperately to correct the imbalance that had knocked his world out of kilter.

Lacy was breathing hard, her chest rising and falling fast as a rabbit's, her cute backside resting in his lap.

Had she felt his arousal? Was she aware of exactly what she'd done to him? How could she not know? The evidence was as obvious as the nose on his face.

What an unpredictable woman. When he had first stepped into the operating suite at Saint Madeleine's and she'd barely mustered the courage to tell him her name, he had labeled her sweet, shy and innocent.

A nice girl. The type of girl a guy took home to meet his mother. A happily-ever-after sort of girl.

A woman to avoid.

But Lacy Calder had fooled him. Completely.

Apparently, she hid more behind that surgical mask then he could have guessed. Beneath that quiet, well-bred exterior lurked a lusty spirit.

Her kiss told him so.

The minute Lacy tumbled into his lap he'd known he was going to kiss her. He'd been fighting the urge for over a month. What had caught him off guard was the realization that she wanted to kiss him, too.

And then their lips had met.

Bennett had been knocked down by the flood of her fervor. Her lips met his with an intensity that caught him off guard and kept him there.

Ravenously, he had embraced the delightful shock of her unbridled desire. Lacy had been the one to introduce tongues into the fray, not he, her warm moistness ambushing him, taking his breath.

Innocent? Not likely. This woman knew exactly what she wanted.

Him!

How could he have read her so wrongly? How had he mistaken this provocative siren for the timid girl next door? The paradox that was Lacy Calder both pleased and perplexed him.

Bennett wanted her as much as she wanted him, and yet something urged him to be cautious.

Be careful, tread lightly, don't lose your head. Or your heart. Remember, you promised Nanna you wouldn't marry until you'd completed your education.

But this was great, wasn't it? To discover that the woman who had so captivated him was not out-of-bounds after all? Learning that Lacy was not the marrying kind, that he could indeed act on these feelings she stirred inside him without fear of karmic reprisal or breaking her heart should have him ecstatic.

Instead, an odd wistfulness crept through him, and he couldn't say why.

He sneaked a peek at her. Her hair was sexily mussed, her lips sashay red and slightly swollen. Lips that brought back the delicious memories of his favorite childhood flavors. Cherry soda and cinnamon jawbreakers and strawberry Pixie Stix.

And those eyes, the soothing blue of Bavarian mist, drilled a hole straight through him.

She desired him.

No woman kissed a man she barely knew that brazenly unless she was prepared to take the relationship to a higher plane.

But before he could accept the invitation her kiss offered, he had to be sure that was indeed what she wanted. He refused to end up with a guilty conscience.

Having a great time in bed was all well and good but it only worked if both partners knew the affair was strictly for fun.

Before he and Lacy took this relationship one step further, they needed to talk. But not in this noisy bar with a throng of nosy rubberneckers.

"Lacy," he said, "would you like to go someplace a little more private?"

4

_____

SINCE THEY'D BOTH ridden to the nightclub with other people and neither had a car, Bennett offered to walk Lacy home via a detour along the river promenade.

A full moon hung in the sky, illuminating the water in a silvery shimmer. This newly renovated area of the hospital district had the quaint feel of a European village. Street lamps lighted their way along a cobblestone path. Here and there, scattered footbridges arched across the river. Trendy shops, locked tight at nine o'clock, sat bunched atop the retaining wall.

A slight breeze softly caressed their skin. From several yards away they could still hear the vibrating bass emanating from the Recovery Room.

Lacy recognized the melody. An old Rod Stewart tune. "Tonight's the Night."

"It's nice out here," Bennett commented.

"Uh-huh."

Since telling CeeCee and Janet that Bennett was going to see her home and leaving the nightclub behind, Lacy's shyness had returned with a vengeance. Without the insulation of CeeCee and Janet, without the boisterous background noises as a buffer, Lacy felt vulnerable, exposed.

She wanted to be here. Oh, yes. Above anyplace else in the world, but she was unsure of herself. Too bad the thunderbolt didn't come with detailed instructions.

She found herself alone with a man she barely knew but with whom she ached to become better acquainted.

Yet in an odd way, she did know him. In her heart. In her soul. If there was such a thing as past lives, then she and Bennett had been lovers in a previous one. Lacy had never felt such an instantaneous connection to another human being.

Her joy fizzed like uncorked champagne.

What should she say? What should she do? What did he expect from her?

But she needn't have worried. Conversation was unnecessary. So was action. Bennett took charge. He reached over and lightly enfolded her palm in his.

It felt so good. Her small hand enveloped in his large one. A perfect fit.

They ascended the walkway in silence, savoring each other's company.

Crickets chirped. In the distance a dog barked.

All anxiety vanished. All doubts evaporated. Peace and contentment stole over her.

"You're easy to be with." Bennett stopped beside a park bench beneath a street lamp. Moths and June bugs flitted through the air. The scent of honeysuckle wafted over from a nearby fence.

"So are you."

"We work well together in surgery."

"Yes."

"It's like a dance."

"A tango."

"You feel it, too?"

She smiled like the Mona Lisa. She didn't mean to be coy; it was just her way.

"I can't help but wonder...." Bennett let his voice trail off.

"What?"

He pulled her close to him and ran a thumb along her jawline. "What it would be like to make love to you."

Lacy sucked in her breath.

No man had ever spoken so boldly to her before. If it had been anyone but Bennett, such a statement would have sent her scampering for cover. But he was entitled to say such things to her.

"Does that scare you?" His eyes glimmered in the moonlight.

Lacy shook her head.

"Because if that's not what you want, then say the word. We don't have to go any further with this...attraction. I know it's mutual. I see my own longing reflected in your eyes."

"Yes," she whispered.

"I want you to know exactly how I feel. You're a beautiful, vibrant, sexy woman. I want to make love to you so badly that I can taste it. But I won't take advantage of you. I won't break your heart. I can offer you nothing but a week.''

Fear raced through her. She peered up, searched his handsome face.

His oaken eyes were serious. Bennett was an honest man.

Shouldn't she be honest with him in return and tell the truth? That she was already well on her way to falling head-over-heels in love with him?

But if she did that, he would bolt. She knew it as surely as her name was Lacy Marie Calder.

''Are you willing, Lacy?'' His breath warmed her cheek.

In answer, she brought his hand to her mouth and gently kissed his knuckles. His skin tasted slightly salty; the hairs on the back of his hand tickled her lips.

''Is that a yes?'' Bennett asked, his voice husky with pent-up emotions.

''My apartment's only a few blocks farther,'' she said, terrified by her unexpected bravery.

Delight crinkled the corners of his eyes, and Lacy's stomach pitched.

What exactly was she letting herself in for?

They strolled along, still hand in hand, gazing at the stars, occasionally glancing at the river. She should have been happy and excited, but Lacy wasn't prepared. Could she really do this? Was she ready to make love to Bennett?

Her body cried yes, yes, yes and her heart leaped with joy at the thought of their joining.

It was her brain, her common sense that held her back. Even though she believed in the thunderbolt and trusted the guidance of her family, a tiny part of her nagged a warning.

Are you sure? Are you truly certain he's the one? There will be no going back. No undoing this once it's done.

"Those shoes look uncomfortable," Bennett said. "You're having trouble maneuvering in those things."

"Me? Oh, no. I wear them all the time," she fibbed, then instantly felt guilty for her additional lie.

"Wearing heels over an inch and a half is bad for your back," he said.

"I thought men liked women in high heels." And big hair and oodles of lipstick and eyeliner. At least that was what CeeCee kept telling her.

He slanted a sideways glance at her calves, and a speculative gleam came into his eyes. A gleam that made her shiver with delight.

"Well, the shoes certainly emphasize what nature gave you," he commented, "but there's no need to hobble yourself for the sake of either fashion or sex appeal."

She almost said, "I couldn't agree with you more." Instead, she simply nodded and took a deep breath.

"Why don't you take them off," he suggested.

"No." She shook her head, despite the fact the shoes were chewing the skin off her toes. She would look too silly padding along panty-hose footed beside him. He was already a good head taller than she. "I'm fine."

"Ready to keep walking then?"

She nodded.

Bennett tucked his arm through hers, and they continued their stroll. Lacy concentrated on each step, cautiously placing her feet on solid ground. She didn't want to break her neck at this stage of the game. Not when she'd finally gotten him alone.

Except she had a major problem.

Now that she had him, what was she going to do with him?

Through lowered lashes, Lacy peeked surreptitiously at him. His profile was cast in shadows but she could still make out his regal nose, his firm jawline, his masculine lips.

She knew zip about seducing a man beyond what she'd seen on television shows or read in *Cosmopolitan*. Game playing was not in her nature, nor was manipulation. She longed for CeeCee and Janet's advice. They had gotten her into this mess.

The wind gusted, snatched at the bow in her hair.

She reached back a hand to hold the bow in place, but it slipped through her fingers and went skittering across the sidewalk.

"Oh, dear," she murmured, anxious to put a little distance between herself and Bennett. Anything to give her time to think. "My great-gramma gave me that bow."

Forgetting about her precarious high heels, Lacy

slipped her arm from Bennett's grasp and charged after her errant hair ribbon.

The bow blew off the sidewalk and tumbled toward the wooden railing separating the path from the river embankment. It hung for a moment on a tall clump of grass. Just as she got close enough to reach for it, the wind gusted again, and the bow took off, seemingly taunting her.

Lacy lurched over the soft ground, damp from recent rains, determined to retrieve her bow before the wind sailed it into the river below.

"Lacy," Bennett called, "be careful."

But his warning came too late. The heel of her right shoe sank to the hilt. She jerked her leg forward in an attempt to extract herself.

The other heel stuck, too.

She stood with her legs three feet apart, barely able to stand.

She tottered to the right. Lacy windmilled her arms, tried to correct and overcompensated. Her balance swung to the left.

The next thing she knew, she was falling forward. Her left foot had pulled free of the infernal high heels, but her right foot, oh, her poor right foot, was still strapped into the shoe, which was twisted at a very odd and uncomfortable angle.

She lay on the ground, face down in the dirt, her bottom sticking in the air, dress hiked around her waist, her black lace Victoria's Secret panties clearly on display.

Ducky. Just ducky.

"Lacy," Bennett exclaimed. Immediately, he was on his knees beside her, his hands going to her foot, undoing the buckle at her ankle.

"I got the bow." She scrambled to pull her dress down and maneuver herself into a sitting position without putting any weight on her foot. She held up the wayward hair ribbon and tried her best to ignore the intense throbbing in her right ankle.

"I hope the bow was worth spraining your ankle over." Gently, Bennett manipulated her foot.

"Ow!"

"I'm sorry."

"How bad is it?" She struggled to peer over his arm, then gasped when she saw her ankle had already mushroomed to grapefruit size.

"Hard to tell. With luck, no worse than second degree."

"Oh, no," she moaned. "I won't be able to work."

"Surely you've got sick time available."

He didn't understand. She didn't care about missing work. What she cared about was missing him. He only had another week left in his rotation at Saint Madeleine's. If she wasn't able to go to work, she'd probably never see him again after tonight.

Her bottom lip quivered at the very thought, and she feared she might burst into tears.

"It's okay to cry," Bennett said. "I know it hurts like the dickens. I sprained my knee skiing one Christmas."

The ankle pain she could handle. It was the other pain, the one deep in her heart, that made her want to cry. She could not let him slip through her fingers. If she had to, she would limp to work on crutches.

"Let's get you home." He slid one arm under her knees, the other around her back.

"Wait, my shoes."

He scraped the mud off CeeCee's high heels as best as he could and handed them to Lacy. They were worse for the wear. Then he bent, scooped her into his arms and rose to his feet.

"Where to?" he asked.

"You can't carry me the whole way," Lacy protested.

"Nonsense. You don't weight much more than a hundred pounds."

"A hundred and seven," she corrected. "And my apartment in the River Run complex is three blocks away. Just leave me here and go back to the Recovery Room and get my friends." She didn't want him to go, but neither did she want to give him a herniated disk.

"Don't be silly. I'm not about to leave you sitting out here alone in pain in the middle of the night." His tone brooked no argument.

My hero, my Prince Charming, my thunderbolt.

He held her close to his chest and started walking.

Her legs dangled over his bulging forearms. By this point, her ankle was pulsing with pain at every beat of her heart.

What a ninny. She had to be the klutziest woman on the face of the earth. But the wondrous effects of being held so close to the man she loved outweighed the downside of a sprained ankle.

"I know you're hurting," Bennett said. "The best way to deal with that is to distract yourself. Close your eyes."

She peered at him.

He looked down and smiled. They had already covered half a block, and he wasn't even winded.

"Close 'em," he commanded.

She obeyed, letting her eyes drift shut.

"Okay," he soothed. The sound of his voice rumbled in his chest, lulling her. "I want you to think of your favorite place. A beach, a meadow, a mountain. Do you have a mental picture?"

Her favorite place? Why, right here in his arms. But yes, she'd play along. "Uh-huh."

"What do you see?" he asked.

See? Hmm, it was hard to visualize when there were so many distractions, the least of which was her sore ankle. Unable to make a picture of her own, she stole one from Great-Gramma Kahonachek.

"A meadow in the mountains with a brook trickling through it." She recited by heart the description of Great-Gramma's girlhood home outside Prague.

"Very good," Bennett said.

What was very good was the delicious way he smelled and the sound of his voice wrapping around her ears like the most lyrical of melodies.

"What time of day is it?" he crooned softly.

"Early afternoon."

"And the time of year?"

"Spring."

"Can you feel the sun on your skin? Can you smell the scent of lilies in the air? Can you hear cattle lowing in the field?"

Lacy tried to concentrate on the mental image, but what she felt were Bennett's arms holding her secure as steel cables. What she smelled was the fresh scent of starch on his crisp white shirt. What she heard was his guiding voice, distracting her from the pain in her ankle.

"Yes," she said. "I'm there."

"And we're here."

"Where?" She opened her eyes, and sure enough they were standing in front of her apartment complex.

"Which apartment?" he asked.

"Two seventeen."

"It *would* be on the second floor." He grimaced but he certainly didn't look as if he'd just carried a one-hundred-and-seven-pound woman three blocks.

"You can put me down. I'm sure I can make it from here."

"No way."

"Please, Bennett, you've already done more than enough."

"Don't argue with me, Lacy." He started up the steps.

She thrilled at his forcefulness. Here was a man who

took care of his lady. No doubt about it. He made her feel safe, protected.

"Keys?" He stopped outside her door.

She fished in the tiny shoulder purse and extracted her keys. She was startled to see her hand tremble. She'd never brought a man to her apartment before. Ever. Not that anything was going to happen between them now that she'd sprained her ankle. Lacy was both relieved and distressed at this realization.

He took the key from her and braced one knee against the door frame. He juggled her against his leg to get one hand free in order to open the door.

A few seconds later he swung the door inward, shifted her in his arms once more and stepped over the threshold.

"Hang on," she said. "I'll get the light." Fumbling along the wall in the darkness, she found the switch and bathed the room in unexpectedly brilliant illumination.

They both blinked, then Bennett kicked the door closed with his heel, effectively shutting out the rest of the world.

"Would you like something to drink?" she asked. "Coffee, tea, soda? I'm afraid I don't have any beer."

"You're not up to playing hostess." He stepped across the room to settle her onto the sofa. "How about I brew you a cup of hot tea and then have a closer look at that ankle?"

"That sounds heavenly," she admitted. The only man who'd ever made tea for her was her father.

Bennett took CeeCee's shoes from her hands and tossed them in the corner. Then he plumped up two sofa pillows around her before peering at her ankle.

"The panty hose have got to come off."

Lacy looked into his eyes. How was she going to get them off by herself? Yet how could she ask him to help her?

He didn't even give her a chance to waffle. He leaned over and ran his hands up her legs.

She squirmed, giggled.

"Ticklish?" His grin made her insides quiver.

They were face-to-face, Lacy leaning back against the couch, Bennett bent over her, his hands under her skirt, fingers searching for the waistband of her pantyhose.

"Good thing there's no one to walk in on us and misinterpret this situation," he said.

"Good thing," she repeated breathlessly.

What if her mother could see her now? Or her grandmother Nony, or her great-gramma Kahonachek. Would they be shocked at her behavior?

Or pleased?

Bennett's unintentional caress built a heated fire inside her. Lacy had to bite her bottom lip to keep from moaning her pleasure. Oh! When would he finish this exquisite torture?

At last his fingers curled around the top of her panty hose, and he began to peel them off.

"Can you raise your hips?"

Using her good foot as a fulcrum, Lacy lifted her bottom off the couch.

Bennett's hands glided over her derriere, sending spirals of delight skyrocketing straight to her bones. He inched the panty hose down, past her thighs, over her knees, then carefully eased them off her ankles.

He rolled the panty hose into a tidy ball and dropped it on the floor beside CeeCee's shoes. He took a third pillow and slid it under her right foot.

"Try to keep your ankle elevated. I'll bring an ice pack along with the tea. Although by the size of that ankle you may have passed the point where ice will be effective. Do you have a heating pad?"

Lacy nodded, too overcome by the tender way he cared for her to even speak.

Don't take it personally, Lacy. He's a doctor. He's supposed to take care of people. That's what he does.

Bennett disappeared into her tiny kitchen, and she heard him opening cabinet doors, running water, turning on the microwave. She leaned back against the pillows, gritting her teeth against her aching ankle. Now that he wasn't coaching her through visualization techniques and his comforting presence was several feet away, the pain attacked with a vengeance.

"Do you take milk or sugar?" he asked.

"Plain is fine, thanks."

There came the sound of her sliding glass door opening. "Hey," Bennett said, "you've got a balcony."

"Yes," she called. "It's what attracted me to this apartment."

"And you've got a herb garden out here. Rosemary, dill, thyme."

"How did you know?" she asked, pleased and thrilled that he was so knowledgeable about plants. Lacy often dreamed of the day when she would have her own plot of land and could raise a real garden.

The microwave dinged, and a second later Bennett came into the room with a cup of hot water and a tea bag in one hand, a makeshift ice pack fashioned from ice cubes wrapped in a kitchen towel in the other hand.

"My grandmother," he replied in answer to her earlier question. "She had a green thumb. Some of the happiest days of my life were spent puttering in the garden with her. Of course she had me convinced I was the world's greatest weed puller." He handed her the cup, then took a seat beside her on the sofa. Carefully, he applied the ice pack to her swollen ankle.

He looked downright boyish with that wide smile and his hair falling across his forehead. Lacy had a hankering to reach over and gently brush the errant lock aside. Instead, she focused on dunking the tea bag into the water.

"I bet you *were* the world's greatest weed puller." She could see him now. Dark-haired and small, smiling at his grandmother, a handful of crabgrass clutched in his chubby palm. She caught her breath at the notion that someday she might have a miniature Bennett of her own, helping her in their garden.

"I smelled tomato plants when I was on the patio, but I didn't see them. Where are they?" he asked. "There's no mistaking that distinctive aroma."

"Along the outside rail." His interest in her garden tugged at her heartstrings. How could her feelings for him be wrong? A man who loved plants as much as she did? He had to be the thunderbolt.

"What kind of tomatoes?" He gently rotated her ankle. Lacy barely realized he was engaging her in conversation about the tomatoes so he could keep her mind occupied while he examined her ankle.

"Cherry and porter. My favorites."

"Mine, too."

"No kidding?"

Their eyes met.

Oh, heavens, she thought. *He's too wonderful. I'm going to ruin this somehow.*

"When do you have the time," he asked, "to garden? I mean between nursing and going out so often."

Lacy gulped and shrugged. She wanted to tell him the truth. That she didn't go out often. That if it weren't for CeeCee and Janet all her spare time would be spent either at the hospital or puttering around her apartment. Instead, she said, "The plants don't take up much time."

"Still," he insisted. "Most of the career women I've known don't have much time for anything else. I haven't quite figured you out."

"What do you mean?"

He waved a hand at her skimpy dress. "You look

like a sultry siren, and heaven knows you kiss like one, but you raise tomatoes, you're very polite and you don't drink much.''

''Those things aren't mutually exclusive.''

''I know, it's just that...'' An expression she couldn't decipher crossed his face.

''What?''

''Never mind.'' He got to his feet. ''You're going to need an anti-inflammatory for the swelling and you could probably do with a pain pill. I noticed there's an all-night drugstore next door to the hospital. I could go there, get your prescriptions and be back in thirty minutes. Will you be okay?''

''Fine. But you don't have to go to all that trouble. My friends should be home soon. They'll check in on me.''

''It's no trouble, Lacy. None at all. I want to help.''

What could a girl say to a gallant offer like that? Lacy smiled and nodded.

''Are you allergic to any medication?'' He paused at the door to ask.

''No.'' She shook her head, distracted by the handsome figure he cut standing in the archway.

''Hang in there, kiddo.'' He smiled, and her heart swelled to capacity. ''I'll be back in flash.''

He shut the door behind him, and Lacy let out a deep breath. At last she had Dr. Bennett Sheridan exactly where she wanted him, and all she'd had to do was sprain her ankle.

But the accident that had produced short-term results in the end boded long-term disaster. If she did not manage to capture his heart tonight, in all likelihood she would probably never see him again.

5

IN A DAZE, Bennett Sheridan wandered the streets of Houston, his mind befuddled, bewitched, beguiled.

He walked down the block, past an all-night convenience store and gas station. He couldn't stop thinking about Lacy and that smokin' green dress and those make-love-to-me-big-boy shoes. And that black lace underwear he had caught a quick peek of when she had taken that tumble in the grass beside the river. Who would have guessed she was a Victoria's Secret aficionada?

And those panty hose he'd had to remove. Whew!

Even at the memory, his body exploded with a sultry heat. He recalled massaging his hands up her silky thighs, peeling the panty hose over her legs like he was unwrapping expensive Swiss chocolates.

And the way she giggled. The sound had affected him like the effervescent giddiness of the finest French champagne.

She'd responded to his touch. There'd been no mistaking her languid movements, the ardent glimmer in her gaze, the deep, whispered intake of breath when his hands had briefly grazed her bottom.

Bennett groaned inwardly and fisted his palm against his forehead.

He wanted her. Too much.

No matter how hard he tried, he couldn't seem to consider anything but those innocent eyes blatantly contradicting that wickedly sexy kiss she'd plastered on his lips back at the bar.

She was as changeable as quicksilver. Shy one minute, strangely bold the next. He couldn't begin to explain her or his dangerously strong desire for her.

He remembered the feel of her in his arms, her soft derriere cuddled against his flesh. He could still smell her scent on him. He held the sleeve of his shirt to his nose and inhaled deeply.

Roses, soap and pure sensual woman.

Paradise.

But why Lacy? Why here? Why now, when his career aspirations prevented him from getting romantically involved with anyone?

What was it about her that so captivated him? This was not a good sign. Not good at all.

It's been too long since you've had a woman, Bennett, old boy. That's all there is to it. End of story.

He did want her. He wanted her badly. But that wasn't the worst of it. What scared Bennett most of all was the way he longed to take care of her.

"Okay," he muttered under his breath. "Here's what you do. You get the pills, take them back to her, make sure she's set for the night, call her friends to come look in on her, then go the hell home. You've only got a week left in Houston. With that sprained ankle, Lacy won't be back to work for at least that long, and by then you'll be gone. You'll never have to see her again.''

Why was that prospect so unattractive? He should feel relieved, not disappointed.

He wanted to be with Lacy, that's why. Wanted to be with her in every sense of the word.

But a woman like Lacy deserved a man who could give her unlimited attention and undying devotion.

"And you, my friend," he said softly, "are definitely not that man."

THE TELEPHONE jangled only a few minutes after Bennett strode out the front door. Luckily, before he'd left he had positioned the cordless telephone within easy reach.

It rang again.

CeeCee? Janet?

She glanced at the clock on the wall. Ten-thirty. Surely her friends hadn't come home this early on a Friday night.

She picked up the receiver.

"Drahy!"

"Great-Gramma. What are you doing up? It's way past your bedtime."

"Pfft. At my age there is no such thing as bedtime. You fall asleep when you're tried, you wake up when you're ready. Besides, Old Blue Eyes has the colic. He ate your father's bib overalls, metal snaps and all."

"Oh, I'm sorry to hear about Frank Sinatra."

"He'll be all right. What I'm worried about is you."

"Me?"

"Don't play coy, *drahy*. Five weeks ago you call me. Great-Gramma, you say, I've been hit by the thunderbolt. Then nothing. No call. No letter. You don't even e-mail your mother. What's wrong?"

Lacy toyed with her braid. "Well, I don't think Bennett's been struck by the thunderbolt. Can this thing be one-sided, Great-Gramma?"

"No. Absolutely not. He's holding back for some reason. When did you see him last?"

"Well…" Lacy began.

"Tell me everything."

It was easy to unburden herself to her understanding relative. She told her everything before adding, "It's hopeless. How can I make him fall in love with me when I can't even be near him?"

"You're saying he will be coming back to your apartment tonight?"

"Yes."

"Hmm," Great-Gramma commented, her voice changing in pitch. Lacy recognized that curious note. Great-Gramma was up to something.

"Hmm, what?"

"Just interesting to know. That's all."

"What are you planning?"

"Me? Planning? I don't know what you mean. I'm a little eighty-eight-year-old lady. What can I plan?"

"I'm not falling for that," Lacy said.

"Good night, *drahy*. Frank is calling me."

And then the line went dead. Puzzled, Lacy stared at the phone for a moment before switching it off.

Ten minutes later two staccato knocks sounded on the front door.

"Come in," Lacy called from her position on the couch.

The door swung open, and Bennett stepped inside. Immediately, her eyes were drawn like a magnet to his face.

"Hi," he whispered, pushing a strand of hair from his forehead as he closed the door. "How are you feeling?"

"The ankle aches a smidgen."

Actually, it ached a lot, but she didn't want him to label her a crybaby. And, truth be told, the pain seemed to evaporate whenever he was near, her mind occupied with cataloging his virtues instead of dwelling on the ankle, which now resembled a lump of pasty yeast dough.

Bennett crossed the room carrying a white paper sack with an apothecary logo emblazoned on the side. He sat on the floor beside her and pulled two bottles from the bag.

"These should fix you right up. This one is to reduce the swelling, the other is for pain." He tried twisting the lid from the bottle of painkillers. It wouldn't budge. He smiled sheepishly. "Darn childproof caps."

"Push down on the lid with your palm and turn at the same time," Lacy advised.

"Guess it's true what they say. Nurses know more about day-to-day patient care than doctors."

"Doctors have bigger problems than opening pill bottles." Lacy tried not to giggle as he continued to battle the stubborn cap.

"Blast it all," Bennett muttered a few minutes later when he still hadn't wrenched the wretched thing free.

"Would you like me to try?" Lacy reached out to lay a hand on his wrist.

"No, no. I'll subdue it."

The pressure of her hand on his must have flustered him—or at least she hoped that's what had happened—because the harder he struggled, the more stubbornly the plastic cap held.

Finally, exasperated but not ready to admit masculine defeat, he stuck the cap in his mouth.

He looked so completely incongruous, this serious-minded heart surgeon gnawing on a plastic prescription bottle, that Lacy began to laugh.

"You tink dis is funny?" he mouthed around the cap, sounding all the world like a mafioso with a mouthful of cannoli.

She nodded.

His eyes twinkled. He growled low in his throat and attacked the bottle with renewed vigor.

"If you jerk your teeth out," Lacy managed to wheeze between gales of laughter, "I won't be able to drive you to the dentist."

"At weast we got pwenty of pain pills," he replied.

"If we ever get the thing opened."

"I never gib up," he informed her.

Bottle cap planted firmly between his back teeth, Bennett gave a finally twist, and the bottle broke free.

"Yes," he gloated, removing the cap from his mouth and thrusting both hands over his head in a gesture of jubilant victory.

Men, Lacy thought with a bemused shake of her head.

Triumphantly, he doled out two pills. One from each bottle. A blue one for swelling, a white one for pain. "Fresh tea to wash these down with?" He handed them to her.

"This is fine." She picked up her stone cold tea from the coffee table and washed back the tablets.

Bennett eyed her. Lacy was the cutest-looking thing he'd ever seen, propped up on the couch. Too cute. Her sweet, incredible scent pushed him beyond distraction, and he couldn't stop staring at those creamy legs. He should get out of here. Leave this minute. Instead, he found himself saying, "Maybe I should stay the night, make sure you're all right."

"That's really not necessary."

"What if you need to get up in the night? You might fall on your injured ankle and make the sprain worse."

She studied him a moment. "All right."

"Can I get you anything?" he asked. "Something to drink? A snack?"

"Well…"

"What?"

"I would like to get out of this dress and into my pj's."

"Your pajamas. Right." He was talking lickety-split, and he knew it, but he couldn't seem to slow down. The thought of sliding a silky nightshirt over her head had him popping out in a cold sweat. "Where are they?"

"In the bedroom." She pointed down the hall. "In the bureau."

"Be right back." Bennett disappeared down the hall, wondering how he had gotten himself into this sticky-but-not-unpleasant situation, and how he was going to get himself out again.

He flicked on the light in the small bedroom. This place reminded him of the Lacy he knew from the hospital. Old-fashioned. Shy. Sweet.

A queen-size bed sat in the middle of the room, adorned with a patchwork quilt. His Nanna had made quilts, and he recognized the pattern. Double wedding ring, it was called, or something like that.

Lacy's bedroom was impeccable. Nothing out of place. No dust or cobwebs or litter in the wicker wastepaper basket beside her computer desk.

Bennett stepped to the antique bureau in the corner. He pulled open the top drawer, dumbstruck by what he saw.

Panties. Dozens and dozens of panties. Thongs. G-strings. Garters. Scarlet lace. Black satin. Purple silk.

Drawn by an irresistible power, Bennett scooped up a handful and held them against his nose.

They smelled of laundry soap and rose-scented pot-pourri. He inhaled deeply.

The Lacy who owned these garments was not the Lacy he knew from the hospital. This was the Lacy who wore skimpy dresses and spike heels to go dancing with cowboys at the Recovery Room.

Then Bennett caught a glimpse of himself in her mirror, a half dozen pairs of thong undies dangling from his hand, an I've-died-and-gone-to-lingerie-heaven expression on his face. Unnerved, he jammed the panties into the drawer and yanked open the second one, his breath coming in hard, short gasps.

All he could think about was Lacy wearing these delicate things.

He was dead meat.

SHE'D SENT HIM into her bedroom. Alone. To rummage through her underwear drawer.

Lacy's face flamed. What had she been thinking? What if he opened the top drawer and saw all her sexy lingerie? What would be his impression of her?

The painkillers were starting to take effect. Not only had the pain in her ankle decreased measurably, but a giddy, light-headed feeling wrapped warm fuzzy fingers around her.

"Is this all right?" Bennett appeared in the doorway, holding a pink satin teddy edged with crimson lace.

Yikes!

The mere thought of lounging on the couch in front of him wearing that scanty number was more than she could fathom.

"Those aren't pajamas," she blurted.

His face fell. "Oh."

"But it'll do," she found herself saying for absolutely no other reason than to see him smile.

He crossed the room toward her.

Lacy's heart began to pound so loudly she heard her blood strumming through her ears.

He sat beside her on the couch, his body angled toward her head, his trousered leg resting against her hip. All her senses strummed with awareness while at the same time a heady warmth loosened her limbs and her tongue. She floated free, untethered, buoyed by pain pills and the giddiness of his nearness.

Her vision narrowed. She noticed everything about Dr. Bennett Sheridan, from the faint laugh lines etched into the corners of his eyes to the beard stubble gracing his manly jaw.

She also noticed that he looked uncertain and uncomfortable.

"Whaz wrong?" She giggled when she realized she'd slurred her words.

"The pain pills are making you a little punchy."

She nodded. It seemed her head bobbed on a string yanked by an invisible puppeteer. "Uh-huh."

Helplessly, he held her pink satin teddy in front of

him. "How are we going to do this? Would you like me to leave you alone while you, um, get undressed?"

This time, she shook her head. "Gotta have help with this darned zipper."

"Oh. Okay."

Still, he didn't move. He sat there with his eyes fixed on her mouth.

"You can touch me," she said, amazed at her own drug-induced audacity. "I won't bite."

Bennett leaned forward.

"At least not very hard."

HOW ON EARTH was he going to undress her without driving them both wild with desire? The painkillers had taken over. The gleam in her eye was too bright, the way she looked at him too bold.

Keep her talking, Sheridan, he told himself, *and whatever happens do not kiss her.*

"If Dr. Laramie could see you now." Bennett shook his head. "He's under the impression that you're a sweet old-fashioned girl."

Lacy lifted a finger to her lips, which looked especially soft and pliant. "Shh. We'll never tell."

He smiled. "No. It'll be our little secret."

"We've got a secret," she said in a singsong voice then thrust her arms over her head. "Clothes off. Teddy on."

What had he done to get himself in such a predicament?

Oh, yeah, he'd given her medicine for her sprained

ankle but his bungle had been leaving the nightclub with her in the first place. He was much too susceptible to her beguiling charms.

"Come on," she urged, leaning forward and twisting her torso so he could see the zipper behind her.

Hesitantly, Bennett reached out a hand and took the zipper between his thumb and forefinger.

Slowly, he inched the zipper down bit by bit, exposing the narrow expanse of Lacy's soft flesh beneath.

Heat swamped him. He bit the inside of his cheek to keep from groaning aloud.

Get yourself under control, Sheridan. Pronto. Lacy's in a vulnerable state.

Gently, he tugged the dress over her head, his fingertips accidentally grazing her upper arm.

Lacy moaned softly and closed her eyes.

"Are you all right?"

"Perfect." She almost purred.

She was sitting on the couch, her legs propped on the pillow, wearing nothing but a black push-up bra and black lace undies. Her long apple-cider hair cascaded over her shoulders, descending to her waist like a golden curtain.

His fingers burned to touch her. His lips twitched to skate along her skin and taste the salt of her. His nose burned to burrow inside the fresh feminine fragrance of her cleavage.

Bennett swore he had died and zoomed straight to

hell. Where else would he have such an exquisite creature at his fingertips and yet be unable to act on his very masculine desires for her?

His eyes ate her up, taking in the soft swell of her breasts, the luxurious curve of her hips.

Torture. Pure torture.

Cover her up. Quick.

Bennett stared at the tiny pink satin garment in his hand. As if it was going to do anything to cloak that magnificent body. Fervently, he wished for a floor-length flannel granny gown to toss over her.

Fumbling in his hurry, he threaded her arms through the teddy's spaghetti straps, then pulled it over her head.

She honed those breath-stealing eyes on him. "Thank you."

"You're welcome."

"I feel...kinda drunk." She rubbed her forehead with her fingers.

"It's okay. The feeling will pass."

Without warning, she reached up and wrapped her arms around his neck. "Kiss me," she whispered.

In an instant her lips were plastered against his. He wrapped his arms around her and held her close. His mouth came down with a fierceness that frightened yet thrilled him.

If anything, this kiss was even better than the one at the nightclub.

Bennett dissolved like ice in a glass of hot water.

He had no resistance to her. Whatever she wanted, she could have.

Her hands roved over his body, gently exploring. She tasted of orange pekoe and smelled of rose petals. Her tongue teased, drawing him out, rousing myriad sensations inside him.

Her skin, her lips, her fingertips inflamed him. He tingled, burned and ached.

Her breasts swelled against his chest. His pulse pounded in his groin as blood rushed to heat that area of his body. He reacted to her contact like a plant reaching for the sunlight. He awakened to the limitless possibilities of what could happen between them.

Breathing heavily, he broke the kiss.

She grinned. "Hi, thunderbolt."

"Thunderbolt?"

Chucking him under the chin with a finger, she giggled. "Don't pretend you don't know."

"But I don't." What on earth was she talking about?

It's just the pain pills. Humor her until they wear off.

"Admit it," she whispered. "Admit you're thunderbolt."

What the heck was thunderbolt? A horse? Anything to pacify her. "Okay, I admit it. I'm thunderbolt."

"I knew it," she crowed and threw her arms around his neck. "Now take me to the bedroom and make love to me."

"Listen, Lacy." He cleared his throat and slowly disentangled himself from her arms. "Much as I would like to, we can't make love."

"Why not?"

"You're under the influence of painkillers and you don't know what you're saying."

"Yes, I do. I'm serious, Bennett."

He shifted away from her. "I won't be in town much longer and while I think we would have had a great time together in bed, maybe your sprained ankle is a sign."

"A sign?"

"That a sexual relationship between us simply wasn't meant to be."

"I don't understand."

Oh, no. That sad, wide-eyed, lost-puppy look.

"I like you. A great deal. In fact probably too much. Too much to make love to you and then just walk away."

THE ACHE in her ankle was nil compared to the sudden stabbing in her tummy.

"Honestly, I'm a little old-fashioned," Bennett continued. "When I meet a girl I really like and I know that there can't be a future with her I prefer not to take the relationship to the next level."

What was he saying? If he liked her *less* he'd be willing to make love to her?

"There doesn't have to be heartache," she insisted.

No heartache at all. They could make love, fall head over heels in love, get married, have a half dozen babies with his amazing dark eyes and live happily ever after.

Oh, why had she let CeeCee talk her into pretending to be something she wasn't?

He reached out a hand and gently caressed her cheek. "Don't get me wrong, cupcake. I want to make love to you so badly I can taste it, but I don't think it would be in either of our best interests."

"Bennett." She spoke his name because she didn't know what else to say. She had so much to tell him, but she didn't know how to begin to explain the thunderbolt to someone who hadn't grown up believing in its mythical powers, and she could barely keep her eyelids open.

And before she could form a coherent thought, Lacy fell asleep in the circle of his sheltering arms.

THE JANGLING PHONE jerked her awake. She blinked, realized she was snuggled tight against Bennett's chest. Lacy sat up straight, a little disoriented. What had happened? Then she remembered the pain pills and falling asleep in his arms.

Bennett yawned, stretched and checked his watch. "Awfully late for someone to be calling. It's after one a.m."

"It's probably CeeCee or Janet checking to see if I made it home in one piece."

She reached over and picked up the phone. "Hello?"

"Lacy, it's Mama."

Immediately her heart sank. Mama never called after nine o'clock at night. Something must be wrong.

"What is it?" Lacy asked, instantly alert. She placed her palm on the arm of the sofa to brace herself.

"Honey, I've got some bad news."

She felt the color drain from her face, suddenly tasted her own fear. "What?"

"It's Great-Gramma Kahonachek."

Lacy's hands trembled uncontrollably, and she almost dropped the phone. "What's wrong?"

"We were up late tending to last-minute details for our booth at the farm exposition when your great grandmother started having another spell with her heart like she did last spring. She's asking for you. Can you come home right away?"

"I'll be right there," Lacy said. Instantly, her nurse's objectivity kicked in. The family needed her expertise. She switched off the phone and started to bring her feet up, but the pain in her ankle stopped her instantly.

"Something's wrong. You're pale as a ghost." Bennett took her hand. "And you're ice cold. What's happened?"

"It's my great-gramma. She's having chest pains."

"A heart attack?"

Lacy shook her head. "I don't know. She's eighty-eight and takes nitroglycerin tablets for angina. Bennett, she's asking for me.''

The look of concern on his face was so touching that Lacy burst into tears. He gathered her to his chest and allowed her to sob. She soaked his shirt, but he didn't seem to care.

''I lo-love her so much.'' Lacy stammered when she was finally controlled enough to speak.

''I understand.'' He squeezed her hand and hugged her tighter. After what he'd told her about his grandmother, she knew that he truly understood.

''I've got to go home. Right away.''

''Where is home?''

''West, Texas.''

''Where's that?''

''About three hours north.''

''You can't drive.'' He shook his head. ''Not with that ankle.''

She worried her lip with her teeth. ''The closest airport to West is in Waco, almost thirty miles away. I probably won't even be able to get a flight out before mid-morning.''

''I'll drive you.''

His offer touched her more deeply than she could express. ''But I looked at the call sheet before I left work, and I thought you were on call for the transplant team in case a heart comes in for your patient Mr. Marshall.''

''I'm on backup call, and the chances of getting

called in are slim. Besides, I'll have my beeper. I can hop a plane back here if necessary. What is it? A thirty minute flight?''

Lacy nodded.

"I'll call Laramie and tell him what's going on."

"If you're certain." She hated to put him to any trouble, but without him she couldn't get to West before noon, and Great-Gramma needed her now.

"Consider me your personal chauffeur."

THREE HOURS LATER, Bennett guided Lacy's Chevy
Cavalier toward West, Texas. When Lacy told him
that her great grandmother was suffering chest pains,
one thought dominated his mind—help Lacy get home
as soon as possible.

He remembered his own nanna and how grief-
stricken he'd been when she had died. The thought of
what Lacy was going through prompted Bennett's decision to drive her.

But the farther they traveled the more he questioned
the wisdom of his impulsive offer. Not that he minded
going with Lacy. Not in the least.

Fact of the matter, Bennett had a knack for rallying
in a crisis. His calm head in the face of adversity had
earned him the nickname Dr. Cool at Boston General.

No, what bothered him was the instant closeness he
felt to Lacy. Sharing a tragedy could create a special
bond between two people. An unintentional sense of
connection. If he wasn't careful, he could get sucked
into the emotionalism of the moment, and he might
start believing the strange tugging in the general re-

gion of his heart had more to do with Lacy and not the situation at hand.

He had called Dr. Laramie and cleared his absence with the chief surgeon. He would try his best to return to Houston if Mr. Marshall was fortunate enough to get a transplant.

Outside, the moon had slipped behind a covering of clouds, leaving the highway bathed in darkness illuminated only by their headlights. At four-thirty in the morning there weren't many cars on the road. Bennett's window was cracked half an inch, and the earthy smell of fresh loam seeped inside the car.

As they'd driven, Lacy had chattered anxiously, telling him that she'd been raised on a farm in West, a predominantly Czech community, and that most of her family still lived there.

Her grandfather, father and brothers were farmers, she'd said. Her mother and sisters ran a general store in downtown West. And her great grandmother Kahonachek ruled the roost.

He sent a quick glance in Lacy's direction. His emotions were in a peculiar scramble. He felt confused, worried and worst of all, desperately attached to this woman. She lay against the headrest, her hair spilling over the seat in a golden cascade.

Bennett's fingers itched to glide through those silken threads, and the urge to inhale the flowery fragrance of her hair overwhelmed him. Did she have any idea how beautiful she was? Did she possess a single clue how sharply his body responded to hers?

Before they had left her apartment, he had helped her pull a casual floral jumper the color of banana custard over the Cinderella-pink satin teddy. The conservative outfit suited her much better than the racy dress she had worn to the Recovery Room, making her appear softer, more inviting.

He'd also wrapped her swollen ankle with an Ace bandage. Cradling that delicate foot in the palm of his hand had almost been his undoing. He had experienced the strangest urge to plant kisses all the way up that shapely leg to her thigh and beyond. Now, every time he glanced over to check on that sexy little foot, he saw her cute toenails painted a provocative pink peeking over the bandage at him, reminding him of that moment in her apartment.

Her eyes were closed, but Bennett knew she wasn't asleep. Lacy rested, taking long, slow, deep breaths, fortifying herself for what lay ahead. Mesmerized, he watched the rise and fall of her well-rounded breasts, then realized his own breath was coming in short, ragged spurts.

Without knowing what possessed him, Bennett reached over and gently patted Lacy's hand. The touch was like an electric shock—intense, energized, startling.

Her eyes fluttered open. "Thank you for driving me," she murmured, her downy voice breaking the silence that had endured for the past several minutes.

"What are friends for?" he asked.

"Is that what we are?" Her tone teased but the look

in her eyes was serious. "I thought we were just co-workers."

Bennett didn't reply. They were just co-workers. They hadn't known each other long enough to become friends, although not seven hours ago he'd seriously been considering becoming her lover.

He was very glad they hadn't done anything more than kiss. Sexual relationships had a way of escalating in the flare of a crisis, even if neither party was looking to get deeply involved. The drama of sudden illness spotlighted the tenuous link between life and death and sometimes led to impulsive actions.

"You're certainly acting like a friend," Lacy added.

Friends. That was good, wasn't it? Far better to settle for friendship than to make love to her and have to abandon her in a week.

His mind knew this was true, but his anatomy balked. His body wanted hers the way it wanted water and food and oxygen. But sexual need and love were two very different things. His parents had hammered home that truth time and again.

"How much farther?" he asked, hoping to distract himself.

"Almost there." Lacy sat up straighter and stared out the window. "Follow the main road until you come to the third traffic light. Then go three miles out of town. Our farm is on the right."

They would be arriving at the house soon, meeting Lacy's family. Bennett winced at the full impact of what he'd gotten himself into. A total stranger amidst a close-knit group. What would her parents make of him and his relationship to their daughter? Did Lacy bring men home often? Were they accustomed to boyfriends popping in and out of her life?

Damn. This was going to be awkward.

When he had started out last evening with Grant Tennison, Bennett had wanted nothing more than to relax, have fun and reduce stress.

How, then, had he ended up in West, Texas, escorting a young woman he couldn't quite figure out?

"This is it," she said.

Bennett turned down the graveled driveway leading to an apple-butter-yellow, two-story frame farmhouse. A bevy of cars scattered across the lawn. Pink fingers of dawn reddened the eastern horizon. He pulled to a stop beside a weathered pickup truck stocked with farming supplies.

Lacy undid her seat belt and opened her door.

"Sit tight until I can get over there to help you."

He got out and from the corner of his eye noticed a clot of people spill from the house and form on the front porch. Trying his best not to let the audience unnerve him, Bennett scurried to the passenger side.

"If you give me your arm, I think I can hobble up the steps," Lacy said.

"I'm carrying you," Bennett insisted. "I'm the doctor, so don't argue."

"Yes, sir." She grinned at him.

His heart lurched. What was it about her smile that affected him more strongly than the joyous satisfaction

of completing a successful heart operation? The notion
that a woman's smile could be as fulfilling as his career was a new concept.

Cautiously, he maneuvered her free of the car seat,
hoisted her high against his chest and started up the
walkway to the house.

Amid cheers and applause, he stepped onto the
porch, packed with what he could only assume were
Lacy's numerous relatives. Over two dozen people
were talking at once, flinging rapid-fire questions at
them. Before he could even put Lacy down, Bennett
found himself introduced to brothers, father, mother,
sisters, grandparents, cousins, aunts and uncles.

The crowd ushered them into the house.

Dazed, Bennett merely nodded to everything. He,
an only child, had never experienced the like. He remembered Nanna's deathbed vigil, with only he and
his father in attendance, so different from this suppor-
tive gathering.

"Everyone, hold on," Lacy laughed, making the
time-out sign with the fingertips of one hand pressed
into the palm of the other hand. "Time out. How's
Great-Gramma?"

"She's in bed, resting," Lacy's mother answered.
She was a very attractive woman, no taller than Lacy,
with short blond hair barely turning gray at the temples
and a welcoming smile. She'd asked Bennett to call
her Geneva and gently kissed his cheek. In another
twenty years, Lacy would look like her.

"Why didn't you take her to the hospital?" Lacy demanded.

"She refused to go," said Great-Grandpa Kahonachek. "She wanted us to go ahead with the farm expo. You know how stubborn my Katrina can be."

The whole clan bobbed their heads in agreement.

"She insisted she'd be fine as soon as Lacy got here," Geneva Calder said.

"I'll talk to her." Lacy nodded. "You can put me down now, Bennett."

"I'll take you in to see her," Bennett said, not terribly anxious to be left alone with complete strangers. While they seemed friendly enough, they were eyeing him as if he was an exotic zoo animal.

Lacy must have sensed his unease. "Okay. Up the stairs, down the first hall." She pointed to the stairway ahead.

Bennett carted her to her great grandmother's room, careful to turn and step sideways down the hallway so as not to bump Lacy's ankle. Her head rested just below his chin. For no good reason whatsoever, his chest tightened, thick with an unnamed emotion. He wasn't comfortable with this intimacy, and yet she felt so good in his arms, he never wanted to set her down.

He looked at her. Lacy stared at him as if he was a gallant knight who'd slain a hundred dragons on her behalf. Her admiration both unnerved him and filled him with an odd sense of pride. No woman had ever looked at him in quite that way.

What was he thinking? Bennett ripped his gaze from her face, stared at the door standing open a crack.

In unison, Bennett and Lacy peeked inside.

A bright-eyed elderly lady sat propped up in bed, a cat-that-chowed-down-on-Tweetie-bird expression on her face. She looked quite healthy for someone suffering from angina and not unlike a queen holding court.

"Drahy," she exclaimed and motioned them forward. "Come in, come in."

"Drahy?" Bennett murmured under his breath.

"It means 'dear one' in Czech," Lacy whispered. "She calls us all that so she doesn't have to remember names."

"Good ploy considering the amount of progeny she's produced."

"Seven children, twenty-five grandchildren, forty-two great grandchildren. But I'm her favorite."

"I can see why," he whispered, his breath fanning the teeny hairs around her ears.

Lacy turned her head and flashed him a smile.

"Don't stand there whispering. Bring your young man here."

Bennett walked across the room and deposited Lacy on the edge of the bed beside her great grandmother. He realized at once that this wizened matriarch had mistaken him for Lacy's boyfriend.

She picked up a pair of glasses resting on the bed next to her and put them on. She eyed Bennett speculatively, then looked at Lacy.

"Yes," was all she said.

Lacy seemed to understand the code, for she nodded in return, then introduced him.

"Very nice to meet you," Great-Gramma said. "You're good to my Lacy, no?"

"Yes, ma'am." Bennett reverted to the old-school manners Nanna had taught him to use when addressing his elders.

Lacy reached out and took the elderly lady's hand in hers. "How are you, Great-Gramma?"

The woman pressed a dramatic hand to her chest. "Not so good at first, but I'm much better now."

"Why don't you let us take you to the hospital?" Lacy asked.

"No reason for a hospital. You're here. You can help me. You and your young man."

"Mrs. Kahonachek," Bennett said, "I'd advise you to seek professional advice."

"But you're a doctor, no? And Lacy is a nurse. That is professional."

"Well, yes, ma'am, but we don't have the equipment here to examine you properly or to make a correct diagnosis."

The woman's color was good, her respirations even, her smile mischievous. Bennett was beginning to suspect she'd experienced nothing worse than a bad case of indigestion. His own nanna had been known to exaggerate her symptoms when she wanted extra attention.

Still, with a heart patient one should never assume anything.

"I'll get the medical kit from the car," he said. "And be right back to examine you."

"That would be good." She nodded.

Bennett hurried from the house, relieved that Lacy's great grandmother appeared not to be seriously ill.

"Oh, *Drahy.*" Great-Gramma squeezed Lacy's hand once Bennett had gone. "Your thunderbolt is so handsome."

"He is cute, isn't he?"

"I knew for sure if he drove you to see me that he was the one. And he even carried you with your poor hurt ankle."

"Don't worry about my ankle. Tell me more about your chest pain."

Great-Gramma made a wry face. "If I tell you something will you promise not to get mad?"

Lacy studied her great grandmother's face, and a sinking feeling settled into the pit of her stomach. She narrowed her eyes in suspicion. "What did you do?"

Great-Gramma looked to the door. "I'm not really having chest pains," she whispered.

"What?"

"Shh. Nobody knows but your grandmother Nony."

"But why would you fib?" Lacy laid a hand over her own heart. "You scared me to death."

"I'm sorry about that. It was a necessary lie. You told me the thunderbolt was going to walk out of your life forever. I couldn't very well let that happen, could I?''

"So you pretended to have chest pain?" Lacy sank her hands on her hips.

"He won't leave you after this. You are in his blood, *drahy*."

"This isn't right, Great-Gramma, and you know it. If Bennett doesn't fall in love with me on his own, we can't force him."

"Pah. No one is forcing him to do anything. We're just getting him in position for the thunderbolt to smack him."

Lacy stared at her great grandmother in disbelief. "For years you've been telling me that the thunderbolt cannot be denied. That it is infallible."

"It is."

"This doesn't sound infallible to me. In fact, this is beginning to feel more and more like unrequited love on my part."

"Oh, he loves you, too. I can see it in the way he looks at you."

"Then why do we have to play games?"

"Games? No games. You're dealing with a man, *drahy*. God bless their souls, they're often hard to convince, even when something is good for them. They are afraid to let go of their bachelorhood."

"I don't understand."

"They all need a push now and then."

"But before you told me not to do anything, that our love would happen of its own accord."

"And it will." Her great grandmother patted her hand. "I just gave the thunderbolt a little shove. Your great-grandpa Kahonachek, he didn't go down easy, either. Your young man reminds me of him."

Lacy pulled back and stared at the wise old eyes peering at her. "So in other words, Great-Grandpa didn't fall in love with you at first sight."

Great-Gramma waved her hand. "Of course he did, he just had other plans and he didn't want to change them. He was going to become a baseball player. Thought he was the next Babe Ruth." She chuckled at the memory. "But the thunderbolt can't be denied. He came around, and we got married when I turned eighteen. We've been happily married for seventy years on my birthday next month."

"He gave up his dream for you?"

Great-Gramma sighed dreamily. "Now that's love, *drahy*. When a man decides you're more important to him than anything else in the world."

"What did you do to convince him?"

Great-Gramma smile slyly. "We got lost in the Longhorn caverns together. Luckily, I happened to bring along a bottle of wine, a picnic basketfull of his favorite sandwiches and a soft blanket. By the time we found our way out of the caverns, he proposed to me and forgot all about baseball."

"But what if he hadn't given up his dream? What if he had chosen baseball over you?"

"Then you wouldn't be here, would you?" Her great grandmother reached up to brush a lock of hair from Lacy's forehead with dry wrinkled fingers. "Because after I'd been struck by the thunderbolt I knew there was only one man for me. If not Kermit Kahonachek, then I would have remained a spinster."

"Really?"

She shrugged. "He is my soul mate."

"How can you be so sure?" Lacy asked.

"How can you not?"

"Because Bennett has a life of his own, a place of his own in Boston."

"His place is with you. In Boston, in Texas, it makes no difference."

"You don't understand. Things are more complicated than that."

"You think things were easy for your grandmother Nony and Grandpa Jim? They lost a baby in 1948 and almost divorced over the sorrow of it. You think your mother and father didn't have problems? Raising six children isn't easy. The thunderbolt doesn't erase all difficulties, *drahy*. It simply tells you who you're supposed to spend the rest of your life with. It's up to you to make love last."

"That's not the story you've been telling me my whole life! You made it sound so easy, so magical."

"It is if you don't try to complicate matters. There, *drahy*, don't cry." Great-Gramma handed her a tissue from a box resting on the headboard. "It'll all work out, I promise."

"Lacy?" Bennett stood in the door, the black medical bag in his hands. "Are you all right?"

She blew her nose. "Fine. Just a little emotional."

Simply looking at him, his hair falling boyishly over his forehead, that concerned expression on his face, tugged at her heart in inexplicable ways. Her entire body buckled at his presence. Her senses were so heightened that his long, lingering gaze brushed her like a caress. She felt as if she'd waltzed off a precipice into thin air, as if she were tumbling in weightless slow motion, spinning helplessly toward a shattering end.

Yes, she had fallen in love with him at first sight, but there was no guarantee he felt the same way. They'd been tricked into coming here by her great grandmother's artless machinations.

Bennett set the bag on the bed, opened it and removed a stethoscope. Several of Lacy's family members appeared in the doorway, watching the proceedings.

"Hey, Lace." Her youngest brother, Jack, held up a pair of crutches. "Look what I found in the attic."

"Thanks," she said. Now Bennett wouldn't have to carry her everywhere. That thought both saddened and relieved her.

"I smell sausage," Great-Gramma said to Lacy as Bennett pressed the stethoscope to her chest. "Bring me some breakfast."

Lacy shot her great grandmother a dirty look. "Oh, no, you're having chest pains. You can't have sausage."

She wasn't going to let her great grandmother get

away with her meddlesome chest-pain stunt without paying some kind of price. But neither was she going to embarrass her by giving away her secret.

But Lacy did have to get Bennett out of here as quickly as possible. Otherwise, the next thing she knew her family would be ordering flowers, sewing a wedding dress and making an appointment with the preacher.

7

"SHOO!" Lacy's great grandmother made shooing motions with her hands. "Everyone out of here but the doctor. You, too, Lacy."

"But Great-Gramma..." Lacy shot her relative a chiding expression.

"Go."

Bennett winked at Lacy. "Go ahead. We'll be all right."

"Are you sure?"

"Go ahead, have breakfast. I'll be there in a minute." Bennett figured Great-Gramma Kahonachek had something to tell him she didn't want her family to hear.

He watched while Lacy hoisted herself up on the crutches, his eyes drawn to her petite form. How long had it been since he'd felt so helpless, so overwhelmed by desire? He remembered all too well what it felt like to run his hands over her well-rounded body, to taste her lips with his tongue. His fingers tingled at the thought, as did other more southern body parts.

"Close the door," Great-Gramma said, yanking Bennett from his fantasies.

"Yes, ma'am." He did as she asked.

"Now, go over to the bureau and open the jewelry box."

Bennett followed orders, humoring her. The heavy wooden jewelry box tinkled a melody when he opened the lid. He expected some Czechoslovakian tune, but to his surprise he recognized the music from a disco song. Something about thunder and lightning and knocking on wood.

"Move those necklaces and rings aside. There's a false bottom. Lift that out," Lacy's great grandmother instructed.

Bennett obeyed. He lifted up the bottom, and beneath lay a pair of gold cuff links in the shape of lightning bolts. They were unique, unusual.

"I want you to have them," she said.

"Oh, no, ma'am." He turned to face her. "These cuff links look like a family heirloom."

"They're yours," she reiterated. "For taking such good care of my great granddaughter."

Bennett shook his head. He felt very odd, and the cuff links lay strangely warm against his palm.

"Please, don't argue."

"I really appreciate the offer Mrs. Kahonachek, but you don't have to pay me for being Lacy's friend."

"You're more than her friend, and you know it."

Her bold statement startled him. Bennett shifted his weight, uncertain how to extricate himself from this touchy situation. He liked the elderly lady. He liked Lacy's whole family. That was the problem. He couldn't have them thinking he was anything more to her than a friend.

"Come, sit down." She patted the bed beside her. "Let me tell you about my thunderbolt."

Thunderbolt. Wasn't that what Lacy had called him last night while she was drunk on painkillers? An edgy panic gripped him. Great-Gramma reached out and folded his fingers over the cuff links resting in his palm.

Clearing his throat, Bennett edged over and eased down upon the bed. Over the course of the next few minutes Great-Gramma told him a wild story about how something she called the thunderbolt had struck her when she'd first met her husband and how she'd known from the moment she laid eyes on him that he was her true love. The cuff links, she told him, had been made in honor of their love.

It was a touching, if somewhat batty, story. The exact opposite situation, it seemed, from what had happened to his parents. Love at first sight that lasted for a lifetime instead of ending in a bitter divorce. What a fanciful idea.

"Your grandsons deserve these cuff links. I can't accept them."

"The thunderbolt cannot be denied. Take them," she whispered. "You must."

THE MORE she thought about her great grandmother's deception, the more exasperated she became. Lacy, an honest person by nature, disliked subterfuge. First she'd allowed herself to be influenced by Janet and CeeCee's advice, dressing sexy, flirting, pretending she was something she wasn't, and now this. Great-Gramma was pulling the strings, and she expected both Lacy and Bennett to dance to her tune.

Thunderbolt, indeed.

It angered her to think that she'd spent her entire adulthood waiting for the legendary whack of love at first sight. She'd even used the thunderbolt as an excuse to hide behind her shyness. She'd put her life on hold. She'd held her figurative breath and waited for the proverbial knight in shining armor.

To realize that all this time she could have been having fun, meeting nice men, coming out of her shell, learning and growing. Just as CeeCee and Janet had been trying to tell her. Yet she'd been too steeped in family tradition to take the chance.

But part of her clung to a belief that the thunderbolt was true. That she and Bennett were indeed meant to be together for a lifetime.

Lacy paced the hallway on her crutches. What was Great-Gramma telling him? She pressed her ear against the door, heard nothing but muted whispers.

Unable to stand not knowing what was going on inside that bedroom for one minute longer, Lacy knocked then pushed the door open. She saw Bennett sitting on the bed beside Great-Gramma.

Her gaze met his. He winked at her, and her heart lurched. They had to leave before things got really awkward. And since Great-Gramma was fitter than a Stradivarius, there was no time like the present.

"Since you're feeling better, Great-Gramma, I think Bennett and I will go back to Houston."

"What's your hurry, *drahy?* We don't get to see you often enough. Besides, you haven't had any sleep. See, your young man is yawning."

Indeed, Bennett was covering his mouth with his palm. He looked sheepish.

"Yes, but Bennett has a patient waiting for a heart transplant. At any minute he could be beeped for surgery. It's better if we leave right away."

Great-Gramma laid a hand across her chest, leaned her head against the pillow and closed her eyes. "Oh! My heart just gave a strange flutter."

In an instant, Bennett had his hand on her great grandmother's wrist, checking her pulse, a look of concern in his dark eyes.

"It's not going to work," Lacy said. "We're leaving."

Great-Gramma opened one eye. "Fine. Scoot. Leave when I need you most."

"If you were really sick you'd let us take you to the hospital." Lacy wasn't going to give in to her great grandmother's maneuvers. Enough was enough.

"Lacy," Bennett said. "Do you really think it's a good idea to agitate her?"

"Trust me. She's fine."

"Could I talk to you in the hall?" Bennett asked.

"Sure."

Once outside the room, Bennett lowered his voice to a whisper and leaned in close. "Listen, Lacy, I don't mind staying awhile longer to make sure your great grandmother is all right. If you want to leave on account of me, don't even consider it a problem. Laramie said it's not vital that I be in attendance if a heart should become available for Mr. Marshall."

"But it's your first heart transplant. If you miss out on this, who knows when you'll have another opportunity to scrub in on one?"

"First of all, the chances are slim that they'll find a match for Mr. Marshall this weekend, but if I do get beeped, we can drive to the airport in Waco then fly to Houston. I can come back for your car later."

"That's really nice of you," she said. "But something tells me Great-Gramma is going to be just fine. We should leave now."

"You never can tell with a woman of her age."

"I already feel guilty enough forcing you to drive me here over a false alarm."

"You didn't force me to do anything, Lacy. I'm here with you because I want to be here."

Oh, Lord, he was saying all the right things. She looked into his eyes and melted. He was a good person. That didn't make him her perfect mate.

"Bennett, I think it's best if we return to Houston. That is, if you feel up to the drive without having had any sleep."

"Are you kidding? I've only been up twenty-four hours. That's nothing. When I was an intern, we worked thirty-six-hour shifts, and plenty of times we weren't able to grab a nap. I can manage.''

Lacy nodded. ''Then let's tell everyone goodbye and hit the road.''

She hobbled inside the bedroom to inform Great-Gramma they were leaving.

''You've got your heart set on this?'' Great-Gramma asked.

''I refuse to force anything between Bennett and me,'' Lacy told her.

''You're a stubborn one, *drahy*. You take after your old great granny.''

Lacy leaned over and kissed her forehead. ''I love you and I appreciate you trying to help. But I can't keep lying to him. If he wants me for me, fine. If not...'' It took everything she could muster to shrug nonchalantly as if her heart wasn't tearing in two pieces at the thought of losing Bennett.

''Could you send your grandmother Nony in here before you go?''

''Sure.''

Lacy bid her great grandmother farewell, and went to where Bennett waited. Together they went down to talk to the rest of the family seated around the breakfast table. Lacy gave Grandmother Nony Great-Gramma's message, then proceeded to tell everyone else goodbye.

''Stay and eat breakfast,'' her mother encouraged.

Lacy shook her head. It was too tempting to stay. Too tempting to eat and sleep and to allow her family to run her life. She'd been doing it for twenty-nine years. It was time she made her own way.

"Bennett, talk some sense into her." Lacy's mother turned to him for help.

He raised his palms and laughed. "Hey, I'm only the chauffeur."

"We really gotta go, Mom," Lacy said. "I'm sure Great-Gramma is going to be fine. She probably had a bad case of indigestion. You guys have fun at the farm expo."

After many hugs and goodbyes, they finally broke away. On the way to the car, Bennett walked beside Lacy on her crutches, opened the passenger side door for her, then helped her slide inside.

Feeling wrung out and discouraged but with an unexplained urgency pushing her toward Houston, Lacy leaned against the headrest and sighed deeply. She needed to get to her apartment, be by herself to sort out her tumultuous emotions.

Bennett got behind the wheel, and it took everything she had to refrain from telling him to floor it. He jabbed the key in the ignition and turned.

Dead silence.

He pumped the gas pedal and tried again.

Nothing.

He looked at her. "How old is your battery?"

"Bought it about six months ago."

"That's probably not it, then." Bennett stroked his jaw with a thumb and forefinger. "Unfortunately I don't know much about cars."

She was about as lucky as a three-legged, one-eyed, bobbed-tail dog. She'd wanted nothing more than to escape the cloying bosom of her well-meaning but interfering family, and here she was stuck right in the middle of them.

Car trouble, of all things.

"Breakfast and a nap are beginning to look very appealing," Bennett said.

"Yes." Lacy sighed. Too appealing.

"Besides, if we stay a little longer we can make sure your great grandmother really is doing okay."

Lacy bit her tongue to keep from telling him that sweet little old lady was lying like a politician and faking her chest pains. If Lacy told him that, then she'd have to reveal why.

And she wasn't ready to see the harsh truth in Bennett's eyes.

That he didn't love her the way she loved him.

"DYLAN CAN HAVE a look at your car when he gets home from the expo. I'm sure it's nothing he can't handle," Geneva Calder told her daughter as she leaned between Bennett's and Lacy's chairs and raked a pile of fluffy scrambled eggs onto their plates.

Blue china plates. Wedgwood. Bennett knew because Nanna had once owned a set. Those blue china plates brought back lots of fond memories.

He eyed the meal spread before them. Sausages and French toast, *kolaches* and buttermilk biscuits, hash browns and fresh fruit cut into bite-size chunks. There was a pitcher of milk, a carafe of orange juice and a pot of fresh brewed coffee. He'd never seen a spread like this outside a hotel buffet line. His mouth watered, and his stomach grumbled.

"But the expo won't be over until ten o'clock tonight," Lacy complained.

"By then you and Bennett will have had a lovely nap and you'll be refreshed for your drive home."

Lacy sighed and Bennett wondered, not for the first time, why she was so anxious to get back to Houston. Granted, her great grandmother seemed to be fine, but her family was so loving, so accepting, he couldn't figure out why she didn't want to spend more time with them. Hell, he would have given his right arm to have a close-knit family like this one.

Lacy sat next to him, her crutches propped against the wall beside her. She kept casting surreptitious glances his way. If he were being honest with himself, he would admit to searching for her gaze time and again.

Here, surrounded by her family, she had changed yet again. She wasn't the shy scrub nurse, nor was she the seductive party girl from the night before. At home, she was the eldest daughter, motherly and responsible.

They were a lively group, jammed around the big table that occupied most of the large kitchen. The air hummed with the sound of their collective voices and clinking silverware. They included Bennett in their conversation about the yearly exposition they were attending that day. Mr. Calder and his oldest son, Dylan, had already left to open the booth featuring crafts and food made by the Calder family. The other family members would be departing as soon as breakfast was over. Except for Grandmother Nony, who volunteered to stay behind and keep an eye on Great-Gramma.

He found their acceptance heartening and yet disconcerting. They made him feel like he belonged. But Bennett had no claim to their affection.

His presence was pure accident. If he hadn't been in Lacy's apartment when the phone call had come, he would not be here.

"So how long have you and Lacy been going together?" asked Mrs. Calder.

"Mother," Lacy said, "Bennett's just a friend."

Yeah, sure. Mrs. Calder's expression was easy to read. She thought they were in a serious relationship. That's when Bennett knew his suspicions about Lacy were true. She didn't bring strange men home to meet her folks. That's why they accepted him so readily. Her family assumed if he was here then their relationship was a serious one.

Bennett gulped. What had he gotten himself into? Lacy was a nice girl with traditional values, just as he'd suspected when he'd first laid eyes on her in the operating suite and told himself—*This one is off-limits.* Seeing Lacy in her home environment told him everything he needed to know. This girl could never be a casual fling. The bold woman he'd met at the nightclub had been a front, a ruse. She'd played a part, pretending to be something she wasn't.

Why?

And yet, those kisses. They'd certainly been real and as hot and passionate as any he'd ever received. They had not been an act.

But he had no space in his life for anything beyond a casual love affair. Pursuing his hard-won career goals prevented him from looking for love. At least for now.

And he couldn't ask her to wait for him. Lacy was in the prime of her life. Surely she would want to marry and have children soon. That's what she deserved. She needed a man who had the time to lavish her with attention, not a harried young surgeon scrabbling to build a career and pay off school loans.

Bennett felt strangely wistful that he *wasn't* going to be part of this loving family, but he also felt claustrophobic, as if something beyond his control was drawing him into…what? For an educated man he was having a great deal of difficulty expressing himself.

Then there were those cuff links that were resting in the front pocket of his shirt where Lacy's great-gramma had dropped them when he tried to give the things back to her. The cuff links with the strange symbolism.

Thunderbolt. Love at first sight. Whirlwind courtship. His parents' bad marriage.

It wasn't that he didn't care about Lacy. He did. Very much. Probably too much. But he didn't want her expecting something from him that he simply couldn't give. Not at this point in his life. He refused to fall in love or to get married before he was ready. His parents had made that tactical error, and it had almost ruined them.

His childhood memories weren't pleasant. Spending Christmas holidays with his mother one year, his father the next. Never a real family, always split between two warring factions. He recalled his parents bickering over who was going to pay for his dental work or buy the Little League uniforms. He remembered long lonely nights spent hugging his pillow and wondering how he could make his folks like each other.

Finally, he'd realized he wasn't to blame. What had caused the problem was physical attraction. If his parents had taken their time getting to know each other, they would have realized they were completely incompatible and that a union between them would never have worked out. Well, if nothing else, Bennett had certainly learned from their mistakes.

"Grandmother Nony," Lacy said, "if we're stuck here until Dylan can look at my car, you might as well go to the expo with everyone else. Bennett and I can check on Great-Gramma."

"Are you sure?" Grandmother Nony perked up. "I was really hoping my apple preserves might win first prize."

"Go," Bennett said, then realized suddenly that he and Lacy would be alone on the farm except for Great-Gramma tucked away in bed. Was that what he wanted? To be alone with Lacy? Yes, he decided. They needed to talk and clear the air between them. And he needed to find out if she believed in this thunderbolt thing her great grandmother had been talking about. Absentmindedly, he patted the pocket with the cuff links.

A knock sounded at the back door.

Lacy's mother waved at a tall, gangly man standing on the stoop. "Lester, come in."

Work hat in his callused fingers, Lester pushed open the screen door and stepped inside, leaving it slightly ajar behind him. "I heard about Granny Kahonachek and I just stopped by to see if she was okay before I headed on over to the expo..." Lester's gaze settled on Lacy and his words trailed off. "Lacy," he said, "you're home."

Bennett didn't like the look in the other man's eyes. Not one bit. It didn't take a rocket scientist, or a heart surgeon for that matter, to figure out the guy had a major crush on her.

Jealousy was a new sensation for Bennett. At least where a woman was concerned.

"Hi, Lester," Lacy said cheerfully, but she didn't meet the man's goo-goo eyes. Obviously, she didn't return his affection.

Bennett felt a spike of triumph, and he had the urge to shout, "Yeah!" Then he immediately wondered why. He had no claim on Lacy Calder. None whatsoever. She was free to date anyone she wanted.

The screen door flapped in the early morning

breeze. Lester stayed posed in the doorway, visually gobbling up Lacy.

Bennett imagined plowing a fist in Lester's face for no good reason other than it pleased him.

"Bennett," Lacy's grandmother Nony said, "try some of my red-eye gravy." She hovered at his elbow, gravy boat in hand.

From the corner of his eye, Bennett saw something streak through the back door and into the kitchen. Several people shouted at once, "Get Frank Sinatra out of here!"

Frank Sinatra?

Bennett frowned at the same moment an evil-eyed goat dashed between Grandmother Nony's legs, heading straight for the breakfast table.

Grandmother Nony lost her balance. Her hands flew into the air.

The gravy boat went up.

And then came down.

Smack-dab in Bennett's lap.

8

"I'M SO SORRY about your pants," Lacy apologized. "And about the clothes dryer being broken."

Bennett glanced at her. Everyone had gone to the farm expo, leaving them alone save for Great-Gramma snoozing upstairs. Lacy was leaning on her crutches watching him hang his Levi's and white long-sleeved shirt on the clothesline.

Being too tall to borrow a pair of pants from anyone in her family, Bennett wore nothing but boxer shorts, his loafers and a bathrobe that belonged to Lacy's father belted at his waist.

"No harm done." He smiled at her. "My jeans should be dry by the time we wake up from our nap."

It was after ten o'clock, and the moderate weather of early morning had given way to eighty-degree temperatures. As a Bostonian, he wasn't accustomed to such a warm spring climate.

"Come on," Lacy said. "I'll show you to the guest quarters above the barn, but don't expect anything fancy. It's where the extra farmhands stay during harvest."

"Hey, all I need is a place to lay my head. I've

slept on exam tables. It can't be any worse than that,'' he chuckled.

"Follow me.'' She crooked a finger then ambled off. She was getting pretty good with those crutches, swinging along at a nice clip.

Unbidden, his eyes traveled from the crutches to Lacy's delicious behind encased so enticingly in that pale floral jumper. He wanted so badly to fill his arms with her lush form, fill his nose with her scent, fill his eyes with the sight of her set free from her clothes.

He realized suddenly she'd gone off and left him standing with his mouth agape like some love-addled teen. Bennett had to take two long-legged strides to catch up with her.

"What's the deal between you and this Lester character?'' he surprised himself by asking.

"Lester's had a crush on me since we were kids.'' Lacy sighed. "He's asked me to marry him about a hundred times.''

"No kidding.''

She nodded.

"He's a good looking guy. Why haven't you ever taken him up on his offer?''

"I don't love him. And sweet as he is, Lester's main interests are cows and corn and not much else.'' Lacy made a face. "Why do you ask?'' She stopped outside the large red barn about a hundred yards from the house and turned to look at him.

"No reason.''

"You wouldn't be jealous, would you?'' She

slanted him a coy glance. She looked so cute in her buttercorn jumper, her hair pulled into a ponytail.

"Me? Jealous?"

Jealous as Othello over Desdemona. Jealous as Popeye over Olive Oyl. Jealous as a kid over Pokémon cards.

Okay, the last example wasn't so hot. But the thought of Farmer Lester with his dirt-stained paws roving over Lacy's tight little body made Bennett's blood run icy.

"I don't do jealousy," he said.

"What?" She frowned at him.

Bennett shifted. Had he actually said that? What a jerk. "What I mean is, well, jealousy is a destructive emotion born of passion, and I try not to let my physical passion get the better of me."

"Oh." She looked damned disappointed while at the same time so much emotion swirled in her eyes. Heat, need, desire.

"I'm trying to explain something to you." He reached out and touched her arm. Despite the words he knew he was uttering in a pompous, all-too-doctorly fashion, he wanted to experience deep passion with her. He wanted to see her wild, out of control, nuts with desire for him. He began telling her about his parents, more as a reminder for his benefit than enlightenment for her. "Lacy, there's something I have to tell you."

"Yes?"

"It's the reason I don't allow my sexual urges to run my life."

She nodded. "I'm listening."

He let go of her arm, too distracted by the softness of her skin. "My parents met at Cape Cod one weekend. On the beach. The attraction was instant. Like being hit by a freight train, my mother said. And like a freight train running off the track at high speed, that attraction ruined their lives." He paused, took a deep breath, ran his hand through his hair and continued.

"They made love the very day they met, and they conceived me. They were both still in college, both studying to be doctors. The last thing they needed was to get married, but that's what they did. Unfortunately med school and parenthood are demanding propositions on their own. Put the two together, and something's got to give. The powerful passion between my father and my mother turned from love to hate. They divorced when I was two. They still can't stay in the same room together. I vowed I would never make a major decision based on physical attraction."

He felt her gaze on his face. Unable to meet her eyes for fear of giving away his emotions, he stared intently at Frank Sinatra, who was blithely munching weeds under the clothesline.

Bennett studied the goat, anxious for something to take his mind off his emotional turmoil. One minute he was struggling against the urge to take Lacy into his arms and kiss her. The next minute he was ready to rip his jeans and shirt off the clothesline, wet or not, shimmy into them and hitchhike to Houston. Because the longer he tarried here the more he yearned to stay.

And no matter how attracted he might be to Lacy Calder, her wacky lovable family and West, Texas, they had no place in his future.

None at all.

Keeping their relationship strictly platonic was in her best interest as well as his.

"Can you get the gate?" she asked softly.

Jerking his head from his worrisome thoughts, he hurried ahead to unlatch the gate and usher her through.

"And the barn door." She nodded.

He did as she asked.

The barn was airless, musty, filled with hay and sacks of grain. Dust motes swirled in the dim light seeping in through the dusty windows.

Lacy sneezed.

"Bless you."

She beamed at him, rested her crutches against the wall. She looked like a teenager, free of makeup, her hair off her face. "Bed's upstairs." She pointed to the stairway at the back of the barn.

Bennett watched, totally mesmerized by her movements. He licked his lips. His pulse hammered. His stomach squeezed.

His body ignored all his mind's earlier admonitions.

He wanted her.

LACY'S INSIDES wobbled like a sailboat in a hurricane. It was official. Bennett didn't believe in the thunderbolt. Question was, did she still believe? Or had she been a romantic fool all these years?

She was having a crisis of faith. First she'd discovered the thunderbolt wasn't quite as infallible as her great grandmother had always claimed. And now Bennett had revealed the horror story of his parents' experience with the thunderbolt. The last thing she wanted was to hurt him in any way.

She should leave the barn immediately, flee from this Herculean force that shoved her inexplicably toward him. She'd shown him where his room was. Nothing good could come of staying.

But she couldn't make herself go.

Okay, what if the thunderbolt wasn't real? It didn't alter the fact that she was very attracted to Bennett. She wanted to make love to Bennett whether he was the one or not. Their affair didn't have to end happily ever after. Sex and love were two different things, and she was beginning to realize that. Perhaps what she felt for Bennett was nothing but runaway lust.

For hours she had been unable to think of anything but kissing him again. In the car on the way here, beside him at the breakfast table, upstairs in her great grandmother's bedroom.

Her lips ached for his mouth, her arms yearned to wrap around his neck, her nose itched to bury itself in his chest. She wanted to smell him, touch him, taste him, feel him.

She wasn't pretending to be a vamp any longer. Nor was she still tied to some bizarre familial myth. The time had come to free herself. To simply be Lacy, with no agenda or hidden motive other than to be with Bennett. For once in her life, she felt no embarrassment over her sexuality, no shame at her inexperience.

In her pocket lay the condom CeeCee had given her the night before. She'd forgotten to take it out of her jumper, and now she was glad.

She wanted Bennett, and she didn't care if he loved her or not. Sure, it would be nice if he returned her affections, but she was tired of believing in fairy tales. Tired of waiting for the perfect man. She wanted to know what it was like to be a woman. To have a man desire her, hold her, make love to her. She loved him, and if he walked away from her after they made love, she would survive.

She angled him a come-hither glance.

And he came hither at blinding speed.

"Be careful." He wrapped an arm around her waist. "You could fall so easily balancing on one leg like that."

His chest was pressed against her back, his hips flush with hers.

There was no mistaking his arousal.

Lacy turned her head. Her cheek brushed his chin. Their lips were so close.

Then indecision struck, and she began to tremble. Her belief in her actions flew away, and she was left with the stark reality of what she wanted and what was about to happen between them.

Bennett groaned, low and guttural.

The barn smelled earthy, rich, sexy. Thick mounds of coarse hay were strewn across the floor not two feet away. The thought of her bare flesh pressed against that rough hay made her tremble all the harder.

Tremble with starving, desperate need.

She'd waited so long for this.

It was warm in the enclosure. Beads of perspiration formed at the hollow of her throat. She saw that he was sweating, too, droplets glistening on his forehead.

She wanted to lick his skin and taste his salty flavor. She wanted to peel back that bathrobe and get her hands on what lay beneath. She wanted to skyrocket to heaven in his arms.

Oh, the things she wanted!

Lacy's lips parted, but before she could whisper a word, his mouth covered hers in a spectacular kiss.

His hands spanned her waist, holding her steady. His breathing was raspy, ragged. His tongue teased and coaxed. His eyes shone feverish with desire.

Lacy turned into his arms, and he lifted her to his chest. Without uttering a sound, he took her to the hay and arranged her gently on the floor.

He ripped the bathrobe from his body and tossed the garment aside, baring his muscular chest. He stood in nothing but his boxer shorts, and the you're-the-most-sexy-thing-I've-ever-laid-eyes-on expression on his face told her that he wanted exactly the same thing she wanted.

Their bodies joined together. Here. In the barn. On the hay. All emotional consequences be damned.

She spread her knees, reached out her hands to him. He lowered himself between her legs, careful to avoid jostling her injured foot, and gently began to kiss her again.

Finally, at long last, she would know what it was like to be a woman.

And if the thunderbolt was real, then he would be hers forever. If it wasn't real then at least she'd have this one moment of exquisite pleasure to treasure until the end of her days.

MAKING LOVE to Lacy seemed the most natural thing in the world.

Never mind the annoying voice in the back of his brain telling him that he was getting in over his head. Never mind that his breath quickened with fear half as much as with excitement. Never mind that he was leaving Texas in less than a week.

His hands were unerring. His lips sure. More than anything, he wanted to give and receive pleasure with this woman.

And Lacy seemed as eager as he to consummate their union. The tension that had smoldered between them from the moment he had sauntered into the operating room at Saint Madeleine's burst into a full-fledged forest fire.

She was the picture of his every adolescent fantasy sprung to life and more wonderful than he had ever dreamed. She was lush and fresh and eager. His hands shook with need. His heart pounded with passion.

Her warm, moist lips clung to his tighter than any embrace. Sensuous lips that were an odd combination of wildness and innocence.

What an intriguing paradox she was. Sweet and naughty.

At times she seemed almost virginal and then in the next moment she would turn into the most tempting of temptresses. His eyes never left hers as his fingers slowly unbuttoned her jumper. She wriggled free from the clothing, and when he saw her bare body wrapped only in that pink satin teddy, he sucked in his breath with admiration.

"You're so beautiful."

She blushed prettily and ducked her head.

"I mean it."

"I'm not used to hearing men talk to me like this," she said softly.

"Well, you should be. You're a spectacular woman, and any man would be lucky to have you. I'm damned lucky to be here with you right now."

"Really?" She raised her head and blinked at him. The tender expression on her face slugged him in the solar plexus.

"Are you sure this is what you want, Lacy?" he whispered. "You know I can't promise you any more than this moment. I can't promise you tomorrow."

"Tomorrow will take care of itself," she said. "Make love to me, Bennett. I want you, I need you...."

Was it his imagination or did the words "I love you" hang unspoken in the air?

Did she love him?

Bennett pulled back and searched her face, saw something suspect in her eyes. The last thing he wanted was to break her tender heart. He couldn't stand the thought of knowing that he'd hurt her.

"Lacy..."

But before he could question her further, she raised up on her elbows, flicked the tip of her hot, pink tongue and licked his nipple.

Bennett inhaled as sharply as if he'd been scalded. Such heat. Such intensity. Such indescribable delight.

Sheer ecstasy.

Moaning softly, he kissed her again, his arms cocooning her.

"Bennett." She murmured his name. "Oh, Bennett."

"I'm here, cupcake, right here."

He lowered his head, nipped and kissed and tickled her skin with his tongue. He visited her neck, her cheek, her eyelids, her earlobes until she was writhing restlessly beneath him.

"Every time I avoided your eyes in surgery it was because I was secretly longing to do this," he said.

"No kidding?" she breathed.

"From the moment you fell off your stool at my feet."

Her cheeks flushed with embarrassment. "I imagined you thought I was the world's biggest klutz, but the truth is, you unnerved me that much."

"I thought you were adorably disarming." He eased the straps of her teddy over her shoulders, then traced an index finger over her tight breasts.

Mesmerized, he watched as her nipples responded to his touch, growing harder, more prominent with each circling caress. When he dipped his head to suckle there, she arched her back and moaned low in her throat.

He ran his hand downward, skimming first her waist, then her flat, firm belly. She writhed against his hand, whimpered for more.

The woman surprised him at every turn. She gazed at him coyly as if completely unaware of what she did to him. Well, two could play that teasing game.

Inch by inch, his hand delved lower, igniting a blazing path of eager response as it went.

"Oh," she whispered when his fingers curled at her most feminine part. "Oh." She grabbed handfuls of hay and whimpered shamelessly, her back arching off the barn floor.

She was the most desirable woman he had ever known. For this brief moment in time, she belonged to him alone.

"Don't stop," she begged, when he moved his hand

to gently rub the inside of one thigh as soft and irresistible as heavenly meringue.

"Do you like what I'm doing to you?"

In answer she fiercely grabbed his hair in both fists and brought his mouth down to hers.

Every muscle in her body tensed as he continued to stroke between her legs. Her flavor filled his mouth in an explosion of epic proportions. Nothing had ever tasted this good. Not the juiciest filet mignon. Not the sweetest birthday cake. Not the finest caviar.

She clung desperately to him, her escalating passion kindling his desire to unbearable heights.

LACY FELT as if she were walking on a piece of string stretched taut across the Grand Canyon. One infinitesimal slip and she would plunge down, down, down into the beautiful abyss.

She was both scared and awed. Wanting to tumble so badly, but frightened of what lay below the myriad sensations assaulting her body at Bennett's every touch.

The power he held in one finger took her breath and her will. She would follow this man anywhere. Thunderbolt or no, he belonged to her, whether he recognized that fact or not. They belonged together. Making love would cinch their connection. After that, could he abandon his destiny?

Then suddenly, without warning, Bennett rolled away from her.

She stared at him. "What's wrong?"

"We...I can't do this."

"Why not?"

"No protection." His voice was a croak. He pulled ragged breaths. "I can't believe I let things go this far."

"Wait." Lacy reached for her jumper, thrown haphazardly to one side in the hay. She dug in the pocket for the condom CeeCee had given her the day before. Silently she said a prayer of thanks for her friend's foresight.

Had it really been less than twenty-four hours since she'd sashayed into the Recovery Room with the intention of learning how to flirt?

Things were moving fast, but she knew it was right. She would not regret this, no matter what the outcome might be. Better to have Bennett for a short while than not to have him at all.

"You're prepared?" He looked astonished but took the foil square she extended toward him.

She shrugged.

"Lacy Calder," he murmured, gathering into his arms once more. "You surprise me at every turn."

"I've got another surprise for you," she confessed.

"Oh?"

She cleared her throat, unsure how to tell him. "You see, I've never really done this before."

"What do you mean?"

"Well...I'm kind of a virgin."

"Excuse me?" He looked incredulous. "Kind of a virgin? How can you be kind of a virgin?"

She shrugged again.

"But why me? Why now?"

She desperately wanted to tell him that she loved him. That she'd been felled by the legendary thunderbolt, and that's all there was to it. But she knew it would most probably send him sprinting off across Lester's back pasture at a speed to rival a Kentucky Derby winner.

And honestly, she couldn't blame him if he did. The thunderbolt was a rather unbelievable story if you hadn't grown up hearing about it day in and day out. Bennett was a doctor. A man with a scientific mind. He would no more swallow the thunderbolt myth than he would believe her if she told him she was pregnant was Elvis's love child.

Especially since Lacy was seriously doubting the thunderbolt herself. But she did believe in her feelings. Surely her heart would not lead her astray. So Lacy said what she had to say to keep him at her side and put that lusty gleam back in his eyes.

"I'm almost thirty, Bennett. I think it's time. I like you, but I'm also realistic. I know you won't be in town much longer, but you make me feel sexy and desirable. I want you to be the one."

"You would give me such a precious gift?" His voice went husky, and she could have sworn his eyes misted.

"Don't read so much into it," she said, struggling to keep things on a light keel. She didn't want to make him feel guilty if he chose to make love to her and then leave her.

She was an adult. She knew exactly what she was proposing. She realized there was no guarantee, no thunderbolt, no myth. Just a woman loving a man to the best of her abilities.

"Lacy..." He looked uncomfortable. "Are you sure? You've waited this long."

"And so far no Prince Charming on a snow-white stallion." *Until you, that is.* She looked at him and smiled shyly. "Please."

"Cupcake, you are the sexiest woman I've ever met, and right now, I want to make love to you more than anything in the world. But as I told you before, I can't make any promises. For the next several years, my life isn't my own."

"I know," she whispered and sudden fear swamped her. "I'm not asking for happily ever after."

She studied the firm line of his jaw, saw the tenderness in his eyes and knew she had to try. Perilous as it seemed, it really would be better to love and lose than never love at all. And who knew? If there was by some small chance a thunderbolt, maybe making love would bind him to her in a way nothing else could. It was a gamble, but she was ready to spin the wheel, roll the dice, pull the lever.

Lacy had spent her life hiding in her shyness, too nervous or self-conscious to reach out and grab what she wanted. Was she going to let Bennett walk away simply because she was too afraid to risk getting hurt?

She thought of CeeCee and Janet and she knew what they would say.

Take a chance.

Lacy took a deep breath and said the bravest thing she'd ever said.

"Make love to me, Bennett. No promises, no strings attached. Let's enjoy what we've got and not worry about tomorrow."

BENNETT capitulated. How could he not, with the sweetest, most honest woman in the world held close in his arms.

Dipping his head, he tasted her lips again, delicious as Nanna's vanilla custard. Then he slid his mouth lower, to her throat, felt the heat of her pulse jump frantically. The force of his need shook him deeply. He feared his knees would not hold him if he tried to stand.

There was no scrambling away from this. From her. He'd dreamed of this moment since the day he'd met her. Dreamed and tried to tell himself it was an impossible fantasy.

Here she was, offering herself up to him without expectations or demands. She was the most understanding female he'd ever come across, and he treasured each moment with her.

In one expeditious movement, he whisked off his boxer shorts.

Lacy inhaled sharply at the sight of him. Pride filled

Bennett, knowing that he had produced such an intense response in her.

He put on the condom, then lay beside her to swirl his fingers at her hot, wet center once more.

"Oh, Bennett."

"Yes, Lacy. Does that feel good?"

"Heaven. I'm in heaven." She clung to his shoulders with both hands. "More. Please, more."

His mouth captured hers. They kissed for one long, earth-shattering moment. Slowly, inch by inch, he slid into her.

When she cried out, he froze, terrified that he might be hurting her, but she shifted beneath him and lifted her hips tentatively.

"I love the way you feel inside me," she gasped. "So strong. So manly."

Her lush naked body was molded by his hands. Those sapphire eyes that had peeped at him so many times over a surgical mask were wide with wonder and desire. He smelled hay and the earthy scent of their combined musk. He was so overcome by sensations that he almost lost control then and there.

"Put your legs over my shoulders. That way there's less of a chance I'll hurt your ankle," he whispered, trying hard to focus on something besides the tremendous fire inside him begging to be released.

This was her first time. He wanted it to be special.

She obeyed, and he ended up with a slim leg resting on each shoulder.

He cupped her face in his hands and carefully began

to move again, his eyes never leaving her face as he watched for any signs of discomfort.

A blinding smile raised her lips, revealing to him exactly how much pleasure he was giving her.

"It's fine, Bennett. Truly fine," she said, reading his mind. "It hurt for a second but now it feels just glorious."

She blinked at him through a fine mist of tears, the smile on her face deepening, and in that moment, Bennett knew he was a goner.

In her eyes, he saw what he feared. Happiness, joy, warmth and affection. Heat and need and hunger.

And love.

No matter that she would deny it, Lacy Calder loved him.

He should have been terrified. He should have stopped, got up and walked all the way to Houston. But he didn't want to stop. He didn't want to leave.

In that instant, Bennett had the strangest sensation that he had come home.

His feelings made no sense. He was in a small Texas town, over a thousand miles from Boston. He was with a girl he'd known barely five weeks. Why he should experience this unwavering sense of belonging, he had no idea.

But he did.

Then Lacy whispered his name, and in the next second a convulsive quiver shook her whole body.

He struggled to hold himself back, fought to hang onto one shred of control, but it was useless. Inside her, above her, he had no will of his own. Her shudder moved through him, overtook him, and he joined her, burying his face in her neck and gently calling her name.

9

WHAT HAD THEY DONE?
Bennett woke with a start and stared in confusion at his surroundings.

Then he looked over and saw Lacy nestled in a tight ball against his chest, one fist curled under her chin.

And he panicked.

He had to get out of here.

Gently he eased his arm, which felt no more alive than a wooden stump, out from under her.

She murmured in her sleep, a lock of hair the color of melted sunshine curling across her cheek. He had the strongest urge to brush that curl away, touch that tender cheek. But if he did, he might awaken her, and he wasn't prepared for that. Before he faced her and told her he was going back to Houston, he wanted to get dressed. A man could make a better case for abandoning the woman he'd just made love to when he was fully clothed.

He found his boxer shorts and borrowed bathrobe—how had his clothes gotten halfway across the barn?—slipped into them and then stumbled outside. He blinked against the brightness of the noonday glare.

His head felt stuffy, his gut empty and his conscience on fire with guilt.

Running out on her, eh, Bennett?

He wasn't a heartless heel. In fact, this was for her own good as much as his. Through his parents he had learned that you couldn't trust emotion, that passion was suspect. The intense feelings he had for Lacy only proved that he must leave her to save them both.

Oh, yeah? Then why did you make love to her even after you found out she was a virgin?

Why? Because he was weak. Because physically, he had wanted Lacy more than he had any other woman.

And because, he admitted to himself, *he* was bailing out before *he* got hurt.

He knew he could not stay in Texas. He had a future in Boston. Obligations there. And he'd promised himself after Nanna's death that he would open up a heart center especially for treating indigent patients. He even planned on erecting a clinic on the plot of land in downtown Boston that Nanna had left him. And he'd promised himself he would never trust love born of intense attraction.

A slight breeze kicked up, blew at the tufts of hair on his chest, making Bennett realize he was standing in the barnyard wearing nothing but his undershorts and Lacy's father's bathrobe.

Get your pants on and get out of here. Pronto. Call a taxi, rent a car, hitchhike. Hurry. Before Lacy's fam-

*ily catches you half naked with this guilty look on your
face.*

Spurred on by that unpleasant thought, he sneaked
around the barn, through the gate and into the backyard. His single goal—his Levi's, hanging on the
clothesline.

Except when he got to the clothesline, Bennett was
stunned to see Frank Sinatra calmly chewing on his
blue jeans. The pesky old goat had already consumed
half of one leg.

"You son of a billy goat," Bennett shouted, and
stalked toward the gluttonous creature. "Get away
from my pants!"

The goat stopped in mid-swallow, a hunk of denim
dangling from the corner of his mouth. Bennett
stormed closer, verbally berating the goat's entire an-
cestry.

Frank Sinatra's back legs stiffened. His eyes rolled
back in his head. Tremors ran through his body, and
then, to Bennett's horror, the goat keeled over onto his
side and lay immobile.

Bennett ran over and knelt beside the goat, who did
not appear to be breathing. His shouting had caused
the old goat to have a heart attack.

Terrific! He'd killed Great-Gramma Kahonachek's
prize possession. He was a goat murderer. A *cabrito*
assassin.

Bennett's stomach pitched as he imagined telling
Great-Gramma that Frank Sinatra had expired. What

if the negative news was too much to take and the elderly lady suffered a heart attack, too?

Lacy would be devastated.

What to do?

He had no choice but to dispose of the carcass.

Bending, he scooped the deceased goat into his arms. Where could he hide the body until he had time to ease Great-Gramma into the notion that she would never see Old Blues Eyes again?

Lugging the heavy animal, he pivoted on one heel. To the right lay the house, to the left the road, behind him the barn.

Think, Sheridan, think.

Goat hair tickled his nostrils.

He sneezed.

Bennett realized he looked totally ridiculous. How had he, a surgical thoracic resident from Boston, come to find himself nearly naked in the backyard of a Texas farmhouse, a dead goat in his arms, his half-consumed blue jeans lying on the lawn?

It was preposterous. Laughable.

He sneezed again.

Great. Super. Stupendous.

Then he thought of a line from his favorite Mel Brooks movie, *Young Frankenstein*.

Could be worse. Could be raining.

It wasn't raining.

But something else unexpected happened.

The goat stirred.

Bennett was so startled, he stumbled backward into the picnic table.

The goat lifted his head, stared Bennett straight in the eyes and bleated long and loud.

Bennett yelled.

The goat kicked.

They both fell to the ground in a tangled heap of hands and hooves.

Quickly, Frank Sinatra recovered, springing to his feet and trotting away.

Bennett stared at the sky, feeling like the biggest idiot on the face of the earth.

"Bennett! Are you okay?"

He looked over to see Lacy hobbling toward him, her eyes wide with concern, her blond hair atumble about her slender shoulders.

"I heard you hollering and came running as fast as I could."

He considered the situation and then started to laugh. So much for a clean, painless getaway.

"What's so funny?" Lacy cocked her head quizzically.

Bennett propped himself on his elbows, waved a hand at the goat. "Frank Sinatra was eating my blue jeans. I yelled at him, and he keeled over. I thought I'd killed him. I thought he was dead. I didn't know how to break the news to your grandmother so I picked him up to hide the body." He waved at the goat, who was in the corner of the yard giving Bennett the evil eye. "As you can see, he's fine."

Lacy slapped a palm over her mouth. "Oh, Bennett, I'm so sorry, I forgot to tell you that Frank is a Tennessee Mountain Fall Down goat. They faint when they feel threatened."

"No kidding."

Their eyes met. Lacy dropped her hand and grinned at him.

"You're a city boy through and through."

"Tell me about it," he said, getting to his feet and dusting himself off.

"That was sweet of you to try and protect my grandmother."

"Hey, I didn't want to have to tell her that I'd killed her favorite pet."

Lacy's giggle gave his heart wings. "You poor thing. You must have been terrified when Frank woke up in your arms."

"Shocked is more like it," he said, not willing to admit how much the goat had disconcerted him. He was a doctor. How could he not have noticed the goat wasn't dead?

How? Well, it wasn't as if he'd performed a postmortem on the darned thing, but mostly it was, because his mind had been filled with sensuous thoughts of Lacy. Thoughts that hit him like the A bomb whenever he dared look at her. Thoughts that could lead them both into serious trouble.

Lacy limped closer and reached up to pluck a piece of straw from his hair. She swayed on her good leg. Bennett put an arm around her waist to brace her.

"Where are your crutches?" he asked, erotic sensations flooding his body at her nearness.

"I was in such a hurry to check on you, I forgot them in the barn."

Her lips were close. Too close. He recalled the flavor of those lips, so recently savored. She had tasted like peaches. Like summer and sunshine. Rich, ripe, expansive. Full of life and energy and love.

He peered into those incredible eyes. She stared at him with such trust, such admiration, Bennett's heart stuttered. His feelings were rushing him down a dangerous path. A path that threatened to ruin all his plans.

But he couldn't seem to help himself. As inexplicably as a child drawn to a magician, he cupped her smooth cheek in his palm.

She smiled at him, her emotions shining clearly in her face—pleasure, joy, happiness.

The panic that had overwhelmed him earlier returned with a vengeance. He was going to have to hurt her. Despite all his precautions, he was going to break her heart.

There was no way they could have a happy ending.

At that moment the beeper in his bathrobe pocket went off.

"THAT WAS Dr. Laramie." Bennett hung up the phone and turned to face Lacy, who hovered beside his elbow. "Mr. Marshall is going to get his heart transplant. They're flying the organ in from Minnesota as we speak. I've got about three hours to get to Houston and scrub in. Unfortunately, I don't have time to wait for your brother to repair your car. Does West have a taxi service?''

She shook her head. ''No, but surely I can find someone to drive you to Waco to catch the plane.''

''All right.'' Bennett nodded.

Lacy rested her hands on her hips and eyed him. ''Since Frank Sinatra made mincemeat of your blue jeans, you're going to need a new pair of pants. We'll borrow from my brothers. What size do you wear?''

''Thirty-two waist, thirty-six length.''

She made a face. ''You're taller than anyone in the family. Dylan wears a thirty-two inch waist, but they'll be short on you.''

''Anything will do.'' His apprehension built. He was anxious to get on his way.

''I'll get your shirt off the clothesline and fetch a pair of Dylan's jeans.''

Just then, Grandmother Nony's car turned into the driveway. ''Hey, kids,'' she greeted them as she got out. ''I came back for more apple preserves. I sold out already.'' She stopped chattering and stared at them. ''Is something the matter?''

''Bennett needs to get back to Houston right away to assist in an emergency heart transplant. With my car out of commission, we need someone to drive him to the airport in Waco. Can you take him?''

Grandmother Nony bared her teeth and sucked in

her breath. "Oh dear. I tried to tell your great-gramma that this was a bad idea."

"What was a bad idea?" Lacy's voice went up a notch. Bennett looked from Lacy to her grandmother and back again.

"Taking the distributor cap off your car."

"What?"

"I'm sorry, honey, I didn't know it would cause this kind of trouble. Your great-gramma insisted you and Bennett had to stay here until he was struck by the thunderbolt. She asked me to disable your car."

"You disabled my car?"

Grandmother Nony winced and nodded.

"I take it the gravy spill wasn't accidental, either." Lacy looked mad enough to spit bullets.

"Well, Great-Gramma said you were pretty mad at her. She wanted to make sure you didn't get away," Grandmother Nony explained.

"The clothes dryer isn't really broken, either, is it?" Lacy asked.

"No," Grandmother Nony admitted.

Lacy smacked her palm with her forehead. "I don't believe this family."

"What's going on? What does this mean?" Bennett asked.

"It means—" Lacy gave her grandmother an icy glance "—that my family has been playing meddlesome matchmakers. You're free to leave, Bennett. All we have to do is reattach the distributor cap, and you can be on your way."

LACY TOOK a deep breath in a vain attempt to calm herself. She'd known from the minute she'd brought him home that she would have to explain her family and their kooky beliefs toward love, marriage and happily ever after to him. She also knew that in all likelihood he would not understand.

She stood beside Bennett while he replaced the distributor cap. He looked like Li'l Abner in Dylan's much too short blue jeans. If the mood between them had been jovial, she would have joked about his being prepared for a flood.

"Explain this thunderbolt thing to me again." He turned his head, angled her a chiding look. "Help me to understand what would make a sweet little grandmother tear apart your car to keep you home."

"It's the funniest thing," she began, purposely keeping her eyes moving so she wouldn't have to meet his gaze. She stared at the oil stains on the underside of the hood. "You're going to laugh, it's so silly."

Bennett straightened, put down the wrench and wiped his hands on a rag. "That's great. I could use a good laugh."

Her palms were sweaty. Her heart raced. "Well, uh, it's like this."

"Yes?" he prompted.

Lacy studied her feet.

Bennett reached out a hand, cupped her chin in his palm and forced her to look at him. His eyes drilled a hole straight through her. "Talk."

Lacy tried to stall. She hemmed and hawed but Bennett was having none of her diversionary tactics.

"Stop beating around the bush and talk to me. I don't bite."

No, but you'll take a powder.

Lacy sighed. Patience and tolerance were reflected at her from the depth of Bennett's chocolate brown eyes. There was nothing left to do but tell him the truth and hope against hope that he didn't find her strange or manipulative or foolhardy.

"It's kinda hard to explain."

"You're a bright, articulate woman." He wrapped a hand around her upper arm. "Give it a try."

"Do you believe in predestination?" Her voice rose on a hopeful note.

"Do you mean do I believe in the concept that we have no free will? That our destinies are mapped out for us even before our births?"

"Well, yeah."

"No. Absolutely not." He shook his head.

"You don't think it's at least possible that you were put here on earth to be a doctor and that even if your life had turned out differently you would eventually find your way to being a physician?"

"I'm not following you."

Lacy wet her lips. "Do you believe in predestined love? That there is one right person for everyone and when you find that person you'll know who they are and they'll know who you are without any doubts?"

"One right person in a planet that houses over six

billion people? Come on, Lacy, that's a bit far-fetched, don't you think?''

''No,'' she whispered. ''I don't.''

''What are you trying to say?''

''I've deceived you, Bennett. I led you to believe that I wanted nothing more than to have a fling with you, but that's not true. My family believes in the power of the thunderbolt.''

Then, in excruciating detail, she told him all about the family thunderbolt legend and how Great-Gramma had fabricated her chest pains in order to get Bennett to bring her to West.

She sneaked peeks at him as she spoke, watched the emotions flit across his face. Confusion, irritation, disbelief and finally disappointment.

''I can't believe your family manipulated me into coming here,'' Bennett said. ''If I didn't know better, I'd say you even orchestrated that sprained ankle.''

''It's not like that. I had no idea what Great-Gramma was cooking up until we got here.''

''But you didn't bother to tell me the truth once you did discover she was playing matchmaker.''

Lacy couldn't look him in the eye. ''That's right.''

''Why not?'' He folded his arms across his chest.

''Because I *do* believe in predestined love. From the minute you popped into the operating suite I knew you were the man I'd been waiting a lifetime for. Call me a fool, but I know you feel something for me, too, Bennett, but I know your career is important to you. I thought if I gave the thunderbolt some time then you would realize I'm the one you're supposed to be with. But I was wrong. You can't force someone to love you.''

The silence lengthened.

Trembling from head to toe, Lacy raised her chin and looked at him.

He met her eyes with a calm gaze. ''Today, I allowed myself to be swept away by my passion for you. And make no mistake, it is a powerful attraction. But that's what frightens me. Something that flames this hot is bound to burn out. I will not commit the same mistake my parents made. I'm so sorry if I've hurt you in any way. You're a truly wonderful person, and I know that some day you'll find this thunderbolt you're looking for. But it simply isn't me.''

Lacy bit her bottom lip and blinked furiously to keep the tears from spilling down her cheeks.

Janet was right. Love at first sight was nothing but a Cinderella fairy tale. Her mother, grandmother and great grandmother had simply been lucky in love, and in turn, they had called that luck the thunderbolt.

For too many years she had listened to their useless advice. Listened and dreamed dreams she had no business dreaming. She'd envisioned a fantasy man who could not, did not, exist.

''Lacy,'' Bennett repeated. ''I am sorry. If I had known… If you'd only told me you really believed in this thunderbolt thing I would never have made love to you. I know it's going to be hard…''

Lacy raised a hand. "Don't. Please, just don't. Okay? I'll be all right."

She had taken a chance. It hadn't worked out. So there was no such thing as the thunderbolt, after all. She would survive. She was stronger than she suspected. One good thing had come out of this. She'd gotten over her shyness. She'd even made love with a man.

At the memory of their tender lovemaking, her stomach roiled. Oh, God, she loved him so very much.

"Cupcake," he whispered.

"Forget it."

He placed a hand on her shoulder, but Lacy shrugged him off. "Let's talk about this some more," he said. "I can't promise you anything, but I do care about you. We had a great time. Maybe, someday, when I've finished my residency and opened my practice, maybe we could see how we feel then."

She whirled on him, sudden anger blooming inside her. She would not be ashamed of or embarrassed by her feelings. She'd made a gigantic blooper in loving him, but she could not regret having taken a chance.

She'd learned a lot and decided that she wasn't going to spend the rest of her life hiding under a rock, waiting for Prince Charming to come kick it over. She was tired of playing Sleeping Beauty. Yes, her lesson was a painful one, but she'd learned it well.

"No, Bennett. If you don't love me now, then you'll never feel it. I can accept that." She pivoted on her good heel then hurried to the house as fast as she could hobble.

10

Bennett sat in the commuter airplane, wearing the ridiculous high-water blue jeans that belonged to Lacy's brother, wishing with all his heart that things could have been different between them.

Lacy was so sweet, so lovable. He hated to think he'd hurt her. Damn. It was the last thing on earth he wanted.

He should have known better. He should have realized she was in love with him. He should never have kissed her that first time at the nightclub.

What he hadn't expected was this hollow, aching sensation in the region of his heart. Had he fallen in love with her, too?

But how could he be in love with her? He barely knew her. Sure, they'd worked side by side for five weeks. Worked in tandem like a well-trained team of trick ponies. Sure, she was one of the cutest, sweetest women he'd ever known. Sure, she aroused him to heights he'd never before experienced. Sure, whenever he caught sight of her, his stomach contracted and his heart flipped.

But that wasn't love.

What he felt for Lacy was simply animal attraction. Love took time.

Lots of time.

There was no such thing as predestined love. It was a precariously romantic concept that led people to do very dumb things.

But still, it hurt to know that he was the cause of Lacy's pain. It was all his fault. He should never have allowed things between them to go this far.

He liked so many things about her. She was good-hearted, warm and generous. Her playfulness helped lighten his seriousness. Before he even knew what was going on inside himself, Lacy perceived his feelings, his insecurities. His best qualities emerged whenever he was around her.

He loved the way her voice resonated in his head, so soft and modulated. It was the kind of voice a man could hear for a thousand years and never grow tired of. He adored her aroma of roses and tomato vines. A cozy scent that could revive a man's heart no matter how often he smelled it. He cherished the sugary taste of her lips that reminded him of home-cooked meals and cold winter nights spent curled by the fire. How could anyone not ache to spend a lifetime tasting such lips?

Any man would be lucky to have her.

But he wasn't the man for her. No matter what she might believe about thunderbolts and soul mates and love at first sight. He didn't buy into any of that.

Relationships were built over a long period of time.

They were based on honesty, communication and friendship, not hot passion, intense hormonal rushes or wayward emotions. Fireworks worked fine for great sex but made for lousy long-term unions.

Besides, how could anything so effortless as his feelings for Lacy be trusted? Yes, they got along like hot chocolate and marshmallows, but that very fact gave him pause. He'd spent his life struggling to become a doctor. It took hard work, long hours and lots of money. He appreciated the fact that nothing worth having came easily, and that included falling in love.

Bennett stared glumly at the clouds. Breaking things off with Lacy was the right thing to do. He should have done so before now.

In fact, he needed to take it one step further. He had to put as much distance between them as possible before his pheromones got the better of him again. He needed to leave Texas for good. After the transplant surgery he was going to tell Dr. Laramie he wanted to cut his study fellowship short.

With any luck, by this time tomorrow he'd be on his way home to Boston.

"IT'S OVER between us." Lacy lay across her bed in her apartment, sobbing into her hands, CeeCee and Janet sat on either side of her.

Dylan had driven her from West two days after Bennett had departed. She'd been unable to tell her family that the thunderbolt had failed.

"What do you mean, it's over?" CeeCee asked.

"When two people love each other there's always hope."

Fat chance for that. Darn CeeCee and her eternal optimism. "Bennett doesn't love me," she countered.

"How can you be so sure?"

"I found out from Jan that Bennett went back to Boston on the first plane out of Intercontinental on Monday morning."

CeeCee's mouth dropped. "He ran away?"

"Fast as a scalded dog." Lacy echoed one of Great-Gramma's sayings, then she burst into fresh tears.

"There, there," Janet soothed, gently patting Lacy on the shoulder. "All men are scum."

"No." Lacy wiped her eyes with the back of her hand. "Bennett's not scum. This was my fault." She told her friends about the thunderbolt. "I never told him about the thunderbolt or about Great-Gramma faking her illness until it was too late. Who can blame him for feeling duped?"

"I can blame him," CeeCee said. "He hurt my friend. If he were here right now I'd kick him in the fanny and ask him what on earth he was doing dumping the best thing that ever happened to him."

"Thanks for your support." Lacy sat up, took the tissue CeeCee offered her and delicately blew her nose. "But really, this is my responsibility. I'm the one who bought into that thunderbolt nonsense. You'd think I would have stopped believing in fairy tales a long time ago."

"It's hard to fight a family legend," Janet sympathized.

"I can't believe I wasted so many years waiting for the thunderbolt to strike." Lacy shook her head. "I was a fool. I should have been dating and having fun. I should have bought a house and planted a garden. I don't need some mythical knight in shining armor to change my life."

"You go, girl," CeeCee sang.

"I took a gamble. You've got to give me credit for that. For once I went after what I wanted. So what if it blew up in my face." Lacy spoke firmly, trying to convince herself as much as her friends that she was going to be all right.

But the hole in her soul whispered that she was kidding herself. Yes, she had learned a lot, and yes, she would survive, but without her other half would she ever be completely whole?

For so long she'd waited for the thunderbolt. Now that it had struck and left her charred to a crisp, she didn't know how to proceed. For twenty-nine years she'd believed that true love would solve everything. She had to face reality.

Bennett didn't want her.

"HOW ARE YOU this morning, Mr. Osborn?" Bennett consulted the chart in his hand then glanced at the spry octogenarian sitting up in the hospital bed at Boston General. His wife sat in a chair beside him, their hands clasped together.

Will I ever have that kind of closeness with anyone? Bennett wondered, then immediately thought of Lacy. It seemed he couldn't stop thinking about her no matter how hard he tried. He'd had such intimacy for the briefest of moments, and his feelings had scared him so much, that he had chickened out.

The elderly man laid his free hand over his chest and smiled. "Thanks for fixin' my ticker, Doc."

Henry Osborn was a native Texan, and his friendly drawl reminded Bennett too much of where he'd just been. Why did fate seem to keep reminding him of what he had left behind?

"I've had sixty years with my darlin' bride here, and to tell you the truth it's not near long enough," Henry Osborn continued.

"I bet you two had a long courtship before you got married—" Bennett nodded "—for your relationship to still be so strong after all these years."

Mrs. Osborn giggled like a schoolgirl and peered at her husband with adoring eyes. "Oh, no," she said. "We had a whirlwind courtship. Henry had come to Boston on business, and we both attended a company party. Our gazes met across a crowded room, and in that instant we both just knew."

Henry nodded, his eyes misty. "I remember like it was yesterday. I walked right up to her and said, 'You're the gal I aim to marry.'"

Bennett's chest tightened. "Really?"

"We were married three weeks later. When it's right, it's right, young man."

"But how did you know for sure?" His mind whirled with thoughts of Lacy, her wacky family and the legendary thunderbolt.

Then he thought of his parents. Two sides of the coin. The pros and cons of love at first sight. What made the Osborns different than his parents? Why did one marriage work and the other disintegrate?

Henry touched the left side of his chest again. "You'll know deep down in here, son. All you've got to do is follow your heart. It will never lead you astray."

Bennett moistened his lips with his tongue. "But how do you keep it going? What happens when things get rough? What keeps you from giving up?"

Mrs. Osborn smiled. "Oh, that one is easy, young man. You remember everything you love about the other person and you never let anything get in the way of that love. Not your job or your in-laws or money problems. You put the other person first. Their needs. Their wants. Their desires. Not yours. Love isn't selfish, young man. If you take care of her and she takes care of you then I promise, everything will work out fine."

It sounded so wonderful. How he wanted to believe.

Could Mrs. Osborn be right? He thought of his parents and how they'd put their own needs above each other. Single-minded selfishness had ruined their marriage, not passion. Not love at first sight.

He reached a hand into his pocket and fingered the

thunderbolt cuff links he'd been carrying around ever since Lacy's great-gramma had given them to him.

Bennett drew in a deep breath as his fingers contacted the warm metal. He held them in his palm, the gold winking in the light from the window.

And then it happened.

He felt something.

Like a zap of lightning zinging through his whole body from his head to his toes, raising the hairs on his arms. In that moment he knew.

He'd been struck by the thunderbolt. Not here. Not now. But eight weeks ago, in a hospital in Houston. And he'd been doing his best to suppress it ever since.

Fear had hampered him from speaking his mind. Fear had kept him from admitting the truth to himself.

His heart throbbed. His body tingled. His soul ached to be fulfilled.

He was in love with Lacy Calder.

And there was no doubt about it.

THREE WEEKS AFTER Bennett left Texas, Lacy was spreading autoclaved instruments across the sterile field when she glanced up and saw him standing in the doorway. He wore green scrubs, a matching scrub cap, blue shoe covers and a mask.

Bennett?

She blinked. Nah.

Surely this must be a mirage. Bennett Sheridan was far away in Boston, doing an important service, saving people's lives. She'd been seeing his face an awful lot in her imagination. Maybe she wasn't at work at all, but at home in her bed, dreaming a dream that was going to make her cry when she awoke and found it all a fantasy. She bit her bottom lip to see if she was indeed awake.

Ouch.

Okay, that was painful. Not dreaming, then. She was wide awake.

His eyes drilled into hers like laser beams melting metal. That crazy, illogical feeling leaped inside her. The thunderbolt. Striking again.

How could it be?

If she wasn't asleep then she must be having a doozy of a hallucination.

"Lacy," he said, his voice strangely heavy.

Auditory hallucinations. That was bad, wasn't it?

She shook her head, returned her attention to the sterile field, determined to ignore this very realistic figment of her overactive imagination.

His shoe covers whispered against the floor. He was coming closer.

Dear heavens. Her heart scampered into her throat. Her hand, wrapped around a retractor, began to tremble.

"Lacy," he said again. This time he was standing right behind her. "Look at me."

She turned on her step stool. Her ankle, healing but still weak, started to give way beneath her.

"Oh." She dropped the retractor and struggled to regain her balance.

But she didn't have anything to worry about. Bennett was there. His arms were around her.

She looked at him. Time hung suspended.

"Is it really you?" she murmured.

"It's really me." He righted her on the stool but kept his hands spanned around her waist. They stood eye to eye.

"What are you doing here?" she asked.

"I work here."

"Since when?" She sucked in her breath and got a mouthful of mask.

"I transferred from Boston General. I'm going to finish my residency at Saint Madeleine's."

"But how?" She scarcely dared believe that this was true. "And why?"

"How?" He reached behind him and untied the top string of his mask so it fell around his neck. "Dr. Laramie agreed to sponsor me."

"You've just broken scrub," she whispered.

"I know."

"You'll have to scrub in again."

"No." He lifted a hand to undo her scrub mask, as well, his arm brushing against her cheek in the process. "We'll have to scrub in again."

"Why did you do that?"

"To show you the reason I came back."

She frowned. "I don't get it."

"Do you get this?" He hauled her against his chest and kissed her with a passion that made her pant.

"Oh, Bennett," she murmured.

"Hey, you two! Stop that and get scrubbed in again. Plus you've contaminated your sterile field, Lacy," Jan barked from the doorway. She clapped her hands. "Come on, we don't have all day."

Bennett took Lacy's hand and led her from the surgical suite to the scrub sinks.

"What's happened?" she asked him.

"I do love you, Lacy. I was just too scared to admit it. I didn't want to repeat my parents' mistake."

"What made you change your mind?" Her eyes searched his face. She wanted so much to believe him.

"I didn't want to live the rest of my life regretting not having taken a chance on us. You're the best thing that ever happened to me, Lacy Calder."

"Oh, Bennett."

"And I'm sorry if I've caused you one moment of pain. All these years I thought love was about passion and that passion eventually cooled and left you nothing but hurt. But I was wrong, Lacy, so wrong."

"How were you wrong?"

"I now know that love is about sacrificing your own selfish desires for the good of another. I learned that if I want to have love, I must first give it. Lacy, I want to spend my life pleasing you. Loving you."

She reached up, traced his lips with her fingers. "I want to please you. Love you. That's how it should be."

He hitched in a breath and paused for a long moment. "You showed me love was about sharing, caring and accepting. It might be rough on us for the first couple of years until I finish my residency and get my practice started, but we'll work it out.''

"Do you really mean it?" She trembled all over. Did she dare hope? "You're not afraid our relationship will end up like your parents'?"

"I finally realized something. I'm not my father and you're not my mother. My parents both have the same tempestuous personality. Both are pretty selfish. Neither of us are like that. We're good together. And there's no rush. No hurry. We don't have to get married as my parents did. When we get married it'll be because we're ready.''

"Are you certain?"

"Absolutely."

"I knew you were the one." She grinned.

"And I always knew it was you from the beginning. I'm just a slow learner."

"Great-Gramma says the thunderbolt is never wrong and that it can't be denied."

"Great-Gramma is very wise."

"She's going to be so happy."

"Not a quarter as happy as I am. Will you marry me, Lacy? For better or worse, I never want to be without you again."

Lacy beamed at him, her heart filled to bursting. "As if I could say no."

He bent to kiss her again.

Endorphins collided with adrenaline. Testosterone jumped like the lords of the dance in his lower abdomen. Sheer joy sprinted through his nerve endings.

He drew her closer to him, tasting every delicious inch of her lips. He knew without a hint of doubt that she was meant to be his, forever and always.

The thunderbolt had struck again. Claiming two more hearts, melding them together for all time.

EPILOGUE

THE PREACHER STOOD at the front of the elaborately constructed altar erected in the Calders' backyard. Bible in hand, he gave the crowd a welcoming smile.

"Friends and neighbors," the preacher began. "We are gathered here today to unite this man and this woman in holy matrimony."

Lacy peeked at Bennett. He winked at her. She smiled shyly into the pink roses and baby's breath bouquet clutched in her hand.

"Do you, Kermit Kahonachek, renewing your vows with your bride of seventy years, take this woman, Katrina Kahonachek, to be your lawfully wedded wife?"

"I do!" Lacy's great grandfather's voice rang out loud and clear as he gazed at the woman who'd been his lifelong soul mate.

"And do you, Katrina, take this man, Kermit, to be your lawfully wedded husband, until death do you part?"

Great-Gramma reached over and took her husband's hand. "You bet I do. I'm not going another seventy years without him in my life."

"Then I now pronounce your vows renewed. Kermit, you may kiss your bride."

Lacy's heart swelled with emotion as she watched her great grandfather draw her great grandmother to him and kiss her soundly on the lips. Pride, joy, happiness and hope pressed against her chest.

A cheer went up from the crowd.

Lacy gazed at Bennett to find his eyes fixed on her face. Eyes brimming with love. Her breath ceased in that fine moment. She saw them together many years down the road with their own family clustered around them as they celebrated their own seventieth anniversary by renewing their wedding vows.

"I'm ready to throw the bouquet," Great-Gramma announced several minutes later. "All you single ladies gather around." She winked at Lacy and nodded.

Lacy's unmarried cousins and sisters assembled in a clump along with CeeCee and Janet. They all grinned and waved.

Great-Gramma turned her back to the crowd and launched the bouquet over her head.

It spiraled into the air.

A dozen pairs of arms reached upward, scrambling for the prize. Despite being disadvantaged by her small stature, Lacy was determined to grab that bouquet. She leaped up.

Gotta catch it, gotta catch it.

If anything, the thunderbolt had taught her a valuable lesson. Never take tradition lightly. Come hell or high water, she and Bennett were going to be the next ones married in this clan.

Then, from the corner of her eye, she saw a streak of white. Someone or something moving faster than greased lightning dashed forward.

And snatched the bouquet.

With a bleat of triumph, Frank Sinatra trotted away, the bouquet firmly between his teeth.

The crowd rolled with laughter.

"Hey!" Lacy shouted. "You come back here! That's my bouquet, you ornery critter."

Old Blue Eyes trotted faster, ribbon streams breaking loose from the bouquet and flying behind him.

"Faint, you son of a billy goat." Lacy fisted her taffeta bridesmaid gown in her hand to kept from tripping over the long skirt and launched herself after him.

"Hang on, there." Bennett took her elbow as she passed him.

"Let go. I'm getting that bouquet one way or the other."

He peered at her, laughter illuminating his face. "You don't need the bouquet, Lacy. Let Frank Sinatra have his lunch."

"But I want to be the next one married," she insisted.

"You will be."

She blinked at him. "Is this a commitment to a wedding date?"

"Yes, ma'am."

"Oh?" She melted against him, placed a hand on his chest. "Do tell."

"A year from today. Same time, same place, same guest list, with a few additions."

"Like your parents?"

"Yes."

"Will you be ready? Are you sure?"

"Honey, I've been struck by the thunderbolt. As you well know, there's no denying it. My residency will be finished. We can start looking for a place to set up my clinic. However, I do have one requirement."

"And what is that?" Lacy asked, gazing into the eyes of her intended.

"Frank Sinatra is to be banned from our wedding."

"Or served up as *cabrito* pâté."

"Either, or." His grin widened. "Have I ever told you how beautiful you are?"

"Not in the last five minutes."

"Or how much I love you?"

"Hmm, you might have mentioned it."

"Well, it's time to make sure you thoroughly understand." He squeezed her tighter, and his eyes misted with unshed tears of joy. "Without you, Lacy Calder, nothing in my life has meaning. You're the whipped cream on my strawberry shortcake, you're the morning star in my sky, you're the tomato plants on my balcony."

"No kidding?"

He turned his face to the sky, grinned and shouted. "Hear me world, I love Lacy."

Her pulse slipped through her veins at his nearness. Everything she'd ever dreamed of had come true. She'd found her soul mate. Only one more thing would make her world complete, and that would be for CeeCee and Janet to find the same kind of love she'd found in Bennett's arms. She sent a silent prayer to the heavens, beseeching the thunderbolt to strike in their lives.

But in the meantime she had her own romance to kindle. Standing on tiptoes, she whispered in his ear.

"Last one to the hayloft is a rotten egg."

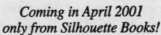

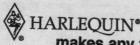

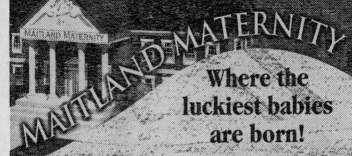

INDULGE IN A QUIET MOMENT
WITH HARLEQUIN

Get a FREE
Quiet Moments
Bath
Spa

with just two proofs of purchase from
any of our four special collector's editions in May.

Harlequin® is sure to make your time special this Mother's Day
with four special collector's editions featuring a short story
PLUS a complete novel packaged together in one volume!

Collection #1   Intrigue abounds in a collection featuring *New York Times*
bestselling author Barbara Delinsky and Kelsey Roberts.

Collection #2   Relationships? Weddings? Children? = *New York Times*
bestselling author Debbie Macomber and Tara Taylor Quinn
at their best!

Collection #3   Escape to the past with *New York Times* bestselling author
Heather Graham and Gayle Wilson.

Collection #4   Go West! With *New York Times* bestselling author
Joan Johnston and Vicki Lewis Thompson!

Plus Special Consumer Campaign!
Each of these four collector's editions will feature a
"FREE QUIET MOMENTS BATH SPA" offer.
See inside book in May for details.

Only from
HARLEQUIN®
Makes any time special ®

Don't miss out! Look for this exciting promotion on sale in May 2001,
at your favorite retail outlet.

Visit us at www.eHarlequin.com   PHNCP01